Praise for

VIGIL

Book 1 of the Verity Fassbinder Series

'Rich and heady as honey mead, potent and earthy as great Scotch,
the sublimely dark tales of Angela Slatter are an addictive delight'
Neil Snowden, Waterstones

'Angela Slatter's ink is full of intimate magic and hard wisdom.
Her characters live and breathe and glance out at you from
the page to question your motives. One of the best dark
fantasy writers working today'
Christopher Golden, New York Times bestselling author of
Ararat* and *Snowblind

'Striking urban fantasy . . . Pleasing and fast-paced'
Lovereading

'We are in the hands of a first-rank storyteller . . . Slatter's voice
is striking. Alternately witty and forthright, Verity leads us
into the weird world with rare and ironic assurance . . . It's a
wonderfully entertaining book'
The Melbourne Age

'Brilliant . . . an original and fresh tale encompassing many genres
that will enthral all readers alike'
Starburst Magazine

'Verity is the best thing about the book . . . she's a surly,
straight-talking, Doc Marten-wearing punch bag who investigates
Weyrd-related crime on behalf of the beleaguered "normal"
police . . . it'll be interesting to see what's next for her'
SFX

'A rich paranormal dark fantasy'
Sydney Morning Herald

'If you like reading intelligent dark urban fantasy, I would definitely
recom

'Slatter can write! Beautifully, stylishly, accurately . . . She conjures the secret and private worlds hidden just inside the curtains of reality, and she does it with sentences as sparse and sharp-edged as unused razor blades'
Jack Dann, award-winning author of *The Memory Cathedral*

'Comes on like a high-octane mix of Jim Butcher's Harry Dresden and Sue Grafton's Kinsey . . . Smart, funny, and engaging. I can't wait for the sequel!'
Jonathan Strahan, editor of *The Best Science Fiction and Fantasy of the Year* series

'A brilliant new urban fantasy with elements of murder mystery and magic - I'm already looking forward to the next Verity Fassbinder adventure'
Alison Littlewood, author of *The Hidden People*

'*Vigil* is a stunning urban fantasy novel, jam packed with action and mystery. Our fair heroine, Verity, is full of wit, courage, compassion and has a penchant for saying the wrong thing at the wrong time . . . An intriguing read and I, for one, cannot wait for more!'
QBD Bookshop

'Angela Slatter is an Australian author who spins beautiful yarns in a musical, fascinating narrative style'
SFSite

'Some of the best setting descriptions I've ever read. I also loved Verity's tenacity and witty dialogue. I thoroughly enjoyed *Vigil*'
SQ Magazine

'I highly recommend *Vigil* for people who enjoy urban fantasy, contemporary faery tales and women telling stories . . . I want more'
Dark Matter Zine

'*Vigil* is fast-paced, quirky, full of twists, and thoroughly grounded in Brisbane . . . I love it and I want more Verity'
Randomly Yours, Alex

'*Vigil* is a brilliant debut novel from an exciting writer . . . Pacy and engaging, it's a book that demands to be finished once it has been started . . . Sure to become a staple of the genre as the series progresses, as instantly recognisable as, say, Sookie Stackhouse or Katniss Everdeen'
Reader Dad

'A darkly fun read that hooked me quickly and reeled me in'
Earl Grey Editing

'*Vigil* dares to be different, eloquent, emotive, and exciting in equal measures; it marks the start of what will become the new must-read urban fantasy series. You will be eagerly awaiting the next trip down under with baited breath; such is the brilliance of this novel'
Ginger Nuts of Horror

'*Vigil* is a great start to a fascinating new series for both urban fantasy and crime fans with a refreshing Australian voice, setting and style. It will be interesting to see where Slatter takes both her characters and her world in future volumes'
Aust Crime

'*Vigil* is an absolute powerhouse of a book. Slatter has taken urban fantasy by the horns, and given it the kick up the arse that it needed. Original, addictive, and a ****load of awesome, *Vigil* is a must read for all fans of speculative fiction'
Smash Dragons

'*Vigil* is a cracking read. I can't wait for the next book, *Corpselight*, and I hope there will be far more books in the series, because I'd love to spend lots more time with Verity and friends in Brisneyland'
A Fantastical Librarian

'An excellent, action filled start to (I hope) a new series with a hero I want to learn more about. And a world with a lot still to unpack'
Blue Book Balloon

'*Vigil* will cast its own spell on you as you read and you will be utterly captivated'
LizLovesBooks

'An engaging read. It moves along quickly, there is barely a moment to catch your breath'
SFF Book Reviews

'So well plotted that everything comes together with a very satisfactory meshing of hip, urban Brisbane and the supernatural. Verity Fassbinder is a classic crime-solving detective but her witty style and self-knowledge make her very endearing'
Holly Gleeson, *The Newtown Review of Books*

'Rich and convincing, and peopled with a cast of odd, frightening, entertaining, and occasionally horrifying creatures . . . *Vigil* is an excellent read, and highly recommended'
Maria Haskins

Also by Angela Slatter

Verity Fassbinder
Vigil

Collections
Sourdough and Other Stories
The Girl with No Hands and Other Tales
Midnight and Moonshine (with Lisa L. Hannett)
The Bitterwood Bible and Other Recountings
Black-Winged Angels
The Female Factory (with Lisa L. Hannett)
Of Sorrow and Such
A Feast of Sorrows: Stories
Winter Children and Other Chilling Tales

VIGIL

ANGELA SLATTER

Jo Fletcher

BOOKS

First published in Great Britain in 2016
This edition published in 2017 by

Jo Fletcher Books
an imprint of
Quercus Editions Ltd
Carmelite House
50 Victoria Embankment
London EC4Y 0DZ

An Hachette UK company

A CIP catalogue record for this book is available
from the British Library

PB ISBN 978 1 78429 404 5

10 9 8 7 6 5 4 3 2 1

Typeset by Jouve (UK), Milton Keynes

Printed and bound in Great Britain by Clays Ltd, St Ives plc

Author's Note

The city is not the city.

Though I do live in Brisneyland and have used it as the backdrop for *Vigil*, I must confess that I've played fast and loose with some details (I'm sorry, West End and I'm *really* sorry, Gold Coast). I'm a writer. It's fiction. So I beg patience of the purists; while the reader will recognise certain landmarks and suburbs, Verity's city is not quite the city you know. It just looks a bit like it, seen through a glass darkly.

Enjoy the journey.

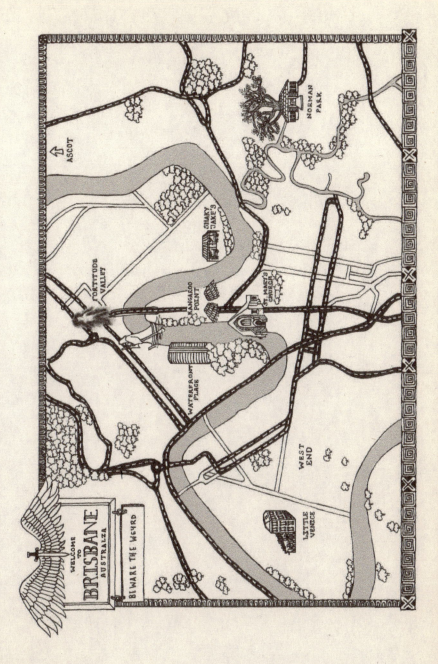

Beginnings

The night moved. Liquid sheets of black spread out then folded back in on themselves. The breeze, seemingly benign, made its way down Robertson Street. It picked up pieces of garbage as it went – discarded newspapers, chip packets, soft-drink cans, cigarette packs. It plucked detritus from the gutters, sweeping all it could find into an ever-growing, swiftly forming body. It looked like a figure, a rough-torn thing: a man of rags and trash and darkness.

Had anyone been paying attention, they might have noticed when it began its journey – turning off Brunswick Street and taking the slow incline – that the sound of footsteps had become audible. But as the road sloped, drawing further away from the lights, as the whirlwind picked up speed and mass, the noise of anything remotely human was lost.

At the bottom of the thoroughfare, almost at the glamour of the James Street precinct, the thing feinted right as if it had no interest in going any other way, then turned a hard left.

The homeless man who'd been sheltering in the curve of the concrete garden wall, praying he would not be noticed, felt only a brief sting of ice reaching into his lungs, then the crushing sensation of too much air all around him as he was lifted from the ground and quickly ceased to be.

At the very end of the strip, where the streetlights bloomed, footfalls were heard once again, a kind of a hiccough in their rhythm this time, as if something *had changed. As if the tread beat out a broken tattoo of unexpected grief. Yet the two who'd watched the procession from their vantage point on the balcony of a vacant apartment smiled, pride palpable.*

They did not see death. They did not feel bereft at the loss of innocence. All they saw was their plan coming to fruition.

Chapter One

The ribbon was judging me, I knew it.

It had become increasingly apparent that wrapping things was not my forte. Even a simple rectangular gift was obviously too much of a challenge. Corners broke through the too-thin tissue I'd bought because I'd thought, *Hey, an eight-year old would love that*! She probably would have, too, if it hadn't developed holes within moments of me trying to swaddle a big book of fairy tales in it. The stiff lace ribbon I'd finally managed to tie around the middle looked self-conscious and a bit embarrassed.

Oh, well. Lizzie would turn the gold and silver paper into confetti in a matter of seconds anyway. I could hear the sounds of the birthday party-cum-sleepover already ramping up next door, and looking through my kitchen window into Mel's garden I could see a circle of small girls in pastel party dresses made of shiny fabrics, glitter and sequins. They all wore fairy wings that caught the last of the sun's rays as they danced and ran, lithe and careless as sprites. It made me smile. Mums and dads were scattered across the grass, some carrying platters of cocktail sausages, fairy bread, mini pies and other essential party foods while others seized the opportunity to laze around being waited on. It would be nice, I thought, to socialise, do something ordinary for a change.

I took a last look in the mirror to make sure I was presentable – or at least as presentable as I was likely to get. I picked up the offering, and that's when the hammering started at the front door. It wasn't the good kind of knocking and my spirits sank. Things didn't improve when I saw who was waiting on the patio.

Zvezdomir 'Bela' Tepes, model-handsome in pressed black jeans and a black shirt, managed his usual trick of appearing ephemeral as a shadow, yet as all-encompassing as darkness. He gave a wave so casual it could have been mistaken for a dismissal. Just seeing him made my leg ache.

'Verity. I've got a job for you.'

'But I'm going to a birthday party,' I blurted, clutching the present like a shield. 'There'll be cake, and lollies.'

He blinked, caught off guard by my unlikely defence. 'I need you to come right now.'

'Party pies, Bela. Fairy cakes. Mini sausage rolls. *Small* food,' I said, then added lamely, 'It tastes better.'

'Kids are going missing,' he said, gritting his teeth, and it was all over bar the shouting. 'And someone wants to talk to you.'

He pointed towards the familiar purple taxi parked at the kerb in the late afternoon light. There weren't too many cabs like this in the city, although I guessed demand would be growing as the population did; it wasn't just people fleeing the southern states who wanted a new start in Brisbane – also known as Brisneyland or Brisrael if you were feeling playful, or Brisbanal if you were tired of restaurants closing at 8.30 p.m. The taxi's general clientele covered Weyrd, wandering Goths and too-plastered-to-notice Normal, though most times even the drunkest thought twice about getting into this kind of car. It was almost like they were snapped out of their alcohol-fuelled stupor by the strangeness it exuded.

Through the passenger window I made out a fine profile and

meticulously styled auburn hair. When the head turned slowly towards me, I recognised its owner, though I'd not formally met Eleanor Aviva, one of the Council of Five, before. It was a bit like having the queen drop in. The driver next to her gave a brisk wave.

My shoulders slumped. 'How many kids?'

'Twenty-five we can identify for sure, but that's out of a couple of hundred a week. Not all those are ours.'

'Don't say *ours*, Bela. They're nothing to do with me.' I regretted the comment as soon as I said it; people had looked out for me when I needed it and I'd determined long ago to try to pay that back. 'Let me drop this off, make my apologies.'

'Don't be long,' he said. As he retreated to the vehicle I made a rude gesture behind his back, which Eleanor Aviva saw. After a moment, her very proper mask cracked and she gave me a conspiratorial smile, then faced forward again.

As I dragged my feet towards Mel's house, I wondered if Lizzie would save me some ice cream cake.

I looked out of the window. My reflection stared back, and beyond that I watched the night speed past. I should be singing 'Happy Birthday', not here with my ex in the back seat of the world's most disreputable-looking gypsy cab. Parts of it had been cannibalised from other cars. Any original white surfaces had been reduced to grey, and the vinyl of the seats was a little sticky with age. The rubber mats on the floor, though so thin as to be almost transparent, were, I was pretty sure, all that stopped me from seeing the bitumen of Wynnum Road beneath us. Instead of the traditional pine tree-shaped air freshener there was a *gris-gris* hanging from the rear-view mirror. It wasn't minty-fresh, but then again it didn't smell bad – it was rather cinnamony, if anything. It just *looked* bad: a shrunken head with dried lavender sticking out of its ears. Scratched along the inside of the doors were symbols and sigils I couldn't read, in a language so old I suspected no one knew how to pronounce it any more. I never looked too close, not since I'd realised that some of the etchings were really fingernail marks. I didn't want to linger on that thought.

'It's only been street kids so far,' said Bela. He didn't even stumble on that bit – he didn't even know he'd said the wrong thing, though no column inches were going to be devoted to those lost children. In the front seat, Ziggi loaded a CD and the exquisite a cappella opening of 'Bohemian Rhapsody' poured forth. Eleanor Aviva made an annoyed clicking sound with her tongue. *Philistine*.

'Turn that racket down,' Aviva ordered in clipped tones, and to my mild surprise, the driver obeyed without argument. The councillor retreated back into silence. Despite Bela's earlier comment we'd not been introduced and I wondered why she was here.

The eye in the back of Ziggi Hassman's head examined me through fine ginger hair. He'd landed in Brisbane about ten years ago and got a job with Bela immediately, thanks to a sheaf of references, so we'd known each other for a long time and I could generally interpret his expressions, facial – and otherwise. But I'd not seen that single orb as inscrutable since I'd ended up haemorrhaging on his back seat after following him and Bela into an abandoned house a few months ago . . . coincidentally, that was the same night I'd lost my enthusiasm for the phrase 'let's split up and cover more ground'. We'd been looking for something that shouldn't have been there – shouldn't have been in this plane of existence. It was a something with claws and teeth and a bad attitude; a something that had been making red messes of pets around the city. Luckily, not people. Not then, at least.

I found it first, and won the fight that ensued, but ultimately wound up in Accident and Emergency. Ziggi had saved my life, wrapping every bandage from the taxi's first-aid kit around my leg to stem the bleeding while Bela had busied himself making phone calls to highly unlisted numbers and reeling in favours while reporting to superiors, which added another couple of layers of resentment to how I felt about him.

'I should be eating ice cream cake,' I announced to no one in particular. 'I should be watching Lizzie open her presents. I really should.'

'Verity, if it's—' Bela started.

'It's not, Bela' I said shortly, pressing down on the rage his voice habitually produced in me nowadays. Before I could give rein to my full displeasure, I was distracted by the vibration of the mobile in my jacket pocket and reached for it.

'Ms Fassbinder, kindly give us the courtesy of your undivided attention,' Eleanor Aviva said sharply and my hand fell away as I instinctively sat up straighter, the response to that schoolmarm tone deeply ingrained.

Bela tried again, and his pitch was softer. 'V, if it *is*, then maybe it's like your dad.' He waited for me to speak, to deny the past, to defend myself. I rewarded him with silence, so he went on. 'If it's a *Kinderfresser*—'

'Well, at least we know it's not *my daddy* this time,' I sniped.

'—then we need to get to him quickly because he – or she – won't stop by themselves. I can't keep this out of the papers for too long. Any undue attention on our community will put everyone in danger.'

There was a time, not so long ago, when I'd been bleeding and screaming in the back seat of this very taxi and swearing I wouldn't ever work for Bela Tepes again, yet here I was, listening meekly to what was expected of me. The weekly retainer was deposited into my account on the assumption that I'd do what was asked. I might not have followed through on my plans to quit – quite frankly, what else was I going to do with an Arts degree in Ancient History and slightly dead languages? – but that didn't make me feel any more biddable.

'Do you really think I don't know that?' My glare was enough to make him look away. Then I felt bad; my temper had become short and my nature less than pleasant in recent months and it was Bela who was bearing the brunt of it. Then again, once upon a time I didn't ache inside with every step; I didn't wake up sweating, thinking something was at my window, and I didn't dream of claws reaching through the gaps in the stairs and tearing so much flesh from my leg that I looked like I'd been ring-barked.

'Perhaps Ms Fassbinder isn't really the person for this task, Zvezdomir?' said Aviva evenly. She pronounced his given name with an assurance and an accent I'd never manage in a hundred years, which was one of the reasons I so seldom used it. That and the Bela Lugosi eyebrows.

'Ms Fassbinder is the *only* person for this job, Eleanor.' Bela matched her timbre, but there was an underlying edge.

Part of me wanted to tell them both where to go, but the sad fact was that I needed money. Though I owned the house, things like food and phone bills didn't get paid with a sunny smile. Things had been quiet in Weyrd-town recently, and the Normal world hadn't been much busier, so the independent consulting assignments I did occasionally had been few and far between too. Bela was a generous paymaster – possibly because his missions were generally the reason I ended up in harm's way – but we'd broken up two years ago and the job meant closure was an issue. Spending all this time together – and not happy fun times – meant I kept wondering when the 'ex' part of ex-boyfriend would kick in.

'Ms Fassbinder, I cannot stress strongly enough how important it is that this matter be dealt with swiftly and shrewdly,' Aviva said. 'And quietly. Any member of our community who risks exposing the rest of us to danger has no rights in the eyes of the Council. There is to be no prevarication, and no mercy for this individual.' She tapped long fingernails on the dashboard in front of her. 'Of course, you know that better than most.'

Behind my head, Freddie Mercury's voice soared, but quietly, as if afraid of Eleanor Aviva's disapproval. I controlled my breathing, counted to ten and remained calm. 'Has anyone thought about asking the Boatman if he knows anything? I mean, all the dead end up with him eventually.'

'I don't think that's necessary, do you?' said Aviva. 'He hardly chats with his passengers. He obeys his own rules, answers to none, keeps his own counsel. He does not come when called.'

She was probably right, but it felt like she was baiting me and I had no idea why. Her attitude wasn't improving my mood. 'I don't mean to be rude, Councillor, but why are you here? The Five have always kept their distance from me.'

'Consider this a performance appraisal,' she answered, not even bothering to look over her shoulder at me. Was she trying to get a reaction? Did she not realise I'd spent my life ignoring stuff like that? I smiled at Ziggi's stare in the rear-view mirror. It had gone from inscrutable to concerned.

Bela, apparently not confident of my self-control, raised his voice to drown out any reply I might have made. 'Eleanor and I are on our way to a Council session and she wanted to take the opportunity to meet you. I assured her you'd treat this matter seriously.' He cleared his throat. 'Where are you going to start?'

'I've got some ideas.' I could feel his gaze, even though I was peering out of the window again. I thought he might be staring at my neck, at the pale curve where the vein pulsed blue close to the surface. I wondered if he was remembering what the sweat on my skin tasted like. I didn't turn around but said softly, 'It's okay, Bela, leave it to me.'

'Ziggi, keep an eye on her,' he said abruptly. 'And V, when you're done with this, there's something else I want you to look into.'

And he was gone, just like that, leaving the seat beside me empty, smelling vaguely of his expensive aftershave, a chill coming off the faux-leather. Eleanor Aviva had evaporated too. That disappearing act was draining in the extreme and only a very few Weyrd could do it. Things were quiet, except for the final coda of Freddie's delicate piano work.

'I hate it when Bela does that. Freaks me out,' said Ziggi, the only other person I knew who got away with using that nickname.

Bela made even other Weyrd uncomfortable. I felt kind of proud, in spite of everything.

'He used to just appear in the kitchen. I dropped a lot of dishes,' I admitted, then bit down on my lip – I hadn't meant that to slip out, hadn't meant to dwell on the past domestic situation. It wasn't as if Ziggi hadn't witnessed all the ups and downs of my relationship with Bela – he once claimed he didn't watch TV for three years because we provided all the drama he needed – but I felt compelled to say, 'It takes a lot of effort, so that's how I gauged how much he wanted to get away.'

'You were a little challenging,' he pointed out. 'You need to cut him some slack, you know.'

I didn't answer; we both knew Ziggi was right. He hesitated, then said, 'How's your leg? I mean, really?'

'How the hell do you think it is?' Even as I snapped at him, I knew

I should have been a bit more gracious. 'I'm sorry I'm being an arse. It still hurts, and that makes me cranky.'

'To be honest, you were pretty cranky before it happened.'

We laughed and the tension dissipated.

'You were trying to annoy Aviva, weren't you?' I asked. 'With the music.'

'What do you think? I don't like uppity folk who think they're better than everyone else.' He sniffed. Ziggi Hassman: melodic anarchist.

'Turned it off pretty quickly though.' I grinned.

'Hey, I'm not stupid.' Then, unable to resist it, he circled back to his topic of choice. 'Should've gone to a healer with that leg of yours.'

'Well, if you remember, there wasn't much time to fiddle about that night and the hospital was closest,' I pointed out. The upshot of my injury was that Ziggi had become my chauffeur, so we'd been spending a lot of time together while doing Bela's assorted jobs. We investigated things that needed looking into, acted as go-betweens and problem-solvers for him – and by extension, the Council – and generally kept an eye on the Weyrd population, trying to make sure it stayed as unknown as possible. This was sometimes a challenge when the community included those who were still looking for a taste of the old days: feline-shaped things who stole breath, succubi and incubi out for a good time, and creatures who swapped their own offspring for babies left unguarded in their cribs.

He gave a grunt that might have been a concession. 'So, where to? You said you'd got some ideas?'

'I might have exaggerated. I have *one* idea. Let's start with Little Venice.'

'Probably should have told me that three seconds ago when I could have taken the turn-off,' he said mildly. 'Now we're going the long way round.'

He cut off a dully-gleaming SUV to change lanes. The sun had fled, and as we drove onto the Story Bridge, the lights of the city down and to the left, and those of New Farm down and to the right, swam in the blackness. High-rise office towers stood out like beacons, standing cheek-by-jowl with the new apartment blocks: all that modern steel and glass juxtaposed with the verdigris dome and sandstone of Customs House and the past it represented. During the day, the river would show its true colour – a thorough brown – but in that moment it was an undulating ebony ribbon reflecting the diamonds of night-time illuminations.

'It's okay. We've got nothing but time,' I lied and hunched into the upholstery, thinking about melting ice cream cake and kids who wouldn't ever know what that tasted like.

Chapter Two

West End was filled with Weyrd.

Most folk thought the Saturday market's demographic was a mix of students, drunks, artists, writers, the few upwardly mobile waiting for rehabilitated property values, religious nutters, common-or-garden do-gooders and dyed-in-the-wool junkies, all mingling for cheap fruit and veggies – or to score weed in the public toilet block in the nearby park. Often these groups overlapped.

But there was also a metric butt-load of Weyrd, who sometimes featured in one or more of the aforementioned groups as well. They were mostly successful in their attempts to blend in, especially in suburbs that already had a pretty bizarre human population – places where it was difficult to distinguish the wondrous-strange from the head-cases. The old guy who yelled at the trees on the corner of Boundary Street and Montague Road? Weyrd. The kid who kept peeing on the front steps of the Gunshop Café? Weyrd. The woman who asked people in the street if they could spare some dirty laundry? Well, actually, she was Normal. The smart ones used glamours to hide what they were, to tame disobedient shapes and disguise peculiar abilities, but some just let it all hang out, not caring if they were mistaken for psychos or horror movie extras.

They weren't a disorganised rabble; any minority group keen on survival soon develops its own leadership. The Weyrd had the

Council of Five, chosen from the old families who'd been in Brisbane since its founding. Convicts, overseers and frock-coated men on the make weren't the only ones doing the invading; lots of folk wanted a new start. In the Old Country – wherever that happened to be – the ancient beliefs and traditions still held sway. Normals were twitchy creatures, but they'd only live in fear of the dark for a limited time. Eventually they got tired of huddling around fires and being scared. As with anything that went on for too long, numbness and fatigue set in, followed by anger, which burned out a lot of the good sense that'd brought on the terror in the first place. They got all brave and started charging around brandishing torches and pitchforks, striking out not just at whatever had frightened them but at *anything* that was different. Problem was, it wasn't really bravery, it was still fear – but it was an *enraged* fear, and that kind wasn't discriminating. As a consequence, the Weyrd – the *different* – from Hungary to Scotland, Romania to Mali, Italy to Japan, the Land Beyond the Forest to several dozen tiny nations that had changed their names multiple times, people like Bela, Aviva, Ziggi or my father, often had to find new homes, or cease to exist . . .

So the first Weyrd came over on their creaking, stinking, packed ships, as stowaways, or convicts, caught by accident or intent, sometimes even as soldiers or governors or wives. Those who survived to put down roots in the new land, who set up shop as the major cities developed, generally became the Councillors, keeping watchful eyes on the rest of the Weyrd population. They ensured peace and dealt with the Normals, using people like Bela – essentially a cross between prime minister and spymaster – to keep the worst 'disturbances' under control. And someone like Bela would employ someone like me, because those of us of mixed parentage can walk between the two worlds. As long as we behave ourselves and don't cause a fuss.

It had gone relatively smoothly until I got injured. Quite apart from my freshly acquired physical limitations, the ancient car I'd inherited from my grandparents had been found burning outside my house a few hours after I'd been admitted to hospital. The insurance payout was just about enough to buy me a second-hand pair of running shoes. The net result of that particular evening had been one dead 'serker, a long-term limp for me, and a new chauffeur.

'You think they'll know anything?' Ziggi had been trying to find a parking space for about ten minutes, although in the grand scheme of things that wasn't a long time in West End. I figured he had maybe ten minutes of patience left, but I had about two.

'There's a good chance. Whether they'll be willing to share? That's the real question.' As we passed Avid Reader for the third time I noticed the snail-trail of people waiting to get their books signed by the author sitting in the window had dwindled. 'Do you know what this *other something* is that Bela wants to talk about?'

He sort of shrugged and made a noise that didn't answer me one way or the other.

'Ziggi.'

'Not sure. He met with Anders Baker today, but that might be unrelated.'

I frowned, but didn't say anything. Anders Baker was a self-made gazillionaire thanks to a variety of import-export concerns, land development and general dodgy deals, including, so rumour had it, brothels, porn movies and some rather heavy-handed loan businesses. He was Normal, so I wasn't quite sure why he and Bela would be having dealings, unless it was to do with his once-upon-a-time wife; she'd been Weyrd, so maybe that was the connection.

We were about to begin another loop around the block when

I decided enough was enough. 'How about you let me out here and I'll text you when I'm done.'

He pulled up, blocking the flow of traffic, and a chorus of car horns began. 'If it's Aspasia,' he said, 'be polite – you catch more flies with honey than vinegar.'

'So my grandma used to say.'

A great number of Weyrd didn't cause problems but lived as quietly as they could. Although many were moon-born and preferred the night, most of them didn't roam the dark hours. They were generally good citizens, paid their taxes, held down all sorts of jobs and kept their secret selves hidden, or at least camouflaged. There were a few places, however, where they could just be themselves, and Little Venice was one of them.

The name was an in-joke, because none of the floods that periodically overran Brisbane had ever touched the place, not even when everything else in West End was under water. It looked ordinary enough: a three-storey building, commercial premises below, private residence above. The café-bar was cute: dingy little entryway lapping the street, long thin corridor leading into four big rooms filled with shadows and incense. Out back was an enclosed courtyard paved with desanctified cathedral stones, not used much during the day except by stray Normals; its tightly twined roof of leaves and vines was enough to keep off the sun and rain, but not quite enough to hide the snakes that lurked there. Through the wide archway I could see the space was packed, everyone swaying along contentedly to a man with a sitar accompanied by another playing a theremin. Two emo-Weyrd waitresses, managing to look both bored and alert, sloped between tables delivering drinks and finger food. Both had Lilliputian horns on their foreheads, just along the hairline; in the Normal world they'd probably be written off as body mods.

They might even have had vestigial tails to match, but Weyrd blood ran wild and it was almost impossible to predict how offspring would turn out.

When I needed information, this was where I generally started. Gossip washed through Little Venice like a river, the three Sisters who ran the place judiciously deciding what stayed behind and what got carried away. They were equally picky about what they shared. But even when I wasn't looking for anything, I still came here, because they did good coffee and amazing cakes: fat moist chocolate, rich bitter citrus, and a caramel marshmallow log that could stop your heart.

In addition to the business of hospitality, the Misses Norn — possibly not their real name — took turns reading palms, cards and tealeaves, each having her preferred method. For twenty bucks you'd get a traditional fortune-telling; fork out a heftier sum and you could see your future in runes, entrails or crimson spatter — in short, the more you paid, the nastier it would get. Maybe the latter were more accurate, but it was hard to know because each choice you made changed something else, shifting Fate like unruly chess pieces. The very willingness to spill blood might be the thing that knocked your destiny out of true.

But one thing remained constant — or constantly inconsistent: no matter which *modus operandi*, one Sister genuinely laid out your choices, one *made* your fate with her words and the third simply lied. Problem was, you couldn't really tell which did which. They weren't malicious, just Weyrd. It was their thing.

I'd been hoping for Theodosia because we got on better, but Aspasia was working the counter, so I kept Ziggi's advice in mind. Behind her was a mirror that looked like lace made of snowflakes. She gave me a cool smile as I limped in. This Sister was all dark serpentine curls, obsidian eyes, occasional prickly personality and red, red smile. When her lips opened I could see how sharp her teeth were.

'Fassbinder. Come to have your fortune told?' Her smile widened and she gave a shimmy and gracefully extended her hand, a belled bracelet making a gentle chime. 'Cross my palm with silver, girly.'

I shook my head. 'My answer's the same as it's always been – surely you could've seen that coming? But I will take a long black, some information and a slice of that caramel marshmallow log. And a super-sweet latte and a piece of mud cake to go.'

She pursed her lips. 'You got a new boyfriend?'

'Hardly.' I considered the idea of Ziggi-as-boyfriend, gave a little follow-up shudder and sat carefully on one of the tall stools, letting my sore leg dangle. Elbows resting on the countertop of fossilised stone, I grinned. I have a good grin, nice and bright, disarming. 'It's lovely to see you again, but this isn't a social call.'

'Colour me shocked.' Of course she wasn't going to make it easy. We might manage to be civil to each other but she's always held a torch for Bela and she's never quite forgiven me for dating him as long as I had. Or at all.

'Kids are going missing.'

'So sad,' Aspasia said lightly, and began caressing the coffee machine – which looked like the console of a spaceship – into doing her bidding. It started bubbling and spitting, a comforting sound that made conversation impossible for a little while. I traced patterns on the stone bench, thought I could make out the impression of a rib or two. After my drink had been assembled, Aspasia extracted the cakes from the refrigerated cabinet, sliced off a chunk and plated it in front of me. I took a glutton's bite, barely letting it touch the sides, then had to chase it down with a big swig of steaming liquid. So much sugar – my heart did a little jig. Aspasia was slower in preparing Ziggi's, maybe giving me time to tell her more, or maybe to show she had no interest in whatever I was going to say.

'Street kids thus far, so pretty much under the radar. Still . . .' I said.

No reaction as she studiously continued to froth milk into a metal jug.

'Still and all,' I persisted, 'it's only a matter of time before some little Normal goes astray and the powers-that-be will sit up and take notice.'

No eye contact; she was jiggling the pitcher around to ensure all the bubbles were evenly distributed. Her attention to detail was impressive.

'When that happens – and you know it will – people in high places will start looking for answers.'

She gave the jug a thump against the counter, as much from temper as technique. 'What do you want me to say, Fassbinder?'

I continued on as if I hadn't heard, 'And you know the Normals: when they want answers, they will lift up every rock and peer into every dark, dank place they can find. And they're not rational critters.'

'You think because some Normal kids go missing I'm supposed to shed tears? When did they ever care about our kind?' For someone whose side business was flimflamming the hopeful, she was pretty bad at keeping her true feelings under wraps. But she was also missing the point: this wasn't about mutual cross-species caring, sharing and handholding, it was about keeping the Weyrd safe: doing what was necessary to keep their existence quiet. In hindsight, I might not have helped things by mentioning Normals. Ah well.

'When they begin to peer into those dark, dank places, Aspasia, this may well be where they start – especially if someone points them in your direction. And that might lead them to take a long, hard look at our kind. Well . . .' I paused. '*Your* kind.'

'Half-breed,' she hissed before she could stop herself. It never did take much: one tiny poke and those nasty hackles always rose like a wave. I watched her hair curl and twist into writhing vipers until she got herself under control.

I gave a cold smile around another mouthful of caramel heaven. 'All I'm saying, Aspasia, is if you know anything, now would be the time to share. And I would be the person to share with. I'll do things quietly, you know that – after all, do you really want Detective Inspector McIntyre traipsing through here?' I let that sink in. 'And let's face it, if word should get out that you're cooperating with the police – or that this isn't a safe haven any more – then where *will* all your customers go?'

I was bluffing – why would I ruin my favourite coffee-and-cake spot? – but fortune-tellers aren't mind-readers and she wasn't sure if I was lying or not. All I needed was for her to be half-convinced. She didn't like being threatened, and I didn't like threatening, even if it was cheap and easy. But I needed to know what was going on, so I didn't stop. 'I'm sure Shaky Jake's would be delighted to pick up the slack, were Little Venice no longer able to guarantee its clients refuge from the *ordinary*.'

Her hands on the shiny countertop blackened and lengthened, the nails turning to sharp points. I tensed, ready to move as quickly as my injured leg would allow – which would, in this case, mean pushing myself off the stool and falling to the ground – then the moment passed and her hands were slender and white again, her manicure perfect.

She fixed me with a hard gaze. 'It's not about flesh. This city hasn't seen a *Kinderfresser* since—'

'—since my father.' I said it so she wouldn't; she'd made quite enough cracks about Grigor over the years and I was pretty sure I could do without one more. But it didn't feel any better to hear the words from my own mouth.

'But I've been offered . . . wine.'

That knocked me back. Of all the things I'd expected to hear, *wine* wasn't one of them. My confusion must have been obvious because she leaned forward and instinctively, I did the same. One of the hair-snakes brushed my left ear, soft as a kiss.

Aspasia spoke low. 'Some of the old ones – they've still got the appetites, the customs they don't want to let go.'

I nodded; I knew it was true, but smart Weyrd had tried to get rid of those habits in the interests of survival. Indeed, the Council had made a point of outlawing a lot of activities the Weyrd once considered perfectly acceptable, even banning *Kinderfressers*, because anthropophagia is frowned upon in most circles. The not-so-smart Weyrd . . . well, they didn't tend to last long these days.

'Kids cry, right?' she continued. 'I mean, they're kids, there's always something to cry over. But enough to fill two, three, four wine bottles? Wouldn't that be a lifetime of tears?'

I stared at her.

'I was offered a case. A *case*, Fassbinder. That's a lot of children, a lot of weeping. You take that . . .'

You take that, and you rob them of all the tears they might ever have. You steal their ability to feel joy, compassion, pain; you take their happiness as well. You remove the things that make them human. You take their lives. Not a *Kinderfresser*, no, but something somehow worse. You don't simply kill them; to get the right quality tears, you subject them to the most utter and lingering despair.

'Who?' I asked. 'Who's been offering?'

She gave a sidelong glance towards a corner table and I didn't turn around, but looked in the mirror. A thin girl sat there, maybe fourteen, badly made-up, her pale floss hair twisted in a clip, twiggy fingers painting patterns in the condensation on her glass. She wore a grey singlet top with an irregular pattern on the front, the design long lost, along with most of the silver sequins. Beneath the table were stickish legs, a far-too-short denim skirt and a pair of green Converse sneakers that had seen better days.

'Normal? Why is she here?'

'Normal. She pays,' said Aspasia flatly.

'When did she offer you the case – you didn't take it, did you?' I added suddenly, feeling a little sick.

'Two, maybe three weeks ago.' She looked me straight in the eyes so there could be no doubt. 'And no, I'm not that stupid.'

As the knowledge sank in, my stomach turned acidic. 'You didn't take it – but you didn't think to *tell* anyone about it?' How many lives had been lost in that time?

'You said it yourself: if word gets around that I'm making nice with the authorities, there goes my business. I've got children to support.'

'No, you haven't.'

'I might one day.'

'Chances are you'd eat them at birth. Christ, Aspasia, three weeks? You waited *three* weeks?'

She looked uncomfortable, but it didn't stop her saying, 'Fassbinder, did you come down in the last shower? You think she hasn't offered it around to others? You think no one's taken her up on it? You think I'm the only one keeping quiet? You think she hasn't been to the old households, for *special* occasions? You think the Council—'

'The Council hired me.'

'No, Princess, *Tepes* hired you.'

I straightened and sat back, digesting her words, trying to assess the possibility of one of the Councillors indulging in this sort of ancient practice. If that really was the case, then my problem was even bigger than missing children – but maybe Aspasia was just messing with me, seeing if I'd bite or head off in the wrong direction; she was pissy enough to try something like that. If anyone on the Council had something to hide, why on earth would they agree to Bela having me investigate? Surely they knew by now what sort of person I was? The sort who compulsively pulled loose threads on sweaters until they unravelled . . .

I flicked my eyes back to the girl's reflection to find she was looking at me. We stared at each other, just maybe five seconds, but that was all it took; she was up and out of her chair and haring down the long corridor before I could so much as turn around. There was no chance I'd be running after her; no way I'd even bother to try. The first step and my leg would be screaming.

'What's her name, and where do I find her?' I asked as Aspasia casually pushed the lid on Ziggi's takeaway latte and snapped the chocolatey chunk of mud cake into a polystyrene box. She shoved them towards me and I forked over a twenty. She obviously wasn't feeling communicative any more. Just as she pulled back her hand, clutching the note, I grabbed her wrist and held on tight, feeling her bones grinding against each other beneath my grip. I may look Normal, but it doesn't mean I've got nothing of the Weyrd about me; every now and then the half-breed blood shows through. I thought about wrapping the other hand around her throat and risking a few nips from the snakes, but I decided she might find it hard to talk.

'I don't want to do this, Aspasia.'

'Sally Crown,' she growled. 'Lives on the streets. Sometimes she sleeps behind West End Library, sometimes in the derelict flats on Hardgrave Road. Now let me go and get the fuck out.'

'You really need to work on your customer service skills. Keep the change.' Who was I kidding? Change from a twenty at Little Venice?

The whole way down the passageway I could feel her eyes boring into the back of my neck. I pulled out my mobile to text Ziggi, who was really not going be happy about my failure to make friends and influence people. A reminder about the earlier missed call flashed, but I didn't recognise the number. It would wait.

Chapter Three

'I'll see you tonight,' Ziggi said, and waved a hand in my general direction as he drove off. We'd given up watching West End Library for any sign of Sally Crown soon after dawn crept over the horizon. We'd also tried the derelict unit block on Hardgrave Road, which had almost got me spitted on the umbrella of an especially grumpy old siren wearing a grubby frock. Her wings had unfurled in shock when she found me in the flat she was using as a squat. After a lot of swearing from both of us – I was still twitchy about strange houses at night – I apologised and backed away. As Ziggi pointed out afterwards, I'd probably have been pretty pissed off myself if I'd found someone trespassing in my living room.

I made my way up the cracked path to my ramshackle home, a pre-war house with moulded ceilings, a huge back garden and a temperamental water heater so old that it might have come out of the Ark. Jasmine was thick on the front fence, lushly green and dotted with white-star flowers like icing. Its scent was heady, and as I felt for the keys in my jeans pocket, warm and fuzzy thoughts about bed danced in my head.

'Verity? Verity! Can you get my ball?' The voice fluted over the side fence. Between the palings was a small face, sharp-chinned, snub-nosed and wide-eyed, with a shock of mousy hair even messier than mine. A little hand pushed through the gap and pointed to a soccer ball lying under the three steps that led up to my patio. Lizzie wasn't allowed out of her yard without Mel, her single-parent, work-from-home acupuncturist mum in tow. She hated the rule, but I told her it was a good idea every chance I got: *There are bad people, baby, bad people*. Some days she decided not to talk to me.

I limped over and picked up the ball. It was new. 'Birthday present?'

'Uh huh.' I could sense a little chill coming from her.

'Sorry I couldn't come to your party, love. I was all ready, and I really wanted to, but there were some people I had to help.' I made a face to let her know that I truly had wanted to be with her, eating party pies and fairy bread until I was set to explode, then asked casually, 'Did you like the book?'

'I love it best of all – but don't tell Mum.' She smiled, defrosting. The fairy tales were the kind we had before Disney got to them: the ones with little girls who are eaten by wolves and bears with no conveniently timed rescue; boys who get lost in the forest and aren't ever found again; the sort where your brother is a danger to you and your sister cannot be trusted; with children whose greatest enemies are their own parents. The volume I'd given her was old, with a tooled leather cover, exquisite line drawings and a long red silk ribbon for marking your place. It was beautiful, though maybe it was a little much for a kid – Mel had frowned when I'd shown it to her a few days earlier. But I told her that forewarned was forearmed. Lizzie read like a champion and had been devouring the contents of my library like a locust. Well, not *all* of it; some discreet censorship had to be applied.

I reached over the fence and dropped the ball into her waiting arms.

'Thanks, Verity. Can I come and visit later?'

I frowned. 'Shouldn't you be at school?'

She rolled her eyes at the idiot adult. 'School holidays. So, can I come over?'

'Aha.' As a non-parent there was no need for me to keep track of such things. 'Not today, my friend. I've had a very long night. Maybe at the weekend?'

'Mmmmm-huh.' She was less than impressed.

'Have a good day, sweetheart,' I said and headed to the door.

Inside, the hot air was smothering. I passed through the front room, which contained a seldom-used asparagus-coloured velvet reproduction *chaise longue*, a desk with a full complement of dust to show how infrequently I sat there, a bookshelf filled with innocuous novels and a pristine waste paper bin. I generally used the room as little more than a place to store furniture, but it also acted as a safe space between the threshold and the rest of the house. I could have used it as a ward-moat, but I'd never really felt the need – or the requisite level of paranoia. And anyway, the aged wrought-iron security door did its job well enough. When I opened all the windows and the double doors onto the verandah, a breeze forced its way inside, and soon the temperature was bearable. I collected a glass of cold water and a variety of painkillers and headed out to plant myself in one of the faded green deckchairs until they kicked in.

My home might be old, but it was comfortable. There were three bedrooms, one of which had been repurposed as a library, a kitchen, bathroom, proper lounge room, a dining room with a table covered with books that hadn't yet found a shelf to live on, and a broad verandah out the back, where I now sat. It had been my grandparents' home, and just about all the furniture was theirs too – I'd seen no reason to change anything when they'd died; I kind of liked it that way. Sometimes I caught the scent of Grandma's Lily of the Valley talcum powder, or Grandy's Old Spice, and the pipe he used to smoke out on the verandah when Grandma wasn't home. She would pretend she couldn't smell it, even though it somehow managed to sneak inside and embed itself in the curtains and cushions. For a long while I thought that was how relationships had to work: you ignored all the things you didn't like, or that annoyed you, in the interests of harmony. Unfortunately, I didn't realise then that each and every irritating thing has its own life, its own limits, its own metre and pace and depth of impact. Like an idiot, I thought I had to tolerate *everything*. Eventually I managed to work out that not *everything* is – or should be – tolerable. I'd put up with a hell of a lot more than I needed to with Bela.

I stretched my leg out and rested it on the battered table my grandfather had cut down to kid-size for me. The top was painted green and the legs were peeling gold – it was garish and a little too short now, but I'd never been able to let it go. Soon the pills kicked in and the pain eased. An extremely fat kookaburra perched in the gigantic jacaranda tree in the middle of the yard. I gave him a nod; he stared back, unmoved.

I needed a nap. I needed to do some research. I suspected I'd need to do other things I didn't want to do. But most of all, I needed a nap – just a few hours. Too tired and comfortable to move, I closed my eyes, dropping my head back until there was a satisfying *crack* and things sat a little more comfortably on my shoulders. There was a chance I might even doze off sitting up in broad daylight.

When you're so tired that dreams come unbidden, when they seep through even though you're still a little bit awake – I hate that. That's the time when I think about my parents. Or rather my father; my mother, Olivia, was just a blur, a framed faded Polaroid on the shelf: a Normal, and dead before I ever knew her.

But I remembered my father; I couldn't forget him in spite of my best efforts. Grigor had no family to speak of; like a lot of Weyrd he came out here alone. There were no aunts, uncles, cousins, parents or grandparents, just him and me.

The everyday things of my childhood were salt in the corners of rooms to soak up the curses that might come our way, blood baked into a loaf of bread and left on the front porch under cover of darkness as an offering once a week to keep the worst of the shades at bay, which were more numerous than I knew for a long while, and dust swept from the footpath towards the house in the hope it would drag wealth with it. My father gave me small lessons in magic, in creating wards and disarming them – nothing that would make me a true witch or a sorceress, for my blood didn't run like that, but helpful for someone with a functioning knowledge of useful protection rituals. And I watched my father transform when he needed more strength, more height, lengthening his limbs and adding muscle. When I was little, I would try to do the same thing because I didn't realise that shifting didn't flow in my diluted DNA any more than witchcraft did. When he explained, I'd cried with disappointment. Grigor told me, *Change transforms, makes things both less and more – different – and we all adapt in our own way. Be patient: you'll find your own way.*

Though my father had no family, he had friends to spare. There were evenings when they'd come over and he'd send me to bed early. They would drink and eat and get rowdy in a language I didn't understand, a tongue that sounded a little like German, a little like Russian. I'd sit quietly at the end of the hallway, just out of their sight, and watch as they told tales and showed off the extraordinary feats they could do: starting colourful leaping fires with a breath; creating whirlwinds that lifted the furniture, then set it back down with no more than a gentle *thump*; shifting like my father, changing size or shape entirely until the lounge room resembled a bizarre zoo. I suppose they were relieved for a while not to have to hide what they were, happy to have a place where they could be free.

I was sworn not to tell anyone — certainly not the other kids at school — about these things, because they were our special secrets. Even then it took me quite some while to work out that there were two cultures and I could walk between them — and not just walk between them but more. I could fool the Normals because I looked like them, and I could step into the Weyrd world because I shared their blood, or some of it, anyway. They were wary, but polite enough, at least when I was little. Truth was, with one foot in each sphere, I didn't belong anywhere; I guess I always knew that.

After my father went, I lost contact with the Weyrd side of my life for a long time.

The angle I was sitting at became uncomfortable and brought me out of my trance state. My jeans were hot and damp in the humidity. I lurched up and rubbed at my hip, then hobbled into the bedroom. I changed into a singlet and a pair of thin cotton pyjama pants that covered my scars but were infinitely cooler than denim. I hovered between taking refuge in the bed where nightmares might wait, or making breakfast and staying awake to think. On balance, bad dreams really did not appeal, so I headed to the kitchen.

Twenty-three years ago my father was jailed as a paedophile and child-killer, but that didn't even begin to touch the skin of what he really was. He wasn't a child molester and he never touched me — that needs to be clear . . . but it doesn't really matter. The lesser of two evils is still evil. What he did — what he was *caught* doing — cast a shadow over the whole community and left us vulnerable. Weyrd memories are long, and sins of fathers need somewhere to go. What Grigor did left me exiled from my old life.

Most folk – both Normal and Weyrd – behaved themselves, through genuine belief in the rule of law, fear or sheer laziness. But there were always those few who didn't care for rules, and that group was split into those who were happy enough to break the law overtly and those who were contented to simply purchase the spoils of the nefarious labours of others. There was a market for everything, and the principle of supply and demand meant that some tables required the most tender of flesh. It was a particular taste, indulged in by the very few and the very old – a leftover from the past when stealing children was an accepted practice, hobby or habit, or sometimes a matter of survival. Back in the once-upon-a-time, children were both less guarded and more numerous in a lot of families, and with so many mouths to feed, sometimes parents weren't too worried if a couple were sold, or went missing. The rich Weyrd who bought those children always promised they'd have far better lives serving as footmen/valets/maids/what-have-you. It was the 'what-have-you' their parents never thought too much about.

In these modern times, that was precisely the kind of conduct the Council had forbidden in the interests of communal safety. Even so, small factions – very private parties, those Weyrd who really didn't like giving up what they considered their *right* – still wanted to indulge, albeit in secret, and someone had to acquire and dress that flesh.

My father: *Kinderfresser*. Child-eater. Butcher to the Weyrd.

To me, he was just my dad. I didn't know what he did when I was at school, or on those nights when he left me home alone with strict instructions not to open the door to anyone. And I never questioned the gifts he sometimes brought me: little bracelets, necklaces or rings. Occasionally there'd be a teddybear or a doll – things that looked as though someone might already have owned them.

I was ten when the police came for him, and I have done my best to wipe the memories of that night away.

Grigor lasted precisely how long you'd think a child-killer in prison would. The Council had made sure he couldn't shift any more. He was a big man, but he couldn't protect himself when six prisoners held him down and jammed jagged wooden broom handles into him. They didn't know what he truly was; they just hated him for what he'd done. His kind of crime meant he was even lower on the societal ladder than any of the other men around him. I wasn't taken to his funeral, nor did I go down to the river to watch my father make his journey with the Boatman.

The porridge in the saucepan began to burble at me and I removed it from the heat to throw in a handful of frozen raspberries. It might be a winter breakfast, but I loved it and it was incredibly healthy – well, at least until I added half a cup of cream. I poured green tea into the porcelain cup my grandmother had used every day for fifty years, carried bowl and cup outside and resumed position in the canvas chair.

The day after Grigor's arrest, my maternal grandparents, Albert and May Brennan, whom I didn't even know existed, appeared and took me into their home. The first months were fraught. I didn't know who they were, I missed my father dreadfully and I was completely uprooted. It wasn't just the new school, new house, new food, new rules, but also the new knowledge: not only that Grigor had done terrible things, that he was gone forever, but also the fact that he had come between my grandparents and my mother, and me as well, for Grigor had kept them away.

I learned 'normal' from them. They cared for me and did their best. Some days I'd catch them looking at me as if I were awful and fascinating, a cuckoo in the nest, and it hurt at first, but in the end I accepted it because I realised that despite that, they did love me. I *was* awful and fascinating, but at least I wasn't stuck with the kind of problems that plagued a lot of half-bloods, like horns or wings or powers they couldn't control. All I got was Grigor's ridiculous strength, which I've been thankful for from time to time, and some useful knowledge of magical practice.

Whenever I'd asked my grandparents about my mother, they'd generally just repeated darkly, *She married badly and ended worse.* How their daughter came to be married to such a man, they refused to disclose. My grandfather would change the subject without missing a beat as my grandmother's lips pursed in the manner particular to little old ladies that so perfectly conveyed both politeness and extreme annoyance. They were even more tight-lipped on the subject of Grigor, except the day they told me, gently, kindly, that he'd died. I let him fade in my memory until he became sepia and easily ignored.

It didn't take long to learn that my grandparents weren't appreciative of magic rituals, that even laying the simplest wards around the house wasn't on, let alone the baking of blood-offering loaves. With Grigor gone, my experience of strange things also faded. The community I'd begun my life in made no contact at all.

The flow of child disappearances stopped for a long, long time after Grigor's arrest – or at least those disappearances obviously connected to unacceptable dining habits. Bela once told me that Grigor's downfall had made the community a lot more alert, a lot more security-conscious: the Weyrd had begun to realise at last that their survival depended on evolution, civilisation, on moving forward and adapting, putting the old ways to rest once and for all.

And Grigor's customers? Those rich, powerful people disappeared like smoke, making it look like he'd been a sole predator, which, by the by, was exactly how the Council wanted it. The fact that he was a *Kinderfresser* never came out, not in the press, not in the courts. And the Normals in charge were just as happy with the result – their justice system had never been designed to cope with stuff like that; it can't even cope with its own mundane crimes. Tell the citizenry there're folk with tails and abilities and strange tastes and there'd be a riot; town squares turned into pyres, sales of garden stakes going through the roof, churches running out of holy water . . .

But now something had changed, and not for the better. A new product, moved by an unknown force, was endangering children and putting the Weyrd community at risk of exposure once more. Something scratched at my back brain and I started to wonder if the past was the place to start. I growled in frustration, heaved myself out of the chair and headed inside to find some grown-up clothes, as most people frowned upon pyjamas as outerwear.

No rest for the wicked.

Chapter Four

The State Library of Queensland resembled West End Library only in so far as they were both buildings. Located on the south bank of the river, between the Gallery of Modern Art and the Queensland Art Gallery, it was an enormous series of rectangles and voids, glass, tiles and concrete, all threaded through with Internet connectivity. International students sat with laptops, taking advantage of the free Wi-Fi to Skype home. Militant gaggles of mothers used prams and toddlers as blunt weapons without fear or favour, laying claim to café space. Determined-looking genealogists headed to the upper floors to trawl through electoral rolls, immigration and shipping logs, convict records and rare manuscripts. Others were there to go through the music, newspaper, film and photographic collections. Some just wandered in to get out of the wind, rain or sun, to nap in the stacks on the appallingly patterned carpet or in one of the almost-comfortable armchairs scattered around, others to sit in the Red Box and watch the river serenely snake past.

Inside, the air-conditioning was set to Arctic breeze. The microfiche reader made a slight hum and gave off a lot of heat and I rubbed my hands in front of it, campfire-style. But I didn't complain about the cold; I was too grateful that I'd been allowed through the door. A few years ago during the floods there had been an 'incident' in which I might have been involved. I was not the *cause* of said incident, but

I was there clearing up a few things and, well, some people got a bit singed, books were damaged and the teacup collection on the Queensland Terrace was irreparably diminished. I was also grateful that old-style librarians — the sort who could turn evildoers to ash with a single glare — were few and far between nowadays.

There was surprisingly little about Grigor's activities in the archival newspapers; that would be down to Weyrd influence in the corridors of power, I supposed. It was all about damage control. But there were pictures of him being taken to and from the Supreme Court: a tall, handsome man in a bad suit, with hangdog eyes and a loose-lipped grin that showed off sharp teeth. Though he looked Normal, I thought I could make out stains on his jacket, right where the sleeves met the body: bleed-through from where they'd inserted the iron nails in his shoulder joints to stop him from shifting. His was the sort of crime that couldn't be entirely hushed up; it had created so much outrage that it could only be shut down by a very public arrest and prosecution. My father was thrown to the wolves — not that he didn't deserve it, but that's how it was done: one scandal amplified in order to cover up a worse one.

I hadn't looked at these reports before, although Bela had occasionally shared some tidbits. I had chosen not to, to ignore it all, as if none of it had happened. During the trial my grandparents had kept the TV off at night so I wouldn't see the news bulletins. If they bought papers, they read them before coming home. They acted as if, somehow, what was happening to my father couldn't touch me if we all ignored it; as if it was nothing to do with me. But there were days when I believed everything I was doing as an adult, the vigil I kept over the city, was a kind of penance. Hidden somewhere in the back of my mind was the thought that one day I'd have to pay for what my father did, and just maybe I had started making reparation.

The clippings ran the gamut from congratulatory front-page features about dropping numbers of street kids thanks entirely to improved Social Services programmes, to a couple of inches on page three about missing kids, then to explosive headlines about the evil at the heart of the city. There were lists of victims' names, and family histories reduced to anaemic sentences that in no way showed the lives of these children before my father had found them. What I did learn was where he'd gone wrong. Grigor got caught because he got lazy and sloppy – he didn't hunt far enough away, didn't harvest from his usual source. He'd taken a cared-for child, one from a happy home in a rich locale, a son for whom someone would – and did – look. Had he stuck to the runaways, the unwanted, who knows how long he might have gone undetected.

I scrolled through for as long as I could, trying to figure out what was important in the wash of the historical irrelevant. Glamorous women smiled out from the social pages, shoulder pads taking up most of the photos; schoolkids brandished trophies after winning debating competitions and football matches; there were outcries over midnight demolitions of heritage buildings and rubber duck races on the river of brown; critics lauded festivals for writers and films, and there were a slew of other crimes just as awful as my father's, but nothing was linked to me or mine.

When even the heat from the microfiche stopped defrosting my fingers, I gave up. Though my brain felt filled to the brim and then some and my heart was sore, it had been a wasted afternoon. Memories made everything hurt. The need for sleep whined in my head like a determined fly, but I was meeting Ziggi at my place at six. I knew he would have picked me up from the library if I'd asked, but I was stubbornly pursuing a dream of some independence. I liked to get myself home using public transport occasionally, even if my sense of triumph was generally outweighed by pain and inconvenience. The ache in my leg suggested I was an idiot even as I hobbled through the sliding doors into the last vestiges of summer heat. In a matter of days, I knew the weather would pull a stunning volte-face and temperatures would drop. Autumn might last approximately seventy-two hours if we were lucky.

The light outside was hard and blinding and I blinked, stunned by the flashes on my retinas. I sensed someone near me before the thump; a violent meeting of shoulders, and for a moment I was sure it had been intentional. Then I was just concerned with not falling over.

'Oh, shit. Sorry! Sorry—' Masculine tones, soft-spoken but sounding genuinely apologetic. Hands steadied me as my sight normalised. The guy was about my height, dark blond, green eyes behind wire-framed glasses, wearing jeans and a grey-blue T-shirt with a top-hatted badger riding a bicycle. Standard geek. He held his palms up to show he meant no harm.

'It's okay,' I said, waving him away. 'It's okay.'

'Maybe I could say sorry with a cup of something warm? It would be over-priced warmth to show my sincerity,' he said.

Without thinking I said, 'No. Thanks.'

I moved off as he gave a *what-can-you-do?* shrug. On a whim that surprised me, I glanced over my shoulder, but he'd already started off in the opposite direction. He looked good in jeans. I shook my head to clear the distracting thoughts and went on my not-so-merry way.

Chapter Five

I limped up the incline from the Norman Park train station cursing and sweating, perspiration running down my face, my back and basically everywhere. The street was deserted, the houses quiet. In the oppressive atmosphere the ring of my mobile sounded overly loud. I fumbled it on, not looking at the number, assuming it was Ziggi or Bela.

'Is this Verity Fassbinder?' Female, the timbre quite musical.

'Who's speaking?' I asked, idly wondering where she'd got my number. It's always nice to know where the referrals come from.

'My name is Serena Kallos. I've been told you're good at solving problems.'

'I have my moments. What's your problem, Ms Kallos?'

'I'd rather not discuss it over the phone. Can we meet? This evening?'

I wanted to say no, but there was something in her tone. 'I have a few things to do tonight, but if you don't mind meeting late? How about Little—' No, it was probably too soon for me to return to Little Venice. '. . . ah, Shaky Jake's, about eleven.' I figured even if Ziggi and I hadn't finished our search for Sally Crown, we could take a break, then get back to it.

'I know where that is. Late is fine.'

I wanted to ask *what* she was, but that wasn't polite. If she knew

39

where the café was, if she knew who I was, chances were she was Weyrd. Though I knew Normal people, lots of them, they generally didn't know what I did for a living.

'Okay, I'll see you there,' I started, but she'd already rung off.

At the top of the hill I looked at the remaining five-hundred-yard downward slope with relief.

Staggering into my yard, I saw someone on the patio, knocking hard on the door.

'Hey, Mel.'

She turned and looked at me with desperate hope. 'Is Lizzie here? She said she was going to read with you.'

Little bugger.

'No, I told her not today. When did she come over?'

'A couple of hours ago.' Her voice shook, and I noticed her hands were shaking too.

'Have you checked the tree?' There was a hollow at the base of the jacaranda in my back garden. Lizzie had comic books, a blanket and a couple of dolls stashed there. Every kid needs a secret spot so her mother and I pretended we didn't know about it.

Mel did that thing with her head, part yes, part no. 'It was the first place I looked.'

My heart thumped and icy little fingers stroked my spine. *No*, I told myself, *wrong neighbourhood. A cared-for child.* Another part of my brain chimed in with, *Grigor did it.* I shook off the anxiety; I was overly sensitive because of what I'd been researching, jumping to conclusions after reading all those news articles. Lizzie wouldn't go anywhere with a stranger; she knew better than to trust an adult she didn't know. At least . . . I *hoped* she did.

'Right.' I paused. 'How about playing up the road with the Thomas kids? I know she's not supposed to, but—' Mel was already shaking her head. 'You've called her school friends?' She was trying not to cry as she managed a *yes*. Panic swelled in my own throat and I swallowed it. *Lizzie was just hiding*. But all the same . . .

'You should call the cops.'

'I don't want to overreact,' she said, but I knew that's exactly what she wanted to do. She wanted to scream until her baby returned. She wanted to kill the person who'd caused her this tearing fear. I pushed her gently towards her house. The police would ask questions, keep her company, file a report, and when Lizzie finally wandered in, they'd give her a talking-to that wouldn't go astray. She wouldn't stay out late – she'd get hungry, that would bring her home.

I told myself this was true.

'Go. Call. Better safe than sorry. I'm sure it's nothing – she'll be back before you know it and getting her bum spanked,' I added, eyeing the gypsy cab as it pulled up. 'I've got to go out for a while, but you've got my mobile number if you find anything – if you need anything, yeah? I can't avoid this appointment, but I'll be back later this evening, I promise.'

She looked really disappointed and I hated having to go; as her tears spilled over, I felt my own eyes welling up. When I hugged Mel I had to swallow my sobs – if I gave in now I wouldn't be able to make myself leave. I held her tight for long seconds, then gave her another nudge. I watched her walk away, narrow back shuddering, still struggling to contain the fear.

Then Ziggi hit the horn and I headed over. I was really trying not to get irritated by the pitying looks he shot me every time I limped. I'd known him almost as long as I had Bela, and he'd taught me a lot of what I knew about the Weyrd and their habits, about tracking and tracing people, and about breaking and entering. In many ways he was closest thing I had to family, kind of like the uncle everyone except kids roll their eyes at. Mostly he didn't judge me, but when he did, I had to admit it was generally deserved. As I leaned in to open the door, something gleaming on the footpath caught my eye: silvery sequins, the worse for wear, shaken from a top – one paired, I imagined, with a too-short denim skirt and tatty green Converse sneakers. Paralysed, I stared across the street at the windows of a vacant house and thought how much they looked like dead eyes.

If it had been me, I would have lain low, avoided my usual haunts for a while, maybe a week or two, until interested parties gave up. Maybe I'm smarter than most people. I was certainly smarter than Sally Crown, who was young and *dumb*.

Ziggi killed the engine and we rolled to a stop outside West End Library. We'd been waiting up the road, watching, careful not to be seen – we were lucky the daylight had given out, considering the car we were in – until a skinny figure flitted under the streetlight outside the redbrick building and ducked down a side path. The community noticeboard out the front was covered with sedimentary layers of flyers no one ever bothered to remove: calls to self-help flocks, book clubs, writers' groups and sewing circles. In a bottom corner, beneath years of leaflet collage and archaeological debris, I spied an enlarged photocopy of a newspaper article, turned brittle yellow by age and elements. I could just make out a perfectly coiffed matron's smiling face beside a feature about the substantial cheque she'd donated to some charity or other. A moustache had been drawn across her top lip.

'You okay on your own?' Ziggi asked around a mouthful of yesterday's Little Venice mud cake. His ability to hoard food never ceased to amaze me.

'Yep.'

'Only Bela said—'

'Fuck Bela,' I snarled.

'He's not my type.' He sighed. 'Look, V, I know you're tired and cranky. I know your leg hurts more than you let on. And because I'm fond of you, I'm gonna say this even though you'll probably yell at me: you gotta let it go.' He fixed me with a stare, lowered his voice. 'I know you don't want Bela back; I know you dumped him, and why, but if you keep carrying around the reasons you left, it's gonna kill you.'

'And why did I leave?' I asked, unable to manage even a lick of sarcasm.

''Cause he wasn't what you thought you wanted. You've gotta forgive him for that. And in all fairness, he's never pretended to be anything other than what he is. Let it go – it's just making you *mean*.'

He wasn't entirely right, but he wasn't entirely wrong. Or maybe he *was* entirely right. I swallowed, tried to answer, swallowed again and finally managed, 'You're right.'

He couldn't have looked more stunned if he'd tried.

'You're right and I hate that, but I am sorry. You're my friend and you don't deserve to be a scratching post.' I rubbed my chin. 'It's just . . . I'm so *angry* with him lately. It's . . .' Ziggi didn't say anything, just waited patiently. 'It's the leg – I blame *him*. My whole fucking life feels like it's been on hold since this happened and I blame him. The pain is just a constant reminder.'

'You think he doesn't blame himself?'

'I don't know,' I said, and I honestly didn't.

'It's always nice to have a break-through in group,' he said, and I punched his shoulder. We grinned like idiots.

'If I yell, then you come running, okay? Otherwise, finish your leftovers – it was expensive and I might not be able to get more for some time.'

43

I struggled out of the cab before he could ask me what I'd done and took the cracked concrete path along the side of the building, moving surprisingly quietly, all things considered. The scent of richly decaying compost from the garden beds perfumed the air. The noises of the city were muffled this far up Boundary Street. I was so tired and steeped in self-pity that I could have cried, and my leg throbbed as though the wounds had reopened, even though they'd been pinkly scarred over for ages. I paused at the threshold of the paved area out back. Overgrown plants climbed the high chain-link fence, pushing bits of it out at odd angles. There were a couple of old metal skips and some broken chairs, and curled on a sofa in the far corner was Sally Crown, all tucked up like a dirty angel, eyes closed, a grubby navy blanket pulled up to her chin in spite of the heat. Mozzies buzzed enthusiastically by my ears, but wisely left me alone.

I was almost across the yard when my phone, which I'd forgotten to set to silent, rang. The sharp squeal woke Sally and she sat up with a start, slashing about with a flick-knife while she tried to scramble to her feet. Fortunately, my own reflexes are excellent. I avoided the blade, grasped her wrist and managed to pull her off the sofa and up towards me, but she was wriggling and slippery in the evening heat and I couldn't get a good enough grip to throw her down, which meant we both stumbled and fell. Luckily, I ended up sitting on top of her; not so great, my bad leg was twisted uncomfortably. The mobile cut off abruptly, as if whoever was calling had thought better of it.

'I didn't get a chance to introduce myself last night, Sally,' I said, snatching away the knife and tossing it over the fence.

'I know who you are, bitch.'

I winced. 'Language.'

She let loose with a few more choice profanities and I lost what little patience I had left and grabbed her face. As I held her jaw and squeezed, she whimpered.

'Now, you will notice that I am freakishly strong. I can and will pop your head if you don't tell me what I want to know.' I gave her an encouraging shake. 'You went by my house – how did you know where I lived?'

She tried to say something, but it sounded impolite, so I squeezed a bit harder. Tears trickled down her cheeks and I felt like a bully, but Lizzie was missing and I wasn't stupid. I let Sally's face go, but stayed on top of her.

'Aspasia. I said I wanted to talk to you.' She spat, red-tinged spittle. I'd squeezed too tight. Aspasia – really? It was hard to know if she thought she was doing me a good turn or just trying to fuck up my day. My money was on the latter. At any rate, we'd be having words later.

'Sally, if you know who I am, then you know what I can do – and have done. This could end several ways, but I'd really prefer it if you'd just tell me what I need to know, then I'll let you get on with your life.'

Her eyes glittered, but she nodded slowly.

'Good. So I have questions. Firstly, who's got you pimping that wine? And secondly, what do you know about the disappearance of a young girl this afternoon?' Her expression clearly said she was considering lying, which ramped up my tightly controlled rage, so I added, 'Think very carefully before you answer. If anything happens to her, I swear I'll be back for you, and you will not enjoy our reunion.'

I gave her time to digest this. 'I'll start, okay? I *suspect* you're collaborating with someone. I *suspect* that you've been leading children astray – no, don't say anything yet; if I only suspect things, you're safe.' I waved a finger at her; it would have looked flippant but for the fact it was shaking. 'For now. If I *know* for certain, then I will not be able to turn a blind eye. But I am willing to ignore all the other things you've done if you answer my questions.'

'She'll kill me,' the child whined, and my conscience pricked at me. Beneath the rat-like demeanour I could see a little girl who'd been ill-used, who was only doing what she could to survive; a child whose humanity had been stripped away until she thought of no one but herself. I felt sorry for her – but that didn't stop me from saying, 'And if you don't tell me, I have another friend called Zvezdomir Tepes and if you don't know who he is now, you will soon.'

She moaned.

Okay, she knows about Bela; someone's warned her good and proper.

'Sally, tell me, and I will stop her so she won't hurt anyone again – she won't be a danger to you any more. I promise.'

She seemed to weigh the odds, and I saw as the scales dropped in my favour, though I didn't kid myself; it was due purely to my proximity, nothing to do with the strength or righteousness of my argument.

'House at Ascot,' she snarled.

'Has this woman got a name?' I asked. She shook her head, but reeled off the address and I decided I believed her. If she was desperate enough to help someone who saw children as an *ingredient* there was no reason to think anyone would trust Sally with more information than they absolutely had to.

I rose stiffly and offered a hand, which she took reluctantly. She stood, poised, as if she couldn't decide whether to try and hit me again or just flee. I pulled out my wallet and handed over the few notes I had in the hope it might keep her from doing anything awful for a night or two. I gave her a business card too, though I was pretty sure it was pointless, but I couldn't help thinking that this might be Lizzie one day, if her life went badly wrong. This girl wouldn't ask for help; she was too far gone, but her face still took on a strange look of wonderment as the tens and fifties crackled into her palm. She stared at me as if I was crazy. She mightn't have been too far off the mark.

'If you've lied to me . . .' I started. I didn't ask how she'd taken Lizzie, how she'd lured her, or *why*, because I didn't trust myself not to lose my temper if I heard any more. This child had already borne too much of other people's anger.

Her expression said, *I know, I know.* 'It wasn't me,' she said. 'I didn't take her.' But she had, though she was lying determinedly, as if saying the words out loud might make them true. Even if I hadn't seen the sequins on the footpath, the way she spoke and the expression on her face told me Sally was lying. I'd known Lizzie wouldn't have gone to a stranger – or an adult, but another child? Of course she'd have gone with another child – she was lonely and wanted someone to play with.

'You should change your shirt,' was all I said. I felt sick with anger – anger at Sally, anger at a world where kids had to live like her – but I walked away before it got the better of me.

Chapter Six

'Ah, Ziggi. How did we not know about this?' I stared at the huge, venerable white architectural mess: two storeys and an attic, a widow's walk between more chimney stacks than looked entirely necessary, a lot of decorative lattice-work and a kind of strange Gothic thing happening with the windows. I didn't remember ever seeing it before. I looked askance at my sidekick: I *knew* Brisneyland, I *knew* all the big Weyrd residences, the places where the moneyed, powerful families resided – or at least, I thought I did. But this . . .

He was still peering at the place. 'Glamoured – a very powerful spell, even I'm struggling. We're only seeing it now because we had the address and came looking for it specifically.'

He wasn't wrong, it was kind of laborious to behold. My eyes kept sliding to the side and I had to concentrate hard for the first few minutes we sat and watched. It got a bit easier, but the building was still, well, *slippery*. I climbed from the cab and leaned against the door while Ziggi hung out the window.

The plot was enormous, even for this area. The house was set far back from the road, in the middle of an overgrown garden with camphor laurels lining the driveway, so tall and close that they formed a loose canopy above the gravel path where we'd parked. Flying foxes squeaked overhead, darker patches against the moonlit sky, like shadow puppets flitting between branches, on course for an evening of stripping people's fruit trees and crapping on their laundry.

'Aw, Ziggi,' I repeated. '*Shit.*'

'What? You don't think it looks right?'

'I think it looks too damned right.' I pushed myself away from the body of the cab. 'You're not going anywhere?'

'I ain't going nowhere,' he said. 'You sure you wanna go on your own?'

I was pretty sure I didn't want to, but if I started making a habit of taking my chaperone everywhere I was doomed; I might as well stop leaving the house and start collecting cats and pizza boxes. 'I'm sure.'

He said hopefully, 'If anyone comes, you gotta secret signal you want me to give?'

'Fuck no! I want you to make a *really* big noise so I can hear you. Who knows, maybe you'll scare *them* away. Just listen out in case *I* start yelling for help. Help would be good. You know, cavalry, et cetera.' I carefully switched my mobile to vibrate.

'Got it. Big fucking noise.'

I gave him a thumbs-up and set off down the drive. I could feel the weight of his gaze. The pills were wearing off and the pain in my leg sharpened; I was okay with that right now, though. It kept me alert.

This house, the whole massive enchantment thing? It would have made sense in West End, but this . . . this was Ascot, home to the important people, with property prices so high they could give you a nosebleed. If the car in the garage wasn't a Jag or a Merc or some high-end 4x4 with bull-bars and spray-on dirt, then you knew it belonged to the cleaning lady. And yet here was this camouflaged mansion . . .

Then again, maybe it did make sense. Only idiots hunt where they live, and no one with half a brain was going to snatch a kid from around here, were they? So maybe someone had learned from Grigor's mistakes.

The five steps up to the verandah creaked under my feet. The red cedar double doors had frosted panels. A white-painted swing-chair sat to one side, a snowy metal table next to it, with three small ceramic pots clustered in the centre, each sprouting some kind of succulent. I pushed the doorbell, listening for reverberations inside, but there was no response. Maybe the battery was dead; it wasn't likely to get much use. Of course, if anyone had answered, some tap-dancing would have been required, but I had standard routines: I'd ask if they were interested in a pyramid investment scheme or if they'd like to be introduced to Jesus. People tended to back away from that sort of approach, though I'd be in trouble if they said yes.

I thought, *What if Sally had lied?* Then, *What if Sally'd told the truth?*

I tried the swirly brass handle but, getting no joy, moved away and peered in the windows. They were clean, as was the swing-chair. So not entirely deserted; someone was concerned enough to keep the place spick and span. I pressed my nose to the pane and squinted: dark rooms, what looked like expensive pieces of furniture, a chandelier catching any stray streaks of moonlight, floor-length curtains tied back with sash ropes. Again I listened hard for the sound of someone moving about, and again, nothing.

I tapped my foot. Maybe Sally had lied and this was just a normal house, so I was wasting my time – but *why* the glamour? I might have given up except for that – that, and the unease in my gut. Where do you hide a whole bunch of kids? How do you make them disappear without a trace? You take them somewhere no one would think to look. Somewhere no one sees properly.

I picked up one of the small ceramic pots, hefted it and broke the frosted glass panel in the left-hand door. Reaching very carefully through the gap I found the latch and let myself in. Ziggi was probably shaking his head at my ham-fisted efforts, but I'd never been able to get the hang of lock picks despite the hours he'd put in trying to train me. There was, I noted with relief, no alarm box on the wall, no little set of lights blinking in a startled fashion as I failed to enter a pin code. There wasn't even the lowest rank of wards – but then, who needs a security system when you've got a honking great glamour around your lair?

The narrow Persian rug running the length of the hallway muffled my footsteps. Halfway along was a staircase covered in thick creamy carpet. To the sides: a lounge and a library, then a dining room and a family room, and on towards the back, where an expansive kitchen waited, all gleaming stainless steel, glittering granite worktops and tiles of Carrera marble. I retreated and took the wide staircase.

On the next level were four tastefully decorated bedrooms, each with a queen bed and chests of drawers, but no cupboards, and no obvious sign of use. Same deal with the cleanest bathroom I'd ever seen; it gleamed. A jungle of very realistic artificial plants gave it a tropical air. A large office lined with filing cabinets had a ridiculously broad desk beneath the window, staring out into the thickness of the trees. I made a mental note to return later and toss the room to my heart's content, but it was apparent there was no laptop, no desktop, no fax, no phone, no nothing. As I was about to head downstairs again, I noticed a hatch in the ceiling above the landing with a thin silver chain hanging to person height. A single tug brought a neat aluminium ladder unfolding easily towards me. I climbed cautiously, but there was nothing in the attic but dust and a few stacked plastic tubs, empty as could be. My leg almost gave way as I descended and I stumbled for a moment until I caught my balance. The limb wasn't thanking me for all this activity.

I returned to the kitchen, the suspicion that I was in the wrong place growing steadily, making it hard to breathe.

It would sound better if I could say I made the discovery because I'm a genius, but mostly I found it because I have this thing for investigating other people's pantries. The slatted wooden door opened onto an area roughly the size of a walk-in wardrobe. Right next to a shelf stacked with salt, sugar, tins of salmon, jars of caviar, bottles of truffle oil and boxes of water crackers was a second door, which was not only unlocked but actually a little ajar. I guess the owner probably thought their larder was safe from hostile incursions.

The steps leading down were brightly lit. At the bottom was yet another door, this one of reinforced steel, also unlocked, which opened into a large white room with a dark grey polished concrete floor that ran the length of the house. This wasn't some dingy cellar with cobwebs and discarded crap as far as the eye could see; this was pristine, *industrial*: a serious workroom. There were banks of timber wine racks on either side with a passage between them. I stopped to examine some of the bottles as I passed: a coat of arms with a big-arsed bird and shield was impressed into the red wax that sealed the mouth of each. When I stepped into the other half of the room I saw it was open, but filled with a row of steel tables. A large furnace sat in the left-hand corner at the back, and to the right was a round vat with a screw-down lid and pipes running into and out of it – it looked a lot like an upmarket moonshine still. The walls were obscured by wine barrels and benches lined with all manner of bottling paraphernalia. And stark against the floor next to the furnace was a tumbled stack of small shoes, all scuffed and dirty and worn, and the air still held a faint hint of cooked flesh.

In the middle stood a woman.

She looked like any Ascot matron, and then I realised she really was familiar: I had seen her face smiling out from the community noticeboard at West End Library just a matter of hours ago. She wasn't much different, except for the lack of a graffiti moustache. She appeared to be in her sixties, but I was fairly certain that her true age was being artfully concealed by a combination of expensive cosmetics, a cunning glamour and a lot of Botox. Even so, the skin on her face and neck was a little too tight, too smooth, as if it had been burned once and a lot of effort had been made to reverse the effects; not even magic and surgery can completely conceal something like that. She wasn't overly tall, but she had a good figure, just a little thick around the waist. Her pale champagne dress fitted impeccably; her hair, an elegant mix of grey and blonde, was immaculate and her eyes a twinkling blue. The get-up was completed by a diamond-encrusted watch, a pendant shaped like the bird-and-shield design on the wine bottle seals, baroque pearl earrings and a selection of knuckleduster rings probably worth more than my house. She looked like the kind of grandmother who wouldn't want to be hugged too tightly lest it wrinkle her ensemble.

'Yes?' she said. She didn't say, *I'm calling the police*, which was telling. She held a pair of thick black silicon gloves somewhat at odds with her outfit.

All I could think to say was, 'You're not eating them?'

The glance she gave me suggested I was as stupid as I felt. 'Oh, no, lovie. If you take their tears,' she answered quite tenderly, 'you can't use the meat afterwards. It's too dry and tough. Really, it's either wine or veal.' She smiled. 'Look at you, Grigor's daughter, so terribly Normal but still causing trouble. Who'd have thought?'

I swallowed, a hundred questions rearing up, not the least of which was, *How did you know my father?* But I didn't need to ask that one at least; it was easy enough to guess. I peered at the child lying on the table in front of her and Lizzie's terrible stillness knocked the curiosity from me. The moments before I detected the faint rise and fall of her chest seemed endless. All I wanted to do was get her out of there.

'Isn't she lovely? I was ecstatic when Sally brought this one! It's much nicer when they're clean and content, but oh, they're so hard to get hold of. I will have to punish her, though, for sending you. I assume it was Sally; she'd sell her mother to save her own skin.' The woman didn't wait for an answer, just beamed at me. 'The little one smells a bit like you, you know. I thought she might be yours. That amused me no end, the idea of harvesting Grigor's grandchild! But when I looked closer, I couldn't see him anywhere in her. Still, a happy mistake; now I can take care of you, too – you've made some trouble for us! Oh, maybe I won't punish Sally after all.'

'Lizzie,' I called, but she didn't stir. I tried again, louder. '*Lizzie!*'

'She can't hear you, dear. I use a sleeping spell right up until I'm ready to put them in the press. You don't want too much panic; that sours things. It's the grief you need, the pain, and it's always best taken fresh. Giving them time to worry just makes things, well, stale and bitter.' Her eyes glittered. 'My, what a vintage you would have made when you were young, girl. What anguish, what unadulterated heartache! The loss of your father, everything you'd known overturned. What wouldn't I have done to take your tears . . . It's so much sweeter, a wine born of deep sorrow.' She clicked her tongue. 'But that grandmother of yours kept such a watch over you! How fierce she was.' Her tone was equal parts irritation and admiration.

'Wake her,' I said. 'Wake Lizzie up and give her to me and we'll walk out of here. I'll tell no one about you. Just give her to me.' I'd have told a million lies if only I could get the little girl away safely, but of course the woman knew that, and it was clear she had no fear of me. I had so many questions and the idea that she might have answers tore at me, but I refused to be distracted, mindful of cats and curiosity.

'Don't be silly,' the woman told me. 'Where was I? Oh, yes, your father. A reliable business partner, a talented *Kinderfresser*, but he could be so rash, so foolish when under pressure to fill orders. He very nearly ruined everything.' She shook her head sadly, a *you just can't get the staff* look on her face.

'Zvezdomir Tepes knows I'm here,' I lied. It didn't matter if I screamed; no one would hear me, not down here deep below the ground. But I wasn't going to tell her about Ziggi. If she got me, I didn't want her sneaking up on him. 'If I go missing, he'll come looking and the full weight of the Council will be brought to bear.' That sounded pretty grand, I thought, though in reality it would really mean both Bela *and* Ziggi.

'I can handle the Council, lovie,' she confided, and her certainty made me shiver. On the table, Lizzie twitched and the woman tut-tutted. 'You've broken my concentration. Enough of this.'

She came at me so quickly I didn't have time to think. In my mind, she was still the sort of woman who was only dangerous if the café ran out of macaroons, but she was old, very old, and infinitely stranger and stronger. Beneath her well-kept skin was something else, something mean and hurtful that writhed and wriggled as if anxious to be *seen*. While I was watching the shadowplay beneath her surface she punched me in the chest with both fists. I felt her rings rip the thin cotton of my T-shirt, pierce my skin and bury themselves into the flesh.

She cackled as I fell straight backwards and hit my skull on the concrete. My eyes closed with shock and I saw starbursts behind my lids, then blacked out briefly.

The agony of being dragged along the smooth cold floor was what woke me; that, and the pain in my lacerated chest and pounding skull. She had hold of my ankles and was pulling me along easily, not struggling with my weight at all. She was hideously strong. When we reached the furnace, she let my legs drop, which also hurt. I lay there trying to make my body and brain work, trying to get to my damned feet and fight. At last I started looking around, and I found Lizzie's terrified stare; with the witch's attention elsewhere she'd woken but, playing possum, not rolled off the steel table. I tried to send comfort, hoping she'd be brave, as I got my thoughts in order.

The old woman yanked open the door of the furnace with a great clank and the heat whooshed out. She meticulously pulled on her gloves and started chattering again, tilting her head towards me. 'Ah, awake. Good. You're quite tall. How am I going to fit you in? Might be a bit of a squeeze. The little ones aren't generally any problem . . .'

She leaned down to grab my wrists so she could heave me forward: Baba Yaga, the witch in the forest, the stepmother offering a poisoned apple. She hauled my top half up and for a moment our faces almost touched. She laughed, her breath stinking like rotten meat, and let me go, then she wrapped her hands around my waist and gathered me upwards. That was when I got my fingers to her throat and she laughed again, and kept laughing until she felt my grip tighten.

'I may look Normal,' I hissed, 'but I'm my father's daughter.'

Then she was gasping for breath and taking me seriously, and I felt her nails bursting through the heatproof gloves and tearing into my back. I couldn't stop myself screaming, but I kept squeezing, watching her face turn purple, her lips cyanotic, as her claws ripped deeper holes in me, closer to organs that would not react well to puncturing.

Then she was went limp. My hands fell away, the agonising pain in my back making it hard to concentrate, then someone – *Lizzie!* – pushed the witch away from me. The woman, reviving, crashed against the open maw of the furnace, pulling Lizzie with her. I almost fell trying to reach Lizzie, but forced myself upright and managed to shove the little girl out of the way as the Winemaker, with smoke already rising from the back of her head, started to shriek. I punched her in the chest, just as she had done to me, and she overbalanced, her beautifully coiffed platinum hair blazing red and gold, in flames.

I grabbed her ankles, lifted and shoved with all my might, and the top half of her disappeared into the oven. I jammed the rest of her in and Lizzie slammed the door shut. I slid the bolt home with shaking fingers.

I hugged Lizzie close as we listened to the drumming of desperate heels and the beating of angry fists for a longer time than I'd have thought possible.

Welcome to the gingerbread house.

Chapter Seven

As the cab crossed the Story Bridge in the soft darkness I felt every bump and dip in the road: a regular rolling rhythm of *thud thud thud*. My wounds ached and itched and the warm leak of blood seeped down my skin. My T-shirt was horribly sticky – the back seat was going to need some cleaning – but I wanted to get Lizzie home to her mother before I did anything else. Sleep called, but I fought it. It wasn't only Ziggi's rear eye intent upon me this time; the two at the front kept flicking to my image in the mirror too. I gave him a weak grin and a wave.

'I know I've asked already, but I'm gonna repeat myself: are you okay?' he asked.

'I'm a human pincushion. I'm sorry about the mess.'

'Not the first time, prob'ly not the last.' He hit the horn as a black Mercedes merged into our lane and came a little too close to cutting off the cab's nose. 'When're you gonna tell Bela?'

'When I stop bleeding.' I paused, then admitted, 'The thing is, Ziggi, I'm not sure what to tell him . . . she knew my father. She knew about *me*. You think this is over?'

He was quiet for a bit, then asked quietly, 'Kid okay?'

I looked down at Lizzie. Her head was on my lap, her body curled beside me. She was sucking her thumb, but I could feel tremors running through her, like a dog dreaming it was chasing a rabbit.

'Yeah,' I said, thinking of all the kids who weren't. 'She will be.'

Ziggi pushed a CD into the player. Harp music fluttered around us, nearly lulling me to sleep.

It was almost midnight when we arrived at Mel's to find her in the company of two police officers; when I'd called ahead to let her know Lizzie was safe I'd assumed the cops would be well and truly gone by the time we turned up. I should have known better. Both were young and hungry – must have been a slow night in the Normal world – and maybe they sensed there was a story not being told. While I knew they were just doing their job, their enthusiasm for asking questions felt overwhelming. While Mel was overjoyed to have her daughter back, and didn't care how it had happened, the officers were not so willing to let things go.

In fact, they were pretty unhappy with my inability to remember important details, like where I'd found Lizzie, and who'd put such a variety of obviously painful holes in me. They wanted to spend a lot of time talking through the evening's events and taking notes, but I *really* needed to sleep. When they threatened to take me to the Watch House so I could think about what I'd done, I insisted on my right to one phone call. They told me I wasn't in America, but I made the call anyway, waking someone who wasn't especially pleased to hear from me at that hour, but who did at least convince the efficient young men to stop asking me questions and go and chase real criminals.

Quietly, Mel asked me if all the blood on me was mine; when I whispered *No*, she gave a short, sharp, satisfied jerk of her head. That was when I gave in to the urge to fall over. The floor was very welcoming, but Ziggi wouldn't let me stay there.

'To the hospital, my good man,' I said weakly, giving in at last.

'Like hell. We're going where you fucking well should've gone in the first place.'

Louise the healer was middle-aged, motherly and pleasant, and the only indication that she was other than she appeared were the vertical slits of her pupils, which she used to great effect over the next few hours, giving me disapproving looks as she worked her magic on my pierced and battered carcase. Through the paper-thin walls of her apartment-cum-treatment rooms, I could hear Ziggi on the phone. He was filling Bela in on the evening's fun and games, which gave me a huge sense of relief. For a while at least, I didn't have to take responsibility for anything.

Louise ground her teeth as I removed my shredded shirt and bloody jeans, as much at the scarring on my lower limb as at my new injuries. A lot of incense was lit, herbs were crushed and powdered and rubbed into wounds where they burned for a while before subsiding to a comforting warmth. Then she made a series of fresh cuts in my recently healed leg and poured a variety of oils – some fragrant, some very much not – into them. On the whole, there was more pain than I'd have preferred, but by the end of it – and after the micro-naps I managed in between the bits that hurt – I felt miraculously improved. When she finally let me get off the table I found I was walking pretty much without a limp, and the bone-deep ache that had been my constant companion for months was just about gone.

It was still dark by the time Ziggi smugly delivered me home. I was so hopeful, as I scrambled out of the cab and waved farewell, that a few hours of sleep was in my near future, but then I spotted the black '74 Porsche 911 Turbo parked a little way up the street. Before I'd even got my front door open I could smell coffee and hear someone rummaging around inside. I wanted to throw myself on the ground and cry. Only one person would dare to break in to make hot drinks.

Bela, buried deep in the pantry, emerged with an ancient packet of Teddybear biscuits. 'This the best you can do?'

'Pretty much.'

'You always used to have TimTams,' he whined.

The case was solved and he'd relaxed. Bela was always more pleasant, closer to human, at those moments, and I remembered what I'd first seen in him. So maybe Ziggi hadn't been entirely right: it wasn't that Bela wasn't who I wanted him to be, just that the Bela I'd wanted to be with was only evident *sometimes*. The divide between *that* Bela and the ultra-focused guy I worked for was an abyss you might never climb out of.

'I also used to have an arse that weighed twenty kilos all on its own.'

He appraised me as if seeing me for the first time. 'You look better than I thought you would.'

'Ziggi's healer is amazing. You should have made me go to her long ago.'

He choked, and managed, 'Because you respond so well to being told to do something . . .'

We waited for the pot to gurgle and he put sugar in my mug, even though I'd told him a hundred times I'd given up; at least he left it black. As he carried the cups out to the darkness of the back deck, I brought up the rear with the world's saddest-looking packet of biscuits. The chairs protested as we settled into them and I thought maybe it was time to get new ones before someone went through the worn canvas.

'So, Bela, what are we going to do?' I asked. The night felt like a bubble around us.

'You know, I really hate it when you call me that,' he said mildly.

'I know. And I hate sugar in my coffee.' But I took a sip anyway. 'Again: what are we going to do, Bela?'

He raised an eyebrow. 'About what?'

'*Her*. The Winemaker. What about tracking down her clients?'

'The kid's okay,' he said. That was apparently the refrain for the day. 'The disappearances will stop.'

'You're not going to do *anything*?' I felt the old anger raise its head and pushed it back down, determined to stop my knee-jerk reactions, no matter how justified.

'What is there to do?' he asked reasonably. 'The beldame's dead. I've told Eleanor and the other Councillors that the problem has been solved.'

'When I threatened her with the Council, that old woman said she could *handle* them – and she wasn't at all bothered. Doesn't that give you pause?'

'V, if the Five had anything to do with her, why would they have me – and by extension, *you* – investigate?'

'Believe me, I've thought about that. If you're a member of the Council and indulging in naughtiness, surely objecting to any investigation is going to paint a big red "Suspect Me!" sign on your chest.' I tried to get him to understand. 'You make your exit strategy first, just in case, but you also let things take their course and hope for the best.'

'Is that why you didn't report in?'

I had the good grace to blush. It wasn't that I didn't trust him; just that I knew that whatever I told him would've gone straight to the Five. 'It wasn't only her,' I pointed out. 'Aspasia said something similar.'

'Aspasia? Person voted most likely to yank your chain?' He gave me a disbelieving stare. 'V, the old woman was just trying to make you despair. These things, they go away—'

'Great. So the bad shit goes on tour.' I shook my head, feeling a pulse building at the base of my skull. 'It doesn't stop being your – *our* – responsibility because it's not in our back yard any more. She wasn't operating in a vacuum, Bela – people were paying for that wine. And you can bet *other* things are being done, too.'

He held up his hands. 'I just meant that without the wicked witch there's no one to ask about her buyers. And it's not like she kept records, or at least, none that I found.'

'What was her name? How long had she been here? She said she knew Grigor, Bela, that he'd worked for *her*.'

'Well, whoever she was, no one's admitting to knowing her. There was no handbag lying around with ID in it. And you kind of toasted her, V – if there was anything on the body, it's ashes.' He reached into his pocket and pulled out a tangle of warped pearls, precious stones and melted golden metal. He dropped the mess into my palm – I thought I still felt some warmth to it and imagined the devouring flames – then ran his hands over his face. 'Honestly, you think I wouldn't know if a Council member was breaking our laws?'

'How *would* you?' I challenged. All I could hope for now was to plant a seed of doubt in him. 'Ziggi drove by West End Library again: Her photo on the noticeboard, the newspaper piece about her donating money? It's unreadable. It was faded before, but you can't even make out her features now. Someone's set an erasing spell.'

'She probably set a general track-covering technique in case she had to make a quick exit. She didn't expect to get Fassbindered.' He paused. 'No one ever does.'

'What about the house? The filing cabinets? What about a title deed? There's got to be *some* kind of documentation. No one can live without leaving any trace at all . . .'

'Look,' he sighed, 'I arrived more than an hour after Ziggi got you and the little girl out of there. *Anyone* could have got in – after *you* broke the door – and swept the place. I can't tell you what I don't know, V.'

'What about Sally Crown?' I knew what I'd promised, but after seeing Lizzie laid out on a steel table and having my own flesh perforated, I wasn't bothered about maintaining Sally's anonymity. Besides, I wasn't entirely sure that she hadn't sent me to the gingerbread house with intent, to win some Brownie points from her boss.

'The Normal girl? Gone. No sign of her.'

I didn't think my cash would have got her very far, but it was clear Sally wasn't too fussy about how she earned an income. She might have had a stash elsewhere. 'But—'

'There's nothing to go on, V. Let it go,' he said softly. 'You did good.'

I was silent, and he took this for agreement, which was a sure sign that he hadn't learned much from our time together. He went on, as if I would be easily distracted by a shiny new object to chase, 'But that other matter I mentioned still needs attention. A missing person case, a private consultancy.'

'No.'

'What do you mean "no"? It's a job.'

'I mean "no" in the traditional sense of "No, fuck off".' I ran a hand through my hair, then noticed I still had blood under my nails. I wasn't sure if it was hers or mine. I *badly* needed a shower. 'I'm really sick of getting stabbed, bitten, beaten and threatened with umbrellas. *Umbrellas*, Bela: what the hell kind of life is that?'

'You haven't been shot,' he offered.

'Yet – *yet!* And how does that help?' I scratched at the new cuts on my leg, which had started itching. 'If you hadn't got me involved, then *Lizzie* never would have been in danger.'

'But you couldn't have known that – *I* couldn't have known that.' He sniffed as if insulted.

'Yeah, you could. You should have had an inkling. And so should I.' I picked at a thread on my jeans. Maybe I was being unfair. I'd resolved to be nicer to my boss; I just hadn't realised how much of a strain it would be. We sat quietly for a bit, eating stale Teddybear biscuits and staring into the darkness, which felt somehow safer.

'You get things done, V,' Bela said at last, softly. 'You walk *between*. There's no one quite like you, and for whatever reason – whether you annoy the crap out of people or charm them – you get to the truth of things. That's why I need you.' He hesitated, as if treading lightly so I didn't tell him where to go again. 'Donovan Baker has gone missing.'

'And he is?' But even as I said the words, I could guess: Anders Baker's baby boy, propped up by Daddy's cash and a tangible lack of anything resembling talent or drive. It was looking a lot like another chance to get lacerated.

'The heir to a fortune, and he's like you – half and half – but no powers to speak of.'

'Thank you for making me sound like a pizza.'

'He is moneyed and missing, and his father wants him back.'

I didn't say anything.

'He's someone's kid, V, someone's little boy.' He looked at me. 'There's been no ransom demand, so he's not been kidnapped. Aren't there enough lost children?'

That was a low blow and we both knew it.

I cleared my throat. 'I really don't like you very much right now.'

He turned his mouth in an 'o' of surprise, but any reply was lost beneath the sound of his mobile. He tilted his head as he answered, and I could hear the rumble of a familiar voice on the other end. I guessed a favour was going to be called in sooner rather than later and tossed the cold coffee dregs over the rail, then went to shower and find clothes that didn't have tears in them.

Bela had hung up by the time I returned and was staring out into the black that was thinning as dawn drew closer. I wondered how good his night-sight was, whether he could see things I couldn't.

'So?'

'Detective Inspector McIntyre says there's a body at Waterfront Place.'

'Of course there is.' I shivered.

'Should I call Ziggi?'

'Nah. Let one of us get some sleep. You can give me a lift in your fancy car.' I stretched. 'I take it Donovan Baker is no longer a priority?'

His mouth said *Yes*, but his eyes said *You're very annoying*. I touched his shoulder lightly. 'Tell his father to contact me sometime. If he makes his case, gives me compelling evidence that it's more than the boy just trying escape from him, I'll see what I can do. Deal?'

'Deal.'

Chapter Eight

There are still some High Places, even in modern cities. *Go up unto the temple; up unto Jerusalem; take your son up to a High Place in order to make the sacrifice.* That's why churches always got the best land when a town was settled, and why so many ancient temples and houses of worship are on the highest hills. Modern ones less so, because people have mostly forgotten magic like that. Of course, High Places are not the only loci of power – important stuff also happens in the depths, the low places. Or Low Places. At any rate, zeniths and nadirs are where the big changes occur; in the middle, not so much; that's just where the consequences play out. So, High Places: religious folk claimed it got them closer to some god or other. Me, I just thought it was because when things fell further, they broke more effectively.

The distance had certainly made a mess of her.

She lay stomach-down, feathers scattered around her in the flowerbed at the foot of one of the city's tallest buildings. A few stakes that had been holding up young frangipani trees poked out of her back, but I didn't think they'd bothered her. She was dead before she hit – she *must* have been, otherwise she'd have unfurled her wings and landed safely. Those wings covered her like a carelessly thrown shawl. They would have been white once, but having been folded away for so long, they were now grey, the only things to show how old she really was.

They were why I was there. Well, and the other bits.

Thanks to the indignity of death, her skirt was all rucked up about her hips, her naked legs on display; right now, just a few cops used to this kind of thing could see that she had the legs of a bird.

Sirens were like that: they could hide their wings – they had this kind of mystic swaddling thing going on – but there wasn't much that could disguise the lower limbs other than plucking out the feathers, which she'd done. It was a nice job, very professional, so maybe there'd been some electrolysis, too. All the same, there was no getting around the fact that she'd had a glorious face and bird's legs. Plumage apart, they were shapely enough, nicely rounded, muscular thighs and calves, right until you got to the ankle, where you found a clawed foot with three toes at the front and one to the back. I couldn't see her shoes, but I was willing to bet they'd been specially made. Sirens propped up the very private custom-made shoe market in most cities. They wore a lot of boots, a lot of special-order Docs.

Dawn had cracked the sky and mist was rolling across the surface of the river. Autumn had been and gone overnight, as predicted, and the dip into winter was fast and nasty. I shouldn't have been surprised, but I always was, just like the rest of the population.

The clean-up crew was working hard to get the evidence tagged and bagged at speed; it was best if no one else saw it. They might have had to tidy things away, but they didn't have to investigate it – that got outsourced to yours truly. The early summons was a real pain and I desperately wanted to sleep, but favours were owed.

I crouched beside the body and stared at her, taking in the awkward angle of her neck that enabled me to look into her blank violet eyes. She'd been *more* than lovely before the fall. There weren't a lot of sirens in Brisbane – the ecosystem could only bear a small flock because they could be voracious in the right circumstances. Too many in one place could lead to a lot of things needing explanation: men, women, disappearances, the usual issues. The exhortation not to eat human flesh had not been popular with the siren community, but the smart ones knew enough to adapt, or at least to be extremely careful.

I didn't recognise this one, and had no memory of her ever presenting a problem. She was probably a serial flirt, because that was what sirens did best, but not a danger to anyone – not one of those who stole citizens away, who might be tracked down by grieving relatives. At least, I'd never encountered her as such. And even if she had been, sirens were damned hard to kill, what with their ability to shift teeth and talons, not to mention the whole being able to fly away deal. There were a lot of white feathers lying around her, presumably plucked out while she was killed.

I took a few steps backwards and turned to face the river, not wanting to look on death any more, even if only for a little while.

'Well?'

The whisky-and-cigarettes voice was too close. I hadn't heard her approach and that irked me. I might have been washed and dressed and upright, but I was also very sleep-deprived. 'Don't do that.'

'I thought you were special, Fassbinder.' It was clear she didn't mean it. That was just rude.

'You called me, Detective Inspector.'

'Actually, I called Tepes.'

'Touché. At any rate, you're taking up my time on a wintery morning when I'd far rather be in bed. Try to be nice.'

'I understand you were pretty banged up this morning. Are you quite recovered?' she enquired politely, mockingly. McIntyre was the reason those enthusiastic young constables had obediently left

Mel's place. We got on okay, might even be described as friends, but that didn't mean either of us would let a chance to be obnoxious go by. Besides, it was cold; we had to keep warm somehow.

'Thank you, yes.'

'Anything about this strike you as strange?'

'Other than the fact that the Colonel would wet himself to see wings and drumsticks like these?'

Rhonda McIntyre grimaced. Rumour had it she'd been a pretty young thing once, but that was before the job took hold of her. Too many late nights, too many fags, too much booze and too many takeaways had contrived to wreak havoc on her face and figure, and now she was configured something like a keg in an ill-cut charcoal suit, just like most cops after a few years on the job. A gold crucifix sat in the hollow of her throat, nestled among shallow wrinkles. She was in her late forties; in a few years they'd become furrows. Her eyes were hard from staring at the seamy underbelly of the city and I suspected her short, iron-grey hair hadn't ever met a hairdresser it liked. She'd managed to rise to a decent rank in her chosen profession, but she must have upset someone important to get landed with what she called (on her good days) the Strange Shit Basket.

'Other than *that*,' she said, teeth gritted, then asked hopefully, 'Suicide?'

'Alas, sirens are unlikely candidates for suicide – especially like this.'

McIntyre paused, cocked her head to the side. 'Should I be talking to what's-her-name in Hobart? Nancy Napoleon?'

For someone with little tolerance for Strange Shit, she knew the right names; still, I wondered how much Bird-Women 101 she would tolerate. 'Different kind of sirens there. Shared ancestors, but these are the first kind, fowl not fish, distinctly non-marine variety.'

'Why can't there just be an ordinary murder?' McIntyre asked wistfully. Whoever she'd pissed off had made it unlikely she'd move beyond inspector. She obviously hated dealing with the weird – and the Weyrd – but if the powers-that-be had intended to irritate her into resigning by making her the Strange Shit liaison, they'd badly miscalculated. She was fully stocked with both piss and vinegar and she clearly wasn't planning on going anywhere until honourable retirement and a sizeable superannuation payout. McIntyre didn't count either patience or subtlety among her virtues: she knew the real story about my father, and for a long while she'd not hesitated to let me know that she didn't trust me; when she'd stopped making digs about Grigor, I figured we'd moved past that.

'Murder always seems pretty ordinary to me,' I said. 'It's mean and petty and sad. Weyrd murders are no better than Normal ones.' All things considered, if I ended up on a cold, hard slab, she was exactly the kind of cop I'd want looking into my death. There was something heroic and old-school about her level of grumpiness; you couldn't help but admire it. That didn't mean she wasn't a pain in the arse.

'Well, fish or fowl, I want it off my books.'

'As I said, the sirens are a small community. I'll ask around, see what I can find out – but no promises.'

'What more can one ask?' She turned her palms upward like a saint in optimistic prayer. 'Keep me informed.'

'But of course. No handbag, no ID, I'm assuming?'

She gave me a look that said, *If there had been I probably wouldn't have called for you.*

I wandered along the boardwalk, ignoring the slap and sigh of the water below. It wasn't far to the CityCat stop at Riverside, where people were already waiting: girls in too few clothes sobering up enough to realise it; young men unwilling to hand over their jackets in a last-ditch attempt at 'romance'. Chivalry's just a bit frosty these days.

I snuggled smugly into my own winter coat, the one everyone said was too thick for the River City, but which they all eyed enviously when the cold winds whistled through the streets. Staring at the revellers made me feel painfully old; soon I'd be starting my sentences with, 'In my day . . .' and yelling, 'Darned kids! Get off my lawn!' I sighed and sat on a bench; swinging my leg back and forth, I was gratified to experience no pain. I did feel the warm tremor of healing still going on, and that made me happier. I had to admit the healer's abilities were pretty bloody spectacular – I hadn't even thought about taking any painkillers this morning.

When I got home I'd check in on Lizzie and Mel, then I'd get some sleep before I became totally psychotic, and *then* I'd make some calls about the dead siren in the garden bed and report to Bela like a good employee. It occurred to me that I should do some research, see if they had any natural enemies.

The CityCat docked with some inelegant bumping and disgorged a few passengers. I walked the gangplank behind the youngsters; hurrying footsteps bringing up the rear told me someone had only just made the boat. The others went inside and settled into the warmth while I took up my usual position in the right-hand corner of the back deck and leaned against the railing like a dog hanging from a car window. It was chilly, but being in the cabin always made me queasy. As we churned downriver, away from the high-rise blocks, I noticed the sun hadn't quite burned off all the mist – in fact, it seemed to have got thicker. Then I realised there was no 'seemed' about it: the air had become a soupy white-grey fog.

I squinted and made out a low dark boat propelled by some unseen force, while a tall figure plied the single oar set in a rowlock in the stern to direct its course. A hand with thin fingers was raised in salute and I shivered. Added to the events of the evening and the dead siren, this really was way too much strangeness before breakfast. I returned the wave all the same; there was no point in alienating the Boatman. I'd read about him, and heard tales from my father and Bela and dozens of other Weyrd who apparently got a kick out of bogeyman stories, but this was the closest I'd ever come to him myself. He ferried both Weyrd and Normal souls off to wherever they went after death, and as I'd ride with him one day, as everyone did, I preferred him to remember me as well-mannered.

I guessed it wasn't a social call, which was pretty alarming considering what a professional one usually meant. The Boatman drew alongside the Cat and kept pace easily. We'd be stopping at Dockside soon so he'd have to talk fast, I was thinking, when I looked around and noticed no one in the cabin was moving. Eyes were glazed, expressions stone as water bottles were caught part-way to mouths; there was a ticket inspector frozen in mid-citing of bylaws, young men forever caught in sly gawks at girls whose nighttime make-up had turned distinctly clownish. Time had been suspended.

It's good to be the Boatman.

I said, 'Hey!' as calmly as I could, hoping to cover both dignified and cool, not to mention *totally not afraid*.

The hood of his cloak flapped, showing cheekbones and a chin, skin as brown as dried wood, a sparse mouth and ruined nose, the cartilage shrunken and sunken. His eyes remained hidden and I was thankful for that much.

'Can I help you?' I asked. 'No offence, but I was kind of hoping we wouldn't meet for a while.'

He cracked a smile, exposing yellow teeth crazed like old ivory. He removed one hand from the oar and reached towards me and my heart clenched until I realised he was offering something, not trying to take me. I felt the cold through the wrapping and quickly tucked the thing into my coat pocket.

Gift horse, meet mouth.

'Thanks?'

He pointed upwards. 'They want to break the sky.'

'Huh?'

But apparently that was all I was going to get. The long hand sailed through the air in a gesture that could have meant, 'These are not the droids you're looking for,' then alighted back on the oar. The world started to move again and the Boatman sped away, apparently without effort.

'Way to be cryptic,' I muttered.

'Hello.'

I turned. Dark blond hair, glasses, thick scarf, battered leather jacket, jeans.

'Standard geek,' I said. The guy I'd run into at the State Library, the one I'd busily dismissed. I saw then what I'd not fully acknowledged before. He was cute.

'Excuse me?' His eyes widened behind the glasses. I thrust my hand at him by way of diversion, hoping he really hadn't heard what I'd muttered. We shook.

'Hi.'

'Hi. I just wanted to say, you know, hello, but without almost knocking you down,' he said.

'Oh. Okay.' My interpersonal skills were never going to win any prizes and I could see my first chance of a date in more than twelve months slipping away – well, less slipping than galloping. It was a mystery how I'd ended up in a relationship with Bela in the first place, really.

'Ah, anyway. Bye.' He began to sidestep, his expression clearly saying that the whole 'Hello' idea had been a bad one.

Wicked witches. Wine of tears. Sirens. The Boatman. Skies breaking. The object in my pocket. I needed a solid breakfast, preferably pancakes, with bacon. Crispy bacon. And syrup. Maple syrup, lots of it. Before I could talk myself out of it I touched his arm and said tentatively, 'So, about that cup of something warm?'

He grinned.

'I'm Verity.'

'David.'

'How do you feel about breakfast, David?'

'It's a meal upon which I look favourably.'

The CityCat began to slow again. We were approaching Dockside, with its fancy-schmancy apartments, overpriced restaurants and plentiful cafés. Surely pancakes, the solution to most of life's problems, could be found there.

Chapter Nine

Several hours and many pancakes later, I was home. I'd even managed some sleep, although by no means enough, and now I was sitting at the dining table and busily failing to open the Boatman's gift. The time with David had blotted out a lot of my concerns, but it was only a temporary fix. Once I was on my own again the chill weight in my pocket brought them all back.

I'd reached out to unwrap it at least four times, but at the last minute my hand had found something else to do: check the spine of a book, flick away a speck of dust, turn over a piece of paper. Frankly, it was a bit of a relief when the knocking started. I answered the front door faster than was my wont – by that point I'd have greeted a toilet-brush salesman with joy.

Reality was considerably less pleasant. I might have recognised my visitor at once, from newspapers, glossy magazines and periodic TV reports about the nation's richest men, but I hadn't expected to find him on my doorstep – at least, not so soon. You'd have thought, with all his money, he'd've managed to get a better dye job, but I supposed the Trump Equation worked no matter where you were: the more cashed-up a man was, the more convinced he was that he could get away with any kind of coif-related quirk. The jet-black hairdo was bad, but the orange salon tan that hadn't reached into the wrinkles on his face, leaving strange white lines deep within the crevasses, was even worse. His eyes were pale blue and his teeth very, very bright. He must have been trying for casual because he was wearing the standard outfit of a man who owned a yacht, but didn't know how to sail; the polo shirt and chinos were perfectly pressed, the deck shoes brand spanking new.

'Ms Fassbinder, I'm—'

'I know who you are, Mr Baker. This is unexpected.' I made sure my foot was wedged firmly behind the door to keep it in place. 'Did Tepes speak to you?'

Anders Baker smiled as if about to offer me candy. 'He did. He said I should present my case to you.'

'I'm fairly sure he didn't say to do it today.' I took a deep breath. 'I know you're worried about your son, and I'll help if I can, but let me be clear: at the moment, your case isn't my top priority.'

'I've employed three separate private eyes but they've had no success,' he said. 'The police are worse than useless. I will pay whatever you ask, just forget your other cases.' He smiled again, as if there was no argument to be had. Presumably Bela hadn't bothered to give him any hints about how to best approach me.

'Sir, from what Zvezdomir said, I'd say the chances that he's gone off on a trip of self-discovery are pretty good. That, or he's making an overdue bid for freedom.'

'Any delay you make will recklessly endanger my child,' he snapped, but I had the distinct impression that the moral high ground was more like a slippery slope for him. And he was a guilt-trip amateur – he hadn't grown up with my grandmother. 'I demand—'

I held up my hand to stop him. 'For a start, the word *demand* does not work with me. Your son is *eighteen*, he's not a child.' I spoke through gritted teeth, but made a point not to raise my voice, which made me feel very virtuous indeed. 'Mr Baker, I don't believe you need me. Any PI worth her or his salt will be able to find your son, but you must give them more time. However, if you do want my help you need to be patient.'

'I told you, I can pay whatever you—'

I grabbed his right pinky finger and twisted it, ever so slightly until he started to gasp and do a little *cha-cha-cha* on the spot. 'You're insulting me, Mr Baker. I am *not* for purchase and I don't care what privilege you think your money gives you.'

'I'm . . . sorry,' he said, breathing heavily. 'Sometimes I can be too pushy.'

I couldn't shake the feeling that (a) the apology was going to cost me, and (b) Mr Baker was less upset about his son's disappearance than my refusal to spring into action immediately. When I released him he shook the injured hand while reaching with the other into his pocket to draw forth a rectangular white card. As I reached for it, there was a scraping sound as someone pushed the gate half open. A thin, dirty face peeked through the gap.

I'd thought her gone for good.

'Sally!' I yelled, and Baker turned. Her expression flickered from timidity to active fear as she saw him; she turned and bolted. I threw myself out of the door, my recovering muscles protesting enough that I had to slow down, but it didn't matter. By the time I got to the footpath there was no sign of her. For a malnourished urchin she could sure make a fast getaway.

I returned slowly, relieved to see that my unwelcome guest hadn't taken the opportunity to step inside.

Baker was staring at me, looking decidedly perplexed, still proffering the business card. Unless he was a really good actor, he didn't know Sally. But she'd obviously recognised him, and something about him had scared her.

'Friend of yours?'

'I'll be in contact,' I said and closed the door, none too gently. After a few moments there was the sound of something being slipped under the thin gap where a draft excluder belonged, and the white rectangle appeared. Then footsteps moved down the stairs and back along the garden path. A motor started quietly, something expensive and highly engineered. I barely heard it pull away as I picked up the card and threw it on the desk.

Back at the dining table the parcel sat in a three-foot-square section where the mess had been cleared away – by 'cleared away', I mean, made vertical rather than horizontal. I stared at the Boatman's gift for a while longer, then pulled on my big girl pants. Gingerly, I undid the frayed red ribbon that was keeping everything together and gently flipped open the edges of the parchment-coloured cloth.

The knife lay in a sheath of intricately tooled, age-darkened leather. Its handle of ebony wood was studded with gold rivets. I bent close and sniffed, but couldn't make out anything except maybe some kind of lanolin. Old though it was, the weapon had been looked after. I hesitated, then picked it up, still sheathed. It was a weighty thing. I drew the blade to find it was double-edged, about twenty centimetres long and engraved with swirls and curlicues. Gold's a pretty soft metal and it didn't look like this'd had too much hard usage. Then again, it might have been an alloy and tougher than it appeared.

Even without the sheath, the dagger was heavier than it should have been, which made me wonder about its core. The thing had started vibrating against my palm and now a humming rose from it. I wasn't stupid; I quickly jammed it back into the sheath. The noise subsided, but I could still feel the reverberation on my skin.

Okay: so not a harmless gift, not an ornament, definitely not a steak-knife-free-with-purchase sort of blade but something that I was pretty sure needed to be hidden – or kept very close – until I worked out what I was supposed to do with it. The sheath had sturdy straps top and bottom, so I could either worry about finding a secure hiding place, or be sure I knew where it was at all times. I tied it to my ankle. I'd have to get used to the weight, but otherwise it felt relatively comfortable. I looked at the wall clock. Time for bed; a few more hours of rest would do the trick before I had to go out again.

I slept like the dead, and if anyone came knocking, I didn't hear them.

Sitting on a bench at one end of the Kangaroo Point cliff walk, book on my lap, I watched the sun set, throwing orange fire on the water in its last moments, some of the tendrils reaching the Botanical Gardens on the opposite bank. Not far from me, just over the other side of a broad stone wall, people with helmets and far too much energy were climbing up and down the cliff face as if it was a good idea. The spotlights at the base of the cliffs flickered on, then streetlamps followed as the dark crept in, but it was officially now too hard to read in my shadowy patch.

I owned a lot of books, a collection built up over the years. Of course, there was heaps of information online but it wasn't the *real* stuff; besides, I didn't trust the Internet. It might give useful hints about where to go when I was researching something, but those were simply leads, and whilst some turned out to be useful, many were completely unreliable. The World Wide Web was just anarchy in a virtual container – there was no *knowledge* there, only data in ephemeral and frequently unsound form. But a book, a nice solid book, a thing you could touch and hold and, more importantly, own – that was *solid*. That was tangible.

Books had shown me that although I was different, I wasn't alone.

My father's library disappeared after his arrest and was probably still mouldering in an evidence locker somewhere. My grandparents had cleaned out Grigor's house, my old home, and disposed of anything that wasn't suitable to be left next to *Women's Weekly*, which covered pretty much everything. They turned out to be very particular about reading material where I was concerned, at such pains to give me a Normal childhood, but I started spending my pocket money on questionable investments such as compendiums of tales about the occult and ghosts, myths and legends . . . weird stuff that would later become Weyrd. I hid my illicit purchases under my bed, behind the old suitcase stuffed with the toys I'd outgrown but couldn't bear to throw away.

My adolescent rebellion might have been nerdier than most, but I found myself hanging out in the sort of bookstores that didn't look like proper shops, the ones hidden down dark alleys, with doors with peeling paint and strangely sturdy locks, or behind hidden trapdoors in the storerooms of shiny new book chain-stores, under which would be *the rest* of the inventory: books as old as breathing, covered in everything from tightly woven hair to human skin, from shaved bone shards to glass, from beaten bronze to blood-dyed silks.

I wasn't like other kids. I knew things they didn't; I'd seen things they never would – and I was strong, so strong. Grandma warned me over and over: *No pushing, no shoving, no fighting, no matter what – you don't know your own strength, Verity*. I really did, though, and I was careful not to use it against anyone – or at least, not until I was older and started recognising and encountering the Weyrd again.

That's where the bookshops came in: I didn't feel as if I was playing dress-up or wearing a suit of armour there. Around the books, I didn't have to be anyone but *me*. That was where Bela first found me – or maybe 'made contact'. He knew who I was. Now I realise that, of course the Council would have kept an eye on Grigor's daughter, but when I was fifteen I was flattered and naturally, I developed a fierce schoolgirl crush. He wasn't interested then (not until I was well into my twenties), but in those early years he showed me my heritage, pointed me towards tomes filled with disguised versions of the truth of where we came from, and others not so disguised. He taught me not to be afraid of what I was.

It's no wonder I loved him for so long.

He'd also been a great giver of books while we were together – a great forgetter of anniversaries and birthdays, too, but random books-for-no-reason helped to smooth that over. Despite those gifts, I'd grown my library mostly on my own, though I only ever bought those volumes I could *afford* to pay for. Some could be had for a lot of cold hard cash, others for a lock of hair, a tiny square of skin, a vial of blood or a whisper of breath, but Bela had taught me that it was unwise to give up any part of yourself, even for knowledge. You never knew what someone would do with something so personal.

The bestiary on my lap was written in bad Latin, which had made it a little cheaper, but it'd still cost me the better part of a month's salary. My Latin was even more atrocious (needless to say my language studies grades had not been stellar), but it had good pictures, which I could 'read', and armed with a dictionary and a basic primer, I managed. Shame about all that effort. The entry on sirens told me nothing I didn't already know.

The winged women with the legs of birds had not been sea-going to begin with. One particular branch of the family had started that tradition, and had also started mating with men. Their appetite for flesh had also increased, and over the years they'd evolved, losing their aerial abilities and morphing into water creatures. The other branch, the older one, stayed aloft and kept their wings – they didn't hold with all that reclining on rocks and serenading their dinner, although they still liked the seduction, the chase. Some liked the murderous habits so much they couldn't or wouldn't give them up; some just liked to tease and flirt, to break a heart or twelve.

I closed the book and contemplated what could kill a siren. Bullets, arrows, decapitation, they'd all do it. Poison wouldn't work – maybe because their own blood was already so toxic. It's difficult to catch something that can fly away unless you're a dab hand with nets. They had fangs and claws, so they could defend themselves pretty effectively. And then there was that whole hypnotic effect: some idiots, men and women both, were dumb enough to fall victim to their lures, rather like a bird being mesmerised by a snake. On the whole, siren bodies were as frail as humans', but unless violence was visited upon them, they simply outlived us. Hell, they'd outlived whole civilisations.

And there had been no marks on the dead siren, whoever she was, apart from the standard fell-from-a-great-height-and-went-splat kind.

The autopsy might show something, but I wasn't going to bet on it. Whoever – or *whatever* – had murdered the siren had probably been smart enough to clean up after themselves. So if there was anything there to be found, I'd have to wait for McIntyre to call once the chopping-up-and-cataloguing part was done. Oddly, I'm squeamish about that kind of thing.

The city's sirens had a regular meeting place: they got together once a month, at the full moon, and fortuitously, we were due a full moon that very Sunday. Sometimes they sang, not the nasty, lure-you-to-your-death sort of singing, which is never conducive to maintaining a low profile, but a nice ladies' choir thing. They gathered together for the same reasons humans do: for companionship, to be surrounded by their own so they didn't feel so alone. Of course, there are edgy loners in every species, and I really hoped that whoever the victim was, she hadn't been one of those, not only because that would make my task more difficult, but because it would mean she wasn't mourned or missed, and that always made me sad.

Mindful of Ziggi's etiquette tip to ensure my continued good health – it was fairly basic: don't be rude, because sirens have a very strict view of what constitutes good manners – I tucked the bestiary into my bag, rose and walked along the cliff path towards the park with its herd of BBQ pergolas sitting in pools of artificial light. Maybe on a non-siren night David and I would go there, bring some Thai food, talk into the wee hours.

The full moon turned the landscape silvery-ash. Everything – buildings, cars, city lights, trees, people, the river below – was washed of colour, rendered ghostly and limned with a strange sort of shine in the winter air. Soon enough I stopped noticing that because I heard the melody, seeping in through my pores and making my belly tingle.

As I got closer the singing got clearer, splitting into lyrics, a version of Greek from before time and history were recorded. I caught the words for *moonlight* and *grace* and *mother*, which was as far as my dodgy translation skills allowed. I figured it for a hymn, the open sky their church. The power was pitched low, so as not to entrance anyone, but I could see figures gathered on balconies in the apartment complexes across the road, and evening picnickers scattered along the cliffs listening, quite still, food momentarily forgotten.

The women were clustered on one of the grey- and white-tiled lookouts, the one closest to the tiny garden of St Mary's Church, at the farthest end of the park. A glass and steel wall kept land and empty air apart. About thirty of them stood in a loose arrow formation, hands by their sides, faces lifted to the moon, mouths moving in unison. They were all dressed differently – anything else would have screamed 'cult' – but without exception each was beautiful. Just behind every one I could see a sort of shimmer effect: the hidden wings.

As I neared, I focused on the woman at the tip of the arrow. She was older than her companions, although still enduringly lovely, ageing gracefully with high cheekbones and a firm jaw. Others looked like extremely well preserved forties, a few in their thirties, but the majority of them appeared to be young, late teens, early twenties. Many of these creatures were ancient enough to have seen the Fall of Troy, but this was a relatively new nest, just over a hundred years old, in a small community, owing to a general exodus when the proscription against human hors d'oeuvres came into effect.

I stopped a courteous distance from them and waited for the song to finish. Slowly the notes dropped away like leaves fallen from a height, and as the music died, so the colour was restored to the cityscape. Then thirty heads turned to pin me with luminous stares until one broke from the group, a glaring adolescent, and approached me.

'You're not welcome. This time is private.'

Mindful of Ziggi's advice, I dipped my head respectfully. 'I understand, and I wouldn't interrupt if it were not important.' I turned and locked gazes with the oldest. 'I'm Verity Fassbinder. May I speak with you?'

She didn't answer immediately and I tugged a sheet of paper from between the pages of the bestiary. McIntyre had emailed me the photo, which I'd printed off in black and white, hoping it might not look so bad. 'I think you might be missing someone.'

A long moment passed before she assented and I loosed a relieved breath. The crowd parted with reluctance; they were nervous, no doubt about it, and there was something they couldn't hide. Their fear had a smell, a scent of warm wet feathers.

I reached the matriarch and handed her the photograph.

It was just a headshot, and the face had been cleaned up as well as they could. She almost seemed to be sleeping, but it was a leaden, hopeless kind of slumber. The woman looked at the image, her expression contorting, and pushed a fist against her mouth to stop any sound. Two of the older females supported her to a bench and I kept pace, refusing to surrender my position to the press of bodies, and hustled my way onto the seat next to her. Shaking, she stared at the photo.

Her child?

'She was found early this morning at Waterfront Place,' I said, gently. 'She'd fallen.'

'No siren falls!' At least three voices joined in outrage until the woman beside me held up her hand for silence.

'We know of you. What is your interest in this?' she asked, amethyst eyes fixed on my green ones.

It's always a bit nerve-wracking when your reputation precedes you.

'Well, if you know of me, then you'll know it's what I do.' I cleared my throat. 'The Normals call me in when things are a bit strange, and the Council expects me to help keep the peace among our kind.'

'We're not *your* kind,' she said, her voice low with contempt. Sirens might like to hold themselves apart, but they are just a subset of the Weyrd. However, opening that particular can of worms wasn't going to get me very far, so I swallowed the urge to correct her.

'I know that and you know that, but the Normals, not so much. So I have been given the job of finding out who she was and what happened to her. I'd appreciate any help you could offer.'

She paused for so long I thought the answer was going to be a big fat 'No', but then, rather surprisingly, she said, 'Serena Kallos. Her name was Serena Kallos.'

'*Serena Kallos?*' Dumbfounded, I felt the blood drain from my face. The missed calls. The forgotten appointment. Rescuing Lizzie had got in the way and I'd intended to ring her to apologise and reschedule. All my good intentions meant nothing now.

The other woman stared. 'You knew her?'

'No, but she'd phoned, arranged a meeting. It . . . it didn't happen.'

She didn't ask why and I was glad. I thought hard before continuing, 'Was she related to anyone here?'

'We're all related at one remove or another,' she said and smiled crookedly, and I was pretty sure she wasn't telling me everything. Tonight I'd get only the minimum, at least until they trusted me.

'Was she seeing anyone? Was she afraid? Was anything happening that I should know about? Is there anything you can tell me? Anyone know why was she calling me?'

'Why should we tell *you* anything?' The question shot from the group and was accompanied by some affronted agreement. Tough audience, this one.

'Because I'm the only one who's going to look into this,' I said evenly, although my temper was starting to fray. 'If you know who did this, fine: off you go, get your vengeance. Just don't put this city in danger, because that will lead to a whole lot of trouble.'

I paused, meeting unfriendly gazes, letting them know I meant what I said. 'On the other hand, if you don't know, then talk to me and I swear I'll find whoever is responsible. This will be put to rights.'

'Nothing will make this right. She will never sing again,' the woman next to me said mournfully.

'I can help. The police won't – *can't* – do anything about this. I'm your only hope.' Even as I spoke I wasn't sure that was entirely comforting.

'I am Eurycleia,' she said, 'and you cannot help. Thank you for bringing this news. We will grieve for her, and deal with it in our own fashion.'

I recognised a dismissal when I got one. Normally, I'd argue for a while, maybe call a few names, but Ziggi's advice, bolstered by the memory of my abject failure with Aspasia, won out. A gracious departure meant the door remained open. Putting one of my cards on the picnic table, I said, 'I'm sorry.'

I left the photo with Eurycleia and headed into the night, my breath frosting.

I didn't think they knew who'd killed Serena Kallos. I *did* think they were scared. And I knew it would be a long time before I stopped playing 'what if I'd made it to the rendezvous?' Something also told me all was not going to be well, but I *would* hear from the sirens sooner or later. At that point there wasn't much I could do except find other places to dig.

I was almost trotting to stay warm and I found myself wondering if it was too late – too soon? *too needy?* – to call David when a movement caught my eye. Near a break in the fence, at the wooden ramp leading into the churchyard, some of the blackness was displaced. A figure retreated from the weak fingers of the park's illumination, gestures wistful, sad as an exile. Someone was watching from the gloom. In spite of my better judgment, I followed.

The church was an English one in miniature, its design, like so many things, transplanted from the motherland, but this was made with convict-cut stone, whetted with the blood of the banished. It was beautiful and uncanny in the moonlight. I circled it clockwise, growing used to the deeper darkness. A paved path led to a side entrance with a shallow stoop and an arched wooden door. Shadows shifted within. I had enough sense not to step into the porch – *be careful of thresholds*, Ziggi always said, *you never know where they might lead* – and retreated a few metres.

Squinting, I could see that there'd once been another wall. Ragged stones clung at the corner, a metre of frayed brickwork hanging against the sky. There were absences in the remaining wall, holes where the masonry had been complete at one point.

I was mid-step, wanting to take a closer look, when a rock hit me hard on the side of the head. The skin broke just above the eyebrow and the flow of blood was quick and warm. Running footsteps crunched down the cracked bitumen drive. Shaking off dizziness and swearing loudly, I followed, but by the time I made it to the main road my quarry was gone. I wiped the wound, winced, searching for the right words. 'Fuckety fucks!'

If someone – one of the sirens? – thought that would warn me off, they'd badly miscalculated. I did recognise that it was time to go home, though. Plotting revenge was always best done with a cold compress on whatever was bleeding or throbbing or aching.

Screw it. I had a name to give McIntyre, and a new burden of guilt that was all my own. That was enough for now.

Chapter Ten

'I hate this place,' Ziggi grumbled. 'When are you gonna apologise to Aspasia?'

We sat outside Shaky Jake's, beneath a comprehensively large sun-sail, but he still wore a cap and big fly-eye sunnies. His skin pinked in the daylight, but apparently that wasn't enough to make him run for cover, shouting, 'I'm melting!' He waved at the waiter, who deftly failed to notice.

'I'm not entirely sure an apology is required,' I hedged. I didn't need to see it to know he'd rolled his eyes. 'Oh, all right! When she's stopped wanting to spit in my food.'

'I'm gonna die of hunger.' He switched from waving to making a gesture that was borderline obscene. The waiter, who was sporting green dreadlocks and a sixth finger on each hand, studiously continued to ignore us.

'If you keep doing that we're going to be banned from this one too,' I pointed out. 'You can't go to Little Venice by yourself?'

'If I'm schlepping you around, it's a work expense,' he explained. 'Just apologise!'

'Yeah, yeah, yeah.'

Given the conspicuous lack of service, the only meal I was likely to get was humble pie. The decor was nice and the location on the river at New Farm to die for, though the food was pedestrian at best – but beggars can't be choosers. No matter what I might have said to Aspasia, Little Venice was never going to be in any danger of losing clientele to Shaky Jake's.

I stuck two fingers in my mouth and gave a high-pitched whistle. The waiter dropped the cup he was polishing and glared. We had a brief staring competition, and when he lost he grudgingly walked over to our table, pulling a pad from his pocket.

'I was on my way over,' he mumbled.

'At roughly the same speed as a glacier. Long black and a blueberry muffin for me, latte and a honeycomb-chocolate muffin for my friend. No spit in our food and drinks, thanks.' I leaned forward. 'I'll know it – and trust me, a withheld tip will be the *least* of your worries.' A throbbing head wound, coupled with hunger and the knowledge I was going to have to apologise to Aspasia sooner rather than later was making me snippy.

The guy stormed towards the kitchen.

'How will you know if he does stuff to our food?'

'I won't, but he doesn't know that.'

Ziggi scratched at his thin ginger mop, then pointed to my face. 'So, what happened?'

'And here's me thinking you'd never notice.' The bruise was blue-black, a ways yet from yellowed edges, and there was a distinct lump, though the cut had scabbed over. 'I visited the sirens without causing a riot.'

'That's good.'

'None of them knew – or would admit to knowing – why Serena Kallos called me. Afterwards, someone threw a rock at me.'

'One of them?'

'Could have been – it was dark. But it could have been someone else, possibly someone I offended.' I glanced across the water at the open mouths of the old rain and sewage tunnels gaping in the bank opposite. They looked like they'd still be there when the skyscrapers turned to dust.

'That doesn't narrow down the suspects.'

'It never does,' I agreed. 'Anyway, have you found anything on the Winemaker? Deeds to the house? Fingerprints on the filing cabinets? Her licence and/or birth certificate down the back of the couch? A convenient scrap of paper that just happens to lead to an important witness? Anything? *Anything?*'

Ziggi had an enviable number of contacts among both Weyrd and Normal, and yet despite having a state-of-the-art mobile phone, he kept everyone's details in an elderly black address book held together with a rubber band. I didn't make fun. The people he knew could ferret out things your average Titles Office clerk couldn't even begin to suspect existed.

'First of all, I've got a question.'

'Mmmm?'

'Who was he?'

'Do we really have to do this?' I groaned.

'I saw you.'

His fatherly tone might have been amusing and endearing if the image of him yelling, *Precisely what are your intentions towards my daughter?* at David, hadn't been strobing in my mind. I shouldn't have been surprised that I'd not even got away with one date.

'Ziggi . . . look, it's all new. David . . . David Harris. He's very nice. No family. Does stuff with computers. Smart, fun, reliable.'

'Normal.'

'*Normal* Normal, which is refreshing.'

'Does he know about *you*?'

'That he might one day want to throw a rock at me?' I grinned. 'Not yet.'

'And?'

'And he turns up when he says he's going to and he doesn't send me on jobs where I'm likely to get stabbed. I'm happy. And no, I don't know if he snores yet – maybe I'll find it adorable or maybe I'll put a pillow over his face. But for now, I'm happy. It's all so new, Ziggi; there's so much potential and nothing's gone wrong yet. Just let me enjoy it.' My stomach rumbled. That humble pie was looking more and more attractive. I held up a finger. 'And I am being careful not to mistake who I *want* him to be with who he actually *is*.'

'Look at you, learning from the past. You make me proud.'

'So, the house? Anything?'

'Nah. Sorry. For all intents and purposes it doesn't exist, although it's still glamoured. Powerful *ju-ju*, to hang around after its maker's death.' He shrugged. 'I'm thinking it's a lot easier to hide than erase. In related news, there are no records of it in the Titles Office, nor of power, gas or water ever being connected. And no one ever registered to vote using it as a residential address.'

'How's that possible?' I drummed my fingers on the tabletop to release the simmering frustration.

'Did Bela come up with anything?'

'Do you think you could avoid telling Bela that I'm still working on this?' As our boss thought it was over I had no desire to listen to a lecture on letting things go.

'I dunno – do you think you could apologise to Aspasia?'

'It's a deal,' I grumbled. I loved Ziggi dearly, but he and Bela had been friends for a long time and sometimes stuff just slipped out. I decided not to tell him about the Boatman or the knife strapped against my ankle either, just in case.

His gaze drifted away from me and he sat up straight, which could only mean one thing: our food was on the horizon, hopefully *sans* spittle. The plates made it to the table in none-too-gentle fashion and the waiter scampered away in case we tried to order anything else. Ziggi cut a cylinder from the middle of his muffin, stuffed a curl of butter inside, then gently massaged it to help the melting process along. It was messy and fascinating. I tried to maintain some dignity as I ate mine.

Then Ziggi came out with, 'Oh!' A little bit of muffin made a re-appearance, but he didn't seem to notice. He grabbed his mobile and waved it about. 'Bela wanted me to show you this.'

He queued the video with greasy fingers and delicately handed me the phone. I hit *play*.

The clip had been taken at night from a rooftop or balcony in Fortitude Valley, further up towards the New Farm boundary. I recognised the glare of the Judith Wright Centre in the distance. The recording was grainy but I could see well enough as a wave of blackness swept along, somehow folding in on itself. Over the sounds of static and the late-night/early-morning city, I picked out the rhythm of footsteps somewhere on the deserted street. A breeze gathered pieces of garbage; newspapers, cans and cigarette butts, and bundled all of it into an ever-growing, rapidly forming body until it looked like a man, a man of rags and trash and darkness.

It turned off Brunswick Street and continued down the incline, revolving madly and picking up speed as the sources of illumination grew fewer and dimmer. Just about at the bottom of the thoroughfare the thing threw itself right, then hard left, and gathered up what might have been a person hiding in the curve of a wall. There was no outcry; whatever – *whoever* – was lifted and spun about in the man-shaped maelstrom quickly ceased to be.

At the very end of the strip, the streetlights bloomed again and the sound of footsteps was clear, but further details were obscured as the video degraded into a haze of grey and white.

'Who took this?'

'A friend saw it and sent it on. It's been doing the rounds on the Internet. Everyone thinks it's part of a trailer for an amateur horror film . . . but it made me nervous.'

'Aw, Ziggi. Why show me this? Don't *add* to the problems!'

'Bela wanted me to suggest that it might have been responsible for some of the disappearances we've blamed on the Winemaker. And he might not be wrong, you know.' He sniffed. 'This stuff – is it just me, or does there seem to be a lot of it happening? You know, strange occurrences, I mean?'

'Ziggi, you've got an eye in the back of your head – you *are* a strange occurrence.' I sighed. 'The amount of wine in that cellar? That was a bumper harvest. Whatever this is . . . I don't believe it was taking those kids. Anyway,' I said, returning his phone, 'until this is *proved* to be something other than an amateur horror movie, it isn't a priority.'

'And the Baker thing? Bela asked me to ask,' he said sheepishly. Bela was obviously anxious to stay out of my reach for a while.

'Also not my top priority. I'll get to it – Baker Père door-stepped me yesterday, for the love of fuck – but I'll put money on the boy having done a runner to get away from his father.' I rose. 'Anyway, I've got to go. I need to buy some hiking boots.'

Ziggi dropped his cup in shock, luckily not from too great a height. The liquid splashed about in the saucer a bit.

'Oh, you heard me.' I stood up. 'See you later.'

'There certainly seems to be a lot of moisture in the air,' I said the next day.

The force of the afternoon storm was massaging my scalp through the cap, which might have been nice except for the icy trickle down my neck. David, a few feet in front, turned his head just far enough for me to see the grin, then continued trailblazing us along the walking track at Mount Holy-crap-I-can't-believe-you-talked-me-into-this.

'And what's that smell?' I asked.

'That would be nature.'

I'd said, 'Sure, an easy ramble would be nice.' With my leg doing so well it didn't need to be *that* easy, but I am essentially lazy. He knew painkillers had formed one of my basic food groups for a while, although he didn't know the circumstances of the injury. The walk itself wasn't difficult, but the unseasonal, very hard, very wet precipitation was making me wonder about my companion's sanity. He'd appeared to be so normal, but I suppose an obsession with the outdoors isn't really as obvious as, say, a pair of wings or elongated canines. At least there was no one else around to see us slogging onwards like idiots through what I was pretty sure could be described as a monsoon.

In all fairness he was, as I'd told Ziggi, not just Normal, but *normal*, and I hadn't realised how much I'd craved that until that first time we went for pancakes. We'd talked and talked, and kept talking. David made me laugh, which still felt like a surprise present being given over and over. He was now occupying a large chunk of my thoughts and I was in danger of turning schoolgirl: lying on my bed, feet kicking around, writing *Dear Diary* notes with a pink pen.

He'd moved from Tasmania to do a computer science degree with a minor in marketing and had ended up staying in Brisbane. He had no family to speak of, no siblings, and his parents were long years dead. We'd established he'd had three serious previous girlfriends;

he'd wanted commitment and two didn't, the last had decided she'd rather go overseas. He was open and unaffected, and not at all embarrassed about answering whatever questions I'd asked. He'd even offered to build me a website, but I couldn't imagine writing the copy to describe what I did – and anyway, it wasn't like I needed to advertise, seeing as jobs found me whether I wanted them to or not.

We'd planned more dates too: lunches and dinners slipped into the cracks of life, between his work and mine, and we spoke about ordinary stuff and we did ordinary things and I liked it. Which was probably why I'd agreed to a bush walk . . . Gods help me, the next thing would be *camping*. I stared at my feet in their embarrassingly new hiking boots, stared past them at the mud and rotting leaves and the yellows, dark crimsons and ochres of berries half-buried in the path. Then I lifted my eyes, blinking against the rain; up beyond the reach of the trees was a sky of darkest grey.

Not that it bothered my boyfriend. Friend-boy. Whatever. He walked on, stoic in the early afternoon light until we eventually hit a sort of walkway in the middle of some crowded trunks and shrubby undergrowth. David pulled back a particularly creepy-looking plant thing and said, 'Wait-a-while.'

'Huh?'

He grinned. 'If it grabs your clothes it takes ages to get rid of them – wait-a-whiles.'

Ah. Nature. Cue shudder.

We pressed on, finally breaking through to a wooden platform hemmed by metal railings and hanging out over a waterfall. The sun put in an unexpected cameo through the clouds, weak and watery. Alongside ran the stream we'd been crisscrossing; it tripped around rocks and dived under fallen branches until at last it threw itself out into the air in one long glorious spray, bursting on boulders far below before reforming into a brownish-olive pool. Moss, the brightest green I'd ever seen, ran riot, even scaling the trunks of the trees circling the pond.

'Long drop,' I said, knuckles white on the rail while my feet tried to sneak away.

David caught my forearms and pulled me close, winding his hands around my waist. 'I won't let you fall.' Then he kissed me, and I didn't care what happened in worlds either Weyrd or Normal or how much rain fell, just as long as no one interrupted us. For a long while no one did.

Until somewhere close by there was a crash, and boughs creaked and cracked. We separated and stared in the direction of the sound. Something heavy, dark and mostly obscured by foliage bounded off, branches and leaves whirling aside as whatever it was disappeared at speed.

'What the——?' I started.

'Mmmm, one of the inhabitants.'

'Mutant wombats?'

'Probably.'

'Ah, nature.'

'You know, you have to stop saying that with such disgust.'

'Meh.'

He ran a finger tenderly across the injury on my forehead. 'Really ran into a door, huh?'

'Really.'

I kissed him again and that kept him quiet.

Chapter Eleven

Inspector McIntyre had provided two addresses for Serena Kallos, along with strict instructions not to leave any prints or destroy any evidence, which to my mind denoted a certain lack of faith. I decided not to take it personally. The Scene of Crimes Officer wouldn't get to either place until later that day, she'd told me, and if I could defuse any magical mousetraps first, everyone would be eternally grateful. So I had free rein for a while, and a little breaking-and-entering was just what the doctor ordered.

Some quick searches showed that the siren was registered to vote, owned property, paid her taxes and generally kept records, which endeared her to me. She had a shop called Birds of a Feather on Oxford Street at Bulimba, close to the ferry stop, so I started there.

Ziggi loaned me his electric pick gun after expressing some concern about my lack of subtlety when it came to locks. The back door gave only token resistance, and it turned out that Serena Kallos, like a lot of Weyrd, didn't bother with Normal alarm systems. There were no serious sorceries, either, just some simple spells that might have been pretty effective against your average burglar, but which took me only a few moments to undo. A chalk mark erased here, a near-invisible thread snipped there, a judicious sprinkling of powdered lavender and marjoram and a whisper of certain words that I understood, a little. Anyone with ill-intent and nefarious purpose would have come down with a nasty rash, not to mention developing a scent the siren would have been able to track. For me, armed as I was with my virtuous designs, a pair of heavy-duty disposable gloves and Grigor's eldritch teachings, I was okay.

A small kitchen at the rear of the building was sandwiched between a stuffed storeroom and a loo so tiny there was barely enough room to sit down, let alone swing any proverbial cats. A sliding door led into the store proper, which was open-plan, with some curtained-off dressing rooms in one corner. A couple of fake Louis XIV chairs, all faded gilt and burgundy velvet, were artfully arranged in between the hanging racks packed tight with vintage clothes. My eyes were drawn to a lovely silk shift; as I stroked the fabric I flipped over the price tag – and immediately let go of the dress, my fingers feeling scalded. Maybe the chairs weren't so fake after all. It took me a while to find the cash drawer, which had been cunningly built into the side of a display case holding a small fortune in sparkling jewellery.

The whole set-up looked less like a vintage clothing shop and more like Lily Langtree's walk-in wardrobe.

I poked around a bit more, but nothing stood out, nothing looked displaced. Nothing reeked of either weird or Weyrd.

I turned to head back through the kitchen – and a flash of bright pink caught my eye. I fished out the *something* from between the sink and the miniscule fridge: a towelling bib, embellished with an embroidered bunny and dried lumps of baby food, smelling distinctly pumpkiny. On the back was one of those iron-on labels mums are so fond of. This one read *Calliope Kallos*.

Curiouser and curiouser.

I locked up and, carefully tucking away my gloves, walked around to the front of the shop where the lurid purple cab was waiting, Ziggi impatiently tapping his fingers on the steering wheel. As I returned the pick gun I wondered whether or not I should get one of my very own. The ethical part of me said *no*; the lazy part of me said *please!* Ziggi examined it closely for any scratches, dents, smudges, or other signs that it had been in my possession too long. Finally satisfied, he put it in the glove box. 'Leave a mess?'

'You insult me,' I grumped, then added, 'Neat as a pin, my friend.'

'Did you find anything?'

'Just this.' I handed him the bib.

He examined it, then sniffed at it, as if that might give him a clue – in fairness, it might have; his sense of smell was much sharper than mine – but in the end he shook his head and gave it back. 'I got nothing,' he said a little sadly.

I read out the next address: one of the more exclusive reaches of the river, great resale value and high enough to avoid flood-waters and keep insurance premiums slightly less than astronomical. He took off at an unhealthy speed just before I managed to belt up; he always did that. I was only a little panicked.

'If there's a baby—' he began.

'I know,' I whispered, horribly aware of what we might find at Serena's home. In an effort to distract us both, I asked, 'Anything more on that clip? The monster-thing in the Valley?'

'Monster? Guess it was,' he mused. 'Thought you weren't interested.'

'Just making conversation.' I drew patterns on the back of the seat in front of me. 'We both know the worst monsters are on the inside of the skin.'

'Truer words never spoken.' He paused, then added, 'Can't trace anything, can't tell where it was uploaded. User ID is FunBoyster, which is to say, useless. People can hide themselves on the Internet.' Ziggi stopped talking to concentrate on the mailbox numbers flashing by. As we approached a high fence of black metal posts topped with fleur-de-lis finials, he tapped the brakes, slowing the cab and we drove through the open double gates. At the end of a longish driveway through a very neat garden landscaped mostly with succulents, we found a white stucco house with lots of tall windows. The front door – Nordic pine, I guessed – stood ajar. Ziggi handed me the box and we both pulled on new sets of disposable gloves before getting out.

The foyer was glacial: the walls were tiled with tiny slivers of mirror, a mosaic that threw thousands of tiny Veritys and Ziggis back at us. A silver-painted wrought-iron hall table held a pot plant; something bushy with pointy red and black flowers. It looked unnaturally healthy, but in my experience plants tended to thrive on benign neglect – or mine had to anyway – and that made me wonder precisely how long Serena Kallos had been gone from this house. As I leaned closer, the leaves, moving of their own volition, reached for my face, and when I jerked away with a very loud 'Fuck!' the thing went into a seizure, like a belly dancer on speed. It eventually calmed down, settling like a cat after an undignified jump. Ziggi and I moved on; it took a while for my adrenalin levels to return to normal.

It wasn't just the foyer; the whole interior was blinding: all high ceilings and alabaster walls, with the back of the house, facing the river, floor-to-ceiling glass. The lounge was mostly occupied by a white leather corner sofa resting on a ruby and charcoal rug, with two matching armchairs. I suspected the pristine ottoman hadn't ever endured the indignity of a pair of clawed feet. The dining area, long and thin and running the width of the house, had a twelve-seater table of raven metal and tinted glass the colour of smoky quartz. Not a smudge nor fingerprint could be seen anywhere. The kitchen, all stainless steel and stone worktops, didn't appear to have ever been used for its intended purpose. There wasn't even a trace of rubbish festering in the bin under the desert-dry sink. Maybe Serena ate out a lot, or perhaps she hadn't been home for days before she died. Ziggi, fairly certain that the place was empty and I was – relatively – safe, went outside to recce the garden.

I tiptoed up stairs thickly carpeted in impractical ivory to the master bedroom, facing the river, with its king-size bed wreathed in linen of some impossibly high thread count. There wasn't much else in the way of furniture, probably because of the *enormous* walk-in closet, which was packed with almost as many dresses as in Serena's store. There were special compartments accommodating jewellery, handbags, belts, hats, scarves, sunglasses and just about every other accessory known to and desired by womankind. And then there were the shoes, so *many* shoes, all custom-made, each pair stored in its own neatly labelled, see-through box. I wasted a few moments appreciating the aesthetics of – okay, drooling over – customised Jimmy Choos and Louboutins I could never afford and wouldn't be able to walk in even if I did decide to mortgage my home and buy a pair.

I tore myself away and went back into the bedroom. There were two more doors to explore. One opened into a spotless, gleaming bathroom. The other revealed a nursery.

The walls were painted with Aegean scenes: whitewashed buildings with blue window frames and doors clinging to dusty green hillsides, water like turquoise and ancient, jagged cliffs. In the sky were figures: winged women, each feather on their snow-brilliant wings picked out in intricate detail. This room had heart; for all the icy elegance and perfect decor everywhere else in the house, this room felt like a *home*, a place where love lived. It took me a moment to realise what the marks on the ceiling were: constellations of glow-in-the-dark stars. A rocking chair in one corner sat beside a pastel pink toybox filled with plushy creatures that would have had Lizzie in a state of cuddle-ecstasy. The cradle, a great thing carved from silvered driftwood, was empty, the bedding cold and unruffled. An immaculate changing table sat against one wall; there was not a single dirty nappy in the lidded bucket.

The rest of the upper floor was devoted to a second bedroom, a larger bathroom and a well-appointed study, furnished with a desk and two four-drawer filing cabinets heavy with folders, a state-of-the-art printer-cum-scanner-cum-fax machine and a slim laptop. A thorough search turned up no sign of either recent habitation or violent ransacking, no sign that Serena might have died in her own home – and no suggestion of what might have happened to her child.

I ran through the records in the filing cabinets; they were about the shop, banking, tax stuff. Her laptop wasn't password-protected, but that too was all business.

Feeling defeated, I wandered back down to the lounge and flopped onto the couch. I lifted my feet onto the ottoman, which squeaked in protest under my Docs, and called McIntyre. She picked up on the first ring.

'I think there might be a baby.'

'And hello to you, too. You leave a mess, Fassbinder?'

'Why does everyone keep asking that?' I looked through the huge windows, watching the ferry making its way across the river. 'I found a dirty baby's bib at the shop and there's a nursery at the house, but there's no actual baby.'

'Shit,' she said vehemently, and I imagined her looking for something to throw. 'Shitty shitty shit-shit.'

'Calliope,' I said. 'The baby's name is Calliope. So where's Calliope Kallos?'

'You think maybe this is about the kid?'

'Hard to tell. Sirens don't tend to breed that often. They live a very long time, and they really don't have much need – or desire – to procreate. I suppose every now and then some of them might get broody . . .'

'What do they do – lay eggs?'

That stopped me. Now I couldn't get the picture out of my head of a grown woman crouched over a nest, straining like mad. 'I am honestly not sure,' I said at last. 'Let me get back to you on that.'

'Actually, I don't want to know.'

'We should try to find the father. You know, someone important and official might be able to get a rush on a birth certificate—'

She snorted. 'Keep me updated,' she said, then cut me off.

I chose to believe she'd get back to me, but made a mental note to follow it up myself. You can never be too suspicious.

A stomping at the front door signified that Ziggi was meticulously wiping his boots. He came into the lounge and announced, 'No recently turned earth, no garbage bags, no dodgy-looking compost, nothing untoward in the wheelie bin. There's a Mercedes in the garage with a baby seat in the back. Nothing here?'

'Nothing here,' I agreed. 'Jesus, Ziggi – she *called* me. Serena Kallos called me and I didn't turn up.' I tugged at my hair, hard, as if pain might cancel out the emotions, or at least distract me from them.

'V, no one's blaming you,' Ziggi said kindly. 'You were kind of busy not getting killed, after all. You might feel bad, but this wasn't your fault.' He patted me clumsily on the back. 'Whatever happened to her started well before she rang you – and remember, they only ever contact us when they're already in deep shit.'

I exhaled. I knew he was right, but that didn't really help right now.

I looked around the room, racking my brain for inspiration. 'You think the kid might have been stolen – by whom, though? The father? Some woman who desperately wanted a child? Baby smugglers?'

'Maybe another siren?' he suggested. 'Why shouldn't they be as nuts as everyone else?'

'Good point. But someone killed the *mother*, Ziggi. Was it so they could take Calliope? And who – or *what* – can kill a siren? Have you ever heard of such a thing?'

'Not in recent years,' he admitted. 'In the old days, well, that was different. There were all kinds of gods and monsters who could do something like that back then.'

'Any chance one survived?'

'Unlikely. When I say monsters, I mean things that were basically ill-tempered, mid-sized dragons: fire- and acid-spitting, tail-spike-flinging, basilisk-gazed nasties – and big, too, way too big to hide. And it's not like they actively hunted sirens – I'm just saying, they *could've* taken one down. So if something like that went after Serena Kallos, or even just came through this house – through Brisbane – we'd know about it. *Everyone* would know about it.' He scratched at his ear. 'Maybe your father could have done it, if he'd shifted and got his timing just right, or if he'd snuck up on her—'

'Thought you didn't know my father?'

He gave me a look. 'I didn't, V. I didn't need to. There are plenty of stories about him – his strength, his shifting . . . and some of his old cronies were still in the city when I arrived. And Bela's told me some things. What, you think I've been lying to you all this time?' He stared at me.

Long moments stretched between us while I thought of Grigor changing, the way he used to grow larger and larger, showing off for his buddies. Finally, I let my pent-up breath go, grabbed his hand and squeezed. 'No. No, I don't think that. Of course not. I'm sorry. And I don't think there's anyone quite like my father left. Are there any neighbours nearby?'

'The houses on both sides are locked up tight and the gardens are huge, with lots of trees; I doubt you'd hear much.' He glanced around, but I could see he'd already dismissed the place. He was right: it was a bust. 'Any more bright ideas?'

'Nope, no ideas, bright or otherwise. I need some percolating time.'

He gave me a look. 'How much coffee you drinking?'

I glared. 'I meant *brain* percolation.'

'Oh. Then we should probably have cake. It helps me think. Besides, it's almost lunchtime.

'It's ten a.m.,' I said.

'Then we've got plenty of time. You're buying.'

'Apparently I'm always buying. Why is that?' I headed into the kitchen and scanned the room until I spotted a spare set of house keys on a wall hook by the phone. It seemed like a good idea to take them. Just in case.

'I'm merely the driver.'

'I thought we were friends.' I locked the front door as we left.

'One of us needs a better class of friends.'

We were both huffing as we made our way back to the cab.

Chapter Twelve

'Where would I find a baby?' I muttered, unfortunately just as David returned from the kitchen, plates in hand. His expression was something to behold, but he managed to set our dinner down without any observable shaking. The aroma of butter chicken mingling with cheese and garlic naan filled the room, and my salivary glands sat up and took notice.

'You getting clucky?' Which was a fair question from a man I'd only just started seeing.

'Don't be silly. I mean somebody else's kid.' That came out wrong. *How the hell would I explain this?*

'You getting kidnappy?'

'I'm ... making some enquiries about a woman who died. It appears she had a baby, and said baby is missing. So, apart from random babynappers and an unknown father, where might the child be?'

'She was a working mum? Before the death, I mean?' He paused. 'Crèche? Kindergarten? Day care centre?'

I stared at him, silently berating myself. Surely I should have been able to come up with that on my own? But we childless, we live in a special kind of happy ignorance.

What David said made sense; of course someone running a business would need time *sans* offspring. And there were definitely crèches and kindergartens in Bulimba.

'Have you ever thought about changing careers, maybe renting yourself out as a back-up cortex?' I asked.

We'd had a talk – not *the* talk, not yet – but *a* talk, which meant I'd told him I was a PI. Well, I was, I investigated things . . . we just hadn't got around to covering for whom, or mentioning which particular sector of the populace employed me. I didn't want to lie outright as that struck me as a very poor way to start a relationship with my first non-Weyrd guy-friend, so all I could do was share as much as I was comfortable with him knowing for the moment. *Sufficient unto the day is the weirdness thereof*, and all that.

I'd spent the better part of the afternoon getting precisely nowhere – company records showed that the Oxford Street shop was the extent of her commercial interests and title-deed searches revealed no other properties under Serena's name. While I was at it, I'd taken a moment to double-check for deeds to the Ascot house, in the faint hope that Ziggi's minions might have missed something, but of course they hadn't. Then I'd wasted the rest of the day phoning round all the upmarket hotels and asking if Serena Kallos had ever checked in; when I'd exhausted that list I moved on to the mid-range hotels before finally hitting the roach motels. But none of this yielded anything, and I was beginning to think that unless she owned another place under an alias, she'd either been staying with a friend when she died, or hiding out somewhere else.

David's invitation to dinner had been the shining light at the end of my crappy day. He had an apartment in the Woolstore, a complex with the kind of architectural strangeness you generally get when someone tries to make a storage space fit for human habitation. Some areas were too large, others too small and almost all of them could be described as 'challenging' in shape. Stairs ran at crazy angles, strikingly ugly carpets mingled with strikingly beautiful polished wood and mediocre polished concrete. On the ground floor, banks of mailboxes requiring small keys lined one wall of the lobby, which I chose to think of as the beginning of the maze: I would not have been at all surprised if I'd bumped into a minotaur checking his mail.

But enough about me.

'What did you do today?' I asked.

'I spent two hours discussing brown with a client,' he answered, his expression pained.

'*Brown?* He's fond of brown?'

'Overly so, I'd say.' He took a bite of naan. 'He wanted his website entirely in shades of brown, of which, it turns out, there are *many*.'

'Fifty Shades of Brown?'

'Something like that.'

'And how'd it go?'

'I stopped listening after the first thirty minutes and sang songs in my head.'

'You are wise.'

I looked around and couldn't help but compare the warmth of David's apartment with the cold refinement of Serena Kallos' place. Though it lurked behind one of many identical glossy cream doors, it had much more character than I'd expected, given the rest of the building. The kitchen was all black granite worktops and gleaming stainless steel appliances; the lounge was resplendent with heavy wooden bookcases, a dark green leather sofa and matching chairs and a Turkish rug about the size of two Mini Coopers parked end to end. At the far end of the room, one whole wall was taken up by the big-screen TV and matching sound system and an enormous desk with a state-of-the-art PC and two monitors. On a charger in the corner of the desk I spotted an iPad, sleeping peacefully. David's tour of the place took in a spare room that was pretty basic, but ready for overnight guests, a fairly large bathroom and a mezzanine platform with a king-size bed and an en-suite bathroom. The place was anything but beige; it was comfortable and cozy, yet stylish in its own way.

I was about to shovel in a mouthful of butter chicken when my jacket, hanging over the back of a chair, emitted a shriek. I gave David an apologetic look and checked the number, thinking it might be Lizzie, who'd taken to calling me before she went to bed – Mel said it helped her get to sleep.

But alas, it was Rhonda's number, and past experience had shown there was no ignoring Detective Inspector McIntyre when she wanted attention. She'd just keep ringing until I answered.

She didn't bother with any of the usual social niceties like 'Hello' or 'Sorry for ruining your evening'.

'Fassbinder, we've got another one of those chicken-women.' She didn't bother to keep her voice down; she was unhappy and she didn't care who knew it. I held the phone away from my ear and could still hear her perfectly, and so, I suspected, could David. 'Have you got any-fucking-thing for me?'

'Tomorrow I'm trying the kindies near her home,' I offered.

'What am I paying you for?' she barked.

'Well, strictly speaking, you're not paying me on this one, Tepes is.' I made the distinction even though I knew it wouldn't make the slightest bit of difference. 'But even I need to eat and sleep and bathe occasionally. Not to mention that kindergartens and day care centres close overnight.' I wasn't doing a particularly good job of keeping the annoyance out of my voice. 'You got any-fucking-thing for me? Something from a birth certificate, perhaps?'

'Nothing yet — apparently I'm not as important as either of us thought,' she snapped, then she calmed down a bit and added, 'Except the autopsy report came in.'

I waited. Her voice sounded a bit odd.

'Apart from the effects of falling from a great height, her heart was crushed.'

I let that sink in, then asked, 'It's not something that could have happened on impact? Wouldn't the internal organs be the consistency of a daiquiri after that sort of plunge?'

'Under normal circumstances I'd agree with you, but these sirens are tougher than old boots. There are finger marks around the cardiac muscle, very clear to see. Someone reached into her chest — *left no trace going in* — and *squeezed*.' She coughed and I heard a lifetime of cigarettes rattling around in her lungs.

'You okay?'

'Nothing a bullet won't fix,' she snorted. 'Get back to me as soon as you find anything. If any more of these corpses turn up I don't know how I'm going to keep it quiet.'

'The new one — you need me to come to the scene?'

'Nope. She's in the Botanical Gardens, caught in a tree like she fell out of a plane. We're cleaning it up and getting her removed.'

'That must be fun to keep out of the public eye.'

'You'd be amazed how much land you can rope off under the threat of a gas leak.'

'Ingenious. Take some snaps; I'll meet you at the morgue in a couple of hours.' I thought for a moment, then asked, 'Any ID?'

'Yep, this one's got a handbag. See you later.' Then there was just dead air.

I went back to the couch. Half of my dinner had disappeared, and anything resembling naan bread had apparently never existed.

David's plate was empty of any trace of food and he wore the look of a guilty dog.

My appetite was gone but I still glared.

'It was unguarded,' he said by way of explanation.

'Okay, this is a boundary issue and we need to talk about it . . .'

I didn't like the morgue. It smelled wrong: the kind of super-duper clean that never quite covered up the fact that there were dead things everywhere. It felt wrong: grief and death had embedded themselves in the walls, in tile and concrete that should have been impervious, and it *sounded* wrong too: the clip of my footsteps so final that I was always vaguely astonished to find I was still alive when I left. Finally, there were the whispers; a gentle, distressed susurrus of the surprised and protesting dead. I was never able to make out what they were saying, mind; I couldn't quite distinguish the words. I just knew the tone, the cadences of despair, which heightened my awareness and made it extra upsetting that I couldn't always help, no matter how much I wanted to.

It was quite a trek to get out to Coopers Plains. Ziggi had taken the night off and the cab fare was hefty – David had offered to drive, but I didn't want the two parts of my life colliding quite so soon. The overly perky night receptionist was new and gave me directions I didn't need to the elevators after she'd handed over a visitor's badge; I was grumpy and definitely did not want to be there, but I managed to bite down on a sarky comment. *Virtue, thy name is Verity.* I took one to the basement and stepped into the long corridor. A breeze pushed at my back, though there was no source, then came a flapping noise and I felt as though feathers brushed against my skin, like wings were being wrapped around me. I tried to rub the sensation away from my arms, much like a junkie trying to remove imaginary spiders, and resisted the urge to run. Fear made me sweat, and for a moment I was glad I'd not had a chance to eat my dinner, as the little I already had in my stomach started roiling.

A door opened a little way down the hallway and McIntyre's dishevelled head popped out. 'Took your time. Finished farting about?'

I shuddered and went over to her. 'You ever *sense* anything down here?'

She looked startled, began to answer, then closed her mouth and retreated into the autopsy suite, leaving me to follow. The room was brightly illuminated and the technician looked like a stain against all the lightness. Ellen was small and thin and shaven-headed, and all visible skin except her face was swarming with tattoos. Myriad designs crawled across the backs of her hands and along her forearms to slip beneath the edge of the sleeve, then reappeared like tendrils from the collar of her scrubs. They wound their way up her throat and the nape of her neck to blossom all over her shaved head: a colourful collage of mouths and faces, tears and roses, pearls and breasts, beasts and bells. Her hairline had exquisitely detailed inking, which made it appear as if her face was peering out from a hole in an eggshell. It was both lizard-like and Bosch-esque, simultaneously beautiful and disturbing. She looked exhausted.

On one of the steel tables lay a dark-haired woman, her pale skin blotched with bruises and smeared with blood. No Y incision marked her chest yet, so I guessed she'd not long been delivered. On a separate table were her wings; their stumps still oozed. I recognised her as one of the sirens I'd seen at the Kangaroo Point nest; she was the one who'd hissed at me and tried to keep me away from Eurycleia. Who – or *what* – had she pissed off?

I leaned in, examining her exposed flesh, and pointed to a trickle of crimson that'd dried on her neck. It led up into her hair. 'What's that?'

Ellen held the black locks back and I took a closer look, McIntyre at my side. A raw red mark sat high behind her left ear, mostly hidden by the luxuriant tresses. It was in the shape of a small square cross, and it hadn't been branded onto her skin, it had been carved.

I straightened, nearly knocking McIntyre over, and asked quickly, 'Is Serena Kallos still here?'

The tech shrugged and turned towards the bank of steel drawers, which earned her a glare from Rhonda, who snapped, 'She means "yes". You'll have to forgive Ellen; she sometimes has trouble using her words.'

She gave me an *it's-so-hard-to-get-good-help* eye-roll while we waited for Serena Kallos to appear from her cold bed.

I tried not to look at the rough stitching holding her torso together. Ellen had to search carefully, shifting individual hairs like a grooming monkey, but at last she found an identical mark high on the back of Serena's skull, dried to a dull rust colour.

'What's it mean?' asked the tech, and it was my turn to shrug.

'If we knew that, Ellen, we wouldn't be here.' McIntyre wearily rubbed her face with both hands, as if she could smooth out the wrinkles.

'More importantly, why didn't *you* find it?' I asked, and Ellen looked embarrassed.

'This one only just came in tonight—' she began, then stopped and admitted, 'It was pretty obvious what killed her – both of them. I didn't think I needed to look for anything else. I'm sorry.'

'Believe it or not, Ellen, we're not only interested in the immediate cause of death,' McIntyre said cuttingly, and I suspected words would be had later.

'Name?' I asked.

'Teles Dimitriou, reputed to be twenty-six. Until very recently, resident in an exclusive block of units over at Sydney Street, New Farm. A lawyer.'

I gestured to the wings. Even though I was certain I knew the answer I asked, 'You remove those?'

Ellen shook her head, earrings jangling in her left ear. When she turned around I saw the wings inked onto the back of her head, reaching up either side from the base of the skull to the crown. I glanced at her feet, but the shoes weren't custom-made, just ordinary Reeboks. 'I know it's hard to believe, but I'm neater than that. These have been wrenched off.'

I touched a finger to Serena Kallos' lovely dead face and traced a raised scratch, thinking of what might have happened if I'd been too late to save Lizzie. I imagined how Mel would look if she'd had to come here, identify her child – if there'd even been a body after the Winemaker had had her way – or worse still, no body, no closure, Lizzie missing like Serena's daughter was now. I thought about Calliope Kallos, out there somewhere in the dark of the night, while her mother lay dead in a freezer.

'You done?' McIntyre interrupted. 'I know you won't want to hang around for the next act.'

'Yeah,' I said, and she started herding me towards the door.

'Ideas?' she asked as we stepped into the corridor.

'Do you trust her?'

'Ellen? As much as I trust anyone.' She gave a wan smile. 'But I think she's harmless. Maybe not too bright some days. And I don't think she's strong enough or mean enough to rip the wings off a fly, let alone—'

'I didn't mean that. I meant . . . Honestly, at this point I don't know what I mean.' I sighed. 'You'll probably find this one's heart in the same shape as the first victim's.'

'Tell me something my questionably competent friend in there can't.'

'Peru once had the world's highest golf course.'

She made a noise that might have been a laugh as we stopped at the elevator and she hit the call button more violently than was necessary. 'Plan?'

'Anything on the birth certificate?' I asked hopefully.

She shook her head. 'I'm not Wonder Woman. Some time tomorrow, maybe.'

'Bugger. Then tomorrow I'll shake a few day care centres and see what falls out. Surely someone would've reported it if a baby'd been left somewhere for days? Maybe someone knows the father and I can have a chat with him, see if he's got Calliope.'

'Ask him if he killed the mother while you're at it. Interested parties need to know.' She was going to say something else, but the coughing began again: an ugly noise, worse than it had sounded over the phone. Her face reddened and her eyes watered and she leaned against the wall, one hand at her throat, clutching at her crucifix as if it might help. I held her for support, ignoring her expression as it flashed between gratitude and impatience, but she wasn't really in a position to refuse assistance.

When she finally recovered and the shuddering had lessened, I let her go. I'd known Rhonda a while and she was a *very* private person: enquiries as to her wellness or otherwise wouldn't be met with cuddles. But still. As she straightened, I said, 'Rhonda, are you going to hit me if I ask if you're okay?'

'Probably.' Her voice was worn, and the exhalation behind it stank wetly. Her breath smelled like the morgue. 'Just a touch of pleurisy. Far less exciting than consumption.'

'Okay, then, I'll respect your privacy if you promise not to drop dead.'

'Deal.' She started back to the autopsy suite.

'McIntyre?' I called, and she looked over her shoulder. 'Anything I can do to help?'

She laughed. 'Yeah, fuck off.'

What a kidder. She disappeared, but I felt as if I hadn't said or offered enough and I turned and followed. The door to the exam room wasn't properly closed and before I barged in I peered through the gap. I could see McIntyre and Ellen standing close as close can be. The tech, looking sad, had her hands cupped around McIntyre's face and I could see traces of tears on the older woman's cheeks. Rhonda clearly wasn't well, but she wasn't on her own.

I felt a little better, but also a lot lonelier. I wanted nothing more than to be back at David's, sitting next to him on his green sofa and breathing in his scent and his warmth, knowing he'd smell like stolen butter chicken and naan. I wanted to touch his face, feel the skin, the stubble, run my hands through his thick blond hair, and see the goofy grin on his face when I said it was time we slept together. Death makes us all want to do something lifeward; sometimes Death got it right.

I turned on my heel and retreated, braced in case the sensation of wings assaulted me again, but this time there was just the cool hum of the dull metal elevator taking me back up – that and the surprise I couldn't quite deny on discovering that I was once more escaping alive.

Chapter Thirteen

'I don't care who you are, Ms Fassbinder,' the woman said, smiling through gritted teeth and glaring at me over the top of her Dame Edna glasses. 'You're not a police officer and I can't give you any personal information about our clients or their children.'

At the first two crèches I had learned what I probably should have already known: you don't get to ask questions about kids, certainly not strangers' kids, unless you have a badge or a degree in social work. Mrs Tinkler, proprietress of Dinky Darlings Day Care, was hammering that message home, and enjoying it way too much. I had the distinct impression she lived only to make other people's lives less enjoyable. The others had at least been courteous in their refusals, but politeness didn't appear to be one of the settings on Mrs Tinkler's dial.

Mrs T. sat at the front counter like an oversized toad, swathed in a pink and white winter-weight caftan. Her hair colour came out of a bottle that hadn't delivered on the promises it had made. Her muddy eyes glittered meanly. The notice boards behind her were covered with artwork from the Retro Glitter and Macaroni School, and sunflowers with faces and speech balloons spouted improving slogans about smiles, kindness and hygiene; at least two of those messages were ones Mrs T. had not taken to heart. To the left was a safety-glass door leading through to an activities room, and beyond that I spotted a playground where hordes of small children were running about like brightly coloured bumper cars. To the right was an office, and a little further along was another open door, perhaps leading to the *sanctum sanctorum*, also known as the staff break room. I thought I saw a shadowy movement there, but Mrs T. dragged my attention back by clearing her throat.

'Is there anything else I can help you with, Ms Fassbinder?' *As if she'd helped me with anything in the first place.*

'Perhaps you could simply nod your head *if* Serena Kallos had her daughter Calliope enrolled here? That would make my job much easier and I could stop wasting your time,' I said, hoping I sounded considerably more polite than I felt. I liked to think of three as a magic number, but as this was the third time I'd asked for help and the third time I'd failed to get it, I was beginning to think the magic was running low. I indulged in a warm, fuzzy fantasy about getting McIntyre down here to tear Mrs T. a new one, but dismissed the idea pretty quickly; Rhonda was clearly not well. I'd try to keep the strain on her to a minimum. At some later date, I could stick a sharp knife in Mrs Tinkler's tyres, but for the moment it was white flag time.

She knew it, too. 'As I said, without a warrant—'

Well, at least I could milk this bit. 'Can you get this through your skull, Mrs Tinkler? Serena Kallos is *dead*. She took a swan-dive off a very tall building, and her child – a *baby* – is missing. I don't need anything from you except a yes or a no.'

Mrs T. was completely unfazed. She gave me a supercilious smile as I placed a business card on the counter and said sarcastically, 'Thank you *so much* for all your help. I'll be sure to mention it to Serena Kallos' family – as well as any journalists I might *happen* to be in contact with in the course of my investigation *into a murdered mother and missing child.*'

It was bullshit, of course – imagine *that* six o'clock news story! – but she didn't know that and her gaze went flat and dark. For a moment I wondered if she might be something less than Normal – the idea of her looking after children didn't inspire confidence in me. I pondered how she came off to the parents who brought their kids here, but she'd probably put on a mask, maybe a cuddly, loving aunty, and suck up to all those mums and dads desperately needing a place to store their offspring for the better part of every day.

What if . . .?

'You don't happen to live in Ascot, do you?'

The question was enough of a change of direction that before she could check herself she'd blurted, 'No. Tarragindi,' then she bit her bottom lip as if to punish it for letting slip. I'd get Bela to check on her.

I let the door slam and was halfway back to the sunny spot where Ziggi was parked before I heard the smack of clacky mules hitting the pavement behind me. Someone grabbed my arm and I swung around, fists clenched – maybe Mrs T. moved faster than expected?

Except it wasn't her but a red-headed girl in her early twenties, maybe even late teens. Her big eyes were caked in mascara and too much black eyeliner, yet she looked kind of sweet. Her nose was reddened, as if she'd been crying, and she kept glancing back towards Dinky Darlings.

'Hi?' I said.

'You were asking about Callie – listen, you can't tell anyone, 'cause I *really* need this job.' She spoke in a rush, as if desperate to get the words out before someone caught her talking to me. 'Serena used to bring her here, just twice a week, so she could have some time to herself and do the stuff she needed to for the shop.' Around her throat was a necklace like the ones I'd seen in the cabinet at the Kallos boutique: black stones with a green fire glowing deep within.

Labradorite, I guessed. Her dress was vintage; maybe 1950s, not really the best choice for working with dirt magnets all day, but I thought the kids would like how pretty she looked. She'd rushed out without a coat and was shivering.

'When did you last see Serena?'

'Is she really dead?'

'Afraid so. Sorry, your name—?'

'Vicki. Vicki Anderson. Serena was lovely, and she was a good mum. I used to babysit for her sometimes, but— Oh God, don't tell Mrs Tinkler!' She wrung her hands so hard the skin started to turn pink.

'No worries there.' I grabbed her wrists to keep her from hurting herself, then let her go, and she left her arms hanging loosely by her sides. 'When did you last see her?'

'Last Thursday afternoon when she picked up Calliope. She was fine then.'

'I don't suppose you know who the father is?'

She tilted her head, her mouth trembling. People always started to clam up after the initial babble, when the relief of telling was overcome by the regret of having let the cat out of the bag. The trick was to distract them to keep them talking, work on whatever guilt got them chatty in the first place.

'Vicki, I just need to find Callie – if her father's got her, then that's fine.' I neglected to say he might soon find himself a person of interest in a murder investigation; she didn't need to know that. 'I just have to make sure that little girl's okay.'

She ran a hand through her messy red curls. 'He used to pick Callie up sometimes – and he was always here for parents' days. He's a nice guy, but honestly, I didn't think he liked girls. Maybe it was an arrangement?'

'Can you tell me what his name is?' I kept my voice soft and restrained myself from punching the air.

'Chris – Christos. I don't know his last name, but he designs jewellery. He's got a store somewhere in Paddington.' She touched her necklace. 'Serena had a heap of his stuff on display in her shop.'

I remembered the price tags I'd seen and must have stayed quiet a moment too long because she said defensively, 'Serena *gave* me this last Christmas.'

I raised my hands to say *I'm not arguing*, but she started to cry, and when I patted her shoulder ineffectually she attached herself to me like a limpet, bawling as if her heart was breaking. It was more close contact than I was used to from strangers and it took all my self-control to make myself relax and emit comforting noises.

When she at last pulled away she looked embarrassed, muttering, 'I'm sorry.'

'You lost your friend. You don't need to apologise,' I said quietly. 'Here's my card. You'd better go back before the old bat notices you're gone, okay? And, thank you.'

She wiped the tears from her cheeks and spread the kohl even further afield. I pointed to my face, then hers. 'You might want to tidy up before she sees you. Give me a call if you think of anything else, okay?'

The sniffling girl smiled wanly and set off down the street, her mules beating out a sad little tarantella as she went.

Facet, nestled in the very chic, very boutiquey, very hilly suburb of Paddington, was one of those expensive stores filled with very little. I'd had to push a button to signal my interest in being let in, so it was a good thing I'd had the foresight to dress well for my second day of trying to extract information from people who weren't necessarily happy to reveal anything to a stranger. My standard attire of faded jeans and an old Cure T-shirt wouldn't have got me across the threshold of this particular shop – it might even have resulted in an uncomfortable phone call to the police – so I was glad I'd opted for my charcoal skirt, granite button-up top, ebony boots (a fashionable way of saying 'a lot of black') and my good winter coat. The fit of the right boot was a little tight with the dagger slid inside, but it was tolerable. I'd achieved quite a respectable appearance, I'd thought proudly as I'd brushed my hair, all the while studiously ignoring the greys peeking through the brown. I even managed to paint on some lipstick inside the lines. Never let it be said we're a society without miracles.

Through the spotless plate-glass window, instead of traditional display cases, I could see eight waist-high pillars spread around the space, each holding a red velvet pillow draped with a single item of jewellery and protected by a glass cover. I spotted security cameras in every corner of the room too, then a figure came in sight and I smiled and waved, apparently looking non-threatening and affluent enough for the lock to click and the door to jerk open a few inches. I stepped inside.

A pale man with light green eyes and long dark hair that kissed his collar gave me a professional smile and began to bustle. His navy wool trousers had dangerously sharp creases and his white shirt looked as if it had just come out of the wrapping. His handshake was gentle, the palm damp and soft-skinned. A heavy bracelet hung about his slim wrist: haematite and dragon-vein agate set in what looked like silver, but I bet was platinum.

'Christos?' I asked. I was willing to bet he'd been born a Christopher.

'And what can I help you with today, my lovely?' His manner was full-blown *dahling*, but he was trying too hard. He was nervous, and

I swear I could smell fear beneath his pricey cologne. He started fidgeting, first checking a cufflink, then a button; stroking his belt buckle, feeling the weight of the bracelet, pulling an earlobe, generally trying to distract himself with a series of busy-nothings. The broad business smile didn't reach his eyes, which were shifting to and fro as if constant vigilance was the only thing that could save him. He might have been right.

And I sensed something else which was really interesting. He was *ordinary*. I could feel it through his skin when we touched: a very solid ordinariness that permeated his flesh and lined his bones: Christos was Normal, and whatever trouble had found Serena, he wasn't able to cope with it. So how was he involved?

Every lie I'd thought of and every cunning half-truth I'd planned to use to inveigle him dried up on my lips. I pitied him, and it made me honest. 'I'm here about Serena and Calliope.'

'I'm sorry, I don't know who you're talking about.' Dread flickered in his face and a muscle started twitching involuntarily in his cheek. He retreated towards a long black velvet curtain at the back of the shop. I didn't follow immediately, just raised my hands, as if that might convince him he had nothing to fear from me.

'Christos, my name is Verity Fassbinder and I'm a private investigator. Serena called me before she died. We were supposed to meet, but I . . . I didn't make it.' My voice shook. 'Do you know what she wanted to discuss with me?'

'She's really dead?' he whispered, slumping against one of the pillars that wobbled dangerously. 'I couldn't contact her while I was away—'

'I'm sorry, Christos, yes. Serena's dead and Calliope is missing.'

He hesitated, as if weighing up my trustworthiness, then, slow as a cat consenting to be stroked, motioned for me to join him. Behind the curtain was a small office; a nappy bag and a baby carrier were piled in one corner. He fell into a chair at the desk and took a couple of deep breaths before saying, 'I was in Sydney on a buying trip. I didn't know anything had happened until I got home yesterday – that awful woman from Dinky Darlings called.'

Mrs Tinkler certainly did have a way about her.

'She demanded to know where Callie was – she started shouting about limited places and fees and waiting lists.' His bottom lip trembled. 'But I don't *know*! Callie mostly stayed with Serena.'

'I don't mean to be rude or offensive, Christos, but are you *really* Calliope's father?'

There was a moment when he looked like he was considering lying – when I could tell he yearned to do so – but I think he knew he wasn't good at untruths. After a pause he shook his head. 'Serena wanted a name to give people, to put on the birth certificate. But I did everything a father could and should. Serena and I are . . . we were best friends; I'd have done anything to help her. And that little girl – *my* little girl – she is just so beautiful. I loved her the moment I set eyes on her.' His smile was tremulous, but I had no doubt it was genuine.

'And you knew what Serena was?'

Again a pause, then he admitted, 'So strange, so lovely. Like a piece of art or something from history, so exquisitely old.' He sniffled. 'I just loved to be around them. I was privileged to be part of their lives.'

'Did she ever tell you who the sperm donor was?' I made a point of not saying 'real father'.

He said sadly, 'She wouldn't talk about it, and I didn't push. I suppose I thought that if I didn't know then I could pretend Callie really was mine.'

Serena would have known that Christos wasn't a keeper of secrets; anyone who wanted to get information out of him wouldn't have to push too hard, so what he didn't know, he couldn't tell.

'And you don't know what Serena was upset about?'

He looked at the toes of his gleaming shoes. 'Either she kept it from me or it didn't start until after I went away.'

'You don't—'

'I don't know where Callie is! I can't even begin to imagine – if the other sirens don't have her . . .' He let the statement hang, the weight of what was left unsaid . . . Serena Kallos had been dead for almost a week. Even though the little girl was half-siren, there was no guarantee she was any hardier than the average infant. Without food, without water, without care she wouldn't last long.

'Please find her,' he begged.

'I'm trying,' I said.

We swapped business cards, and then I opened my mouth to give the usual exhortation to call if he thought of anything, but what actually came out was, 'Christos, maybe you should go away for a break.'

Tradition dictated that people be told *not* to leave town, but I didn't think he'd do well against whatever had killed Serena, and I really didn't want a call from McIntyre telling me this gentle man – or parts of him – had been found in a tree or scattered across a park somewhere. If I could do something positive for at least one life I'd feel better about myself.

It was almost five by the time I left Christos and the day was pretty much gone. What little progress I'd made was nowhere near enough and that was lying heavily on me, as was the suspicion there would be some tail-chasing in my future, and while I was wandering around in the dark, that little girl's time might have already run out. I wasn't sure I was even asking the right questions, or looking in the right places.

I said as much to Ziggi as he negotiated the traffic to get me home.

'Can't think like that or you might as well just give up breathing,' he said firmly. 'You're annoyingly tenacious. You've got a brain. Use it,' he ordered.

Watching the vehicles around us, cars moving back and forth like a high-speed game of Tetris, I realised there was one place I *might* learn more: someone who knew a hell of a lot about a hell of a lot of things. But the privilege of talking to her was going to cost me. I'd be rearranging my priorities. I pulled out my mobile and resentfully thumbed a contact.

Chapter Fourteen

Every so often Mel had clients on a Saturday for acupuncture, cupping, Thai massage and other natural ways of leaving bruises, so I occasionally acted *in loco parentis* — after unsuccessfully trying to convince my charge that it did not mean *crazy parent*. That often meant schlepping Lizzie to relevant sporting events, for which Ziggi appointed himself fairy god-chauffeur — he claimed that if he was driving me it counted as work, for which Bela would pay, but I think he just liked the kid. Given the whole Winemaker business, I was lucky Mel still trusted me with her daughter.

That was how I came to be watching a game of under-tens soccer, a sport I'd previously understood to be non-contact. The noise generated by the crowd was phenomenal, but not enough to drown the voice in my head shouting that I wasn't doing enough to find Calliope. But I reminded myself sternly that I didn't have too many options: my dearly bought appointment wasn't until the next day. I was praying it would yield some leads, but in the meantime there was nothing to do except worry about a missing child whose mother I'd failed, while trying to immerse myself for a while in the flow of the ordinary world of a child I *had* managed to save . . . nothing to do but wonder, foolishly, if one day I'd be sitting here watching my own mini-me run after a stupid ball, to wonder if David would be beside me.

Mind you, observing those grownups at close quarters as they yelled violent advice at their children was not the best advertisement for parenthood. I pondered how and when life had changed for them – when they'd stopped thinking this was all meant to be *fun*. And when they'd stopped hoping for themselves and started dousing their offspring with their own dead ambitions, as if enough might soak in and resuscitate lost dreams. They might as well have been shouting, 'Let Daddy re-live his youth through you!' or, 'Become a star and keep Mummy in the manner to which she should already have become accustomed!' because that was clearly what they were seeking. And however much they loved their progeny, they had no true idea of their value – and they wouldn't, not until one was gone forever.

Watching all those cared-for kids made me think about the ones who had no one to worry about them: the ones who'd been lured to the gingerbread house and never got away, and the others, like Sally, who'd do anything to survive, no matter how awful. I was definitely conflicted about that little guttersnipe. Part of me felt desperately sorry for her, but the rest of me couldn't forgive her for the appalling harm she'd done. And that started me wondering: why'd she come by my place, only to disappear when she saw Anders Baker? Or was it me she was afraid of? Had she changed her mind at the sight of me? Perhaps she hadn't known I'd got to Lizzie in time and was terrified I'd failed and that I'd blame her? I tried to put the questions aside, before my mind started to feel like an out-of-control hamster wheel, and focused on the game.

Lizzie and I had had a long talk about good sportsmanship and she was following the rules to the letter – and doing an impressive job of keeping her temper in check, which was all the more remarkable since it appeared no one else had bothered to give their darlings a similar spiel. In the space of ten minutes she'd taken three falls, tripped by the same little grub each time, yet she'd neither popped him one nor grabbed him by his mullet and twirled him around like a streamer. I, on the other hand, was verging on enraged. I'd have given someone's right arm for the power to hex, so it was probably a good thing I had no magical talent whatsoever.

I glared at the people gathered around the field and in the stands, taking note of those who were especially vile; I might not be able to do anything, but I could dream. A few seats over from me sat a man with soft white hair and a bushy moustache and beard. A silver-tipped walking stick was propped next to him. He wore a navy and red chequered flannel shirt, grey tracksuit bottoms and a pair of expensive brown Polo loafers that looked out of place; the sort of gift a determined daughter-in-law would give, trying to smarten up the old man. At first I thought he looked familiar, until I realised it was the seen-one-seen-them-all phenomenon: he was standard granddad fare. He was also a single point of calm in an ocean of crazy. I couldn't tell which kid he belonged to and he wasn't yelling, just smiling gently, and I appreciated his dignity in the midst of the uproar. When he caught me staring we exchanged nods, then directed our attention back to the game.

Lizzie got possession of the ball and danced it towards goal, with me making encouraging noises even though there was no way she'd pick my voice from the cacophony. Someone bumped into me and sat too close, setting me off-balance until I realised Ziggi had returned from his quest for food. He shuffled about on the bench and I considered warning him about splinters when I noticed he'd bought *one* hotdog and *one* Coke. I was about to start on him when the shouting went up a level and my attention was drawn back to the pitch.

There was a fight, and when Lizzie was nowhere to be seen in the circle of small bodies I knew right where she'd be: in the middle of it, on her way to three-match suspensionville.

Leaving Ziggi to his lunch – and hoping heartily that it would be disgusting – I headed towards the cluster. When I finally managed to separate Lizzie from her opponent, she had scratches on one cheek and a blossoming bruise on the other. Her knees had dirt and grass ingrained in them and her hair was sticking up at all angles, a real pin-up girl for *Bedraggled* magazine. She gave me a shamefaced look, while her foe – the brat who'd been tripping her all afternoon – wailed like a recently neutered cat over his broken nose.

I looked from Lizzie to the group of glowering parents and back again. There was only one thing to say. 'Good shot.'

Being sent off the field in disgrace required the liberal application of ice cream. Had I been an actual parent, I might have worried about positive reinforcement of negative behaviour and other grown-up buzzwords; instead, I tried to salvage something fun from the day for Lizzie while I figured out how to explain it all to Mel. Perhaps some kind of martial art would be a safer – and less violent – weekend activity?

After a Cold Rock sundae big enough to send an entire kindergarten into a sugar frenzy, we pulled up outside my place and Lizzie ran from the cab like a rabbit on speed. She was at her front fence before either Ziggi or I had managed to haul ourselves out, but as I watched she stumbled, then froze, her right hand reaching for the gate.

'Lizzie, what's wrong?' I hurried over, and within a couple of steps I heard what had stopped her: two people yelling from inside her home. One was Mel, obviously trying to be calm and placating, but shouting in order to be heard; the other voice was also female, but this one was screeching, and refusing to be either calmed or placated.

'*Always so fucking perfect!*' came next, at impressive volume. 'But you never want to help *me*! What about *me*?'

'I think it's Aunty Rose,' Lizzie whispered, and I was afraid she was right.

Rose Wilkes, Mel's older sister: in no particular order, an alcoholic, the stealer of Mel's husband, and not a little bit insane. Lizzie's father had waltzed off to Thailand with Rose four years ago, deciding freedom and wild adventure beat marriage and fatherhood any day. She'd left him five months later, in monstrous debt, and with a bankrupted business. Who says karma's dead? Rose reappeared every eight to twelve months to demand money from her sister; there'd be a new commercial scheme, or another round of 'rehab' at some top-of-the-range health spa, or a donation to whichever fashionable new spiritual leader was touting a path to enlightenment paved with hundred-dollar notes. Mel's sense of family made her an easy mark; she had made the mistake of allowing herself to be guilted into 'helping' the first time, then realised that Rose didn't understand the phrase 'Just this once'.

The front door flew back on its hinges and Cyclone Rose powered along the little elevated bridge leading from the verandah to the footpath. She wasn't particularly big, but neither was a shithouse rat and I didn't want to tangle with one of those either. Any prettiness Rose had once had was long gone, eaten away by bitterness. Now she was all wrinkles, orange tan and white-blonde-bleached hair as brittle as desert-dried bones.

I pulled Lizzie out of the way, because her aunt was showing no sign of slowing down as she stormed towards us. She barely gave the little girl a glance, though I got glared at while she headed to a car that had seen better days, and a long time ago at that. The engine started unwillingly, roaring with all the conviction of a dying lion. As she took off the muffler scraped on the asphalt.

I heard footsteps on the verandah and turned back to see Mel, looking exhausted. She held out her arms and Lizzie ran to her.

'Money?' I asked, and my neighbour laughed bitterly.

'New guru, new needs. She thinks it's a good idea I take out a second mortgage.' Her home was the single thing Mel had managed to keep from her marriage other than Lizzie, and it was all she had. When I was little, I'd sometimes yearned for a sibling, but Rose Wilkes was the perfect demonstration of the benefits of being an only child.

'You can choose your friends—' Mel muttered, stroking her daughter's hair.

'—but not your relatives,' I finished.

'More's the pity. Lucky my last client had gone before Rose showed up,' she said, then looked down as Lizzie's head. 'So how was the game?'

I figured the suspension issue wasn't going to matter after this.

Chapter Fifteen

'Ms Fassbinder?'

The phone had dragged me from sleep, but I made a noise that must have sounded positive because she went on, 'It's Eurycleia — Eurycleia Kallos.'

Kallos? Aha.

'I need to talk to you. Can we meet?'

'When? Where?' I peered over the David-shaped lump at the clock on my bedside table. The lurid red numbers said five a.m. On a Sunday, no less. Evidently the powers above and below had determined I should never sleep in again. 'What's open at this hour?'

'Oh, is it early?' She sounded surprised, and I wondered how often she slept, whether Circadian rhythms ever touched her.

Instead of 'Yes, it's *bloody* early!' I managed to say, 'I'll meet you about six at the café at Kangaroo Point.' Experience has taught me to take chances when they offer themselves, because you never know how long they'll hang around. Surely the Cliffs Café would be open, given the number of cyclists the city had spawned in recent years? As far as I could tell they were all always riding to or from weekend breakfasts. It would also keep me occupied until my nine a.m. appointment, although I'd rather hoped David would be doing that.

I hung up and texted my driver, feeling petty satisfaction that I wasn't the only one whose morning was being ruined. Snuggling back down, I pressed my nose in between David's shoulder blades as he snored softly and closed my eyes. Fifteen more minutes, that was all I wanted. But I couldn't get back to sleep, no matter that it was still dark outside. Five minutes later I surrendered and went to have a shower, keeping the water as hot as I could stand in the forlorn hope of staying warmer for longer out of doors.

David didn't stir while I clumped around getting dressed in the outfit I'd carefully chosen last night, not even when I kissed him goodbye and left a red lipstick mark on his cheek; he was still snoring contentedly as I closed the front door.

On the porch I paused and watched my breath turning into frosty curlicues rising in the reluctant morning sun.

Ziggi dropped me off, then went in search of a fare or two to justify rising at sparrowfart while I ambled towards the café. I spotted Eurycleia at the best of the cliff-edge tables, the one with the great view of the city and the river. In the daylight she looked nearer to what I imagined her true age to be. Her faint smile was sad, but that might simply have been regret at asking me along. She was still beautiful, though, all cheekbones and eyes, long hair twisted into a silver chignon, body encased in a close-fitting, knee-length, sky-blue cashmere coat. In spite of my tailored navy woollen dress and expensive coat I felt a little dowdy. Her ebony leather boots were handmade, and so well done that there was no way to tell that hers contained clawed feet and mine did not, and the handbag on the table looked so soft I wanted to stroke it. I guess you don't live thousands of years without learning something about investment pieces. Idly, I wondered if she'd had her legs done the same as her daughter, the feathers plucked or lasered away until there was only smooth skin wrapped about warped feet.

She looked up as if sensing my presence, and her smile became strangely formal; almost as if it was something she'd learned, like she had to remind herself every day not to eat the humans. I slid into the seat across from her, but before I could say *Hello*, a waitress had appeared, glaring at me and flicking her notepad with the tip of a pen. One of the youngsters from the nest. I ordered pancakes and bacon with maple syrup (one needs some constants in life), hoping she and Aspasia had nothing in common. Around us, the winter wind kicked up its heels everywhere – except in the space where we sat. Neat trick: the air surrounding our table was distinctly warmer than it should have been.

'Thank you for coming,' Eurycleia began.

'I didn't think you'd call,' I lied.

'I gave it a lot of thought. With Teles gone . . .'

Her voice drifted off, but her smirk said she wasn't going to tell me who her source was. Plainly the grapevine had been in overdrive since Serena's murder, and the sirens were smart; they'd surely have sources in the Police Department. The conclave must be on hyperalert now another of their number had dropped from the sky.

'How can I help you? I'm assuming this isn't just a girly catch-up.'

'Delightful company though you are, no.' She cleared her throat. 'I was wondering if you'd found out anything about my daughter.'

I looked down to make sure I wasn't wearing a *Gormless Idiot* T-shirt, as Eurycleia had obviously decided I was some kind of easy mark. She'd gone about it all wrong if she wanted to know what I knew: no one milks me for information, especially not before I've had my first coffee. This meeting would be *quid pro quo* or nothing.

'Do you know where the baby is?' I asked. Her lips twitched, her expression tightened and I could tell she was reassessing me. 'That little girl's been alone for a long while. Are your secrets really worth her life?'

She said mournfully, 'No. But I don't know where she is, and I fear I never will.'

'You should have told me there was a baby. You should have told me whatever you knew then,' I said. 'I could have moved faster. Now I'm following cold trails.'

'I didn't – I don't know why Serena called you. I didn't – don't – know if I can trust you,' she admitted. There was an edge to her tone; I was getting the impression that Eurycleia Kallos didn't like not being in charge and she certainly didn't like anyone or anything she couldn't control.

'*I'm* the person – the *only* person – trying to find out who killed your daughter. *I'm* the only person looking for your granddaughter,' I pointed out.

'Well, have you discovered anything?'

I sighed and shook my head. 'I've been right through her house and her shop and I've been to Callie's crèche, but I've found no leads, no nothing. Do you know who the father is?'

Her mouth twisted in distaste. 'No, but it's certainly not that jewellery designer.'

I studied her face, then said baldly, 'I think you're lying. I think you know very well who the father is. And for your information, *that jewellery designer* is the one other person who I am certain has Calliope's best interests at heart, which I don't believe you do.' My breakfast arrived and I made use of her silence to start on the maple syrup-covered pancakes and crispy bacon. Silence works its own magic on people, makes them blurt things out to fill the void, so right now, breakfast and confession equalled two birds with one stone.

'I . . .' She seemed to be weighing things up.

I didn't offer encouragement, just waited.

'I didn't know there was a child, not at first.'

I raised another forkful: *more bacon, more pancake, chew, chew, chew*. David would find next to nothing for breakfast at my place, but any guilt I might have felt was smoothed over when I thought about the extra sleep he was getting. I decided I could live with myself.

'I hadn't spoken to Serena for a year or more. We . . . fell out.' For a tiny fractured moment she shifted, showing me what was beneath the beautiful façade: the teeth, the talons, the fire in the depths of the eyes. *Remember not to eat the humans*. She'd been – and was still – *so* angry, in such a rage that it had caused a breach between mother and daughter that would never have a chance to be mended.

I finished my mouthful. 'Why?'

'No reason that concerns you,' she almost spat, then got control of herself, stirring the cup of tea in front of her: classic displacement activity.

I blew out a maple-fragrant breath. 'Is there anyone who might know more? The other sirens? Did she have close friends in the nest?'

'Teles and Raidne were like her sisters. But Teles won't be telling any tales . . .' She broke off and looked down at her teacup before continuing, 'Serena . . . When we fought, she stopped coming to the conclave. I don't know who else she might have stayed in contact with – no one would've dared tell me.' She lowered her eyelashes and I thought it might be to cover her shame.

'Where might I find Raidne?'

'I'll give her your details so *she* can contact *you*; I doubt she'll be very receptive to a cold call from the likes of you.'

'Lady, *I'm* not the one trying to kill you. *I'm* the one trying to find out who crushed your daughter's heart, then threw her off a building. Don't be getting uppity.' I scribbled my address onto yet another business card and flicked it across the table. As I stood up I pointed to the bruise on my temple. 'Did you send one of your little fledglings to teach me a lesson?'

Her stare told me not, but I wasn't quite sure I believed her. 'Don't take too long about getting back to me. Siren corpses are piling up and it appears I'm the only one worrying about it.'

I left Eurycleia with the bill.

I could only hope Raidne would be more accommodating – Hell, I could only hope Raidne would get in contact. I'd have tried to find her myself, but without a surname to research, even Ziggi's connections wouldn't be able to do much.

The air was icy outside Eurycleia's little bubble and the wind picked at me as if to get revenge for having cheated it for a while. I needed to walk off the pancakes, clear my head and get things straight. Stone steps cut into the cliff led down to a path beside the river. People wearing too few clothes and tied with too few ropes for my liking were already clambering on the sheer rock walls. Groups of middle-aged men wearing Lycra, that most unforgiving of fabrics, rode past on expensive bikes as less fit individuals puffed on the grass, throwing medicine balls at each other, doing sit-ups and skipping ropes, while very fit instructors yelled at them in a manner meant to be motivational. I took the long way, meandering along the mangrove walk, stopping from time to time to watch the river roll past.

Out in the middle of the current was the Boatman, his cloak, roughly the same colour as the water, flapping lazily in the breeze. In the bow of the boat a huddled pair of souls clutched at each other. I couldn't tell who they were – a married couple, carried off together, or simply two strangers finding the only comfort available to them on this last journey?

The Boatman raised his head casually, found me and gave what might from anyone else have passed as a jaunty wave. I raised my own hand politely, and watched the mist rise around the vessel as it continued its journey out towards the sea. In a few seconds I couldn't see him any more, nor even the movement of the water where his oar dug in deeply to steer the course.

I returned to the road at the base of the cliffs and continued on downriver, until pinpricks started running across the nape of my neck; I sensed I was being watched. Looking around, I discovered I was somewhere below the garden area of St Mary's Church. I started craning back and squinting, trying to find my watcher, but there was nothing to see but the rock face and some determined climbing vines. I thought it was entirely possible my imagination was working overtime.

My head ached, a combination of insufficient sleep and excess frustration. Thoughts chased each other around and around while I kept walking, not really paying attention to where I was going, conscious only of the river on one side and the cliffs turning into houses and apartment blocks on the other. When I reached the outskirts of the park beneath the Story Bridge, the path wound through a maze of trees and bushes. Far above, traffic rushed and clattered, the noise drifting down to mingle with the busy sound of water flowing past. On my left was a railing, and below it, a small beach. I leaned my arms against the metal piping, which was cold even through my coat sleeves, but it took me a moment to realise that on the sand below an almost clothed young couple were rolling to and fro on a tartan picnic blanket, apparently oblivious to the winter breeze coming off the water. I was about to retreat, meaning to give them privacy, but another movement caught my eye.

At the base of the bridge was a wall of stone and cement, and in its face was a dark hole; one of the old tunnels. Something spun out from the darkness, but it took me a few seconds to realise I was looking at the thing that had appeared on Ziggi's dodgy phone video, now much bigger. Maybe it had gathered stuff to itself from the drains and sewers. The courting pair were so caught up in each other that they didn't smell the dreadful foetid stench wafting up from the beach, or hear the awful *whirring* as it hurtled towards them. I opened my mouth to yell, then felt a cold hand press over my lips and an arm around my waist pull me backwards.

As I struggled, the grasp didn't relax, but someone hissed in my ear, 'You can't do anything for them. Be quiet or it will come after *us*.' Bela's voice was so low I could barely make out the words, but I recognised the urgency in his tone, and something else: fear. If Zvezdomir Tepes was afraid, the world should be crapping its pants.

We watched as the thing first bundled up the girl, then the guy; inside the maelstrom of its form I saw bodies pulled apart, limbs flying, then finally absorbed into the whirling darkness. When it was done, the creature moved back to the open mouth of the drain and disappeared within, leaving only a crumpled tartan blanket and a few crushed cigarette packets on a disturbed patch of sand.

When Bela's grip finally loosened I could feel the imprint of my teeth against the inside of my lips.

I swallowed before saying, 'So, is there something you want to tell me?'

Chapter Sixteen

Brisbane's City Hall is a beautiful old sandstone building, fully equipped with a clock tower, auditorium, marbled floors, myriad offices, moulded ceilings and chandeliers, not to mention the Shingle Inn Café. Apparently said café was so beloved of Brisbanites that when a fit of urban renewal necessitated its removal from the original location, the whole thing – from dark wood panelling to padded booths, scarred tables, comfy armchairs and dainty doilies – were put into storage until they could be reassembled in a new spot.

Now it looked as if nothing had changed: all terribly normal, and Normal – and a useful place to hang out if you were waiting to be summoned . . .

If you stood in the City Hall's aforementioned auditorium, right in the centre of the mosaic depicting the city's leopard-between-two-gryphons coat of arms, and whispered the right words, then the space around you would shiver and shift, opening a door in the air right in front of you.

I didn't quite have the pull to enter unaccompanied, hence Bela, my chaperone. Access to the seat of power was carefully regulated and jealously guarded. Normals didn't have the monopoly on bureaucratic mechanisms or paranoia, and sometimes the Weyrd could be positively Byzantine.

'Remember: the Archivist seldom receives guests. The only reason

143

you're here is because of my intervention.' Which was Bela's roundabout way of telling me to behave myself. 'Don't speak until spoken to,' he continued, and I had to stop myself checking to see if he was ticking off the points on his fingers. 'Don't touch the books. Don't ask her about anything other than the sirens, because that's the only subject she's agreed to talk about. Understand?'

'Don't put my hands or arms outside the moving vehicle? Yes, Zvezdomir, I understand,' I said, and as he winced I felt a twinge of guilt. After all, he'd just kept me from getting eaten by whatever it was we'd seen by the river, so I thought I should probably be a bit more amenable. I could do that. I smoothed the front of my dress to make sure I was tidy, then touched his arm and said, 'Just messing with you. I get it. I promise I'll follow the rules.'

The Normal section of City Hall was perfectly well lit, unlike the Weyrd area into which we stepped: that was distinctly dim. Suits of armour lined the round foyer, surrounding the central glyph in the floor, a mosaic made of precious and semi-precious stones forming two gryphons but without the leopard, just to distinguish it from the Normal coat-of-arms. The polished metal reception desk, looking rather out of place, was manned by two Weyrd guys who probably wouldn't get far down the street without causing a riot: one was hirsute and distinctly fangy; the other was so thin and wispy he could probably slip under a door unimpeded.

'Weapons?' the hairy one asked.

I shook my head, wondering if anyone ever said 'Yes' and handed over their knives, blackjacks, hawthorn stakes, crucifixes, swords, holy water, et cetera. The skinny one looked as though he might try a pat-down. Bela had warned me that could happen, and we both knew it wouldn't end well – I objected to being treated like a potential criminal. The guy was probably very fast, but I was strong; I only needed to get hold of one of his digits and pop it out of its socket—

My escort held up his hand and said, 'That won't be necessary.'

Phew.

I thought it spoke volumes about the state of Weyrd politics these days that this level of security was deemed necessary, that not even Bela could walk right in. Seats on the Council of Five were inherited and members, though long-lived, seldom had 'old age' listed as a cause of death. Memories were enduring things, and feuds between Weyrd families never simply died out, not unless the families died with them. The Weyrd hadn't ever really taken to any sort of democratic system of protest, preferring older, more permanent methods of change: assassination was considered a perfectly valid form of social revolution, not to mention an effective way of silencing dissent. And not everyone was happy with the way the tribe had to live now.

Mr Wispy led us along a corridor and stopped so abruptly in front of a steel-banded door that I almost ran into him. When he finally got all the various locks undone he gestured for us to go in. *How does the Archivist get out at night?* I wondered. Did she knock three times and wait to be released? Or did she just never leave? Maybe she had a secret tunnel somewhere. A memory rattled in the back of my mind: Ziggi mentioning that the old woman lived in, with a room somewhere in the bowels of the earth. A set of surprisingly well-lit steps led downwards, and I noticed a set of dimmer switches on the walls. The gentle flicker of flames might be the preferred illumination for mostly nocturnal creatures, conjuring reminders of the good old days, a time when people were rightly afraid of the dark, but fire and paper weren't such a good mix, so for the Archivist at least, practicality apparently overcame nostalgia.

We stepped into an enormous room with rows and rows of steel shelving stretching before us. It was cold – climate-controlled, I'd bet – and remarkably hi-tech. I could hear a server whirring contentedly somewhere nearby; there were a few whispers from the books shelved along the walls too. As we approached the far end I could make out a line of desktop computers taking up one corner, and a couple of microfiche readers not dissimilar to those at the State Library in the other. In between sat a large wooden desk blackened with age, like a kind of oversized mediaeval lectern with a tilted tabletop. It was the oldest thing in the room.

Well, the second oldest.

She was tiny, wizened; sitting on a high stool of chrome and plastic so she could reach her work surface, which held an illuminated manuscript. She glared over her hunched shoulder as if our echoing footsteps had disturbed her, then closed the book, pushed away from the desk and stretched as if she might reach the ceiling, her bones giving cracking protest. As she swung about to face us I noticed her ears were tiny vestigial flaps of skin. Her eyes were a deep pinkish red, her nose small but kind of squashed, and showing a little more nostril than I was used to. The battered leather orthopaedic boots she wore had once been burgundy, though her khaki overalls were pristine. A skullcap sat on her thick white curls. A cane was propped against the wall. She wore no jewellery of any sort; nothing so frivolous. She'd not bothered with a glamour as far as I could tell, she was unalloyed, without vanity, proud of what she was . . . then I thought again: if the Archivist didn't go out, she didn't really have a need to hide anything, so perhaps it was less bravery and more lazy arrogance. She gazed at me as if she had some serious reservations about my presence. In spite of myself, I felt a chill run up my spine.

'Honourable Ursa.' Bela intoned the name as one might a prayer. 'This is Verity Fassbinder.'

'Zvezdomir Tepes. And Grigor's daughter,' she said, narrowing her eyes, considering me. Her accent was not especially thick, not easily definable, but it certainly said 'Old Country', wherever that might have been for her. 'What do you want?'

If that was a warm welcome, I was likely to get frostbite.

'Err,' I began, my promise to behave warring with my natural urge – sadly, never far below the surface – to tell someone who was rude to me to fuck right off.

'You are here to waste my time?' she sneered, crossing her arms.

The legacy of being Grigor's child is this: many Weyrd, the elders especially, those who were around at the time, remember my father. They remember what he did and, most importantly, they remember that he *got caught*. They remember how their lives changed because of that. And in remembering that, they apparently cannot forget to number my breeding amongst my sins, most especially the fact that I'm neither purely one thing nor the other.

The Archivist was obviously one of *those* Weyrd. I bowed my head so she couldn't see the anger sparking in my eyes and said humbly, 'I've come seeking your aid, Honourable Ursa. I beg your indulgence if I appear nervous: the depth and breadth of your wisdom is spoken of with great awe and respect. You will forgive someone who feels daunted at the prospect of speaking to you.'

I waited a little longer to look up, and it was to see her positively preening, something that might even have been a smile hovering at her thin lips. I was pretty sure I could feel the weight of Bela's gaze on me too, and equally sure his mouth was hanging open, just a little.

'Ask your questions, girl.'

'Sirens.'

'Sirens?'

'What could kill one? Not anything big and nasty, not something even Normals couldn't miss. It must be something subtle, something that might slip beneath the notice of the Council.' I buried my hands deeply in my coat pockets, though I knew I wouldn't find warmth there either. 'Something that could reach into a siren's chest and squeeze her heart until it stops.'

She slowly scratched her chin while I tried not to stare at the downy cluster of white hairs growing from it.

'It doesn't leave a mark,' I encouraged.

She shook her head slowly. 'If I don't know, I don't know,' she said rather tetchily. 'No book contains everything, just as no mind can hold every piece of knowledge. Sirens – I don't know!'

I couldn't help but wonder why she'd even agreed to speak with me if she had nothing helpful to say, but I managed not to pout, even though that meant all of my wheeling and dealing with Bela was for naught, *and* I was still going to have to uphold my end of the bargain.

'*But*,' she added after a moment, crooked index finger raised, 'but it doesn't sound like an ordinary hunter, not unless they've managed to summon something particularly vile and vicious for this task, like a 'serker.'

'With respect, ma'am, I've seen a 'serker up close and personal, and they don't do their wetwork tidily. They like tearing and rending and smearing – smearing is a big thing too.' The memory of the ravening creature in that dark house made my leg ache in spite of all of Louise's excellent care. 'Whatever's killing these women is relatively neat.'

'Humph.'

Despite my promise to stay on topic, I couldn't resist pushing my luck – after all, she'd given me nothing. I figured I could try and get at least one of the other gaps in my knowledge filled. 'I went for a walk by the river—'

'Verity,' warned Bela, but Ursa waved his unvoiced objections away. Her gaze was fixed on me as if weighing the worth of my words, as if I were suddenly of greater interest than first assumed.

I told her all about the creature; not just how it had made the amorous couple vanish, but how it looked, how it sounded and moved and smelled. Ziggi'd sent me the link to the clip of the Fortitude Valley incident and, ignoring Bela's silent fuming, I pulled out my phone and played it for her. I could've sworn her eyes shone as she watched the whirlwind of night and garbage at its endeavours, then she leaned back and made a humming noise, as if deciding where to start.

'Well, *that's* definitely not a 'serker,' she said at last.

'The thing that kills the sirens at least leaves bodies behind; this — this *whatever-it-is* — leaves not much at all, just a few bits of rubbish that fall off it. Quite frankly, if there wasn't the risk of a horrible death, I'd hire it to clean my place, 'cause it can't do worse than I do.'

Bela made a strangled noise as Ursa turned to the book on her desk and for a second I thought myself dismissed. With painstaking care she flipped through it until she found what she wanted, then, gently, angled the volume so we could see the illustrations.

A clever hand had drawn five figures, all of them vaguely human-shaped but none of them human. One appeared to be made of earth, the others of ice, fire and water. The final one, a cyclonic form of wind and collected dross, had cartoonish marks around its edges, as if to indicate motion. There were paragraphs beside each sketch, brief descriptions in Latin and Ancient Hebrew, which I struggled with, so long after university.

'What do you know about golems?' asked Ursa, and it sounded as if she might be gloating a little at redeeming herself so spectacularly after the siren washout.

'The Prague kind or *The Lord of the Rings* kind?'

Another noise from Bela; this one might have been a sob. Ursa stabbed at the image of the tempest-thing and glared at me.

'Sorry,' I mumbled, then, 'I thought the Prague golem was made to protect people?'

'Oh, this much you know?' She curled a lip. 'All well and good, little miss, if its creator has admirable purpose in making his "weapon". But a gun is a thing without will, either righteous or ill, and the damage it does comes from the heart of the one who holds it. So too the golem: it's a tool and has no more – or less – moral compass than the person who controls it.'

'So you think what we saw is a golem?'

'Made of intent and excrement and foul things, all wrapped around a human core.'

'There's a *person* at the centre of it?'

'With the right spells, the right curses, it's possible. A powerful mage or witch could do it. It takes much energy, much blood-cost.'

'That thing doesn't look like it would happily take orders. How could anyone control it?'

'An iron will might master it. You must remember that a person surrenders part of themself to another when they become golem. You need to consider the heart of the thing, who it *used* to be: if they gave themself up willingly, then the desires of creator and creature may well align. That would certainly make the beast more malleable.'

My breath caught as I shuddered. 'Human underneath.'

'Such a working must have a mortal nucleus because anything uncanny is already so touched by magic that enchantments of this sort would be diluted. They would not function correctly.'

'Then what does it want?'

'The thing itself? Now? To feed. That desire will grow stronger as its mortal element shrinks and is consumed. This . . . this is a *transformation*. Each time it happens, the human within will find a little less of themselves to return to. Depending on how often it's occurring—'

'—it will burn out?'

She blinked slowly, considering. 'Eventually.'

'How long?'

The shrug took her entire body and made it shudder. 'It depends entirely on the individual, what spark first set it on this path, how brightly that yearning still shines . . . it may be days, weeks, months . . .'

I looked at Bela. 'It doesn't really matter how short its span, does it? It will continue to suck the life out of whoever crosses its path. It's not like we can wait it out.'

'No,' he said.

'As you say.' Ursa's expression combined horror and fascination. 'This is what they *didn't* write down about the Golem of Prague: that it was a real man under the mud and clay. A real man gave his life and soul to protect the people there. But even a little wickedness in the service of good darkens the soul and robs you bit by bit, because each time the evil actions become easier.'

'How can we stop it?'

'As with most things, you must find its maker. Identify the magician and the magic, then find the spells to undo it.'

'What if we just kill the magician? Will that work?' I asked.

'Possibly, though it's crude,' she said with distaste. 'But I'd not rely on that alone. Sometimes the creature's desire to feed is strong enough that it will continue without its master's hand.'

So I could live with Plan A, killing the mage, but I'd still need to spend time coming up with a Plan B.

'Thank you,' I said, truly grateful, and not a little surprised to have been given so much information.

Beside me, I felt rather than heard Bela's own sigh of relief. All in all, it hadn't gone anywhere near as badly as it might have.

'Oh!' I said as if something had just occurred to me. 'One more thing: were you by any chance offered wine a month or so ago? Made from the tears of children? Someone of your vintage might have been a target market.'

Bela sounded as if someone had punched him in the gut and my conscience prickled, but I could always apologise later. The Archivist froze and gave me a killing glance, though I'd have thought it obvious by now that I didn't shame easily.

Through clenched teeth she hissed, 'Such a thing is not allowed.' Then she turned her back on us.

By the time we'd returned to the reception desk Bela had recovered enough to say tightly, 'I thought you'd dropped that? The Winemaker?'

'You thought wrong.' I stared at him for a long moment. 'Really? After all this time, you thought I'd drop something because you *told* me to?'

He kept his tone level and I had to admire his restraint. 'And did you find anything? Apart from dead ends?'

'No,' I said sulkily. 'Not yet.'

When we finally stepped back through to the Normal hall, he continued, 'So you'll speak to Anders Baker now? And I mean *now*, as in prioritise his case so he stops calling me every hour on the hour?'

I might not have been enthusiastic about paying back the favour he'd just done me, but a deal was a deal. 'Ziggi's waiting for me outside' – no doubt illegally parked – 'so you can let Baker know we'll head down the coast as soon as I'm out of here.'

'Do you think you could manage to be polite?'

'I promise to really try,' I said, and at that moment I truly meant it.

I hated the Gold Coast. It never felt like a real place, and there was a reason for that: it was a threshold, a crossing place from this plane to dark ones, and out the other side. Or at least, it used to be. Once upon a time, those people so inclined travelled along the corridors between the light world and the not-so-light and thought it worth the risk. But then the things that live in perpetual shadow learned to find their own paths through, and started to bleed into the everyday. Such breaches put both Weyrd and Normal at risk, so the ways betwixt were sealed, and scarred over – the Gold Coast was one of those scars. That wasn't to say that there were no remaining doorways, or that they couldn't be opened, but it took a lot more effort than previously, and the cost in blood was a lot higher. Yet again I found myself wondering who'd paid the price to bring over the 'serker I'd killed months ago.

The Gold Coast wasn't entirely ugly. As a holiday destination it had appeal – white sands and beautiful blue ocean, fantastic weather – but both seafront and suburbs were so jam-packed it felt like room to move was a luxury add-on. The housing was a mix of old- and new-style short-lets and brittle surf shacks in between the ordinary homes where residents tried to get on with life in the face of the constant swarms of tourists and backpackers. There were myriad restaurants and shopping malls, and hundreds of souvenir shops, all filled with the same crap imported from China, alongside rip-off attractions like Ripley's Believe It Or Not™, all shouldering each other, making the most of their piece of the glitziest, tackiest strip of real estate in town.

No matter what the promotional photos promised, there were no deserted beaches, and every inch was at a premium. You had to get up very early to stand a hope in hell of finding your own little patch of sandy heaven, beating the onslaught of determinedly vacationing families, teenagers skiving off school, mad keen surfers and militant retirees, all flocking to the seaside for a tan on the pink side and a taste of salty water.

Other bits of the coast, like the Sovereign Islands, were entirely man-made. This estate for the rich and infamous began life as big boys' mud pies, not even real landmasses, just piles of landfill dumped in the ocean until even it couldn't keep swallowing the crap. Once it'd all been teased into a carefully connected archipelago, the developers rubbed their hands in glee and started building concrete-and-metal monstrosities for the *nouveaux riches* and *Mafioso* of various stripes to snap up.

One good cyclone and the whole area would be awash with sand and blood and glass. I was really hoping that wouldn't happen on the very day I went to visit, but given my luck, who knew?

The Islands were reached by a bridge from the mainland, the Sovereign Mile. Ziggi braked gently as we approached the security gate, which was firmly closed, presumably to keep the *hoi polloi* at bay.

'What do you reckon, Ziggi? Should we go with charm or intimidation?'

'S'okay. I got this,' he said, sounding relieved he didn't have to make that decision, this time at least.

A middle-aged man in an uninspiring uniform — too-tight brown trousers and beige short-sleeved shirt with straining buttons paired with a brown, shapeless, non-uniform cardigan — stepped out of a guard hut. He squinted and shaded his eyes with a hand as if the combination of sun and purple paint-job were too much to bear, then his expression cleared, he gave my driver a curt, distinctly covert wave and returned to the booth. The iron barrier rose silently and we slid through, feeling rather like a shark entering someone's nice, well-appointed pool.

Ziggi drove slowly, as if there was some chance we might go unnoticed. The winding streets were overlooked by high fences and higher houses, some mere mansions, others hoping to grow up to be full-on castles. Each abode was a signature piece; not one resembled its neighbour in even the smallest of ways. Materials, form and colour were all unique, but in those desperate attempts at individuality, all sense of architectural harmony had been lost. Expensive vehicles lounged in Taj Mahal-standard carports like big cats. I could almost hear the purring. It didn't look like somewhere to live, but rather somewhere to be *displayed*.

We took the long road down the right arm, making our way out to the most remote of the islets, until we sat outside a driveway. Access was blocked by an artistically beaten panel of copper set in a soaring wall of ecru render and secured by the modern equivalent of a gatehouse, from which stepped yet another security guard. This one was youngish and female, a concrete blonde with a dark red birthmark up the right side of her neck. She stared at the cab as if it were a blot on the landscape. I could see her point.

Everything about her looked muscular, and her white long-sleeved shirt and navy trousers had creases that were obviously *meant* to be there, as if no fabric would dare wrinkle on such a hard body. Her straw-pale hair was pulled into a tight bun, and the lines around her eyes and mouth made me reassess her age upwards; she was more thirties than twenties, and maybe even a passably preserved forty. I spotted a Taser that I was pretty sure shouldn't have been hanging from the belt of a private citizen – Ziggi owned one too, and he wasn't meant to have it either. Maybe she was a cop making a bit extra on the side, just using departmental equipment to make her life easier. Of course, that immediately raised the question of *why* Anders Baker might need extra security.

Ziggi craned his neck to exchange glances with me. 'Wish me luck,' I mumbled, and opened the door. Climbing out, I pasted on a smile that felt like quick-setting plaster.

'Can I help you?' She stood too close – we were roughly the same height, but I was glad of the inch or so I had on her – and breathed spearmint gum-scent into my face. There was neither warmth nor friendliness in her voice, but I decided to give her the benefit of the doubt; I might be decently dressed for a change, but I couldn't deny Ziggi and his car did look pretty rag-tag.

'I'm Verity Fassbinder. I've got an appointment with Mr Baker,' I said, searching for a flicker of recognition and was vaguely miffed to find none.

Blondie stared back, then walked past me and inspected the taxi, leaning down to peer in the windows. Ziggi gave her a two-fingered salute, the affable kind, but it didn't expedite matters at all. I waited for as long as I could, which wasn't very long, then said, 'So, you going to call up to the big house? Let the boss know I'm here?'

A ripple went through well-trained jaw and cheek muscles as she clenched down on a retort. With that kind of strength I reckoned she could spit and cause an injury. I gave in and said, 'Please.'

She might not have moved any faster, but she did at least amble over to her hobbit hole and pick up the phone. I could hear muttered queries, then pauses while answers were given. She didn't bother to step out again, but the gate swung open. I got in the car and Ziggi hit the accelerator.

Baker's cash was new, barely out of the wrapping, and his home was proof, if ever it was needed, that money couldn't buy taste. Misplaced orange faux adobe met and mated unwillingly with white wrought iron and a butt-load of thick tinted glass in someone's nightmare idea of Mediterranean-style architecture, with some extra attitude thrown in. The rolling gardens weren't much better: a manicured mix of Australian natives with imports like foxgloves looking horribly out of place, all surrounded by a legion of palm trees growing along the fence line, leaning a little drunkenly over the top. A six-foot-tall bronze of Poseidon, complete with trident, bulging budgie smugglers and leer, stood manfully in a massive fountain, eternally drenched by multiple water jets. A circular drive of stamped black concrete curled around it.

The whole set-up was eye-achingly frightful.

The bright blue front door had panels of green and red tile down its middle, for no reason that I could discern. It opened before I was even out of the vehicle. Baker sported a grey linen suit that any star of *Miami Vice*, circa 1984, would have been proud to wear. Mindful of my promise to Bela, I loaded my 'Miss Manners' software program, took his outstretched hand and managed a smile.

'Ms Fassbinder. I'm so pleased you're able to give my son some of your valuable time.'

Though it sounded suspiciously like sarcasm, I let it go. Baker was little more than a thug with a lot of coin; I doubted his manners had yet been finely tuned. I'd cut him some slack, at least until I was proven wrong.

'Let's talk inside, shall we, Mr Baker?' I used his handshake to pivot him around, then pressed the small of his back to steer him through the entrance, smirking to myself when he looked startled. Rich people are so used to being deferred to that they get quite a shock when someone else takes charge. You usually only get away with it once or twice before their sense of self-importance reasserts itself, but sometimes you just need the upper hand for a little while.

The enormous hall had a chessboard pattern of black and white marble tiles underfoot. In the centre was another fountain, this one an oversized bronze mermaid, though not quite as big as the god of the sea. She held a hairbrush poised over her flowing locks and a mirror in front of her face, so she could admire her own beauty with the bluest of glass eyes.

Baker led me into a sunken sitting room that overlooked a lap pool. The place was a symphony in creams and browns that might just have worked, if only someone hadn't installed a naked-brickwork bar at one end, allowing the Seventies to live and breathe again. The carpet was thick silk shag and I felt self-conscious about letting my boots touch it. A fireplace with a mammoth hunk of camphor laurel as a mantelpiece took up half a wall. I chose a single butter-coloured leather armchair to ensure there was no chance he'd try to sit next to me for a cosy chat.

'Drink?' he called from behind the bar, waving a bottle of something amber.

I stared at the label. 'Err, no thanks. A little early for me.'

'The sun's past the yardarm somewhere in the world,' he said cheerfully, and splashed himself a good five inches from the forty-year-old bottle of The Macallan. It occurred to me then that he might be more nervous than clueless – or perhaps as nervous as he was clueless. He sat across from me in the middle of the three-seater couch, leaning forward, elbows on knees, crystal tumbler cradled between thick fingers. Under his spray tan his nose had an unhealthy pink bloom, which made me wonder how long he'd been pouring his own drinks; I suspected the intake had increased recently.

When he spoke again, the tone was a little petulant. 'I'm glad you came to your senses.'

I stiffened, tamping down the urge to make a *very* rude gesture, and said, as politely as I could, 'Mr Baker, I am looking into a number of matters at the moment, including several missing persons, not one of them less important than your son, although they may not be as rich. They deserve my attention as much as Donovan does.'

He held up his hands as if backing off and said hastily, 'I'm sorry, I didn't mean to imply . . . Verity, I just want to say how grateful I am for your help.'

We eyed each other for long moments before I gave in. 'Mr Baker, I'll do what I can, but I need to be honest with you: I think your son's missing of his own free will. He's young and a bit aimless, and I gather he's financially independent?'

'Trust fund from his mother,' he answered curtly.

'Right. So, what makes you think he's not just gone off to "find himself"?'

His mouth puckered as if he were sucking on a lemon and the false bonhomie dropped away, leaving the truth of him exposed. The man was all hard desire to have his own way and punish those who denied him. At first I thought the bitterness was directed at me, until he said, 'Because the boy's too gutless to do anything for himself.'

The contempt hung in the air. I considered then that it might be less about concern for his son and more about irritation at being defied, about having something he owned taken away from his influence. The boy had left under his own steam, or been removed, and both were equally unacceptable to Anders Baker.

I cleared my throat. 'Maybe you should tell me about Donovan. What was he doing with himself?'

'He was doing as little as possible at Bond University. Doing nothing seems to take up all his time.'

'What was he studying?' I asked.

He shrugged, all fatherly despair. 'He started a business degree, but kept changing – I've paid more withdrawal fees than I care to think about. I believe he finally settled on leisure management – what the hell does that even mean?'

'Beats me. What about friends, from school or uni, maybe?'

'No friends. The losers from high school who let him tag along because he paid for everything finally dropped him. At uni even the leeches stayed away.'

'A girlfriend, then?'

'What did I just say about leeches?' *Ouch.* 'Apparently my son's spinelessness, coupled with my money, still wasn't enough to attract even the most determined gold-digger.'

He took another swig of his drink and I noticed the whisky was almost gone. There was a good chance his mask would slip further and his level of aggression would rise. I didn't fancy being around for that, although not because I couldn't handle him. Mindful of his reputation, I just preferred not to.

'How about any enemies, either yours or his? People who might try getting to you through your son? Any disgruntled employees?' He shook his head. It occurred to me that any enemies Baker had probably didn't last, and ex-employees wouldn't stick around for fear of being kitted out in a fetching new concrete bathing suit. 'Do you have a housekeeper, or other domestic staff?'

'No. I like my privacy. I eat out mostly. An agency sends cleaners once a week.'

I pursed my lips. 'The guard on your gate – how long has she worked for you?'

'Almost fifteen years; don't worry about her.'

That sounded like a fair while for a private security guard to hang around. Maybe Baker offered really good benefits. 'What was Donovan doing last time you saw him?'

He hesitated, and that immediately confirmed my suspicion that he didn't take much notice of his child. It told me he hadn't seen Donovan for a few days before he realised the boy had disappeared.

'I . . . I think I saw him one night a few days before . . .'

I didn't make him go on. 'Did he have any hobbies or special interests? Talents?'

'Wasting money? Taking everything as if it's his right? He's as spoilt and useless as his mother.' The hostility rose a couple of notches and I followed his gaze to a portrait hanging over the fireplace. A slender blonde stared out from the canvas. 'Haughty' just about covered it.

I knew a little bit of the gossip from Bela, a lot more from Ziggi. For ten years or more, Anders Baker had been half of one of those mismatched power couples you saw all the time in the social pages: Dusana Nadasy, the elegant Weyrd beauty, alongside a man whose only recommendation was the size of his wallet and his willingness to open it. They'd played together nicely for a while, long enough to have a child, at least, then things had gone south as battle lines were drawn and the fights started escalating: she would change the locks on the house, he'd cut up her credit cards; they'd make up for a bit, then it would all start over again: Dusana sliced the crotches out of his Armani suits; Anders made a bonfire of her Ferragamo shoe collection . . .

Despite that, Anders Baker remained relatively tolerant, by all accounts – until the year (or even the month) of the pool boy, the gardener and the tennis instructor, when his patience was finally exhausted. There was an explosion at their Bridgman Downs mansion, which not only took out the missus, but also said pool boy, gardener and tennis instructor. It was a messy business, but according to Ziggi, everything was soon settled by a liberal application of funds in the right places. An inquest verdict of 'death by misadventure' was handed down and the newly widowed Anders Baker took his young son to live at the new family home on the Gold Coast. Since then he'd kept a string of increasingly young, blonde and not-very-bright mistresses, each of whom was replaced the moment they mentioned marriage or put on weight.

On the drive there Ziggi told me the boy, Donovan, had no power to speak of, and I knew personally how that must have hurt – when you're a mixed child, the best thing you can hope for is some kind of ability so the Weyrd will at least pay attention to you, not write you off completely.

'Kid seems like a bit of a vacant space, V. Gotta feel sorry for him.'

And I did. I'd lived long enough straddling two worlds; I knew how easy it was to fall between. Donovan Baker had had no one to offer him a hand, to pull him back up when he fell. And my sympathies didn't lessen, hearing his father talk about him. It was becoming clearer and clearer that Baker Senior didn't know much at all about his son, and it was getting harder and harder for me to repress my dislike for the man.

'Can you think of anyone – *anyone* – your son might go to if he was in trouble?'

Baker's head moved from side to side and his eyes drifted away from the portrait and back to the bar. If I didn't distract him he was going to be chugging down another five inches of boozy peaty goodness and that would be my interview done.

'Relatives?' I asked loudly.

'What?' He looked at me, confused.

'Are there any relatives Donovan might have gone to see?' I enunciated.

'I'm an only child and my family was wiped out in the Second World War. Donovan didn't have siblings or cousins to grow up with, no uncles, no aunts, no grandparents.'

'What about the other side? The Nadasys?'

He snorted. 'Old families – old and dignified Weyrd in particular – don't like to acknowledge anyone who marries out of the fold. They sure as hell don't like the children of such marriages.'

I couldn't disagree with that, but I managed to refrain from saying that not too many Normal families were delighted by it either.

'My wife was disowned and neither of her parents ever came to visit our son. No one came to his christening; no Christmas or birthday presents ever mysteriously appeared on the doorstep.' He stood and paced. The Weyrd weren't too keen on either christenings or Christmas, but again, I kept my trap shut. I was doing so well.

'My son is without anchor, Ms Fassbinder. He's found no place to belong. Perhaps if his mother had . . .' He broke off.

I said softly, 'And what did you do, Mr Baker? To help him?'

He didn't look at me and he didn't answer. I thought I had a fair idea of Baker's parenting style: all the expensive gifts in the world, pocket money equal to a middle manager's weekly salary, a car – everything except love, approval and support. Everything except friends, the ability to fit in, a place to feel at home. All this made me even more convinced the kid had run away – but I could see Anders Baker didn't want to admit that, because then it would mean having to take the blame.

'I'd like to have a look in his room,' I said. 'And I'll need a photo of your son – if you've got one.'

He ignored my snipe and led me back to the hall and up the curving stairs, along so many hallways and turns I was certain I'd never find my way out again. I'd have to phone Ziggi for assistance, but he might not make it soon enough. I could only hope I wouldn't need to go full-on *Lord of the Flies* and kill and eat Baker in order to survive . . .

There was nothing out of the ordinary in Donovan's room – well, nothing for a rich kid. The furniture – sleigh bed, bookshelves, desk, the doors of the built-in wardrobes, dressing table – was all dark cedar, and none of it looked like something a kid would have chosen for himself. There were no posters hanging on the walls, but a Stratocaster with Eric Clapton's signature on its white face, a Turner, a Van Gogh and a Rembrandt charcoal sketch made for interesting viewing. There was an enormous flat-screen TV connected up to every games console imaginable, and discreetly recessed speakers in the ceiling said the space was wired for sound. Interestingly, there was no computer; Baker said it was the only thing missing, so presumably the boy had taken it with him.

'There's been no ransom demand?' I asked.

'Nothing. If he'd been kidnapped, surely that would be the first thing they'd do?'

I answered with a question: 'No withdrawals from his bank account, no credit card usage, no calls on his mobile?'

'I told you, nothing.'

'What did the police say?'

'Like you, they think he's just run away from home.'

'Mr Baker, surely you've got enough contacts within the department to get some pressure applied?'

He looked away as he replied, 'I didn't want . . . A police investigation might—'

—might reveal things he didn't want uncovered. Things connected with his business interests; things more important than his son. It must have been killing him not to be able to lord it over the cops.

'Right. Hence the private investigators.'

While Baker reached for one of only two photo frames on the desk, I quickly went through the drawers and cupboards. The place was clean, with not even the tiniest hint of illicit drugs, no hidden bottles of booze, no cigarettes, either traditional or wacky, no painkillers in the bathroom.

A quick glance at the remaining photo showed Dusana with a very young, white-blond Donovan on her lap. Baker handed over the picture he'd pulled from the frame. It looked recent: father and son were smiling in that awkward manner of men who really didn't want to touch each other. Donovan, even with his hair turned middling brown, bore more of a resemblance to his mother: a pretty kind of boy with no outstanding features.

I stared around the room, then looked closely at the king bed. There was a lump at its foot, tucked under the forest green duvet. Few things in the world are less appealing than a young single man's sheets, but I steeled myself and pulled them back. A pile of dirt, threaded with shreds of rubbish, sat on the crisp white, inordinately high thread-count Egyptian cotton sheets, almost as if a scrub turkey had taken up residence and started making a nest.

I glanced at Baker, but he shrugged and waved his hands as if to say, *What are you gonna do? Boys, hey?*

'And you're *sure* your son has had no contact with his mother's family? Or with anyone else from the Weyrd world?'

'I told you, no,' he snapped. 'The Nadasys showed no interest in either me or my son. Besides, they disappeared years ago, after Dusana . . . They've got to be dead by now.'

I moved towards the door and he grabbed at my arm, fingers pinching into my flesh. 'What are you going to do?'

I wrapped a hand around his wrist, applied just enough pressure to remind him how strong I was, and peeled his fingers away. 'Mr Baker, don't touch me again, or we're going to have a problem.'

His eyes narrowed; he wanted to hurt me, but he was at least smart enough to realise that wasn't a battle he'd win, at least not without some kind of large gun and a head start. He rubbed at the spot where bruises would soon come up, and repeated, 'What are you going to do?'

'Be patient, Mr Baker. I'll be in contact.'

Outside I tried to breathe in fresh air, but the breeze carried nothing but stench, probably from the mudflats, where stranded fish were doubtless bloating in the winter sun. Though I hadn't bothered to shake Baker's hand as he saw me out — not that he'd offered it — I thought I'd mostly done a pretty good job of playing Miss Manners, especially in the face of some challenging behaviour. Baker was a shitty parent, to say the least; in fact, I'd say he was a shitty human being all round. I'd have walked for good, but my conscience wouldn't let me. I had a feel for the boy now, for what his life had been like, and sympathy got me every single time. I could have ended up like him, as unloved as he was, if my grandparents had been any different. If they'd had smaller hearts and narrower minds, if they had not simply accepted me for who and what I was, I too could have been Donovan Baker, with a Weyrd's strength and a hateful attitude to the world.

The guard had left her booth and was standing beside the taxi; it looked like she and Ziggi had been chatting. I couldn't say she looked any more pleasant, however, and that was definitely the evil eye she was giving me as I approached.

I chose to smile; I was becoming the queen of affable. 'I was wondering what you could tell me about Mr Baker's son?'

Her pissy expression wavered; she was still reluctant to share.

I tried again. 'That's why I'm here, to try to find him, and I could really use your help. Let's face it, parents don't know their children, but you – you see the boy coming and going, and maybe he talks to you 'cause you're youngish, you're pretty—'

She wasn't sure whether to take offence or not, and frankly I wasn't certain either, but I kept going. 'Does he have any friends his father doesn't know about? Anyone he was hanging out with before he went missing? Anyone he might go to?'

Relenting, she said, 'Look, he's a lonely kid – there are no friends. A few months ago he mentioned wanting to find his grandparents – his mother's side.'

'Baker said they were dead.' Then I remembered his exact words . . . *got to be dead by now.*

'I don't know what the boss told you.' She was shutting down. 'All I know is that's what the boy said to me.'

'Where was he looking?' I tried to draw her out, but she was closing in again.

'He didn't say and I didn't ask. It's not like we were best friends, okay?'

I clasped my hands together behind me to keep from wrapping them around her throat. 'Did anything unusual happen the day he went missing?'

'Lady, he went out one night and didn't come home. Just had the laptop bag over his shoulder, nothing else.'

'Thanks for your assistance,' I said, and couldn't help but note Ziggi's astonishment at my restraint.

As I settled onto the back seat I asked, 'What were you talking about?'

'New-model Tasers,' he replied, then followed with, 'Are you on Valium?' which I didn't dignify with a response.

We left the Islands faster than we'd entered and I recounted my conversation with Baker. Repeating the story confirmed to me that there was no proof anything untoward had happened to Donovan Baker, but the sense that something wasn't right had only increased.

'So what are you thinking?' Ziggi nodded to the guard at the main gate as we hit the Sovereign Mile.

'Everything. Nothing. I'm thinking about what the Archivist said about golems, about the sort of person who might lend themself to such a being.'

There was a long pause before he said, 'That's a pretty big leap, if you're thinking what I think you're thinking. The kid didn't have any contact with the Weyrd.'

'You heard Blondie: he talked about looking for his grandparents. If they aren't extant any more, maybe some of Dusana's old crowd kept an eye on the boy . . . like Bela did with me.'

'You were different. This kid has no power. The Council generally don't concern themselves with duds.'

The word might not have been aimed at me, but it was dismissive and cruel and it still hurt. I expected better of Ziggi, and I was about to tell him so when my coat pocket vibrated. The name flashed across the screen and I started tossing up whether to answer or ignore. All I wanted was get back home and back to David, to feel his arms around me, to smell his scent, to have him make everything seem ordinary. To remind me that I wasn't a version of Donovan Baker.

Against my better judgment I gave in. 'Yeah, Bela?'

'You need to get here. We've got a mess.' He sounded strange, distant, and a tremor shook his voice.

'Are you okay?'

'Just get here.'

'Here being?'

'Pullenvale.' He rattled off the address.

'What kind of mess, Bela?'

'The golem-related kind.'

Chapter Seventeen

Pullenvale was a patchwork of big rural properties about thirty minutes from the city centre, in good traffic at least. The houses were huge, but so much more refined than those on the Sovereign Islands, the overall style countrified elegance rather than *look-at-all-my-money*. Pools, discreetly concealed spas and well-used tennis courts were de rigueur, and most places had stables for spoilt little girls to keep their ponies, and garages for equally spoilt little boys to park their quad bikes and other assorted toys.

Perched on a fifteen-acre block surrounded by gums, acacias, banksias, casuarinas and a high stone wall, the Greenill dwelling didn't particularly stand out. The three-storey building was an architect-designed, eco-friendly delight in jarrah weathered to silver. Solar panels basked on the roof and several of the walls were nothing more than thick green-tinted glass. I counted four decks of varying heights, one to each compass point and all of them with a wonderful view. The structure sat comfortably in its landscape, and far enough from neighbours that anything short of a riot wouldn't have been heard.

There was no overt sign of a break-in, but the front door was open. We pulled in behind Bela's black Porsche, which was skewed across the driveway. Ziggi and I exchanged a look. We went inside, not commenting on the stray pieces of garbage marking out our path; a lack of precision from the boss was a cause for concern.

We stepped into an enormous space: a bright and airy interior with exposed beams and polished timber floors. The lounge held comfortable leather couches covered with colourful throws and cushions, and all the usual clutter associated with a large family: discarded dolls and Matchbox cars, charging iPads and a Nintendo DS console. Magazines were scattered around, books left opened and face-down on footstools, ghostly cup circles beside a stack of unused coasters on the glass-topped coffee table.

The dining room had built-in shelving which housed awards; when I wandered closer I could see there were as many for sporting events as Eisteddfods. A long ironbark table with ten matching chairs waited for the family to sit down to a meal that would never be served. Its rose and chrysanthemum centrepiece was wilting.

In a kitchen filled with appliances that were expensive but not new, we found our employer. Bela leaned against the sink, looking even paler than usual. The man I'd never seen remotely dishevelled, even in the midst of passion, had a speck of vomit on his bottom lip and a couple of substantial splashes on his navy shirt. His grip on the edge of the bench top was so tight his knuckles looked set to poke through the skin.

Ziggi and I approached as if he were an animal likely to flee.

'Adriana?' asked Ziggi softly.

Bela looked around at us, coming back to himself. He turned on the tap and doused his face with water, then drenched his shirt as well.

'Oh, Bela – I'm so sorry.' I found a clean tea towel in one of the drawers and handed it over.

'All of them,' he said, his voice hollow as if his heart had been scooped out. 'All of them. Adriana, Zendan – *the children* – all.'

Zendan Greenill owned a Mercedes dealership and made enough

money to keep his family in very nice style. More importantly, Adriana Greenill was a member of the Council of Five, and one of Bela's oldest friends. I'd met her a few times socially and she'd always been nice to me, smiling as though she'd meant it, never making snarky remarks about my parentage. She always seemed to be genuinely interested in the world, and unlike many, she didn't regard the Normal part of it as just a nasty crunchy coating around the core of wonderful Weyrd. She didn't appear to think human life was something to be merely tolerated.

Now, she and her family were no more than a memory, and a few fragments of stray trash.

'Are you okay to . . .?' I started to ask as Bela pushed away from the sink and strode towards an internal staircase leading off the dining room.

Upstairs were seven bedrooms, each with a different coloured feature wall: blue, green, pink, a darker pink, purple, primrose and russet. We worked alone, so that every room was searched three times, each hoping fresh eyes might pick up a clue another had missed. All the beds had been disturbed, the covers thrown back and sheets rumpled. Pieces of golem spoor – a lolly wrapper here, a shred of newspaper there – were the sole evidence of what had happened. In the primrose room, the only one with a queen bed, there was no sign of a struggle, no indication that either husband or wife had awakened and tried to save themselves or their children. They'd been asleep – and then they were gone.

'How'd it get in?' Ziggi asked when we reconvened in the hallway.

'The sliding door leading out to the pool was open. Adriana was always complaining about the kids forgetting—' Bela started, and then he stopped and pointed to what looked like a cupboard at the end of the corridor. 'Panic room.'

The door was reinforced steel, with a range of locks and latches to keep out Normal threats, and wards and sigils against the Weyrd ones. It wasn't locked, though, and none of the enchantments had been activated. No one had had a chance to get in there and find safety.

The windowless space was big enough for a family of eight to wait out a home invasion or a cyclone. Armchairs and sofas, a large bar fridge, some books and board games made it as comfortable as a lockbox could be. From one wall, closed-circuit TV screens stared blankly back at us. Bela sat in the creaky leather chair in front of them and fiddled with the control panel. The monitors flickered to life and Ziggi and I watched intently as he ran through the night's recordings. Feeds came from the open-plan living area downstairs, the front and back doors, the pool deck, the internal staircase, the balconies and all of the bedrooms. It might have looked like overkill, but all the Councillors had similar set-ups. Paranoia kept you safe in the upper echelons of Weyrd power . . . although apparently not always.

The golem's hunger might be mindless, but the creature was surprisingly smart: it seldom went in full view of the cameras, generally sticking to the walls and the corners, so mostly all we got were brushes and blurs of it shifting through the house. The only time we got a full view was when it went to one of the beds and took a sleeping figure, but I couldn't watch the kids disappearing, so I watched Bela instead as he stared hard-eyed at the screens.

'It's changed prey: Normal to Weyrd,' I said, pondering the dietary adjustment. Had the city's homeless, sensing a tremor running through their cold concrete territories, found new places to hide, like rabbits realising a fox had moved into the neighbourhood? With the streets empty and need clawing at its centre, had the golem wandered further afield, seeking something new? Was it all a coincidence or was this something else? Something more targeted and purposeful?

How long would it be before the golem lost its remaining skerrick of humanity?

Bela shut off the images and pressed his palms against his eyes. Ziggi's fingers hovered at his friend's shoulder, descended, landed brief as a butterfly, then lifted off. I touched the blacker than black hair and lowered my voice. 'Do you think this was intentional?'

'Attacking one of the Council?' His fists slammed on the console and he shook my hand away.

'Yeah.'

'I don't know.'

'Coincidence, then?'

'I'm too old to believe in coincidence.'

'Then I think we need to err on the side of caution, treat Adriana as if she was the intended target.' I didn't say, *And the rest of the family was just collateral damage*, though I suspected we were all thinking it. 'You'll want to tell the other Councillors that they'll need to rethink their security measures.' I paused. 'And I'm sorry, Bela. I really am.'

He said nothing.

I left them in the panic room and went back to the stairs. I examined the pieces of garbage as I descended: Mars wrappers, cigarette butts, old tissues, carpet fibres. Those last, the horrent twists of a most abhorrent shade of bright orange, scratched at a memory, one I couldn't quite pull up. Down on the lower floor the house opened onto the pool area. Wards were scrawled over the frame, but because the door hadn't been closed and locked, they hadn't mattered. I stepped onto timber decking which still held a little of the sun's warmth, though the breeze whistling by was chill. Plastic chairs and sun loungers dotted a wide terraced garden that surrounded the far end of the blue-tiled pool.

The golem must have come over the perimeter wall or the front gate, across the lawns and then through here. A sizable pile of rubbish was caught in the green metal palings of the pool fence, so it must have entered there, leaving behind more debris than usual. I remembered the day David and I had gone bushwalking and how there'd been an awful lot of rubbish scattered on the car park asphalt, with twists of bright orange mixed in. I'd joked about mutant wombats, but now I wondered if something had been watching me even then.

I sat on the end of one of the striped loungers and stared at the grass stretching into the distance.

My phone bleeped with a text message.

You never write, you never call.

David. I smiled and typed a reply.

'Are you gonna tell him?'

'Ziggi, don't creep up behind me like that!'

'Sorry,' he said, not sounding sorry at all as he sat heavily beside me. 'Are you gonna tell him about Baker's boy?'

'You said it yourself: it's a pretty big leap from runaway to death-machine. And I've got no proof – besides, Bela's suffering at the moment and I don't think it's the best time to share my cockamamie ideas with him.'

'You're maturing,' he said approvingly, so I gave him the finger.

'What are you doing?' Bela's tone was weary, and Ziggi and I both jumped.

'Do I have to put a bell on you two?'

I swallowed a couple of times, trying to work out what to say. 'What's next here?'

He stood by the pool, the highly polished tips of his Zegnas hanging over the edge. 'What is there to do?'

Bela was right: a quick vacuum and the house would be spotless. There were no bodies, no burials to arrange and no closure to be had. All he could do was lock the doors and send me off to do my best bloodhound impersonation. He asked, 'What are *you* going to do now?'

'I . . . I'm going back where we first spotted the golem, see if I can find anything. And I need to talk to the sirens again.' His expression told me that my ability to prioritise was questionable. 'I'm juggling several things at once, Bela, and I'm trying to do my best. Just let me get on with it, hey?'

He remained silent, but dipped his head. He didn't ask about my meeting with Baker and I didn't volunteer anything. He'd remember later, when he stopped aching.

I stretched in frustration and considered kicking the park bench in front of me, then thought better of it. Thanks to the healer, I was walking as if I'd never been injured; it would have been stupid to abuse that. 'How's this damned thing getting around the city?'

Ziggi muttered something I didn't quite catch.

'Huh? Speak up, Zig.'

'I said *tunnels*. Normals live their whole lives above; they know nothing about what's beneath.' He sounded fed-up; he sounded as though he thought I was Normal.

'Tell me, oh wise one.' My tone didn't improve matters.

'Tunnels. Sewers, storm-water drains. They run all over, built when the place was first settled. They go to the river. Some are big enough for a man to stand in; others are small and choked by years of mud and neglect. Tunnels. That's how you travel this city without being seen.'

The golem had come from a conduit near the river. I'd thought it had only been hiding there. 'Is there some kind of Weyrd underground network?'

He gave me a look, the same sort you might give a conspiracy theorist, the one that said *Go home and take your medication.*

'Maybe we prefer the dark to the light, but we don't prefer the damp and the dirty. Who lives in sewers apart from rats? Some days . . .' He broke off, muttering, just to make sure I knew his opinion in no uncertain terms. As he wandered off towards The Lone Cartman, the only vendor in the vicinity, I called, 'Long black, thanks for asking.'

We'd reached the tired and cranky part of a long day about half an hour ago and sniping was unavoidable. The spot by the river where Bela and I had first seen the creature was a bust; I'd also found that even the surly waitress from the conclave, the one who worked at the café, had made herself scarce. I had a sneaking suspicion all the sirens were laying low – not that I blamed them for that. Ziggi and I had wandered back to the park at the base of the cliffs.

I squinted at the water; in the afternoon sun the glare flashed silver. Across from Kangaroo Point were the Gardens, a mix of huge ancient trees, thick shrubs and buildings belonging to Queensland University of Technology, some old and ugly, some new and uglier. I could see tunnels there, too, lurking under the boardwalk like toothless mouths.

Ziggi's mood had lifted when he returned, which I put down to the caffeine. He handed me a large takeaway cup and we stood for a while, drinking and staring at nothing in particular.

'Ziggi?'

'Mmmm?'

'You think Bela will be okay?'

'He's hard to know.'

'Not what I asked.'

'Look, the thing is, he's *old*. He and Adriana were friends a long time. You're a blink of the eye to him. No offence.'

'None taken.'

'Bela's kind, they age slowly, but they do age, and sometimes they go a bit strange. You gotta consider how they feed, too, on human energy and emotions – those things change as the world does, and leave nothing familiar for them to hold onto. If you've got touchstones, at least you have a sense that something remains the same . . . it's easier to hold it together. He knew Adriana from *before*, before coming here.'

The meaningful tilt of his head stumped me until I realised what he meant. It hadn't ever occurred to me that Adriana might have known Bela rather better than I had. Once upon a time the idea might have turned me green and a little psychotic, but now even thinking back to the way his real name rolled off her tongue, the way she'd sometimes touched his cheek and laughed up into his face, I just felt sorry for him. 'Oh. Sometimes I forget he doesn't tell me everything.'

Some days I think I will disappear up my own fundamental orifice.

'Secrecy's natural to him – you don't survive without keeping things close. It's nothing personal.'

'It would have been nice to leave the relationship feeling like I knew him better than when I went in.' I held up a finger and said proudly, 'But I'm not angry, see? This is me, not being angry and bitter.'

'I can see that. The person you know in bed isn't *all* of the person.'

'I knew more than his bed-side,' I protested, but my words sounded empty, even to me.

'Maybe some of him, sure, but if you'd known more you'd have realised it was never gonna work, you and him.'

I hesitated. 'You didn't think to tell me that at the time?'

'Would you have listened?' He continued when I gave him a shamefaced look, 'He was never gonna be the Bela in your head, never going to be who you thought he was.'

'Ziggi—'

'I watched. I ached for you, V; you're like my little girl, but you were always gonna get hurt.' He sighed.

I grabbed his hand and squeezed it. 'It's all good now, Ziggi.' And it was. I thought about what an open book David was and felt a rush of relief. So many things in my life had to be kept hidden; so many things shrank from the light of day. It made me uncomfortable, though, to consider what else Bela might not be telling me. 'So, my friend, tunnels.'

'Tunnels.'

The battery on my mobile was dangerously low. I wasn't going to risk using the torch app. 'Got a flashlight or two?'

'In the cab.' We waited a little while longer until he said, 'Let's get moving, do this while there's still some sun. Never know what darkness might bring.'

I had a fair idea, but I kept it to myself.

Liquid refuse trickled sluggishly past my boots and I prayed they were watertight; I wasn't dressed for urban spelunking and for a moment I deeply regretted not going home to change. The bricks were slippery underfoot, kind of green and nasty, and I had to step gingerly. The weak torchlight was about as useful as a firefly's bum and I wished Ziggi would hurry up with the fresh batteries. In hindsight, of course we should have tested them while we were still near the cab.

The mouth of the tunnel was tall enough for me to stand straight. We'd walked until we'd spotted one of the drains – though *not* the one where I'd seen the two young lovers taken up. Behind me was a mud bank with my bootprints embedded in it and a little beyond that lapped the river. The tide was coming in, deceptively slowly. The circle of sky at my back was a late-afternoon dark blue. Kids played in the park above me, their shrieking laughter dulled, as were the shouted warnings from parents who were cooking sausages on gas hotplates, trying to enjoy themselves while simultaneously checking on the children. Life went on as usual.

Down here were things that had been around for too long, and the scent of rot was overwhelming the BBQ aromas. Further in, other unidentifiables splashed and plopped. Liquefied household debris whooshed from holes high in the walls and with it came another rush of stench. There was a limit on my breath-holding abilities, and breathing through my mouth seemed like a terrible idea. I looked over my shoulder, hoping to see Ziggi, but met only the sight of the Gardens' boardwalk in the distance. People moved along it, small coloured Lego figures.

I faced the darkness again. *Just go a little way*, I thought. *It's better than doing nothing*.

One foot moved, then the other; filth squelched under my soles. My dress suddenly felt uncomfortable, its hem constricting, and my right boot too tight, as if the dagger had somehow swelled. To distract myself I aimed the dull torch beam at the brickwork around me. It was superbly made, cut from something that might have been Brisbane Tuff: some blocks were buttery-hued, others a delicate pink and all of them fitted closely, the mortar still bonded and firm, belying its age. They don't make drains like they used to. It wasn't as if I wanted to set up home there, but I admired the workmanship.

Somewhere ahead of me there was a noise: too big to be a rat or other small sewer-dwelling critter, and if the air had been bad before, it suddenly got much worse. There was a shifting in the gloom, almost a swarming.

'Uh, hello?'

Whatever it was didn't come any closer, but instead began to move away. I took a few steps backwards, wanting to bolt towards the last of the light and sun, but my determination not to turn my back on what was waiting in the deeper dark won out.

I kept retreating, a fragile moment of hope that it would let me be swelled in my chest . . . then the thing sped forward, shadows whirling, bits of wet mess and plant matter, newspapers, tin cans, plastic bottles, all orbiting around limbs that were roughly human-shaped, though with no discernable features.

Then it was on me, surrounding me: I was *in* it and I was cold and the air in my lungs stopped and froze and the atmosphere around me moved slow as molasses. I fought, throwing punches that seemed to connect, because I heard a grunt and what might have been a curse. The attack lessened, and for a few seconds I could breathe.

I took those precious beats to fumble at the top of my right boot, to find the knife and *pull*. The Boatman's dagger came free, heating up in my hand, and I lashed out. The creature made a sound between a bleat and a roar and dropped me like a hot potato.

I managed to land on my feet and stumbled backwards, trying to stay upright. A hand behind me grabbed at my shoulder and I began to turn, yelling, then lost my balance and fell. My face hit the water, then continued down until it smacked against the stone beneath. There was a sudden burst of stars and I sank into a black sea.

'You are a danger to yourself.'

'Did you see it?' I sat up very slowly. My head hurt. I was damp and smelled really, *really* bad. When I coughed, something stagnant erupted. But more than anything, I was really, really cold.

'You've gotta stop doing that wandering-off-on-your-own thing. I can't keep taking you to hospitals or someone is gonna report me. Keep scaring an old guy like me and I'm gonna have a heart attack.' Ziggi's hand on the small of my back was the only thing keeping me upright.

I coughed again, and a mix of liquid vile flecked with orange came out. Why was there always carrot? It came up again and again until there was nothing left, just the thin yellowy nastiness your stomach releases when there's nothing else to expel: the digestive equivalent of a white flag.

We were on a patch of grass and hidden from the general thoroughfare by trees. The land dropped away to the left and met the river, which was making soothing sounds. My head was pounding, my throat was raw and I was fervently wishing to be elsewhere. On the ground beside me was the knife, gleaming.

'I can't leave you alone for five minutes.'

'It was closer to fifteen,' I protested. 'Did you see it? And have you got any gum? Mints? Toothpaste? Anything?'

He handed me a bottle of water so I could rinse and spit, then a crumpled packet of PK gum. I noticed he was staying upwind and not getting too close. 'Yeah, I saw it. Or bits of it. It hesitated when you fell and I thought it was gonna come after me.'

'Didn't though, huh?'

'Nope. You still think it's Donovan Baker?'

'I've got no reason to think it wasn't. Why didn't it take us? Me?'

'Maybe you taste bad. Or maybe it had something to do with *that*?' Ziggi pointed towards the Boatman's blade.

'It certainly didn't seem to like it.' I regarded the dagger with new fondness, then realised that it was shining with dark blood, tinged green. 'Did the golem say anything?'

'Nothing recognisable, just the screamy bit when you stabbed it.' He pulled up handfuls of grass like a kid in a sulk. 'Surely it couldn't still be hungry. It ate eight people last night.'

'Apparently eight isn't enough. Man, I need a shower. Take me home, please.' I rubbed at the abrasions on my cheek where I'd scraped against the brickwork; they'd complement the bruise on my forehead nicely.

'You're not getting in my cab like that.'

Chapter Eighteen

We negotiated. I found a toilet block with a functioning – albeit cold – shower, but I was so chilled that the water felt warm. I stood under it for a while, though I wasn't sure if the smell went away or just morphed into something marginally less offensive. Afterwards, examining my reflection in the polished metal mirror, I considered how to best explain my latest stunning facial addition to David.

Wrapped in nothing but a scratchy grey blanket, I shivered and coughed in the back of the taxi, ignoring Ziggi's ostentatious sniffing; he'd already made it quite clear I was stinking up his pride and joy. My clothes had been stuffed in a number of plastic bags and banished to the boot. Intensive cleaning would be required, and even then I wasn't convinced anything could be salvaged, not even my poor coat.

By the time David knocked on my door a couple of hours later, I'd showered again – three times – washed my hair until it squeaked, and loofahed myself so enthusiastically that I showed signs of remaining bright pink permanently. Ointment had been liberally smeared on the new scratches, but I couldn't truthfully say I was an attractive proposition.

David lifted a hand to my cheek, but didn't touch the wounds. 'Walking into walls again?' he asked gently.

'Bricks. Bricks are not my friend.'

'Do we need to have a talk? Only I feel like you're keeping something from me.'

'I guess there's no time like the unavoidable time.' I sighed.

'You're not a superhero, are you?' he asked as I led him into the lounge room. At that point, the idea of a life spent wearing my undies on the outside was sounding distinctly enticing. He eyed the bottle of red I'd opened earlier and watched as I poured more than the recommended daily dose into very large glasses. I took a sip for courage, then began the tale of a wine made from tears, just to ease into things.

All things considered, he took it remarkably well. He clearly didn't believe me, but he took it well. He also didn't break up with me, which was a major plus. There was something heart-warming about the fact he didn't run away screaming, but rather stayed and worked on trying to convince me that I was nuts.

'Did you hit your head when you fell?'

'See, this is why I didn't want to tell you about myself.'

'Well, it is kind of hard to swallow.' He was genuinely apologetic. 'See, if you were a superhero, you could just show me your superpower as proof. But this stuff? I'm kind of waiting for a camera crew to appear and tell me I've been Punk'd.'

I pulled up the right leg of my second-best pair of jeans and showed him the pink scars, those little cuts made by Louise barely perceptible now. 'You've seen this, yes? Can you think of any native Australian animal that might have done this? Do not say dropbears.'

'I'll grant that's a pretty impressive injury. Escaped tiger?'

'It's called a 'serker. Something from the nasty side, something that doesn't normally come through on its own, 'cause it's not that smart – it has to be summoned. It likes its hamburgers human and super-fresh.' I shivered. 'I went looking for it, although at the time I didn't know that's what I was looking for, otherwise I'd have thought twice about taking the job.'

'Why *did* you take the job?'

'That's another long story for another long day.'

Silence, then, 'So, you're what? Magical?'

I shook my head. 'Nope, no enchantments in my skin. I'm very strong, but not magical. I can perform rituals and some spells – but so can anyone with enough belief and willing blood – but I'm not inherently . . . *spooky*. Some Weyrd are, and if they combine that power with a spellbook – we call it a *grimoire* – and a bad attitude, well, you're in a shit-load of trouble.'

'And magic wands are—'

'Handy. Places to store your power, a tool to amplify it when you send a bolt out into the world. Again, not inherently spooky.'

His look of disbelief didn't shift. I ran fingers through my hair, hard across my scalp. *Maybe I should break something?* I opened my mouth to try a new tack, but realised I didn't actually know what that tack might be. A thudding at the front door saved me from saying something stupid, but my gratitude was tempered by the knowledge that thudding never bodes well.

A body was sprawled on the patio, bleeding quietly into the prickles of the welcome mat. The siren had lost one wing – it was completely gone, leaving only a bloody stump – and the other was still clinging on, but only by a few tenacious tendons. Her clothes were ragged, as if many hands had been trying to tear them off, her face was a pulpy mess and she was bleeding from a lot of cuts. Yelling for David to get towels, I scanned the street and the garden quickly, trying to see if anyone was lurking, then dragged her into the front room before going back and locking and bolting the door.

I wedged a cushion under her head, then tried to wipe away some of the red. The wetness made my palm tingle – not an acidic burn, just a kind of fizzing. I didn't recognise her, but I could make an educated guess.

'Raidne?' I asked, without much hope of an answer, but her eyes opened. Her lips parted and she coughed up scarlet, trying to speak.

'What's that? Sorry, I couldn't—'

'The baby,' she gasped. 'Got . . . to get . . . baby.'

'Calliope? Where is she? Have you been looking after her?'

'Ligeia. Teles. We took turns . . .' She coughed again and the sound almost drowned out David's shocked cursing as he covered the injured woman with the towels. I held her head, gently moving my fingers across the base of her skull, and was rewarded by a congealing cross-shaped void. Raidne hacked and barked and shuddered, dying noisily.

I slid her lids closed over staring eyes.

Silence reigned for a while. Another death, and I was no closer to an answer or a baby. But I did have a new name, which was something. *Ligeia*. Taking a deep breath, I looked at David and couldn't resist saying, 'Superpowery enough for you?'

I dialled McIntyre, really not looking forward to telling her who was in my front room and what state she was in.

While I dealt with the cops, David retreated to the kitchen, taking refuge in cooking dinner, guessing quite correctly that if the task were left up to me, said dinner would take the form of a second bottle of wine. He was muttering to himself, obviously trying to rationalise what he'd seen and heard, and it was sounding very much like the last straw meeting the camel's back. So maybe he wasn't going to hang around. After the meat-wagon took Raidne away, I made my decision.

'David, we need to talk.'

'That's never a good start to any conversation.' He gazed at me reproachfully as he stirred the spaghetti bolognaise he'd whipped up. It struck me as nothing short of a miracle as I hadn't even realised I had the right ingredients in my woefully stocked larder. 'And don't you think we've had a peculiar enough chat for one evening? I'm prepared to admit you were right and I'll never question your knowledge of strange shit again.'

'Appealing though that is . . . Look, I know I went to all the trouble of opening up to you in the interests of an honest relationship, but—'

'Are you trying to break up with me?' he asked calmly.

'It's just – you know – I don't—' Painful experience had taught me that once you got to the babbling stage you'd already lost.

'Are you trying to break up with me *badly*?' He laughed, retrieving two bowls from the cupboard.

I slapped at his shoulder. 'David, what I do can be *dangerous* – Exhibit A just got carted off to the morgue: Exhibit A, who had *wings* and *claws*, and *many* ways to defend herself. What are you going to do when the monsters come calling? Write code at them?'

'I don't write code – well, not all the time.'

'My point is: I don't want anything to happen to you. I don't want *that* to happen to you.'

'V, I'm afraid I'm going to have to reject your break-up. It's too incompetent to take seriously.' He put his arms around me and nuzzled my neck. 'Besides, being single is too much hard work. Everyone's got baggage – although I will admit that yours is a bit more exceptional than most.'

'My baggage is a little more bitey than most.' I pushed him away. 'I spent part of the day at a house when an entire family was eaten – I was almost eaten myself. And remember what happened to Lizzie? Because of me?'

'It wasn't *because* of you – that old bat would have taken any child. She could have seen you talking to a kid at the shops and decided to take that one.' He brushed the hair back from my face. 'Lizzie was endangered by someone else's crazy, but she's *alive* because of you.'

I didn't think his logic would stand up to scrutiny but I kept my mouth shut. The truth was, I really didn't want to be without him. When I'd walked away from Bela it was because that was what I wanted to do more than anything. This time, leaving was the last thing on my wish list. Besides, he was right, both about the suckiness of being single and the incompetence of my break-up, and at this point, knowing that I was loved and loving, that my life wasn't one great gaping hole, was very, *very* important.

As I set the table, I couldn't remember the last time it had been used for actual dining rather than book storage. It felt weird. But good weird.

Chapter Nineteen

Later that night, after David had gone to sleep, I tried Eurycleia, but the number rang out. Then I called Bela to tell him about Raidne. He was curt when I asked how he was, more like himself; it sounded like he was rapidly rebuilding his walls. There was a lot of put-upon sighing at my failure to make at least one dilemma go away, and I felt like a kid pulling at his coat for attention. Zvezdomir Tepes, Patron Saint of the Mortally Inconvenienced.

'V, I'm not saying the sirens aren't an issue, but I've – *we've* – got bigger problems. Another of the councillors was targeted this evening. Mercado Wright? Lives in one of those big old Art Deco apartment blocks in Spring Hill? Luckily, he owns the building, so he's the only tenant.'

'Dead?' I asked, hoping there was no hint of longing in my voice. Wright was one of *those* Weyrd: on the single occasion I'd met him, he had looked through me as if I wasn't there. Not that I wished him ill; I just didn't like him.

'No – he was woken by the motion sensors going off, then he heard his bodyguards being eaten and ran while the golem was distracted.' I could hear Bela tapping on something at his end. 'I've stashed him and the other councillors in a safe house.'

'Is his place near a stormwater drain or sewer?' I asked, and waited for an answer. If I'd held my breath I'd have passed out. I tried again, 'Did the wards go off at Wright's?'

'He didn't say.' His tone told me he was annoyed at himself for not asking.

'I'm willing to bet they didn't. Ziggi and I walked straight in at the Greenills' place – am I right in thinking you'd disarmed the protections over the front door when you arrived?' He grunted, which I took as an affirmative. 'If they'd remembered to set the Normal security system, they might have had a chance.'

'Your point?' he asked sharply, and I realised a reminder that something so mundane might have saved his friends was probably not what he needed at that moment.

'Wright didn't say he was woken by his wards doing whatever they were meant to do, did he? He said it was the motion sensors. Remember what Ursa said? The golem has a Normal core. So the Weyrd stuff around it is just a wrapping, not strong enough to set off magical barriers – but the mortal part, its *essence*, still affects Normal things. Let's face it, a lot of apotropaic power doesn't work on me either.'

There was a lengthy pause, then, 'You've been working on your vocabulary.'

'Sometimes I'm not as stupid as I appear.'

'Ziggi told me about the tunnels,' he said obliquely. 'Are you okay?'

'I'm alive, but I fear I'll never get the smell out of my nostrils and a very expensive dress will never be the same again.' From the bedroom came the sounds of David's contented snoring and I wanted nothing more than to join him. 'You know you might have to go underground?'

'By *you*, you mean *you*, correct?'

I realised he was right, and sighed. We'd both have given our right arms for a team of dumb, gun-toting Normals willing to go beneath the city and flush out the golem for us. Alas, all we had was me.

'Do you think you can get me back into the Archives tomorrow?'

'Is that a good idea?'

'Hey, I remained polite with Anders Baker *and* his surly security guard. Mostly. I'm growing as a person. Ask Ziggi.'

'He mentioned it already – he seemed to think you might have been on drugs. Why do you want to see Ursa again?'

'Location scouting,' I hedged. 'I thought I might see if she has more detailed maps of the tunnels than those available through Normal channels. It might give me some hints about something, *anything*.' It sounded convincing. After a few moments I said, 'So, can you get me back in? I promise I'll be good.'

His groan told me that he really didn't want to but had no choice. Life had taught me a lot about doing things we didn't want to do, but I didn't think he'd appreciate my insights just now.

I headed over to Little Venice bright and early, preparing myself for the taste of crow. The bar area was deserted, but the Sisters had unearthed winter braziers, which were now dotted around the courtyard so those patrons who felt the cold could still sit outside comfortably. One of the Norns was moving between tables, putting candles into Moroccan tea glasses of yellow, orange and purple etched glass. At night they would be lovely.

The long fall of auburn corkscrew curls dropping to a slim waist dissipated some of my tension: it wasn't Aspasia. Boyish hips were encased in skinny jeans and a black skivvy covered barely-there breasts. I called, 'Hey, Theo.'

She swung around, the cataract of hair moving like a velvet curtain. Her free hand made its way to one hip as she assumed her best you've-got-a-lot-of-nerve pose.

'You bruised Aspasia's wrist.'

'I really don't know my own strength,' I offered, and considered walking with a limp I no longer had in hope of sympathy. Deciding against it, I went with the truth. 'And I have come to apologise.'

Above me there was a displeased chorus and looking up, I saw three small serpents, one red, one blue, one green, entwined in the canopy of vines. They didn't look happy. I pointed. 'You wanna call them off?'

'Aspasia's babies. Don't worry, they're not so poisonous. And you're doubly in luck: she's not here.' She grinned, sat at one of the tables and gestured for me to join her. Theodosia didn't make me too nervous; she thought I was cute. 'You want your fortune told? I think I've got my cards around here somewhere.'

'No thanks, but I admire that you Norns never give up.' I sat. 'I'm after information.'

'This got to do with the sirens?'

'Why am I not surprised that you know about that?' I asked. 'But no – unless you know something, of course.'

She shook her head. 'Other than they're turning up dead with startling regularity? No, I know nothing.'

'One of them, the first one to die, had a baby. Said baby is missing, and I have to admit I'm not holding out much hope at this point,' I admitted.

She threw her hands in the air. 'What is it with you and children?' She *tsk'd*.

'Used to be one myself. If you hear anything—'

'Unlikely. You know the birds like to keep to themselves . . .' My pitiful expression must have had some effect because she said, 'But I'll ask around . . . if that wasn't what you came for, what is?'

'Years ago a Normal named Anders Baker married a Weyrd woman, Dusana Nadasy.'

She looked at me as if to say, *And?*

'She and her house blew up. The hired help too.'

Her face lightened. 'Oh, *that* Dusana Nadasy.'

'The very same. Her son's gone missing and I'm trying to find him.'

'Wouldn't he be an adult now? A bit old for your super-nanny attentions?'

'You know, it hurts me when you're sarcastic like that.' I crossed my arms.

'I'm sorry.'

'Anyway, he is indeed all grown up, but his daddy wants him home.' I rubbed at the back of my neck where the headache was starting. 'Before Donovan disappeared he might have been looking for his grandparents on the Nadasy side. Don't suppose the kid ever came in here, asking questions?'

She tilted her head and studied the photo I held out. 'Never seen him. You think maybe he found them?'

'His father seems to think they're dead, or should be, anyway.'

'But you're naturally suspicious.'

'Comes with the territory.'

'Vadim and Magda Nadasy were very traditional; if there was such a thing as Old High Weyrd, they were it. Not necessarily well-liked; but then people who insist on rigorously maintaining standards seldom are. Don't know why they came to Oz; maybe the Motherland got a little too dangerous. Here, no one believes in the old monsters so it's easier for us to hide in this godless modern society, bless it.'

'So where could I find them, if they're alive?'

'Don't know.' She frowned. 'They've been gone a long time, Fassbinder. Maybe once the daughter went pop they dropped out of sight. Or maybe they'd already decamped. Did Magda die? I think she might have – oh, don't look at me like that, Fassbinder, it was a *long* time ago.'

'Sorry, sorry. Can you remember anything else?'

'They apparently used to hold court, the full deal, quite grand. I'm repeating gossip, of course: *we've* never been good enough to score invitations to that sort of event. Whispers had it that your father supplied their table.'

'My father supplied a lot of tables, Theo. I guess if they were gone it would explain why Baker got away with killing Dusana,' I mused, storing the other information away. The Winemaker had said she'd known Grigor – so had she known Vadim and Magda too?

Theo's mouth dropped open. 'Really? He *murdered* her?'

'I don't know for sure, but it was strangely convenient timing. Anders Baker doesn't strike me as the kind of guy who'll take an infinite amount of humiliation. But if the Nadasys are still around, why is Baker still alive?'

'What if Baker had something they wanted more than revenge?' That hung in the air.

'Like what?'

'How should I know? You're the investigator.' She rubbed at a mark on her skin. 'If they're alive and if the kid found them——?'

'You know how popular mixed marriages are – I'm not sure how warm his welcome would have been. *If* he found them.' I cleared my throat. 'I am, of course, clutching at straws. It appears to be my specialty.'

She grinned and tapped a long nail against the tabletop. It sounded like glass hitting tile. 'The great thing about rumours is that they never quite go away, and at the heart of every rumour—'

'—is a kernel of truth.'

'I'll see what I can find.'

'There's something else.'

'Isn't there always?' She pouted.

'Well, this is more of a public service announcement. There's a golem roaming the streets – and not a helpful one.'

She looked away. 'I heard about the Greenills. Shame. Adriana was nice.'

News travelled fast. 'It went after Mercado Wright last night.'

'He's no loss.'

'Sorry to say he survived. Wagons have been drawn into a circle, and the Council is in lockdown. I don't want to panic peeps, but forewarned is forearmed – put the word about, hey?'

'Wasn't a problem when it was taking Normals,' she grumbled, and I shook a finger at her.

'Look, thinking it's all fine and dandy as long as the bad things are happening to Normals is not okay. Consider this: eventually they'll be gone and the bad things will look for new targets – as evidenced by the Greenills' extinction.' She gave me a flat stare and I resisted the urge to grab her hand and squeeze. 'And what happens when the sirens' nest is cleared out? There's no guarantee whatever's doing that will leave town. Then the rest of us are in the firing line.'

'Shit.'

'Not to mention that if this golem keeps going, keeps feeding, we won't be able to keep it quiet: if what's happening spills into the open, we'll be in real trouble, Theo. A bunch of panicking Normals looking for scapegoats is not a pretty future.'

'Double shit. I really don't want to have to move again.'

'Then *help* me. Keep an ear to the ground, and if you hear anything, let me know.'

'In everyone's interest, isn't it?' She grinned. 'Aspasia's going to be pissed off when they tell her you were in here.' Theo's eyes rolled upwards to the serpents, who'd subsided and were listening carefully. 'She'll be even more pissed off when I tell her she missed your apology.'

'I'll be back – but you might want remind her that the last person who aggravated me got shoved into an oven. Tell her not to give my address to strays.' I hadn't forgotten she'd told Sally Crown where I lived, and I hadn't forgotten that was how Sally had found Lizzie. Theo's cheeks flushed, and I knew she hadn't forgotten either. 'I'll come back to apologise in person, if she promises not to spit in my food.'

'It's a deal.'

I tapped the tabletop, mirroring her rhythm. 'Any chance of a piece of marshmallow caramel log before I go?'

At City Hall, the guards let me through without comment, despite my lack of chaperone, which was nice, but Ursa – today in baby blue overalls – was less welcoming. She gave the jeans and T-shirt under my leather jacket a disapproving stare; obviously supplicants were meant to be well-dressed, no matter her own sartorial style. Yet she brought me the books and maps I asked for, and she showed me how to search the database, though it was obvious she wasn't happy to have me there. She gave off a funny smell, like an animal does when it's distressed, so I was surprised when, about an hour after setting me up at a desk as far away from hers as possible, she broke the silence by asking, 'Do you remember your father?'

I froze. On the List of Unexpected Things to hear, that was close to the top. I'd made a point, most of my life, to talk about Grigor as little as possible, and I made a special point not to ask about him, because it's harder to suppress memories if you're constantly dredging them up. Clearing my throat, I said, 'Some things. I've jettisoned a lot.'

'But he was your father,' she insisted. 'An important person to a child.'

'Certainly important to the children he murdered,' I said, keeping my eyes on the fat register of Council minutes in front of me and hoping she'd take the hint.

'Did he teach you things? The protections, the spells, the offerings?'

I shook my head – not because he didn't, but because I didn't want to discuss it. Bela and the Council might have watched me from a distance, but it wasn't the same as being included. It wasn't the same as *belonging*.

'Your heritage? After he died—'

'After he died my heritage disappeared. It vanished along with all the Weyrd who'd once been his mates. All the people who wanted to forget they ever knew the *Kinderfresser*, or that they'd bought meat from him, or drank with him and laughed at his jokes,' I said tightly. My hands were shaking, the pages in my fingers making rustling noises. 'After he was gone, all I had were my mother's family. None of his fair-weather friends stopped by to see how I was after my world broke apart.'

'Really?' she asked, feathery eyebrows raised. 'No one?'

'No one.' With an effort I got my tremors under control.

'No one?'

I bit back a shout and opened my mouth to calmly repeat, *no one* . . . then I felt the itch of recollection: one night, a full moon hanging in the sky, a knock on the door . . . my grandmother answering, while my grandfather waited out of sight, a cricket bat in his hands, just in case. Me, supposed to be asleep but sitting at the top of the stairs, watching as a well-dressed visitor tried to convince Grandma to let him in . . . to see *me*. Now I recalled her refusal, despite the man's insistence, and Grandy stepping forward, solid, nuggetty, the muscles from his years as a coalminer still firm, still evident.

'An old man,' I said slowly, 'after the trial, after Grigor was dead. Not one of the Friday-night drinking crowd. My grandparents sent him away; he never came again. There might have been some unusually salty language from Grandma.'

'Then perhaps you weren't as deserted as you have always felt. We have long memories,' she said.

'Who was he?' I asked.

'Who knows? Someone concerned for you, for Grigor's daughter.'

Well, since we were friends now . . . 'Did you know Vadim and Magda Nadasy?' I asked.

Her face twitched as if slapped. Guess I'd said the wrong thing. Again. Maybe it wasn't just me. Maybe the Nadasys had been even more unpopular than Theo had implied.

Ursa turned away very deliberately and fixed her attention firmly on her work, discouraging any further conversation.

That was okay by me.

I didn't bother with the subterranean maps – I'd asked for them just in case Bela checked up on what I'd been doing. The golem was using the sewers to move around some of the time, but it wasn't living there and it sure hadn't travelled to Pullenvale that way, because they only stretched as far as the edges of the inner city – the outer suburbs were decidedly tunnel-free. Instead, I looked for any mention of the Nadasys. There should have been records, some documentation of their arrival in the city, interactions they'd had with the Council, any disciplinary matters, notification of their deaths . . . but there was nothing, not even a photo.

I was about to give up when I finally found a trace of Donovan Baker's mysterious grandparents. Careless shelving had pushed a slim journal inside one of the property registers, making one page fold back on itself. The paper was thin and the crumpled folio was easy to miss. I smoothed it out and found Vadim Nadasy's name halfway down the long list – but that was not what made the breath catch in my lungs. *That* was the address.

The register dated back about fifteen years, when it had been a prime piece of bend-of-the-river real estate on a long, wide strip of land. Now it was an abandoned house, still smelling of the mud that had been carried inside by floods a few years ago. I'd assumed nothing had been done to fix it because insurance companies were arguing about paying out, but maybe that wasn't the case at all.

Maybe the owner of the dark, empty abode in Chelmer had neither any need nor intention of making a claim. Maybe there was no desire to fix the place up, for it was better fit for purpose in its current state. It was, after all, the house where we'd found the 'serker.

Chapter Twenty

The day had waned while I'd been in the Archives and by the time I made it to the Botanical Gardens, darkness was falling fast. Teles' body had been discovered there, hanging from one of the Moreton Bay figs, so that seemed as good a place as any to go and re-direct my thoughts back to the sirens. The air was cold and I wouldn't have been surprised to see the fountain frozen and icicles forming on branches, but there was nothing more wintery on show than my breath frosting. I didn't bother sneaking around; without wings I was unlikely to be in danger from whoever was hunting Eurycleia's clan, and I hoped the golem would be wary of approaching me again any time soon. The dagger, no worse for wear for its impromptu dip, vibrated gently against my ankle.

As I wandered, I tried to put my thoughts in order. Where was Donovan Baker – and *what* was he? Were his grandparents still alive? And who or what was killing the sirens? Where was Calliope Kallos? Was *she* even alive? Who was the Winemaker – and who were her clients? Was Sally Crown still hanging around? And how the hell could I go back to the abandoned house without a skinful of liquid courage and a gunned-up posse?

Meandering didn't magically produce answers, but it did make me realise someone else was lurking, though it took a while. I was down on the boardwalk, considering heading home to David, when I finally heard stealthy sounds behind me. The promenade led over the water, zigging and zagging amongst the mangrove trees. When I reached a point on the path where the canopy of leaves overhead broke and let the moonlight through, I stopped and turned.

'Come out,' I said quietly, half-expecting Eurycleia.

For a moment there was silence, then a shuffling, all unwilling, until she stepped into the light. Not Eurycleia, not even close.

This one was ragged, with none of the manicured beauty of the conclave sirens. Age sat heavily upon her: hair grey-white, skin dirty and carved by the centuries, eyebrows thick with feathers, lips as cracked and canyoned as a heavy smoker's, eyes as ancient as the world, and black with it. Her dress had once been a summer frock; even in the moonlight I caught hints of yellow, lavender and blue remaining, though it was filthy. Her wings were grubby silver, their plumage scant, almost skeletal, and she wasn't bothering to hide them with any kind of enchantment. Her legs were fully feathered, with patches of chicken skin showing through where she'd moulted. In one hand she held a tattered black umbrella.

Even if I hadn't recognised her, I'd have known that umbrella anywhere: I'd been almost spitted upon its tip not long ago at the Hardgrave Road squat.

She smiled, and her teeth caught the moon's glow. Something moved there, reflected in an expanse of surprisingly clean dentition, and I remembered the legends of bygone sirens, those who'd never given up the taste of human flesh. Sometimes, it was claimed, the souls of their victims could be seen in the sheen of their fangs; something of them always remained, a memorial, like a hint or a stain.

'You're an exile,' I ventured.

She gave a quick dip of the head, birdlike, but birdlike as a hawk, predatory and alert.

'One of the veterans who didn't stop.'

Again, that sharp affirmative. How many of the city's homeless had kept her fed over the years? As if the poor sods didn't have enough to contend with. And add the golem to the equation . . .

'They cast you out because you're a danger; your habits risk attention.'

Grief now, and anger, a refusal to acknowledge any wrongdoing. Could she help herself? Was eating mortals a choice, or was she simply so ancient, so set in her ways that she *couldn't* change? Her eyes glittered darkly, and there was something in the regal, defiant angle of her head that made me realise she wasn't so entirely different from Eurycleia.

'The Boatman said you'd come,' she crackled, her voice like an ancient gramophone record.

'Really? Then he told you more than he told me.'

'We're old friends, he and I. We've travelled far together.'

'I'll bet.' I frowned. 'He said they're trying to break the sky.'

'Did he now? He's not supposed to interfere, you understand.'

'Do you know who *they* are?'

She didn't answer, just smirked and sidled closer until I held up a hand. 'Do you know who I am?' When she nodded, I said firmly, 'Then you'll know there's half a chance I can take you in a fight. And even the mozzies don't touch me, so I probably don't taste very good.'

She pouted, stopped.

'Surely you didn't come to make a snack of me?' I said and her top lip curled, caught between a sneer and a snarl.

'Stop looking for the child, girl. Stop asking questions, or next time it'll be worse than just a warning,' she said and made to leave.

I started to yell, but stopped myself, instead saying more calmly, 'Wait!'

She paused and said almost tenderly, 'What do you want, little half-blood?'

'I know there's a baby somewhere, and I hope someone's looking after her. I want to know why sirens are being murdered. I want to know what the fuck this golem wants, and where it's hiding. And I want to know what the Boatman means for me to do with that knife.'

'So many questions.' She laughed. 'So few answers.'

'Do you know where the child is?'

She didn't speak.

I took a breath. 'Did Raidne know where the baby is?'

'Raidne? Raidne is a good girl. Raidne doesn't judge. She understands the old customs.' Clearly she didn't know about Raidne and I wasn't going to be the one to tell her. She began to shuffle back to the shadows.

'Hey, hang on. The baby?' *Please don't let her have eaten it.* For a moment I didn't think she'd reply, but then in a gentle voice that had a hint of beauty, she said, 'The child is being looked after. She's safe.'

'Are you Ligeia?'

She hesitated, her mouth open as if to answer, then her head jerked to the side as if she'd heard something beyond my range. She slipped into the darkness when I stepped forward — then I too heard the rhythmic beat of heels on the boardwalk: something corporeal, not the golem with its insane whirling. I waited.

'To whom were you speaking?' Eurycleia demanded, coming into sight.

'I have no idea,' I half-lied. 'What are you doing here?'

'Looking for someone. Not you.'

'Story of my life,' I sighed.

'Did Raidne find you?'

'She came to me, but I didn't get much out of her.'

'Well, I did warn you,' she said dismissively. There was something mean and triumphant in her tone and I wanted to knock the smug out of her.

'You didn't warn me she'd die on the floor of my house.'

'*What?*' Even in the near-dark I caught a flash of something *other* in her eyes.

'She came to me last night, but something had already got to her. She didn't last long. I did try to call; you should pick up.'

Eurycleia crouched as if she'd been hit and I felt sorry then, and petty. But not petty enough not to ask, 'How many more must die before you tell me what I need to know?'

She started keening and after a moment I made out, 'It's all her fault!'

'Whose fault?' I didn't move any closer; I couldn't trust her not to strike out.

'There was no *reason*,' she blurted, terribly distressed, 'no need for her to be seeing that *thing*. There were humans aplenty to play with – it's simple enough, a good life, follow the rules, don't draw attention. Even an ordinary life as a siren is still so much more than the most extraordinary existence of a mortal.'

'But she wanted something else,' I stated, wondering what 'that *thing*' was. I understood that sometimes 'enough' never was.

'She wouldn't obey, just like those who refuse to let the old eating habits die – and just like them she has brought catastrophe upon us. She kept seeing him, and we argued, she and I, so *terribly*, the last time, and we never spoke again.'

'Serena.' Had Serena been stubborn, or had she simply fallen in love? And with what?

'My own daughter did this to us. *Mine!*'

'Do you know who he is?'

'His name, when he walks the earth, is Tobit.' She looked at me and smiled, tight as a pulled bowstring. 'We don't socialise with his kind.'

'What kind, Eurycleia? You've got to help me out here.'

'The perverts, the watchers, the voyeurs.' Her bitterness soured the air. 'The writers, the note-takers, the self-righteous, the law-givers. The ones left behind.'

I threw my hands up in despair. 'Still not getting it, Eurycleia.'

'Angels! He's an *angel*,' she yelled at last. 'God's shit, they are, yet they think themselves better than everything else in creation!'

Chapter Twenty-One

I knew very little about angels except this: they don't like us. For all the Good Book paints them as glorious deliverers of tidings of comfort and joy and protectors of the innocent; for all the illustrations of handsome, calm-faced men glowing at you from the pages of Improving Children's Literature, they thought we were a little lower than insects. The Heavenly Host, according to legend, at least, were the right hand of the Deity, doing some of the Lord's creational buffing and polishing, and even – apparently – some of the actual heavy lifting: the angels spoke, and words became worlds. They had beauty. They had power. They were not just given dominion over the earth and the sea and the air, they were given wings – and let us not forget the flaming swords for vengeance and all the smiting.

Mortals, on the other hand, were made last and least perfect: an amalgam of clay and stolen ribs. We were the spoilt-and-not-very-bright kids as far as the angelic hordes were concerned, the most oblivious and yet the most privileged. We warranted a sort of low-level contempt; they didn't like us, but at least we didn't *offend* them, not so terribly. In the greater scheme of things, we were *tolerable*, the way ants are tolerable.

The thing was, as belief in an Almighty deity declined, so the angels began to diminish too. They no longer covered the globe as they once had. They needed places where large crowds of the faithful gathered, sending nourishing waves of worship upwards – although it didn't matter what *flavour*; faith was faith, after all. So St Peter's, St Paul's, Lourdes, Mecca, Jerusalem, the Bible Belt, Tibet – in fact, most capital cities with decent-sized populations – generally had one or two angels hanging around. They were a bit like sirens: the piety ecosystem could only support so many of them. Being dependent on *us* might not make them happy, but mostly that was resentment, not an active hatred.

They didn't like the Weyrd things either, though they tended to ignore them. But at least one celestial being had managed to put aside natural enmity long enough to get close – in a Biblical sense – to Serena. Was he on his own? How long had he been in the city? Long enough to make a baby, it looked like, but how long before that? Did he have Calliope now? Maybe that was what Ligeia meant when she'd said the little girl was safe . . . Had he repented whatever impulse had attracted him to Serena and turned all murdery, or was there something else entirely? If anything could kill a siren, I guessed it could be an angel . . . but I came back to *why*? Eurycleia's hatred of this Tobit hinted at a far deeper loathing . . .

'Great, just great, because things have not been bizarre enough.' I clenched my fists. 'Don't suppose you know where to find him?'

Eurycleia shook her head and straightened, clearly closing herself off, regretting having shown her pain and her rage and her shame. There'd be nothing more from her, not tonight. I turned and walked away.

'You'll keep me informed,' she demanded.

I didn't bother to respond. She wasn't the boss of me.

'So.'

'So,' I repeated. My eyes felt full of grit after yet another sleepless night. I glanced at Ziggi, who had beads of sweat forming on his forehead in spite of the chill. I knew how he felt. Bela, though still pale, was his normal immaculate self, poker face firmly in place once more. He didn't say anything, and he certainly wasn't sweating. He just stared at the house, which was impossible to distinguish from a shit-heap. I'd filled them in on my encounters from the night before, which might have been why we were all a bit nervy. Things were piling up – and not just bodies but *nasty* things.

The neighbourhood used to be a good one, but it had been devastated by the deluge of a few years back and was taking a long time to recover. Thanks to hefty insurance payouts, most of the very expensive houses on that bend of the river had been renovated to within an inch of their lives and had then been sold on by gleeful owners to folk who actually believed all that hype about 'once-in-a-century' floods. Buyers had been tempted with colourful paint jobs, sparkly new kitchens and polished floors, and sometimes it had worked and someone decided the bargain was worth the risk. But a lot of these abodes hadn't been snapped up; instead, they'd been left standing empty, their families long-gone to higher ground. The houses looked all bright and shiny, like kids scrubbed up at the orphanage, desperately hoping someone would take a chance on them and love them.

But *this* place was decidedly unloved, and what's more, it looked like it didn't want to be loved, thank you very much. Even out on the footpath I could smell the damp, earthy stink of rot. The house was high-set, reached by an ornate but sturdy staircase at the front, though some of the steps were now missing and there were gaps in the verandah rails where palings had disappeared. Someone had hosed the whole place off at some point and the French doors on the ground level had been boarded up, but the walls were the faded, cracked colour of mud, and around the base was a nasty kind of black-brown layer that looked almost like it was trying to pull the building down.

Upstairs was another wide verandah that ran around the whole structure, with more French doors and wide bay windows, also boarded over. The front door was shut, and that was noteworthy because last time we were here it had been left hanging open after Ziggi and Bela had carried me out. My leg ached at the memory. Then again, maybe it wasn't so noteworthy – a good strong breeze could have blown it closed, or a concerned neighbour might have tried to be helpful . . . although it was worth remembering that the last time we'd been here there'd been a definite lack of those in the vicinity.

'Looks different in the daylight,' Ziggi commented.

'Not better, though.'

'No,' he agreed.

I thought it was telling that our fearless leader hadn't put a stop to the procrastination party and charged on ahead. He spoke now, his first words all morning, surprising me. 'V, you don't have to do this, you know. We can take care of it.'

It was such an incredibly tempting offer that I almost salivated. But after a moment, I said, 'Thanks, Bela, but if I don't do this now I will never be able to walk anywhere dark and scary ever again.' I pushed away from the cab and walked up the garden path of blue-grey pressed concrete. Determined weeds were already poking through its weakest points. The trees in the yard looked like they'd been badly buffeted by the flood-waters and never really recovered; they leaned to one side as if drunk. The 'lawn' stood thigh-high. If it had been summer I'd have been tiptoeing for fear of snakes.

Behind me reluctant footfalls sounded as my companions trailed after me. I stopped at the bottom of the staircase and lifted one boot onto the first step, then bent forward and pretended to retie the laces, although I was actually checking to make sure the Boatman's knife was still there, ensconced in its sheath. My heart was going a mile a minute and adrenalin heated me up as surely as an open fire. Then I moved fast, because if I didn't, my nerve would break and I'd be bolting down the street like a howling cartoon character. It also made Ziggi and Bela increase their own pace, and by the time my hand was reaching for the tarnished doorknob they too had reached the verandah.

I gave the door a push, and it surprised me by not squeaking. A pungent rush of decay rose to greet us as we stood shoulder to shoulder at the entrance and peered in. It was unexpectedly light too, pouring in through the doors at the back. The boards that had been nailed there last time had been torn off and thrown across the enormous deck. The interior had originally been a triumph of open-plan design: the left-hand side the lounge, dining room and kitchen, each large space once defined by the furniture that was no longer there. All that was left in the kitchen was the long chef's island, and above it a stainless steel rack where pots and pans used to hang. To the right, three doorless gaps ruptured the wall, leading into huge ex-bedrooms. Bela flicked on his torch and shone it across the debris to give us that extra bit of clarity. It certainly looked like there was a lot more garbage on the floorboards than last time.

'After you,' I said, gesturing. My gung-ho had been exhausted – and besides, Bela held a hefty Maglite that doubled very nicely as a cudgel. I moved behind him, and Ziggi brought up the rear. I'd seen him take his Taser out of the glove box, but I wasn't sure how much good it would do against whatever was – or hopefully *wasn't* – there. Stepping inside, I felt the craquelure of dried mud under my Docs.

I was a little surprised to see there were paintings still hanging, crooked on their hooks, brown tidemarks partway up some of the canvases.

The only out-of-the-ordinary thing was in the back bedroom: a stained mattress that hadn't been there previously, with a hillock of rubbish and dirt and twigs, looking like an outsized nest. Bits of it had been compressed, presumably by the weight of a heavy body.

'That's the same kind of thing I found in Donovan Baker's bed,' I said. 'Except bigger.'

Bela's head swung towards me, his gaze questioning, and I remembered I'd kept that information back. I'd been trying not to overwhelm him after he'd discovered the Greenills were gone. But he didn't attempt to extract more from me, not then. I moved closer and crouched down, then, grabbing a thin branch that looked marginally less grubby than the rest, poked about in the mound. I was about to give up when I saw a glimmer of gold picked out by the beam of Bela's flashlight. I dug a bit more and managed to hook the thing. I held it up.

It was a Rolex, that deep almost greenish gold, a traditional design best suited for a slim wrist – not really something a young man would buy for himself, but rather a gift imposed by an older man, perhaps a father. I flipped it over, checking for an inscription. No warm sentiments, no message, just the name: Donovan Baker, and a date two years ago; his sixteenth birthday present, probably worth more than Ziggi's cab, and discarded, neither needed nor wanted, and no longer fitting on a slender wrist in a life newly remade.

The knoll on the mattress heaved and gave a squeak—

It was only by sheer force of will that I kept myself from scaling the walls and clinging to the ceiling. I half-staggered to my feet and was pulled back by Bela and Ziggi as three of the biggest rats I'd ever seen burst forth, protesting the disturbance – and probably also the theft of their shiny-shiny-pretty-pretty. They reared up on hind legs, a nightmare soundtrack of screeching erupting from their toothy mouths. Ziggi hit one with a bolt from the Taser and the other two scampered away through a hole in the corner, leaving behind the scent of singed rat and the echo of their fury.

'We need to check downstairs,' said Bela.

I groaned. 'I knew you were going to say that.'

We didn't get far, just halfway down the internal staircase at the end of the kitchen. The sound of squeaking was overwhelming, and when Bela angled the Maglite towards what used to be a family room, he lit up a jumping, writhing sea of fur: rat city.

Everyone has their limits and we'd found ours.

Outside in the cold sunshine, the air was decidedly fresher and the sensation of having travelled to an outer suburb of hell slowly lessened. We all sipped peppermint tea from the Thermos David had handed me as I'd left home: a surprise, and an unexpected pleasure. I leaned against the hood of the cab, contemplating what I knew lay beneath the rug of rodents: a bright orange carpet, a monumental failure in taste in every way. I knew this because my face had been pressed into it just a few months ago as I fought for my life against the 'serker. My blood was probably embedded into the weave still. Identical carpet fibres had been left at the Greenill house and, now I had some context, in the car park the day David and I went bushwalking. We silently refilled our mugs; no one wanted to start the conversation.

In the end I bit the bullet. 'I think it's safe to say we've located Mr Baker's son, or his new digs, at least.'

Bela protested, 'That's crazy – we only found his watch, a trace of him. There's no evidence that he's the golem—'

'You think he's a victim?' I asked, disbelieving.

'Maybe.' But he didn't meet my gaze as he spoke.

'Bela,' I said gently, 'you saw what the golem did to those kids by the river. And there was nothing left of the Greenills: hair, jewellery, clothing – *everything* was absorbed. I don't think a Rolex is proof against that thing's digestion.' I examined my nails, scraped a stubborn bit of dirt from under one. 'And there was the beginnings of a nest in his bed at Baker's.'

'Maybe he's the one controlling the creature?' ventured Ziggi in a tone that acknowledged he was grasping at straws.

'You said it yourself,' I replied. 'He's a blank slate, precisely the kind of person who'd give himself up to a stronger will. It would take a much more forceful personality than Donovan. *If* the golem is being controlled at all, it's by someone else. Someone powerful.'

'Doesn't mean the boy's . . .' Bela trailed off, then said, 'That kind of magic isn't a simple enchantment, V, not something you buy at the corner spook shop. He's barely had contact with the Weyrd since his mother died.'

'He was trying to find his grandparents, the Nadasys,' I said, then, 'Wait – what do you mean, "barely had contact"?'

Again, he looked away.

'Bela' – I kept my voice low and even, though I felt my resolution to be nicer to him ebbing fast – 'what do you know about this? Is Anders Baker pulling your strings?'

'No one's pulling *anything* of mine and I don't owe *him*. I . . .' He paused.

'What's this boy to you? Tell me now, or I will become very unpleasant, and that's something neither of us wants.'

He kicked the grass at his feet and came to a decision. 'I knew his mother. She was a . . . friend. I promised I'd look out for her child. It's nothing to do with Anders; it's a matter of honour.'

I crossed my arms. 'So if you knew Dusana, you knew her father.'

He looked away.

'Then why the fuck didn't you say so before?' I yelled. 'I thought this was just another job, not something personal!'

'That shouldn't affect how you do your job. Does it matter?'

'Of course it bloody matters! The son of your "friend" goes missing after he's been trying to make contact with his Weyrd grandfather? The husband of your "friend" may be guilty of her murder? You knew these people and didn't think to offer this relevant information? Jesus!'

'Time out, you two,' said Ziggi. 'We won't get far if we're fighting among ourselves.'

'We won't get far if we keep secrets!' I shouted, but with marginally less volume. I pressed my fingers against the bridge of my nose and prayed for painkillers. 'So, have you seen him? Nadasy, I mean? Since he disappeared?'

'No.' Bela wiped his palms against his jeans. 'Vadim dropped out of sight a few months after Dusana died. We had been close once. He had . . . helped me a long time ago. When his daughter was gone he changed, became especially hateful of Normals. And yes, he blamed his son-in-law, but there was no evidence Baker had anything to do with the death.'

'Baker said Nadasy had cut his daughter off; that she'd become a pariah.'

Bela shook his head. 'It was Magda, she was the one who refused to speak to Dusana. Vadim kept in contact, and that drove a wedge between him and Magda. She left Australia.'

'Right. And where's she nowadays?'

'Dead — a road accident in the Swiss Alps maybe a year before

Dusana's death. I didn't know her very well. After that, there was just Dusana. Vadim doted on her.'

My stomach began to rumble and I realised it was well past midday. The hungries were threatening to make me say things I knew I'd regret. With a deep breath I reminded myself that Bela carried his history tightly rolled up inside. All his griefs and losses were well-hidden, but that didn't mean he didn't feel any of them. 'Okay. First of all, Ziggi, please find us somewhere for lunch, while *Zvezdomir's* having a *really* good think about everything he's neglected to tell us. *And by that I do mean everything.*'

Chapter Twenty-Two

After food, a thorough grilling and a fair bit of castigation, it turned out Bela really didn't know much more than he'd just told us. We went our separate ways, and I had Ziggi stop at the corner shop on the way home. When he drove off I headed over to Mel's, carrying the bottle of milk I'd borrowed from her earlier in the week.

As I wandered along the walkway, the hairs on the back of my neck stood to attention. The front door was open. I could see a discarded pair of Birkenstocks, and puddles of something dark and viscous-looking with flecks of heart-stopping orange in them. Moving carefully, I went inside, listening intently but hearing nothing. In the dim light I could see sticky footprints where someone had stepped in the puddles and splashed on the lounge room floor. I called Mel's name, but only the shadows answered.

I crouched and sniffed at the fluid: an iron tang. Some of it was blood, but not all. Some of it looked like dirty water and sludge.

I searched the rest of the house: three bedrooms, one treatment room, all redolent of bergamot and lavender and all empty. Cupboards neatly packed with clothes, blankets, linen and scented candles, massage oils, acupuncture needles, cups and other accoutrements required by any natural therapist. The bathroom was spotless and smelled of roses, with a multi-coloured pyramid of guest soaps next to the basin and several bottles of rainbow bath salts on the shelf.

I checked under beds and in wardrobes and went through drawers as if somehow the occupants might have shrunk and hidden there, but all for naught.

By the time I moved through the kitchen and out onto the tiny back deck overlooking the tidy yard, my throat was constricted. Even so, I charged down the stairs, yelling so loudly that I barely heard the little voice that piped from the other side of the fence: Lizzie was standing right where the land between the two properties had sunk and the palings were low enough for her to see over the top. Her face was pale; she obviously thought she was in trouble. I realised at once what she'd done: she'd snuck out to my hollowed-out tree with her books and dolls and some snackables – when I lifted her over the barrier and hugged her fiercely I smelled salt and vinegar, and her sweater was flecked with shards of crisps. Being disobedient looked like it had been the only thing that had saved her; scolding her was the last thing I was going to do.

'Where's your mum?' I asked, and she looked bewildered.

'Inside.'

I didn't have the heart to tell her that wasn't so. I put her back into my garden and said, 'Go to my front door. I'll be there in a second.'

Later that night, after Rhonda McIntyre's people had gone and Lizzie had taken refuge in my spare bedroom, I set wards around the house. There were already basic, everyday spells to keep out the general low-level magical shit you have to contend with – curses were easily repulsed, most unwanted visitors couldn't just waltz in – but I needed something more stringent, so nothing even vaguely Weyrd could enter. The new wards would bounce any intruder away and, if s/he continued to ignore them, s/he would be shredded by winds until s/he either sensibly gave up or was turned into a form of butter.

Unfortunately, it also meant neither Bela nor Ziggi would be able to cross the threshold. Alas, equally unfortunately, it didn't cover the golem. It was, however, the best I could do.

I sliced the palm of my left hand, the sinister one, and mixed the blood with salt and sulphur. I took a paintbrush and scripted the intricate symbols required to keep unearthly things from my door across the lintels and over the window. I baked four loaves of bread with stalks of lavender inside and buried one in each corner of the yard. Next, I took a piece of thick cartridge paper and wrote a spell that would keep the bearer safe on it in tiny letters.

I left it to dry and went outside. Ziggi was slumped behind the steering wheel, ostensibly asleep, but I figured at least one of his eyes was open. Bela was waiting beside the fence. We sat on the footpath while we discussed what might have made this attack different, and what Mel's chances of survival were.

'You think she's still alive?' he asked.

'I really don't know. But there are three sets of footprints in there, one barefoot and the other two sneakered. That blood's not right either – it's not human, or not entirely.' I scratched at my cheek where the wounds were scabbing over and starting to itch. 'Something went wrong, whatever the visitors intended.'

'She might have been—'

'I know. I'm preparing myself for that . . .' I shuddered. 'If that's the case, I don't know how I'll ever be able to tell Lizzie. So until I know for sure, I'm going to believe Mel's alive.'

'I'm always amazed by your optimism.' But I knew he wished there was even a shred of doubt about the Greenills' disappearance, that he might have some hope to hang onto. We didn't speak for a while until he came out with, 'I've been thinking about your dead siren.' At my look he added, 'The angel?'

'Yes?'

'That's new.'

'What part of it? And please get to your point quickly, I'm ageing rapidly here.'

'Angels don't like sirens.'

'They don't like us either.'

'I mean, they *really* dislike them, as in "more than anything on a very long list". They seldom even reside in the same areas if they can help it.' He answered my questioning look with, 'Sirens have wings and no need of faith. Angels have been cut off for a long time. It makes them bitter.'

I opened my mouth to ask more, but was distracted by the haunting sound of Lizzie's sobbing.

'We'll talk later,' he said, but by the time Lizzie finally calmed and went back to sleep, he was gone.

The parchment had dried. I folded it into a tiny origami bird and enclosed it in my grandmother's glass-fronted locket – Lizzie'd always loved it. She was curled in the middle of the bed in the spare room, as if the linen moat might provide protection. Gently, I slid the pendant over her neck, thinking her asleep, but when I sat back her bright eyes were upon me.

'Hey,' I said.

'Where's my mum?'

'I don't know, honey.'

'You'll find out, right?'

'I'll try.'

'You found me.'

'Yeah. I did. I promise I'll find your mum,' I said, writing a cheque I wasn't sure I'd be good for. I kissed her on the forehead, wishing I could ensure a dreamless sleep, but I knew she was in for the sorts of nights I'd had after Grigor's arrest: fitful napping fractured by bad dreams that either seemed endless or returned you to wakefulness with a shriek, sure there was a monster under the bed until you remembered why you were upset – and then reality felt infinitely worse.

I tucked her ancient teddy bear in beside her and pulled the covers up. Though Mel's sister was notoriously difficult to find on those rare occasions when she was actually needed, and though she really, *really* wasn't wanted, police procedure said she had to be looked for, so McIntyre's team were trying to trace Rose in case she could help with enquiries. I was absolutely certain Mel wouldn't want Rose to be taking care of Lizzie, though – and even if Rose wanted to, which was highly unlikely, I sure as hell had no intention of handing the kid over.

The kitchen was cold and I wrapped my fingers around my mug of hot chocolate, trying to absorb the warmth. I wasn't convinced that whatever had come a-calling was really after Mel. This wasn't an ordinary home invasion. No one had any reason to take her. She had no enemies – her ex was still in Thailand and the worst Rose would have done was steal her wallet. I couldn't imagine a disgruntled client doing anything like this.

Poor Mel.

On closer inspection, the flecks of bright orange in the goop on the floor had looked very much like carpet fibres. But I took comfort – a very tenuous, anorexic kind of comfort – from the fact that Mel's shoes had been left behind; as I'd said to the boys hours ago, the golem hadn't been leaving anything on its plate, and those Birkenstocks had been thrown off in a struggle. As far I knew, I was the only person who'd had a chance to fight against the golem, and I was still alive. It was proof of nothing, really, but I had to hold onto *something*. Strangely, it was easier to believe Mel'd been taken to get at *me*, and if that really was the case, she had no value if she was dead. Ergo, she was currently safe. Maybe they'd come for me and I hadn't been home, so they'd tried for Lizzie, and not being able to find her, had taken her mother instead. That would be a sign that whoever it was knew that both mother and child meant something to me.

My phone rang. *David*. He'd headed back to his own place after he'd seen me off, and I had to admit that I'd been somewhat put out, walking in and not finding him in my home, even though I *knew* he'd gone. Then the thought that he hadn't been here when the kidnappers came to visit helped me get over that one.

'Hey,' he said, and hearing his voice almost made me cry, though I fought the impulse. It felt like he'd twisted open a valve and let out all the tension and worry I'd been holding in. I told him first about Mel and then we talked about small things, normal things, tiptoeing around all the weird shit of my life that was going to flow into his if we kept seeing each other.

'So, date night?' he asked, which made me smile. *Brave man*.

'I'm going to be a bit jammed up for a while with this surrogate mum deal.'

'If you ever need a babysitter—'

'Got any experience with kids?'

'None.'

'Yeah, I could tell from the way you offered so willingly.'

'You've got to give me points for being helpful.'

'I bet you've got a badge for assisting little old ladies across the street.'

'Why did I call you again?'

'Because you missed me and in spite of everything I'm adorable.'

'Yeah, no.' He blew a raspberry. 'How about dinner over here tomorrow night? Mainly because your cupboards are so bare the mice are planning to protest the conditions.'

'I choose to ignore your facetious commentary and graciously say *thank you.*'

I hung up and ran my hands through my hair, which needed a wash – I could have sworn I still smelled river muck. There was a good chance the odour, like the mud itself, was invasive: it got into the cracks and stayed there, hidden in plain sight.

I looked at the phone's screen and saw a missed call. I didn't recognise the number, but hit call-back and got the answering machine for Dinky Darlings Day Care. It was nine p.m. so I figured it could probably wait – after all, Ligeia had said the baby was safe. If Mrs Tinkler was calling, it was only because she wanted something, and I wasn't feeling generous.

'An angel?'

'An angel,' I said for the second time. We'd rehashed Mel's disappearance and now I was reporting my progress, or lack thereof, on the Kallos case.

The detective inspector didn't look good. Her office at Headquarters was a corner one with big windows on the sixth floor, overlooking the junction of Roma and Makerston Streets. Her career might have stalled, but the digs were testament to the fact she still had some clout, although she didn't appear to appreciate it. The bin was overflowing, unfiled paperwork teetered on tops of cabinets and her in-tray looked like it had vomited all over the desk. Any kind of corporate uniformity had been totally defeated by the force of the owner's personality. I was a little in awe.

McIntyre's leather chair made comfortable groans every time she shifted. I, on the other hand, was perched on the edge of a visitor's seat designed by the people who furnished the Spanish Inquisition offices; it wasn't meant to encourage long stays. But Rhonda looked worse than I felt. Her skin was a decided shade of grey, the shadows under her eyes had turned into bruises and her hair looked thinner, as did her face – I'd have sworn her cheekbones were trying to push their way out. And she'd been coughing a lot, especially when I'd first said 'an angel'.

But I didn't get the derision I'd expected. The small gold cross around her neck gleamed at me as if to point out what an idiot I was, but I knew full well that icons didn't necessarily correlate to faith. I hadn't ever pegged the inspector as much of a believer, but maybe she had hidden depths. Maybe she was a dyed-in-the-wool disciple and that was why she was so impatient with all things Weyrd: they were an irrefutable big finger to the traditional tenets of Creation, a sure sign that the Bible had more than a few missing chapters. Or maybe I was misreading things entirely and she was just feeling so sick she didn't have the energy to be angry any more.

'So, where does one find an angel? And more importantly, how does one detain and question one?' she asked.

'I bet it's a bitch trying to get the cuffs on them.'

'I repeat: *where does one find an angel?*'

'Don't know. They're not like the sirens, who are visible. As far as I can tell, angels are unseen, unless they want it otherwise.'

'Can they be detected any other way?'

'Based on my brief research last night, only by the crazy, the blessed, the dying, and sometimes by the Weyrd and the mythical.'

'Can you see them?'

'No matter what you think, I don't actually fit comfortably into any of those categories. So no.'

'*Any* idea where to start?'

'Like I said, they mostly gather over sacred places, where there are a lot of the faithful, so I'll try churches. But if he doesn't want me to see him it won't matter where I go. Besides, as far as I can tell, Tobit was here to be with Serena, not to do anything miraculous. I'm assuming Brisbane already has its own angel. One more added to the mix shouldn't make much difference, at least if it's just a couple feeding, but I don't know if Brisneyland could support a whole host for any long period.'

'You've got a faithometre?'

'I wish.'

'Any of your strange little friends got a clue?'

'I am planning to do some polite asking today.' I shrugged. 'McIntyre, I've never dealt with angels. You need to remember these things don't really like us . . . and they're not *fluffy*.'

She closed her eyes and leaned her head back – the exhalation she gave sounded like steam pouring from an engine – then rubbed her eyes. Her fists thumped on the blotter and the assorted pens and stapler jumped. Finally, she calmed and took a deep breath. 'Anything else? Anything on the kid?'

'Nothing so far – apart from the old siren trying to warn me off.' I hated admitting that. 'And I had a missed call last night from that day care centre; I rang this morning and couldn't get anyone to admit to making it, but the lovely Mrs Tinkler hasn't reported for work.' Both Bela and McIntyre had done some digging on Mrs T., but nothing Weyrd or otherwise had popped up. 'So perhaps—'

'You want me to send someone around to check out her place?'

'Gee, Rhonda, would you? I'm a little busy, what with looking for angels and all.'

She gave me the long flat stare that regularly cracked the men and women under her command before remembering it never had much of an effect on me. Instead, she started drumming her fingers on the desk and almost relaxed.

We'd reached an impasse, and there were neither doughnuts nor danishes to keep me longer.

At the door I turned back. 'I . . . I don't know if we're going to find the baby, Rhonda.'

'Not like you to give up.'

'I'm not giving up,' I said, setting my jaw. 'It's just, if the old lady was telling the truth, then someone's got her and is looking after her. They're also doing a good job of hiding her. If she was lying, if Calliope's dead . . . well, there're a lot of places a body can be disposed of.'

'And her mother's killer? Find the killer, find the baby?'

'Maybe. Maybe not. Maybe, find the baby, find the killer. Maybe find the father, find the baby. Maybe find the baby, still don't find the killer and vice versa.'

We sighed simultaneously.

'Go on then,' she said. 'You're not doing much good here.'

'I know you really like me, McIntyre.'

'Keep telling yourself that.'

I was barely out of the office before the coughing started again.

Chapter Twenty-Three

'Where the fuck is my niece?'

It wasn't exactly a refreshing change from 'hello', especially when spittle from the woman's mouth made it an impressive distance to land on my jacket. She couldn't have done better if she'd been trying. Not for the first time, I *really* wished I could hex.

So much for going home to drop off much-needed groceries before heading out again; I should've known that was a rotten plan. But at least I knew where Rose Wilkes was now, and it was obviously providing some entertainment value, as Ziggi'd climbed out of the cab to watch. Up close, she looked a lot older than Mel, and the aroma of stale booze travelled on her breath and wafted off her skin.

I tilted my head and stared and she began to fidget, as if suddenly realising her approach maybe hadn't been ideal.

'Where's Lizzie? I'm here—' She broke off to hiccough, then burp: a warning hint of vomit soon to follow.

I took a couple of precautionary sidesteps.

'I'm here to take care of my niece.'

'Rose, you have difficulty taking care of yourself.'

She swung at me and I swayed back; she missed me, smacked her fist into the doorframe and lost her balance, going down like a sack of potatoes. It took me a moment to realise she'd passed out.

She clearly knew Mel was gone, which meant the cops must've

found her. I noticed she'd had no word of concern for her sister. If she wanted to look after Lizzie, she must've thought there'd be some sort of financial benefit to her. There were fairly strict limits on my tolerance at the best of times and they'd been well and truly reached. I yelled, 'Little help?' to my driver and went back inside to grab Mel's spare keys from the hook in the kitchen.

With the limp, beery-smelling lump of Aunty Rose over Ziggi's shoulder, we went next door, ducking under the blue and white chequered crime scene tape announcing POLICE and giving the Crime Stoppers contact number. We dumped Rose unceremoniously on the leather couch and I covered her with a throw against the cold. I didn't like the idea of leaving her unsupervised in Mel's home, but I was even less enamoured of the thought of her being in *mine*, supervised or otherwise.

'You have interesting friends,' said Ziggi as I pulled the door closed behind us.

'If she's my friend, I'm in more trouble than I thought.'

I was pretty sure Rose would be safe; in a clear-cut case of shutting the gate after the horse had bolted, I'd set a few basic wards over Mel's place after she'd been taken. It was unlikely anything or anyone would come back there since they already had what they wanted, but frankly, anyone who took on Rose Wilkes deserved what they got.

'So, no ransom demand?'

'No contact, no nothing. I think taking her was just a warning to me – a kind of ambiguous warning, 'cause I don't know what I am or am not supposed to do.'

'What are you *gonna* do?'

'What I always do: my best impersonation of a bull in a china shop until someone tires of the damage and gives me what I want.' I stretched, then pointed to the cab. 'Let us set sail for the Gold Coast.'

'The traffic will be murder. You can't just call him?'

'Sometimes the personal touch is required, my good man. Add an inconvenience fee to your mileage claim.'

He grinned slowly, as if the idea had never occurred to him before but he liked it very much indeed.

The Concrete Blonde was nowhere to be seen and Anders Baker's mansion looked unattended, waiting only for a good breeze to push it over. I pressed the buzzer a few times, then peered through the glass panels on either side of the door. There was a quick rat-like darting across the foyer and someone peeked from behind the mermaid fountain.

'I can see you, Mr Baker,' I yelled. 'Don't make me break something.'

I waited a full thirty seconds before surveying the garden for nice hefty rocks. He must have seen the intent on my face because he gave in: the door cracked a sliver, security chain still in place, and Baker's head filled the gap. I pushed hard, and the very expensive, very sturdy links snapped, a piece shearing off to hit my client. He stumbled back as a red line opened up on his face and began to seep like a bloody tear.

'Sorry,' I said, and I almost was.

Stepping inside, I got a whiff of his body odour, and then I really was sorry as I started to cough: the stench of unwashed male, rank booze and boxers that had probably witnessed an unfortunate accident. How had he fallen so far so fast? What did he know now that he hadn't before? I was beginning to have a good idea.

'What do you want?' he snarled.

'Mr Baker, I'm sensing a chill in your welcome.'

'I don't want you here.'

'You're a contrary bloke: one minute you simply *must* have me on the case, the next you're positively uncontactable.'

'Tell fucking Tepes I don't want this to go any further.'

'You can't tell him yourself? I'm reporting in as requested.' I fished the Rolex from my pocket and dangled it in front of him. He made a grab and childishly, I snatched it away. 'Where's your guard?'

'Gone.'

'Did she jump, or was she pushed?'

'Bitch hasn't shown up for work.'

I feared the reason and hoped the Concrete Blonde had put up a good fight before the golem got her. 'Mr Baker, has your son come home?'

He shook his head, but I'm nothing if not persistent; besides, it's all in the phrasing. 'Did you *see* your son?'

A hesitation, then what might have been a muffled '*Yes.*'

'And when was that?'

'Last night.'

So that was the end of the Concrete Blonde. Baker made another grab for the watch and this time I let him have it.

'Did it *look* like him?'

He sobbed. 'No, Christ, no! It – *he* – said things . . . I couldn't understand much of it, but I understood enough. It was Donovan.'

So the golem could still talk. Was there a house on this man-made island or in the mainland suburbs where no trace of the inhabitants would ever be found? How had the golem managed to get to the Gold Coast and back? Train or bus didn't really seem like an option, so it must be being chauffeured around; that would also explain how it had made it to the National Park, and Pullenvale.

'When did you realise he was changing?'

'I didn't – not until last night . . .' He trailed off and started putting his son's watch on, rubbing it as though to smooth the metal. 'Maybe it's not him – it could be someone else, someone pretending, couldn't it?'

But he knew as well as I did that the thing was his son. Donovan had whispered to him, the words of an angry child who'd finally found the strength to rebel against a loathed parent. My only surprise was that he hadn't taken Anders Baker out – then again, the rage required to answer back didn't necessarily correlate to patricide.

He began wheedling, 'But you can *help* him, can't you? He'll get better, won't he?'

Reluctantly, I said, 'I think it's too late. He's been transforming for too long. What's beneath – the real Donovan – is being eaten away. Soon he might not be able to change back at all. You're lucky to still be alive, Mr Baker.'

His eyes bulged, his head jerked, a panicky movement. 'He wouldn't hurt *me*.'

'He's hurt a lot of other people. If he survives, he'll be brought before the Council – or what's left of them.'

'That bunch of *freaks*! My son doesn't have to answer to them!' His face twisted with a hatred so intense it was difficult to believe he'd once married into the Weyrd. But then, maybe he'd only learned to hate them after he'd said *I do*.

'A Normal court won't be able to try him, but he needs to answer for what he's done.' And I saw from his expression that was exactly what he'd been counting on: a Normal court, somewhere he could influence the outcome. So Dame Rumour had been correct; he'd purchased justice before. If he'd got away with murder, why shouldn't his son?

'Did Donovan contact his grandfather?'

He looked at me blankly. 'I told you before, my father's dead.'

'Not your father. Your wife's.'

He paled, his lips thinning. 'Why would he do that? He knows nothing about them.'

Maybe not from you, I thought. 'You said it yourself: he was lonely. Mr Baker, how stupid *are* you? It's only natural he'd seek out family members.'

'*I'm his family*,' he shouted, and when I didn't answer, he felt the need to go on, 'He didn't know *anything* about Nadasy.'

'Well, someone told him.'

'Who?'

I shrugged, ignoring the vibration in my pocket. 'Look, even if your son could be changed back, he might not *want* to be. Whatever you know about Nadasy, you'd better share. Is he alive? Have you seen him recently?'

He began to bawl, inconsolable as a child. Shaking his head, he cried, 'He's taken my son, my only boy, hasn't he?'

'In all fairness, you did kill his daughter. But I have to ask, why didn't he just slaughter you?'

He snorted, eyes sparking up. 'I showed that old fucker! He'll never see his precious little girl again, but she's mine forever.' He leaned forward, snakelike, and spat, 'And that's all you fucking need to know!'

My back felt tingly, the way it does when something with eight legs is taking a day-trip along the spine, and I looked at him in disgust. 'Mr Baker, a friend of mine is missing – I'm not saying you're involved, but if I find out you or Donovan had anything to do with it, I swear I'll send your son back in a Jiffy bag.'

As we pulled up outside David's building, my mobile buzzed again, like a vaguely annoyed wasp. It was McIntyre, telling me she'd had the blood work from Mel's place rushed through and, consequently, I owed her big time. The red stuff wasn't Mel's — she was A positive — and whatever had spilled was, well, not quite anything. It was corrupted, mixed with mud and deteriorated from age.

After she'd finished describing the analysis, she asked if I'd had any luck on either angel or baby front. My negative answer displeased her, but I didn't have anything else to leaven it.

Before he took off I shared the latest with Ziggi and asked him to let Bela know. I just couldn't face talking to my boss that evening. Then I made my way inside the complex, thinking it might be wise to set some protective spells around this place, too.

I'd barely even knocked when the door flew open and a wide-eyed Lizzie appeared, giving a damn good impersonation of a child who'd temporarily forgotten her sole parent was missing.

'Oh, Verity! You won't *believe* what he's got here!'

'I probably will, honey.'

She'd obviously been communing with the Wii. The image on the TV was paused, partially pixelated, and I raised an eyebrow at David, who was hastily trying to hide the fact that (a) he'd been playing a game in which a cartoon cat with a handbag beat up Godzilla, and (b) he'd been losing badly to an eight-year-old. I didn't say anything. Then I noticed two mugs sitting on the kitchen bench, cold grounds in the bottom. I frowned.

'You didn't give her coffee, did you?'

Lizzie answered for him, throwing the words over her shoulder like an ice bath, 'Bela came to visit and the boys had es-peress-os.' Oblivious to her bombshell, she switched to single-player mode and continued smashing Tokyo.

I felt like someone had stuck a steak knife under one of my

fingernails. I looked at David for clarification, while I auto-corrected Lizzie. 'That's Mr Tepes to you.'

'We had a chat about guy things. He left this for you.' David's tone was carefully neutral; it was never easy to meet the predecessor. In my defence, we had briefly covered the topic of Bela when we'd had 'the talk', but still . . . also, I might have glossed over precisely how handsome my ex was. On the one hand, if Bela ruined this for me, I would kill him. On the other, if David was the kind of guy who was rattled by Bela, then I'd kill him. He handed me an off-white envelope with my name in old-fashioned cursive script scored deeply into the thick paper. I slid it into my pocket, saving any nasty surprises for later.

'So.'

'A bit Vlad the Impaler, isn't he?' David tried for flippant but the snark was there, oh, it was there, just enough to make me relax and grin.

'Jealous?'

'No. Judgemental. Look, I can't say I like the idea of you working for your ex, but it's not my choice.' He caressed my face. 'Besides, I trust you.'

'You're jealous.' I was gloating a little, I admit. Then I put my arms around his neck and was relieved to feel him pull me closer. We held each other tight, watching the stars pulse and sparkle in the sky outside his window.

Chapter Twenty-Four

'So, Zvezdomir Tepes, do we need to talk about boundaries? Specifically, you *not* visiting my new boyfriend.' I did my best to keep my voice level, but I wasn't sure I'd succeeded.

Bela's brows went up, black caterpillars on their way towards his hairline.

'How did you even know where he lived?'

'Ziggi.'

I glared, and Bela looked uncomfortable. 'Don't be too hard on him – I bribed him.'

Of course: my faithful sidekick's only weakness. How sad it wasn't some sort of heroic weakness; instead, I'd been sold down the river for a piece of chocolate cake. Okay, so *very* good chocolate cake, but cake nonetheless.

'Bela, listen, I need to have a life, an ordinary life outside of the work I do for you. Or at least part of one. And I need high fences around that part of my existence. Don't screw this up for me, or so help me, I will—'

'I wasn't . . . That certainly wasn't my intention.' He scratched his head. 'I wanted to check on Lizzie, to ask her a few more questions.'

'Stuff you think I wouldn't have asked?'

We were sitting at a McDonalds, which wasn't my first or even twelfth choice of venue, but Lizzie had begged for an Egg McMuffin and I couldn't bear to say 'no' to a currently motherless kid. Lizzie, having gobbled her food at frightening speed, was now running around the play area, making friends. Bela was glaring at a pile of hash browns as if he couldn't quite understand what they were doing on his plate and I was picking over my pancakes with not much appetite. Neither of us were drinking the black sludge.

'She believes in you, you know. Utterly,' said Bela, gazing at her as she climbed up the slide instead of using it in the more traditional manner. 'That's why she's not *too* upset. Yet.'

'What do you mean?'

'She told me so. She misses her mother, but she absolutely believes you'll bring Mel back. I think she's told herself her mum's away, just for a bit; she has no doubt she'll return.'

'No pressure then.' I shuffled in my seat, which gave McIntyre's office furniture a run for its money in the discomfort stakes. 'In other news, Baker's seen his son and knows the boy's not the way he used to be. His security guard is missing, too – probably another victim.'

He was silent, but at least this time he didn't deny what Donovan had become.

'And Bela, someone has to be helping the golem move around. There's a fundamental lack of tunnels between here and the coast, and here and Pullenvale too. And it has to be someone confident of their hold over the creature, not scared of being eaten. Do you have any reason to think it's not Vadim Nadasy?'

'Other than no one's seen hide nor hair of him for roughly fifteen years?'

'Other than that, yeah.' Lizzie was hanging upside down from the monkey bars, her face going red. 'Did you look for him when he went missing?'

'Of course – he'd been my friend, V. He helped me out of a

backwards Eastern European country filled with people who liked to shove stakes through *anything* they didn't understand. We lost contact for many years, but when he wanted to move his family here, he found me and of course I assisted.' He sighed and looked at Lizzie again. 'When Dusana died I tried to talk to him, but he didn't want to listen to anyone. There was no proof she'd been murdered and the Council refused to let him go after Anders. They told him to wait, see how the inquest came out . . . he got no satisfaction there, but by the time the verdict was handed down something had changed. I don't know why, but he let it drop.

'A while after that, Vadim disappeared. All I could discover was that he'd purchased a one-way flight to Budapest. His arrival was logged by Customs there, and then he immediately dropped out of sight. I enquired about him, on and off, for a couple of years, but he was gone, and he'd left no trace.'

'He could have come back, though, right? He's loaded? So little things like international borders aren't going to stop someone like him getting where he wants to go.'

'Very true. Vadim was always very persuasive, and on the right kind of mind even the slightest mesmerist power can work.'

'If he's that persuasive and Donovan's that weak-willed, it's a match made somewhere creepy.' I flicked my cardboard cup distractedly and almost upended it. 'You didn't know he owned the house at Chelmer? You didn't know that when we went there the first time?'

'I didn't know, V, truly. Believe me, if I had, I'd have been more careful. Vadim was a mage of considerable force and I wouldn't have put it past him to booby-trap the place.'

'He didn't need to; he'd brought the 'serker through. It mightn't have been for us specifically — maybe it was just like a big fuck-off guard dog.'

'You're probably correct.'

'What about Baker? Why are you working for him?'

'Strictly speaking, I'm not. This isn't – *wasn't* – a Council matter until Adriana . . . I got to know Anders pretty well. I didn't like him, but that didn't stop me feeling sorry for him. Dusana . . . she wasn't very nice.'

'The fact he'd probably killed her didn't annoy you a little?'

'You want to hear this or not?'

'Okay, okay.' I raised my hands in surrender and buttoned my lip like a three-year-old.

'There was no evidence, V. He appeared to be genuinely cut up over her death, and I helped because of the child. No matter what, Dusana loved her little boy, and he was devastated when she died. I used to talk to him. He . . . he thought his mother was going to come back. He asked me to bring her home. And I couldn't.' He paused, then said quietly, 'I failed.'

It was the gentlest, the saddest I'd ever seen him. He'd been upset about Adriana, but he'd also been angry. In that moment, he was just sad. He was dealing with losses that I'd known nothing about. Believing him to be heartless had made disliking him easier for a long while, but he wasn't and I knew it really; he wouldn't have set Ziggi to watch over me otherwise. He wouldn't have kept an eye on Grigor's daughter otherwise. I thought about how Baker's obsession with his deceased wife hadn't dimmed with time; maybe Bela's sense of failure was equally tenacious.

He added, 'I did try to keep in contact with the boy, but his father made it pretty clear that was not desirable.'

'So when Baker turned up asking for help, you saw a chance for redemption?'

He nodded.

I changed the subject. 'Ever met an angel?'

'V, this thing with the sirens – can't it wait a little? The golem needs to be our priority—'

'Multitasking is an essential quality, Bela. I know we have a lot to deal with, but do you really want more bird-lady corpses littering the city?' I stared at him until he shook his head. 'So why is the angel Tobit here? Are there more? 'Cause the way those sirens were ripped apart, I'm thinking many hands were making light work. What do you know about angels?'

'I met some in Byzantium, a very long time ago. They weren't as grumpy as they are nowadays, but back then they still had hope of being called home.'

'And they're grumpy because—?'

'They lost track of their boss sometime after the Middle Ages.'

'And when you say "boss" you mean "God"; and when you say "lost" you mean . . .?'

'I mean *lost*. Fewer and fewer of the angelic choirs were getting directions from On High, and eventually they stopped altogether. The Archangels tried to maintain some kind of order, but there was no hiding the fact that the body was having trouble surviving without the head. No one's really sure when it happened, but divinely inspired writing has been thin on the ground ever since. Whatever created them – and I'm not saying it was any kind of deity, no matter what *their* apocrypha may say – deserted them and left good-sized chips on their . . . wings.'

'Stranded angels?' I said, amazed. 'As lost as the rest of us, and faith keeps declining, and so do they?'

He nodded. 'Don't forget they think they're superior, better than everyone and every*thing* else. They can't accept that they've fallen, that the world has moved on. They tend to roam, looking for meaning, for something to prop up their self-worth – quests, stuff to *do*. They're looking for a god.'

'And they don't like sirens?'

'Congratulations, V – you've mastered the art of the understatement. Angels are *bound* by a belief in their own mythology; their writings, rules and stories chain them inextricably to their lord and master, to his will, because they believe *implicitly* that he raised them above all others. They accepted the binding because they were *unique*. But well before the Creator got bored and went wandering there came the off-cuts, the misbegottens, the so-called *mistakes* from the stray enchantments flying around.'

'All the making, all the magic, as if someone had forgotten to turn off the tap?' I guessed. 'Every mythical beast from the ancient world sprang forth: cyclops, dragons, lycanthropes, manticores, mermaids, rocs, rusalkas, unicorns, vampires, water monkeys, wendigos, zilants and zombies . . . The Weyrd things.' There was no black and white in matters of dogma, no matter how much churches would like it to be that simple. Faith, any sort of faith, was multicoloured.

'All of whom the angels found annoying and worthy of a good deal of contempt, but nothing roused their fury, their jealousy, their envy until—'

'The sirens,' I breathed.

'The sirens: equal in beauty, in voice, in *flight*. But beings with no obligations, who recognised no rules; they served no will but their own.'

'Sibling rivalry.'

'Angels do not admit to envy; they think it beneath them. However, I've read some of their jottings and they've hated the winged women since Adam was a boy. The two just don't mix *at all*. Though angelic numbers have dropped, the sirens have flourished, comparatively speaking. They're arrogant, free, happy as Larry – and blessed, without any cost.'

'Why would an angel fall in love with a siren?'

'Not every species is filled with bigoted psychos.' He smiled. 'Romeo and Juliet with wings?'

'And we know how well that turned out for the kids.' I scratched tentatively at the half-healed cut on my temple. 'If there are more than one, more than Tobit, why are they here? Would they be attacking sirens just for the fun of it?'

He was quiet for a moment, considering. 'Angels aren't really fun-focused. I think the answer is Serena's and Tobit's child: a rare and unparallelled thing.'

He was right. The baby was the key, somehow. I just needed to find her. 'They feed off faith the way you feed off people's energy?'

'Similar,' he said reluctantly. He'd never liked to discuss the mechanics of his Weyrdness, it felt too personal, too private.

'Are you related?'

That made him laugh. 'I'd be a very poor angel.'

I couldn't argue there. 'I'd better get Lizzie home.'

'And you'd better organise your babysitter for tomorrow too.'

'Am I going somewhere?'

'The Council – what remains of it – wants to talk to you.'

'Well, that can't be good.'

'It seldom is.' He stood. 'Ziggi will pick you up at six p.m.'

'No exhortation to behave myself?'

'Would it do any good?' he asked bleakly.

'It might if you asked nicely,' I said, which surprised us both.

'Oh.' He pushed a lock of black hair out of his eyes. 'And did your new boyfriend give you that note, or did he burn it in case it was a love letter?'

'You're an idiot. I got it.' But I'd forgotten, and it was still in my jacket pocket. I tore the flap open and drew out a piece of parchment, thicker and older than even the best I sometimes used, with age spots dotting its surface. I felt bad about crushing it and tried to smooth it flat on the table.

The sketch was done in charcoal and coloured chalk: a portrait, head and torso of a young woman wearing an old-fashioned headdress, a kind of gabled cap decorated with what looked like seed pearls. The pendant at her throat was a bird-and-shield, strung on a thick black ribbon, and her earrings were baroque pearls. Her dress had a square neckline, tight bodice and tiny waist embellished with an elaborate stomacher, again the same intricate bird-and-shield design . . . *and identical to the seals of the wine bottles in the Ascot house cellar.* All around her had been shaded, as if she sat in shadow. She smiled, her expression mocking, as if she knew better than the watcher, better than everyone. It wouldn't have bothered me as much if she hadn't been so familiar.

It was the Winemaker.

She was younger, *much* younger. Her skin was smooth, unblemished, but those were her pale blue eyes, hinted at with a stroke of chalk, those were her cheekbones, the set of the head. And all of her jewellery was now a cold, hard, congealed lump in a desk drawer at home. I looked up at Bela, waved the parchment helplessly. He sat back down again.

'All your yelling at the Chelmer house on Tuesday made me wonder if I wasn't being pigheaded, and as a result, missing something important. I thought about Vadim, and then Magda. I can't say I remember her having any dealings with Grigor back in the old days, but she always did like using go-betweens. I found *that* and showed it to Lizzie while your boyfriend was powdering his nose.'

I ignored the jibe. I couldn't believe she hadn't mentioned it, the little monkey – that she hadn't woken from sleep with nightmares screaming after her. She really was incredibly resilient. 'Where's this from?' I whispered.

'Papers from Nadasy's office. I had to clear out his home when he disappeared. I didn't keep much, but this was amongst them.'

'It's the Winemaker.'

'It's Magda Nadasy.'

'Less dead at the time than reports would have had us believe.' I frowned. 'Why isn't this erased? Everything else has been taken out by whatever spell she set.'

He shrugged. 'Its age? It might not be something she thought to include in the enchantment – she might not have made it far-reaching enough. It's hard to remember every trace we leave in life, and she was probably only thinking of modern records being here. There was no reason to assume a Rembrandt sketch would be lying around her estranged husband's discarded documents.'

'Right. So if Vadim Nadasy is behind the whole golem thing, I killed his wife—'

'Yes, you did.'

'But again, if it's Nadasy, then *why* is Anders Baker still alive? What's he holding that's staying Nadasy's hand?'

'Add it to the list of things we don't know.' Bela gave his hash browns one last unforgiving look. My pancakes could have been used to line a rubber room.

Bela gave us a lift home; Ziggi needed a break, not to mention a chance to sleep somewhere other than the front seat of a vehicle. I mulled over angelic hatred for sirens and what a mating of the two species might have produced, while Lizzie sang along to some pop earworm on the radio, a Britney or a Taylor or a Jessie, that Bela – less grudgingly than I'd expected – tuned in to for her. Calliope was presumably normal enough to go to the crèche, so no chicken legs. I wondered about her wings. Her mother must have bound them, but what happened when Serena was killed? Had her magic died with her, or was there something more tenuous about such witchery?

'Shit, shit, shit,' I said in frustration.

'Mum says you shouldn't swear,' came a small voice.

'Me in particular, or adults in general?'

'You know, people.'

'Uh huh.' We drove past a school as all the kids started tumbling out onto the playground for recess. Vacation time had obviously ended with me none the wiser. We non-parents usually revelled in our ignorance of school terms, but I had new responsibilities now. 'Hey, shouldn't you be at school?'

She blushed and looked away.

'I'm calling your principal, young lady. Who is that, by the way?'

Bela snorted.

Chapter Twenty-Five

'Interesting décor. A certain *je ne sais quoi* to it.'

The *je ne sais quoi* was actually excessive amounts of chintz, doilies, hall tables, sideboards, woven rugs, wood panelling, coat racks, umbrella stands and vases containing dusty silk flowers. Essentially, it was an antique store with no cash register. Ziggi was out in the taxi, apparently not good enough to meet the Inner Circle. We waited in a small parlour just inside the front door which was dark and cool and smelled of mothballs and incense. Two large Weyrd, each roughly the size of double-door refrigerators, stood at attention in the hall; in my head I'd named them Hairy Jerry and Monobrow Mike.

'We've only had access to this place in the last couple of years, so no one knows about it except me and the Council,' Bela said.

'And me. And them.' I looked meaningfully at the heavies, who ignored me Coldstream Guard style; I kind of wanted to poke them but I doubted they shared the restraint of their martial counterparts.

'*Yes.*' Bela rolled his eyes and checked that his gold cufflinks were perfectly aligned with the pristine cuffs of his perfectly tailored shirt and his perfectly tailored Armani suit. Though my contrarian instincts had urged otherwise, I'd once again dressed as presentably as I could manage, though honestly, my wardrobe was getting a bit thin. My pinstriped trouser suit in light grey was a classic cut, so no one could really tell how old it was. The rebel in me won out when it came to footwear: black Docs with red roses embroidered on the sides.

I looked around the room again. This was a pretty good hiding place – after all, who'd look for the Weyrd Council in a *rectory*? The golem had breezed through magical wards and protections, but sometimes holy ground presented barriers that things which had started out as human couldn't – or wouldn't – cross. Maybe it was a genuine mystical barricade or maybe it was just in the mind, playing on every bit of religious mumbo jumbo stuck in the psyche. St Barbara's Church, located in the far-flung suburb of Waterford, ministered to a small flock of devout ageing dowagers, repentant old men and a few very enthusiastic youngsters. The house was big and creaky, once a seminary designed to hold about twenty priests. The encroachment of worldly things meant it hadn't been able to fill its quota of blokes-in-training for a long time.

Our host, Father Tony Caldero, had been a member of the Vatican's adjuristine-exorcism squads. That either made him an unlikely ally, or at least the sort of man who understood there were more things in Heaven and Earth than were dreamed of in a tidy philosophy. Bela had explained the situation to him and he'd quickly realised that the golem was a threat to both Weyrd and Normal, religious and heathen alike. He stuck his head around the door, and said, 'They're ready for you, Zvezdomir.'

Father Tony was a tall, thin man with bright blue eyes and iron-grey hair sticking out at all angles. White and brindle cat fur stuck to his black trousers, and his dog collar was prominently displayed above a pilled old camel-coloured jumper.

He led us into a sitting room, the walls of which were covered with framed *petit-point* tapestries of flowers, no two the same, as far as I could tell. The housekeeper, Miriam, patting her shellacked lilac hair, gave a kind smile as she stood beside a rickety drinks trolley that, sadly, contained not a trace of booze.

Eyes lit on us, but nothing was said while the priest and his housekeeper served very late afternoon tea. Miriam stroked the old priest's hand as they distributed the floral-overload porcelain cups and I had to hide my smile.

Once Bela and I had taken the only free seats and everyone was balancing a teacup and a scone piled high with cream and jam, they left us to it.

Sitting across from us in an assortment of antediluvian armchairs were the remaining Councillors, glamours firmly in place so no one could tell what made them different: the thin and very nervous Mercado White; Sandor Verhoeven, corpulent and calm; Titania Banks, who looked precisely like my idea of a gypsy fortune teller, and the ever-elegant Eleanor Aviva, who gave an off-handed wave of acknowledgement. They were all well-dressed in an understated fashion, but the outfits were tailored, the kind of expensive clothing that didn't need a label, and even Titania's myriad Stevie Nicks skirts showed signs of designer construction. They also looked, each and every one, sleep-deprived, not just Mercado White, who shifted in his recliner, jiggling a leg; occasionally his left eye twitched. His unease was entirely reasonable given that Adriana Greenill was now no more than a few smears on a carpet square and he himself had come close to the same fate.

My sympathy was short-lived, however, the moment he opened his mouth.

'I don't understand why you haven't caught this thing yet.' He wasn't looking at me; in fact, I appeared not to exist, which made me wonder what I was doing there at all. The Councillor stared at Bela, whose face was blank as a piece of marble. 'Are you even taking this seriously?'

'Mercado,' said Eleanor Aviva, her tone that of a scolding mother. Her fingers, weighed down by large rings, fidgeted with the clasp of the expensive-looking handbag in her lap. 'Be nice. What have we said about good manners?'

He turned a fervid gaze on her. 'Aren't you *worried*? Don't you think it's taking a long time? Don't you think it's all very *convenient*?'

'What do you mean?' Verhoeven's chins wobbled, his voice rasping like sandpaper on old painted wood.

'This thing is picking us off while *he* bides his time. What's his plan? Zvezdomir Tepes takes over when we're all gone?'

Bela's expression changed in a split second, became thunderous, his voice the crack of a whip. I'd never seen him get so angry so quickly, not even at me during our worst fights, not even when I was a revolting teen who thought she knew better than everyone, especially him. I could have sworn his eyes turned a little bit red. A glance at his hands, clenching the armrests of his chair, showed the fingers had grown longer, the nails sharper.

'I have served this Council since before you inherited your father's position on it. You are the only one who hasn't earned his place here, White. You might remember that.'

Titania giggled like a schoolgirl – if anyone wasn't taking things seriously, it was her. Mercado spluttered his outrage but didn't actually manage to produce any words; I thought it was probably best he didn't, not if he wanted to stay intact.

'Ahem,' I said, and five heads turned towards me at exactly the same speed; four of them gave me precisely the same look you'd give a dog that had suddenly addressed you in fluent Chinese. 'Yes, you. Hello. You invited me, remember?'

Eleanor Aviva raised one perfectly plucked eyebrow as if granting permission to speak. I imagined her assiduously practising that move in a mirror.

'Right. Being in danger as you are, I'll assume you'll be a little more forthcoming than usual. Each of you knew Vadim Nadasy?'

Vague acknowledgements all around, although White was still stiff with umbrage. Verhoeven admitted, 'He once sat on this Council.'

'So did his wife,' added Aviva.

I gave Bela a sideways glare and he raised his hands, palms up: *sorry*.

'Why did he – *they* – leave?'

'She had to save face in light of your father's disgrace,' said Mercado gleefully, as if he'd been waiting for the opportunity to bring it up. The others looked away; had any of them supervised the application of iron nails to Grigor's body to make sure he couldn't defend himself? I hadn't wondered about that before; I had been too busy not thinking about him and what he'd done. But now . . .

'You didn't tell me that,' I said to Bela.

'I knew about Vadim, but I didn't know about Magda,' he replied. 'I swear.'

'Zvezdomir – your dear *Bela* – was very new to his job when Grigor fell from grace. We did not tell him everything in those early days; he had yet to earn our full confidence,' said Eleanor Aviva smoothly. 'Magda's involvement with your father was scandalous; it put our treaties with the Normals in jeopardy. We believed the fewer who knew about it, the better.'

But how much did they tell Bela nowadays? How fully did they trust him? I was pretty certain he was starting to ask himself that very question. Perhaps his faith in the Council's integrity was getting a little less solid.

'As for Vadim, we had a falling-out,' Verhoeven offered, which sounded like an understatement to me.

Titania appeared to agree. 'What a very polite way of putting it!' she shrieked, and leaned towards me, saying confidentially, 'He said we were traitors to our own kind; that we were cowards. Vadim was . . . very attached to Dusana, and very determined she be avenged.'

'And you refused . . . So he probably feels he has good reason to go after you with his pet monster.' A long game, though, and a dish served very, very cold. 'But he didn't do anything at the time. He gave up.'

Titania sat back. 'He might have stopped talking about it, but I didn't trust him. The Nadasys never did let anything go lightly.'

'You're being hunted by a golem. We think it was created by Vadim Nadasy – out of his own grandson.' I wished I could have seen some kind of shock on their faces when I added that last bit, but alas, not a blink, not a twitch. Some Weyrd were definitely more cold-blooded than others.

'Nadasy disappeared. I believe he died,' said White dismissively. 'You're wasting our time.'

'I'd point out that his wife was supposed to have taken a dirt nap long ago, yet there she was, peddling wine made from the tears of children – well, she was before I pushed her into an oven. Don't feed me shit and tell me it's chocolate.'

Bela cringed while everyone but White guffawed; his face spasmed – he was no poker player, this one – and he blurted, 'How can you know—?'

'—that it was her? That's my business. But I'm willing to bet you knew who you were dealing with when you bought the wine, didn't you?'

It was a shot in the dark but it produced the desired effect: indignant expressions from the others and stuttering from Mercado White, who'd lost all his colour and broken out in a sweat.

Bela gave him a look that made me wonder if White might just be about to burst into flames.

'I never saw the woman – I didn't know who the supplier was, I swear.' That sounded about right: she'd be the sort to keep a layer between herself and her clients. After all, she'd not even trusted her identity to her sole employee. It didn't change the fact that he'd happily quaffed the tears of dead children.

'You must have suspected, surely, when something like that was offered? You must have realised it wasn't some youngster with an interest in specialised viticulture.'

The way his eyes slid away told the truth, but he continued speaking, 'It was my housekeeper – he made the contact, placed the orders. There was a girl, he said, some Normal girl—'

Good old Sally.

'I'd like to talk to your housekeeper,' I said.

'He's dead.'

'How *very* convenient.'

Bela cleared his throat to tell me I was getting off track.

'Right. So if the woman was alive when everyone thought her otherwise, why shouldn't the disappeared husband be around and going after you lot?'

No one made eye contact until Sandor Verhoeven said, 'When Dusana died, Vadim made his demands of us, but we would not give permission for such retribution. Even had there been proof, the potential for backfiring was too great. Nadasy said we were putting the lives of insects above those of our own kind.'

'I'll bet,' I muttered. 'No wonder he's got no reason to like you lot.'

'Nor you,' murmured Eleanor, 'after your treatment of his wife.'

'But if it's Nadasy,' interrupted Titania, 'why isn't Anders Baker dead already?'

'Lady, I have been asking myself that.' I slumped in the overstuffed armchair, feeling a coil give and poke me in the back. That was one way to ensure good posture. I straightened up and said, 'There has to be something Baker's got that Nadasy wants: something that he can't get without Anders' help.'

But apparently no one knew – or was admitting – what that might be; blank expressions were my only reward. I tried my luck with another topic. 'Have any of you noticed anything angelic occurring?'

'Is this about the sirens Zvezdomir has mentioned?' asked Verhoeven.

'The dead ones, yes. Has anyone heard anything about an increased presence of angels over Brisbane? Anything at all?'

Eleanor said, 'We cannot see them. They do not speak with us, not even at the best of times. And this is not the best of times.'

'I've heard nothing,' grumbled Verhoeven; he sounded angry that the city was changing around him, and without his permission. No one mentioned the baby, which made me think Bela hadn't passed that juicy bit of info on, so I didn't either. Had he been having doubts about the Council? I was happy not to discuss Calliope, because that would have to lead to the matter of Ligeia, a creature who was happily defying the Council's decrees. I didn't agree with her ways, but equally, I didn't want to be the one sent to hunt her.

So the plan was for them to stay safe and sound in the rectory and for me to continue risking my life looking for nasty things. I pointed at Mercado White, who was sitting there shaking, and said, 'You're going to do something about him, right?'

'Yes.' Sandor Verhoeven's voice rumbled across White, who whimpered. His terror told me the fat man would be true to his word. No one liked being put at risk by a trusted colleague.

The moment Bela and I left the room, Hairy Jerry and Mono-brow Mike stepped in. It looked like justice would be swift.

Chapter Twenty-Six

'We've got a visitor,' said David as he met me at the door all dreamy-eyed, and not in a 'he's so dreamy' way. If I hadn't known better, I'd have said he was high, but that wasn't his style – even during our brief acquaintance I'd worked out he was a lightweight as far as booze was concerned. So unless someone had fed him some very special cookies, my boyfriend had been bewitched, and I couldn't figure out how that had happened since he'd been in my ward-bound home for the last four hours looking after Lizzie.

'Who is it? *What* is it?' I was starting to get worried about who our guest might be, especially as Mercado White had somehow managed to give the goons the slip and was now in the wind. The guy was an idiot – he'd've been better off taking his chances with the Council than with the golem. I'd politely declined the chance to take part in the search for him.

'You need to see for yourself.' He had a really goofy grin now.

I followed David into the lounge room, calculating how fast I could pull the dagger from its sheath if required. Across from the sofa was a single, wide-seated armchair, and in that armchair sat the most beautiful hobo in the world. He'd obviously been living rough and his jeans and jumper were ragged and pretty grotty – but not a trace of dirt clung to his skin. A leather coat lay on the floor beside him, neatly folded.

I looked at him and I knew how he'd got past the wards.

When he saw me and stood his head almost scraped the ceiling. The tips of his wings *did* scrape the ceiling. He had masses of black hair, and silver eyes. The air around him shimmered. He really was perfectly, exquisitely lovely, in a real 'manly man' kind of way. My protection spells couldn't do much against the angelic.

And poor David had been angel-struck. I'd learned in my research that this was a common phenomenon whenever someone had an encounter with them: men, women, children, dogs – not cats, though, never cats – all fell in love. I reached out and held my beloved's hand. Weyrd and half-breeds generally don't suffer from it as we're fantastical enough ourselves, so I hoped touching him might help, willing him to take in a little of my immunity. His eyes started to clear, but he still looked punch-drunk.

I glared at the angel. 'Could you turn the glory down a bit, please? I don't want him completely addled.'

The angel blushed. 'Sorry. I had to convince him to let me in quickly. I didn't fancy being left outside.'

The shimmer around him stopped and and he shrank back down to a reasonable size, which was about six foot three. David stumbled as if released. I gave him a kiss and he focused.

'Where's Lizzie?'

'Asleep,' he said.

'No, I'm not,' came a little voice from under the dining room table, then a small form crawled out to sit directly across from the angel and stare at him. 'He smells *really* good.'

'Doesn't he?' I agreed.

'Odour of sanctity,' rumbled the angel.

'Thought that was just saints.' I offered a hand that got swallowed by his large palm.

He shook his head. 'Who are the original saints, do you think? Suffering with nothing in return.'

'Good point. Tea? Coffee? Holy water?'

'Beer? And maybe a sandwich?'

'Right. David, you okay?'

He rubbed his eyes, then got up to make for the kitchen. 'On it.'

The incongruous sight of an angel with a Corona in one hand and a hastily constructed ham and cheese sandwich in the other chased away most of my weariness. David and Lizzie sat on either side of me on the couch and we just kind of gazed at our guest until it became uncomfortable for everyone. As I'd said to Rhonda McIntyre, angels aren't *fluffy*. This one looked like a warrior: a down-on-his-luck and exiled warrior, sure, but stick a lance in his hand and a demon beneath his feet, and they wouldn't have looked inappropriate. He was obviously exhausted, with bags under his eyes and an overwhelmed kind of gaze.

'So,' I began, 'you're an angel. How's that working for you?'

He took a swig of beer, the shadow of a grin passing over his face.

'I'm guessing this isn't a social call,' I continued.

He shook his head and finished off the sandwich.

'And I'm guessing you're Tobit?'

Aha! He looked surprised by that. 'Yeah.'

'What are you doing here?'

'I heard you might be nosing around about—'

'Serena Kallos?'

His face convulsed with grief and he lowered his head. 'What happened to her?'

'Her heart was crushed and she was thrown off a building.' David nudged me, but I wasn't in the mood to be kind. Tobit remained silent, downing the last of his beer before dropping the bottle. It didn't fall over, just neatly floated to the floor.

'You've got a daughter. You know that, right?'

Still the silvery eyes didn't meet mine.

'You know she's missing? Do you *care*? I mean, I know your lot think you're better than everyone else, but this is your *child*.'

Tobit nodded again. David's don't-annoy-the-angel grimace was in full bloom.

'And Teles and Raidne are both dead. They had their wings ripped off. I'm assuming they died to hide your secrets.'

'Raidne said you were looking for me,' he said. He perched on the edge of the chair, elbows resting on knees. One hand grasped the other tightly, making the knuckles as white as bone. Tobit looked as though light might shine through him. 'She and Teles were taking care of the baby, but by the time I ran into Raidne—'

'Where?' I demanded.

'Where?'

'Where were they looking after Calliope?'

He shrugged. 'They wouldn't tell me. I don't think they trusted me.'

Apparently not all the sirens had Eurycleia's distaste for the angelic, but it looked like they still didn't entirely accept him. 'What or who have you been hiding from? Eurycleia? Ligeia?'

'Serena's mother?' He laughed wryly. 'Hardly. I don't know who the other one is.'

'Then what?'

His obvious reluctance to speak was starting to really irritate me. Why would *no one* give me a straight answer to *anything*? I didn't have much patience left. 'Serena called me the night she died. She didn't tell me why, just that she had a problem that needed solving. I'm guessing that problem got her killed.'

Still he didn't answer.

'Look, if you're just here for a free feed then you can fuck off now.'

'You shouldn't swear,' chimed Lizzie.

'You can *leave* now,' I corrected, 'because you're no use if you won't give me the information I need to find your daughter.' I sat forward. 'Who are you hiding from?'

'The Arch.'

That drew a blank from me.

His wings trembled a little. 'Archangels. You might know there aren't a lot of us common-or-garden angels left. Well, there are even fewer Archs – those remaining Archangels have a hard time rallying the rest because they've lost the will to be good foot-soldiers. Most of us wander, but there are some zealots, those who took the desertion harder than others, and they like to *organise*. Any more beer?'

'Not yet.'

He sighed. 'I've been around for aeons and I've seen a lot, but it's been a long time since I've met a fanatic like this one.'

'But what is an . . . *Arch* . . . doing over Brisbane?' asked David.

'Good question,' I said. 'It's not like we're a normal pilgrimage destination.'

'Somehow he found out what I did, who I was with.'

'Serena.'

'All those millennia and I never loved anyone but our Lord,' he said. 'Then I wandered here and found her. And I got her killed.' He paused, then said, 'More importantly, the Arch found out about the baby.'

'Why should it bother him?' asked David.

'Apart from the fact we're not meant to have anything to do with sirens?'

'Doesn't like inter-species breeding programmes?'

'To put it mildly. There're a lot of things the Archangel doesn't like.'

He probably wasn't keen on the whole angels-taking-the-daughters-of-men-to-wife thing either. 'Is he alone?' I asked, figuring that was too much to hope for.

'I wish. He's got half a dozen of the brothers – all but one he brought with him.'

'What's he offering them?'

The angel snorted. 'A new Crusade? To be honest, I haven't got close enough to chat.'

'And you don't have any friends you can ask?'

'Not amongst my kind.'

'How did he know about Serena?'

'I told you: Brisbane's angel has joined him. We are, for the most part, watchers. What's the point in watching if you can't tell someone?'

Angels carrying tales. A crusading Archangel. A baby who was still lost. I hadn't thought it possible, but my day had just got darker.

'Do you have Calliope?'

'Is that her name?' He smiled, and it was like a sunburst.

'Serena didn't tell you?'

'Serena and I had a disagreement and I left before the baby was born. When I heard the Arch was coming, I returned, but it was too late and I . . . hid.'

'Why you? Who are you in the bigger scheme of things?'

'Way to belittle the angel,' murmured David, and I made a mental note to not let him sit in on my Q&A sessions again.

'I'm no one. Just a watcher. Just in the wrong place at the wrong time.'

'That's all fine and dandy, but you're part of this, so what's so special about you? About Serena?'

His wings shifted the air in a kind of augmented shrug.

'Do you know where your daughter is?' I asked again.

'No, and I didn't try to force it out of Teles and Raidne in case—'

'In case you got caught.' I scratched my head. 'But you didn't, and they did. Yet they managed to keep their mouths shut. Have you even been looking for Calliope?'

The angel hung his head. 'Hiding's taking up all my time.' He gave me a glance that begged pity and I wanted to slap him. Just my luck: a deadbeat dad angel. He hadn't left to keep Serena safe; he'd left to keep himself safe. I wondered if she'd known, before she died, that she'd been in love with a coward. I wanted to turn him out, to send him back under unsafe skies, because that's what he deserved.

I sighed and stood up. 'Is there *anything* useful you can tell me?'

'I don't think so.'

'Is there anyone I can talk to? Anyone who might have Calliope? Anyone Serena might have trusted? I note she didn't hand the baby over to her mother.'

He laughed coldly. 'Eurycleia's more like the Arch than she'd like to admit.'

'Well, you despise a people long enough, they'll start to despise you back,' I said, though I wasn't sure why I was defending the woman. 'But I take your point; she can bigot it up with the best of them.'

'Sorry I can't be more helpful,' he mumbled.

'You can sleep on the sofa. Your feet will hang off the end, but it's more comfortable than a park bench.'

'I've been dossing in the tunnels. Believe me, a short couch isn't going to be a problem.'

I shuddered. Still, if sleeping in the tunnels was the worst he'd suffered, he should consider himself lucky. I was going to tell him so when my mobile did a little jig on the kitchen bench: Rhonda McIntyre letting me know that Mrs Tinkler — or rather, the bits of her that were left — had been found in her home. She hadn't gone peacefully, but whatever she'd had to tell me was lost. There were no shreds of garbage in evidence, but there were white feathers everywhere, some in her fists.

Remembering the feathers that had lain around Serena in that garden bed, I suggested they be tested against those of the dead sirens. I hoped like hell the bird-women hadn't started hunting for the baby themselves, uncaring for anyone who got in their way, but I was willing to bet that the plumes belonged to something else entirely; that Mrs T. had managed to irritate the Arch and his friends so much that they'd claimed their first Normal victim.

I didn't tell McIntyre — she'd started coughing again and I decided she had enough to contend with right now. That could wait.

After everyone else was tucked in bed and the house was still, I sat out on the deck, bundled in a flannelette dressing gown that used to be my grandmother's and could have been promoted as an aid to contraception, and tried to fit together all the bits of information that I'd gathered. But there were still too many gaps, too many pieces that were the wrong shape, and my full picture came out as a Picasso when what I needed was something photo-real, with helpful captions.

I counted the positives: if the old siren had told the truth, Calliope was being well cared for. The Boatman, inscrutable bastard that he was, had ensured that I had a knife the golem didn't like. It had kept me from being digested, and not being dead made me charitable, even if he was friends with Ligeia and I still didn't know why I had said knife. I finally knew who the Winemaker was, and that was a weight off my mind too. And David and Lizzie were safe.

When my fingers went numb with cold, I made a decision. Tomorrow, I would head back to Little Venice. There was one last Sister I needed to see. I wanted to cherish the illusion that Aspasia wouldn't be in, but that was akin to wishing for a unicorn for Christmas.

Chapter Twenty-Seven

Little Venice had two upper floors. I'd visited them once or twice in the past, but only when I'd really had no other choice. The first was the warren Theo and Aspasia shared. There were too many walls and corridors and the rooms were small and crowded with furniture and knick-knacks any decent Antiquities Department would have killed to get their hands on. The light was kept low, the windows mostly covered with thick tapestries and shawls. Underfoot, the carpets were dense, hand-woven, ancient and exotic.

The uppermost storey was reserved for the third Sister.

I made it to the top of the stairs, puffing only slightly after trading insults (which began as a reasonably heartfelt apology and went downhill from there) with Aspasia while Theodosia laughed. The door opened and two shaken Normal women exited. They'd come to have their fortunes told and hadn't liked what they'd heard – apparently no one had warned them that the Sisters Norn couldn't be trusted with the future.

The door stayed ajar like a mouth waiting for a morsel to drop in. I let the shuddering women stumble past, back towards the light, then strode over the threshold. The atmosphere shivered around me and the woman in the middle of the room shivered too, as if her connection to the air was so intimate she could sense its every distress. She looked up with eyes like the sky and a smile as cold as a Norse winter.

Thaïs was white-blonde and tall, but she was also large – and not just carrying a little extra weight. Theo was whippet-thin; Aspasia was voluptuous; Thaïs was *fat*. She might have modelled for the Venus of Willendorf; come to think of it, there was a very good chance she had. Her hair was plaited into a complicated braid: one to each side, a third at the back, and then all three woven together until they looked like nothing so much as a macramé plant-holder, like those once produced in bulk by schoolchildren and offered as gifts to unsuspecting mothers, aunts and grandmothers. Her dress, sprays of pinks and greens with a splash of white and a few spears of black, made you understand precisely what a caftan was. She was reclining front and centre on an old brown velvet three-seater, taking up roughly two-point-five seats, her legs twisted underneath her in some miraculous yoga manoeuvre. The way the couch bowed testified to this being her favourite spot. The room was thick with the scent of incense and a body that had a lot of places where sweat gathered, no matter how many showers were taken.

Candles flickered here and there. The only enclosed space was a bathroom in one corner; the rest of the area was warehouse-spare, with a bed resting on a raised platform to one side.

Thaïs' sofa sat in front of a low coffee table, which was actually a chest of drawers of various sizes, filled with all the sorcerous paraphernalia she might need. The eternal four-year-old in me wanted to sit on the dusty floor and go through every compartment, just to see what was there; I imagined strewing everything around me until nothing remained hidden and I had no idea where anything went. Luckily, grown-up me stayed in charge, which was probably for the best. Three other low and equally over-stuffed sofas made up a square around it.

Thaïs squinted across the distance, then smiled. 'Hello, little strangeling,' she piped in a sweet voice.

Strangeling seemed a bit rich considering the source, but I let it pass and approached with more confidence than I felt. Truth was, I didn't like being near any of the Norns without either witnesses or back-up. After so long managing to avoid having my palm read, I was especially uneasy being alone with one of them in case something got blurted out, some stray strand of the future I really didn't want to hear. But Thaïs wasn't an outdoors kind of girl, so everyone had to come to her. I didn't want to know what might be in the stars for me, but if there were any answers to be had, then Little Venice was the most likely place to find them, for the Sisters always pooled their tidbits of gleaned knowledge. Thaïs might not go out, but intelligence came to her as surely as the noise of a fridge opening transmitted itself to the ears of any cat within a half-mile radius. She dipped into and out of the otherworldly streams as easily as a mermaid duck-diving in the ocean. I didn't need the future, but some hints about the past and the present wouldn't go astray.

'Hey, Thaïs. How's life?' I sank deeply into the sofa opposite her and was left with my knees almost at my shoulders. Trying to stretch out, I kicked the table, then finally settled for loosely crossing my legs at the ankles.

'Comfortable?' she asked, one snowflake eyebrow raised.

'Absolutely not.'

'Good.' She collected the Tarot cards that had been laid out in a Grand Cross spread on the gold-fringed purple cloth covering the table. It was a Rider Waite deck, but hand-drawn, not one of the mass-produced sets, with edges worn and soft, the colours muted from years of handling, sweat and natural oils. Thaïs moved slowly, as if the longer she left them there, the more I'd be tempted, but I remained still until she'd stacked them, making sure they were sitting flush, then wrapped everything in a square of black silk. The bundle went into a plain brown cardboard box, and thence into one of the niches on her side of the table.

'And what brings you to my door, Verity Fassbinder? I'm surprised Aspasia let you in.'

'Theodosia likes me.'

She sighed. 'Theo's an optimist. She still thinks you'll sleep with her one day.'

'Surely you can peer at some entrails and put her mind to rest on that score?'

'She won't listen. We've been at this so long we've forgotten who lies and who doesn't.' She smiled briefly.

Norns with Alzheimer's? I shook off the distracting concept. 'Theo told you about the golem?'

'And the sirens. And the baby. And Aspasia told me about the Winemaker — and everyone else told me how you dealt with her. Very summarily.'

'It's not like she was an innocent, Thaïs. She was a murderer — and she was also Magda Nadasy.'

She looked as though she'd been slapped. Ah: the satisfaction of knowing something a Norn didn't was rare and wonderful. Magda had kept herself *very* secret indeed if not even Thaïs was aware she'd returned. I wondered if the Norns had tried to dig for details back when Sally Crown had first offered wine made from children's tears and come up against a brick wall.

I continued, 'As I've explained to your Sisters, anything that risks exposing this community to the gaze of panicky Normals — anything that exposes panicky Normals to the threat of flesh-hungry Weyrd — needs to be dealt with quickly.'

While most Weyrd acknowledged the requirement for policing

their interactions with Normals, and while they knew people like me and Bela and Ziggi were the thin line between them and danger, they still resented it. Normals might have all the high technology of a geek's wet dream at our fingertips, but essentially, humanity reverted to its strike-out-at-anything-different mentality at a moment's notice. That was knowledge all Weyrd shared.

'So: we've got the golem – who is Nadasy's grandson, by the way – attacking Normals, and any Council member he can get his hands on. And there are the sirens, who are being murdered wholesale. There's the exile, Ligeia, who may or may not be protecting the siren's child and, just to complicate things further, there is now an Archangel over Brisbane leading a posse of lesser angels in a crusade of some description. Know anything about any of that?'

'Sounds like you know a whole lot,' she mused.

'Nope,' I admitted. 'I've got bits of a broken mirror that I'm trying to put back together, and the edges are *very* sharp. The glass is smudged, and slippery to boot.'

'Ooo-kaay.'

'Nothing is fitting together properly, and the Arch particularly is bothering me.'

'Me, too,' she admitted. 'Brisbane really isn't the kind of city one of them visits, not without a good reason.'

'Someone – and let's say for the sake of argument that it's an angel – is taking out sirens at a rate of knots. Last night, the first Normal victim was claimed – you might have appreciated Mrs Tinkler's taste in clothes,' I added as an aside, 'which means it's a real problem. Fixing it is now my problem, and if it's my problem—'

'It's going to be everyone's problem until you get answers. I know how you operate, Fassbinder.' She paused, considering, then said, 'Bottom drawer on your side, far right.'

The bowl was a flat-bottomed shallow brass thing. Its rim was sharp and I cut a finger dragging it out; fat droplets of my blood spattered into the base. Frowning, I rested it in the middle of the table.

Thaïs handed me a matching brass ewer, carved with snakes and branches, and pointed me towards the bathroom, which turned out to be magnificent and pristine: white marble, fluffy towels, scented soaps, one wall mirrored, the others covered in a lavishly tiled design of girls jumping over bulls. Even the loo looked majestic. I filled the jug, then washed my bleeding digit and wrapped a piece of toilet tissue around it. When I returned, I noticed Thaïs hadn't cleaned the vessel of the red droplets. She impatiently took the water, noticed the direction of my glare and said, 'You know nothing comes for free.'

'I know. That's why I brought these.' I struggled to get the two large bars of Valrhona dark chocolate from my inside pocket, where they'd been slowly melting. Thaïs eyed them greedily, then snatched the booty away.

Muttering, 'Better than ichor,' she filled the basin. I watched the fluid swirl and circle and settle, relieved the blood was so diluted; that was the only reason I didn't kick up more of a fuss. In that state it would be no use to anyone afterwards. Thaïs sprinkled a handful of what I suspected was grave dust over the surface and it slowly dissolved and sank. When the liquid had turned an impenetrable charcoal, we both leaned forward.

All I saw was a great big mish-mash of white wings, spinning garbage, the Winemaker's press, large pale hands with neat nails tearing at equally white feathers, and an empty cradle. Oh, and the stern of a long thin dark boat piloted by a figure in a dead brown cloak. It meant nothing to me, other than flashes of the past, but I wasn't a scryer, nor an interpreter.

Thaïs eyed me. 'Anything you're not telling me?'

I took a gamble and reached down to slide the knife from the sheath, carefully placing it on the table between us. Air hissed out of her, not in an angry way, but more in a surprised loss of steam way. It was a relief to think someone might know exactly what the thing was.

'The Boatman gave it to me. Along with some cryptic wording about someone wanting to break the sky. I don't know what I'm supposed to do with it, but I found out purely by happy accident that the golem doesn't like it.'

'Naughty Boatman.' She didn't touch it; she reached out and wiggled her fingers in its direction, but didn't make contact. 'It's the Dagger of Wilusa, which was a Bronze Age settlement sometimes mistaken for Troy. The dagger is older, but that's where it was found once, then lost again. It's also known as the God-slayer. Some say it was what Zeus used to kill Kronos. Abraham used it on his son – oh, yes, there was a sacrifice, no matter what the Biblical press release says. Others insist it belonged to the Amazon queens of old. There are lots of stories, not many of them written down, certainly not in schoolbooks. Whatever it is, it's got some power in it.'

'What am I supposed to do with it? Any ideas?' She shook her head slowly, and I thought it was looking like my very expensive chocolate investment was a bad one, but I waited. Maybe she was picking through what to tell me, which meant I might need to shake information from her sooner or later. Preferably sooner.

Impatiently I said, 'Look, anything you've got. Anything that might help me find the baby? Find the golem? Stop the angels?'

'I don't think the baby's dead. I can tell you don't trust the old siren and you're probably right on a lot of issues, but the little girl's not as helpless as she may seem.' She rubbed her chin and sighed.

'Look, leave this with me. I need to do some reading. I'll call if I find anything.'

'That's what Theo said and I didn't hear from her.'

'That's because she likes you to have to come here and see her.'

I hadn't thought of it that way.

'And, Fassbinder, keep *that* close. It might be the only thing between you and pushing up daisies.'

'This has not been reassuring.'

'It seldom is. I *promise* I will contact you, little strangeling.'

'I hate it when you call me that.'

'I know.' I rose, but her voice stopped me at the door. 'The Archangel, he's searching, that's all I can tell you.'

'I figure he's searching for the baby.'

'Better hope he doesn't find her,' she said, and would say no more.

It was one in the morning when the phone rang again. Though Lizzie, Tobit and David had gone to bed ages ago, I wasn't asleep. I'd just finished talking to Ziggi, whose mate on the Sovereign Islands had reported that Baker's house was deserted. It had been ransacked and its occupant-of-interest was gone. Ziggi could barely cover his relief that he didn't have to drive down there again.

On the first ring I thought it might have been him again, that he'd forgotten something, but the voice was coarse, sick-sounding. 'Fassbinder?'

'Yes. Rhonda, what's up?'

'St Stephen's.'

'Yes?'

'You might find one of those angels you're looking for.' She gave a laugh bereft of humor, then clicked off before I could ask who'd seen them and how she knew, or indeed mention that the location of at least one angel was already known to me. Her phone went straight to voicemail and I left a terse message, then pulled on my coat. I stuck an explanatory-but-hopefully unnecessary Post-it note on the fridge for anyone who might look for me and snuck out of the house.

I took pity on Ziggi and got a 'real' cab. I wasn't planning for it to become a habit, because I didn't much like the Normal drivers. Too talkative, too opinionated, too sleazy, too creepy. That night I got Barry, who loved cricket, football and beer, and was passionate about the world, but hated everyone in it who wasn't white. In the end, I had him drop me on the corner of Elizabeth and George Streets because I couldn't stand to listen to him a second longer. Music spewed forth from the nightclubs and gambling dens of the Treasury Casino. I paced along the mostly empty streets towards the cathedral, which was currently hidden by the high-rises. I kept my head down, the low level burr of minimal traffic the only sound as distance drained the music away.

I walked on the opposite side of the road, but as I came alongside St Stephen's, I ran into something: a large, invisible something. If it hadn't been for the steel grip clamping around my upper arm, I'd have bounced to the pavement. Being half-dragged across the street, then up stone steps, was disconcerting, but I was smart enough not to struggle. Anyway, this was what I'd been looking for, although probably with less of me being frog-marched. The precinct, bordered by Elizabeth, Edward and Charlotte Streets, contained a small but neat cathedral with an even smaller chapel to the south, the old school-now-admin building and another larger structure where more administrivia was conducted.

In between was a green space, empty for a while, and then much less so when five angels, in addition to the one holding me, shimmered into view. No jeans and T-shirts for these – they all wore white chitons, short enough to show off muscular legs that ended in lace-up booties, all very Greek, and about their torsos were wrapped worked silver breastplates. Each cuirass boasted a bas-relief heart surrounded by flames, a little off-centre, right where I assumed the angels' own hearts were situated, and set in the middle of each was a different coloured precious stone. All wore thick silver rings on their index fingers, and I stared at the one on the hand around my arm: the cut-out detail showed a quadrate cross. They were, without exception, male, very tall, beautiful, and with red hair that shone like something in a TV advert. The one sporting a ruby demanded, 'Where is it?'

I couldn't help myself. 'Ginger Liberation Front Annual General Meeting?'

That earned me a good shaking from Sapphire. Ruby didn't bother to answer, just glared as if he could make me shut up by thinking about it. The air around us was thick with a sickly-sweet odour; too many angels in one area apparently makes the place smell like a badly ventilated florist's shop. I was beginning to feel a bit faint.

'Where is it?' asked another, Emerald.

'You're going to have to be more specific. I'm looking for quite a few things at this point in time. How about a hint.'

'The double-winged.'

I paused; that was a new one on me. 'Yep, looking for a lot of things, me, but that's not one of them.'

Again with the shaking, and this time I cried, 'Honestly, I don't know!' Although I was beginning to have a suspicion; I just wanted them to say it. 'What *is* the double-winged? And use small words.'

'The child. The child of an angel and a wingèd whore.'

'That's very judgemental.' I lifted a finger to my minder. 'And do *not* shake me again. It's lost its appeal.'

'They speak of you – the tribes here. They say you keep the peace, keep a vigil.'

Keep the peace seemed like a bit of a stretch, but my current lack of sleep could very well be translated into a vigil. 'Sure, why not?

'They say you find lost things.'

'Don't believe everything you hear. Half the time I can't find a matching pair of socks.' I surveyed the wall of cold beauty towering above me. They were near identical, and I didn't imagine the Arch would want to look like one of the herd. 'Where's your leader?'

'The Archangel will not show himself to the likes of you,' Amethyst boomed.

'But he's around.' I smiled, trying to pick out a spot where the air shifted and broke a little, a sign of something standing just on the other side of perception. 'I bet he is, but he prefers to send his lackeys.'

'The Archangel will not speak to you,' said Topaz.

'You are *beneath* us,' said Amethyst.

'Which one's the local boy?' I hoped fervently that they couldn't smell Tobit on me. We'd been in the same house for more than twenty-four hours and I wondered how much might have rubbed off. I had no idea how keen an angel's sense of smell might be.

The one who still held me lifted his chin in the slightest acknowledgement.

'Shame on you,' I said, 'getting dazzled by these new kids. Turning on your city as if it hasn't fed you, nurtured you, for all these years.'

'The Arch will bring us home,' he said, but there was a faint blush on his marble-perfect cheek.

'At what cost?'

And he turned away. He might feel guilty, but he was beyond caring; whatever loyalty he'd had to Brisneyland was gone. They were all lonely and heartsick and lost without their parent; they wanted to find him, no matter what. Everyone and anything else was just collateral damage.

On a hunch I said, 'You're planning to break the sky?'

To a man – to an *angel* – they looked shocked. They were so used to being the bringers of tidings that they hadn't considered that others might know what was going on. Not that I really did, but I was doing my best to work it out on the fly. Did Tobit know what they were planning? Did he know more than he'd told me, or was he just afraid they were hunting his daughter to wipe her out? I had him down for a wimp, but I didn't think he was like these *things*.

'The Arch will open the way and take us home. The double-winged is the doorway,' said the Emerald angel, then corrected himself. 'The key. We will bask in the glory of His face once more.'

I didn't like the sound of that, even though I didn't feel any more illuminated. 'You killed the sirens because you're looking for your key? Which one of you did it?'

'We all had that honour,' said Ruby.

I felt ill at the idea of those large hands tearing at Teles and Raidne, ripping feathers and flesh and wings. I thought of Serena, her heart stopped in her chest, then thrown off a building like so much rubbish, all because these guys were homesick.

'Honour?' I struggled, and the Brisbane angel let me go. I didn't kid myself it was because of my strength, just that he'd lost interest in hanging onto me. 'Break the sky? What will that do to the world? You want to go back to the Mothership and you don't care what happens to the rest of Creation? How pleased do you think your Boss is going to be when He sees you've let His goldfish die?'

'There will be a Darkness,' said Emerald, as if it was nothing to him.

'We were created first and best,' chimed Topaz. 'He will rejoice to see us.'

'Here's a thought: if He was that fond of you, He wouldn't have left you behind.' In my imagination David was launching into the 'Why Baiting a Flock of Angels Is a Bad Idea' lecture. 'And what about Mrs Tinkler? Why kill her?'

They gave me blank looks until Emerald's face cleared and he said, 'The fat woman.'

She was an old bat, but she still didn't deserve to be treated as though her death was inconsequential. And she certainly didn't deserve to be shredded. 'Why her?'

'She was unhelpful,' said Amethyst. 'She fought.'

And I could see that therein lay the sin: she'd *rebelled*. My rage blossomed and I clenched my fists, contemplating whether I was strong enough to actually break an angelic neck. The increase in their number must have been stretching the city's faith thin; none of these creatures would have had a decent feed in a couple of weeks so they wouldn't be at their best, their peak.

In my head, David's voice said, *They're freaking angels.* I swallowed my fury.

Sapphire frowned, mystified. 'She fought so, yet she knew nothing.'

All those millennia watching humans, dealing with them, and it was apparent these creatures had not a clue about what made us tick, how we would fight in the face of hopelessness, refuse to be pushed around, even if we had no information to give. They didn't know that many of us would refuse to beg; that not all of us would cower. I felt a headache coming on – or I thought it was a headache, then I realised it was more like someone simultaneously drilling a hole in my skull and ransacking inside.

I glared at Ruby. 'What the fuck are you doing?'

Sapphire replied, 'What you will not give, the Arch must take. If you have knowledge of the prophecy, we will have it.'

I screamed, trying to block the intrusion, trying to keep all my thoughts – all of *myself* – together, like someone juggling too many parcels. It felt . . . it felt as if my recollections were being randomly pulled from the shelves like library books – as each came out, the memory flashed. Luckily, I didn't know much. I mean, I knew a lot, just not a lot that was connected or coherent. The lack of order was enough to cause whoever was paddling around in there to hesitate, only for a moment, and that was enough: I pulled down the shades, imagined the intruder gone and my mind locked up like Fort Knox. *Get out!* The effort left a dull thud in my brain and a trickle of blood from my nostrils, but no unwanted guest.

A deafening silence fell, then a voice came thrumming from the air with no discernable source. 'She knows nothing of the double-winged.'

I fell, proud of myself for managing not to vomit, and lay curled on the grass until the worst of the pain had subsided. When I opened my eyes I was alone. Though I might not have known anything about the double-winged, I knew where Tobit was, which meant his brethren did too. They'd left me alive, and I could only imagine it was because, like the rest of my kind, they thought me no threat. I also took it as hard-won proof that I wasn't as annoying as others claimed.

Fumbling for my mobile, I stumbled up the street, wiping the scarlet from my nose and looking for a cab.

Chapter Twenty-Eight

With its arteries unclogged by traffic, the city shrank at night, so we made good time. I fell out of the taxi and scraped my wrist on the raised gutter, feeling bones grind unhappily against each other. The front door of my house was wide open, though not kicked in – I figured angels probably didn't need a key for *this* sort of B&E. All the lights were on. I moved through the rooms, heart in my mouth, hoping I'd called in time. There was no sign of violence, no sign of struggle. Most importantly, there were no bodies.

It was obvious the angels had beaten me here, but with any luck they'd arrived after David, Lizzie and Tobit had fled. I started shaking and couldn't stop. Sitting on the couch and breathing deeply helped, as did swallowing until the lump in my throat went away, though my head still ached and my nose was still blood-encrusted. When my heartbeat slowed and the tremors eased, I carefully locked up, then sneaked down the rear stairs. Under the cover of darkness, I scrambled over the fence into Mel's yard, then crept to the back door.

I knocked hopefully, heard a nervous shuffling on the other side and whispered, 'It's me.'

David held me tight. He and Lizzie had been at the table in the dark kitchen, drinking hot chocolate and eating comfort biscuits.

Lizzie held onto my waist like a limpet. 'We saw them,' she said in a rush, eyes wide. 'More angels.'

'I know, honey. Remember, they're not fluffy.'

She inclined her head sagely. 'They looked so angry, not like ours.' So she'd already adopted Tobit. So much for *not fluffy*.

'I didn't know how much time we had, so this was probably the safest place, the least likely place,' said David as he microwaved a cup of milk, then added enough chocolate powder to make the spoon stand up.

'Where's Tobit?' I asked, accepting the warm mug, happy that my risk had paid off.

'Gone. He said they'd know he was around if he stayed this close.' He ran his hands over my shoulders. 'Where did you go, by the way?'

So much for my Post-it note of awesome. I told him about the cathedral adventure and how fruitless it had been, except for the certainty of some kind of angel-induced apocalypse.

'Double-winged,' he mused. 'If a child has two parents with wings, you might call her that.'

'But I wasn't. I was thinking of her as "Callie", not as some object. I wonder if that's why they thought I didn't know anything?'

'Obtuseness for the win,' he said, and kissed me.

'Do you reckon Tobit's aware they wanted her for this prophecy deal? If he is, why wouldn't he tell me?'

He thought for a second. 'Maybe it's because he doesn't know you very well. Maybe he's worried you'd give the baby up. Or maybe he really didn't know.'

'Thaïs said the baby was still alive, and the angels obviously believe that too, or they wouldn't be hanging about.' I sipped my hot chocolate. 'I'm getting tired of vague hints. I'm pretty sure Thaïs wasn't telling me everything and I'm damned sure the Boatman's got more to say.'

'Don't blame yourself. You can only get so much out of people without thumbscrews. You want me to get Lizzie to school tomorrow . . . well, today?'

The little girl dozed, head on the pillow of her crossed arms. 'No, I don't think she'll be up for much after this night's escapades. And maybe it's best she stay home, which is a shame since I just got her back to school. You probably need to go to work?'

'I have a lot of leave. It's okay.'

I smiled at him but didn't say how wonderful he was. I didn't say that I probably loved him in that moment. I didn't say anything, but I hoped he realised it all.

Then I had a thought. 'Hey, was Rose Wilkes here when you arrived?'

'Nah, the place was empty.'

'I should have tied her to something,' I sighed.

Although Lizzie slept in her own bed that night, we were all displaced in one way or another. In Mel's guest room, David warm beside me, I closed my eyes, but my mind kept whirring, shifting and shuffling pieces, trying to work out how to get what I needed from people who weren't willing to play ball, either because they didn't appreciate the stakes, or because they were just arseholes. It was hard to tell which, sometimes. And I wondered, oh how I wondered, how Rhonda McIntyre had known where I might find the angels.

I'd spent a fruitless chunk of Sunday morning on the riverbanks, waiting for the mists to swirl and the thin dark boat to appear, but I was out of luck. Either business was slow or the Boatman was just plain avoiding me.

Bela and I met briefly for mutual recriminations and an update on Mercado White, who'd been seen at the airport, boarding a plane for places unknown. Or rather, unknown-for-the-moment: it would only be a matter of time before networks were activated, contacts tapped, favours reeled in. What happened then wasn't my concern; the Council took care of its own sinners.

My boss' reaction to the news that I'd attracted the attention of the angelic choir was to moan, 'You're in so much trouble.'

It was no comfort to hear Bela say that. 'Tell me something I don't already know,' I muttered.

'But you didn't see the Archangel?'

'*See*, no. Hear, yes.'

He'd blanched to a shade that I didn't think had existed before. 'What did they get?'

'Where I live and the fact Tobit was there. That I don't know where the baby is, or anything useful about their prophecy. Lots of golem stuff, which will be irrelevant to them. But I think I shut him out before he learned about the Boatman.' Bela did a double-take, which I naturally interpreted as criticism. 'It's not an exact science, y'know. I've never had anything like that in my head before.'

'No, you said *the Boatman*,' he interrupted sharply, and I remembered he wasn't the only one who'd held things back. Obviously Ziggi had kept *schtum* about that too. 'What about the Boatman?' That's where the recriminations came in. 'If you'd mentioned the Boatman earlier—'

Once I'd filled in the gaps and he was able to speak civilly again, he said, 'So, where to from here?'

I sighed. 'Thaïs, for a few more stern and probing questions, because after last night I am pretty sure she knows more than she's saying – then again, who doesn't? After that, Rhonda McIntyre, to establish how she knew about the angels. And Anders Baker – I need to find him and work out why he's still alive . . . assuming he still is.'

'Ziggi's on the hunt for Baker, so don't worry about him.'

'Do you think it – I mean, *Donovan* – worked up the courage to kill his father?'

He shook his head slowly. 'I think after we disturbed its nest it went home again to hide. I think Anders got scared and bolted.' He added, 'Are David and Lizzie okay?'

'Hiding at Mel's.'

'The angels got David's address?'

'I'm not sure but I suspect so, so I couldn't risk it.'

'If you need a safe house—'

'You'll run out of rectories. Besides, I don't imagine there's anywhere safe from those things.'

'Okay, be careful.'

'You don't need to tell me twice.'

I was so sick and tired of being lied to. I hit Little Venice in a royal temper. There was a buzzing in my head, an electrical hum that became stronger the closer I got. The main bar area was deserted, except for the two bruised and beaten emo-Weyrd waitresses cowering behind the servery. The bodies of Aspasia's three serpent babies were lying on the flagstones, surrounded by the splintered remains of chairs and tables; the snow-lace mirror was in shards. A few large, gloriously white feathers floated on the breeze. They didn't belong to a siren.

'Where are they?'

One of the girls pointed upwards, her hand shaking wildly. The other had crimson running from her mouth and her trembling hands were cupped around something pink and fleshy.

'Get out. You know Louise Arnold, the healer in Franklin Street? Go there. Don't come back here until you hear from the Sisters.' If, of course, the Sisters hadn't become extinct. The girls scurried out, terrified little gothic mice.

I moved swiftly and silently up the staircase. On the second floor I found Theodosia and Aspasia in a disarrayed sitting room, bloodied and battered, but breathing. Theo's eyes flickered open when I knelt beside her. She hugged her ribcage tenderly, then whispered, 'Thaïs?' I made to stand, but Aspasia's hand snaked out and grabbed my wrist in a grip that belied her pummelled state. Her eyes bored into mine, so black they were abysses, and she spat, 'Angel.'

I shook her off and slid the Dagger of Wilusa from the ankle-sheath. I had no idea if it would have any effect, but it had stopped the golem in its tracks and other options were limited. Even with the weapon and my freakish strength, I wasn't the odds-on favourite here.

The noise in my head got worse as I ascended, but at least the nosebleed didn't start again. The door to Thaïs' sanctum had been wrenched off its hinges and half-blocked the hallway.

I sidled into the gap and stared.

As with the rest of the place, the furniture had been thrown around. The couches had been gutted, all exposed stuffing and broken springs. The chest of drawers coffee table had almost entirely disintegrated, its contents spilled across the polished timbers. Vials, cards, bronze bowls, athames, jewellery, tokens and charms, powders and dried herbs, gris-gris and fetishes, were all lying about as if a whirlwind had been through.

But what really drew my eyes was the sight of an angel holding Thaïs aloft. She hung from his fist like a captive kitten tired of struggling. Her face had turned a strange cherry hue and her lips were blue-tinged. The angel was shouting, and Thaïs' ears were bleeding.

I took advantage of the racket to creep towards them, cherishing the notion that he was too focused on trying to make the Norn talk to notice me; so much for that fond thought. As I got within arm's length – *his* arm, not mine, more's the pity – he brought his free hand up, incredibly fast, and swatted me away. My teeth and ribs rattled when I hit the wall and a rush of blackness threatened to wipe me out, but I fought it. Turns out nothing makes you focus quite like the sight of an enraged angel charging at you.

He'd dropped Thaïs' great bulk and was concentrating on me now. He didn't look too angelic any more, not with his gaze emptied of everything but fury. I stayed where I was, waiting until he bent down to scoop me up, then I side-scrambled as fast as I could. In reaching out to grab me he exposed the soft flesh of his left armpit and I jammed the dagger's long shaft into it, angling it down, in the hope it would reach his heart.

I didn't know whether it did, or whether the mere touch of the Boatman's knife was enough to undo him, but whatever the reason, he stopped yelling and his wings started jerking convulsively. He gave a surprised grunt, disbelief flaring brightly in his eyes, and elbowed me in the head as he slumped to the floor. I shuffled away quickly, terrified he would move again.

But he didn't do anything except smoulder briefly, then burst into fast-burning white flames. Soon he was gone, leaving nothing but a gleaming sapphire atop a large pile of grey ash. It was still hot, singeing my hand when I reached in to retrieve the dagger, which turned out to be completely undamaged. Blood started leaking from my poor abused nose and the cinders hissed as a few drops hit it.

Brisbane was down by one angelic watcher. That would teach him to betray the city that had fed him.

Thaïs lay on her side, gasping and spitting teeth. I crawled over to her, not yet ready to commit to standing myself. From the doorway came swearing, which meant Theo and Aspasia had made it up the stairs. The Misses Norn were obviously tougher than they looked, black eyes, broken smiles, cracked ribs and all.

I helped Thaïs to sit as the other two staggered in and flopped beside us. I contemplated the Sisters, and they stared back. Aspasia looked as if she didn't quite hate me any more, or at least less than she had. Without a word she handed me a scrap of cloth and I cleaned the dagger thoroughly. It still scared the crap out of me, but I was getting rather fond of that knife. The Norns all sported punched-out quadrate crosses: Aspasia on her left shoulder, Theo at the base of her throat and Thaïs high on her right cheek – not hidden away as with the sirens, but on display. Even when they healed, they'd be scarred. Somewhere in the mound of ash was the silver ring that had done that damage.

'You okay to talk?' I asked Thaïs, and when she nodded, I said pointedly, 'There's some stuff you left out when I came to see you last time.' Her blue eyes slid to the side, but I grabbed her chin and made her look at me, ignoring her when she winced – I supposed I was hitting places where the angel had bruised her, but I didn't really care at that moment. 'Because when the angels had a little chat with me very early this morning, they mentioned a prophecy: the prophecy of the double-winged. I would like all the information you have, please. I reckon that's the absolute bare minimum you can do, seeing as how I just saved your life. *All* of your lives.'

The truth of those words sank in for all of us; I could see the understanding bloom on their faces. I'd turned an angel to ash: one of the First, the Chosen, the Angelic Host, was dead by my hand, which probably wasn't going to do wonders for either my karma or my chances of surviving the next few days.

Thaïs said nothing, so I went on in an encouraging fashion, 'The Boatman said they want to "break the sky". The angels say their Arch is promising a return home – or at least a way out of this world. Got anything you want to add?'

'The blood of the double-winged will break the sky. It will let the angelics pass through – not literally the sky, but it will split open dimensions and let them out, leave them free to travel,' Thaïs replied at last.

'And the child of Serena and Tobit is the double-winged?'

'You know she is.'

'They're not planning to just prick her finger, are they?'

'They do love a blood sacrifice.'

'If they succeed, what are the consequences for us, Normal and Weyrd?'

'Darkness. A perpetual darkness.'

No daylight, forever night. The Normals likely wouldn't be able to handle such an inversion; they might not survive at all. The Weyrd would reign, those who wanted to, those with an axe to grind. All balance would be gone; Normals would become fodder for those revelling in an eternal eventide.

'And you didn't tell me this because—?'

'I thought maybe it wouldn't be such a bad thing.' The admission fell like a glass.

'*For fuck's sake!*' I heard myself shout. 'Every idiot wants immediate revolution with no consequences for themselves. Everyone wants an apocalypse that benefits *them* – but how do you not realise that change just brings new problems? If the sky is broken, if the angels leave – then *what else comes back in through the cracks*? Where do you think the 'serkers wait? And worse?' They all paled at that thought; even the Weyrd didn't much like their chances against the things that lived in the between spaces. 'You'll happily give up all the Normals just so you can play in the dark? *Seriously?* As if there haven't ever been mortals who've helped you somewhere along the line? As if each and every one of you hasn't owed your life to a human who didn't hate and hurt blindly? And *this* is how you want to repay them all for the sins of a few?'

I heaved myself upwards, heavy with despair. None of them would meet my eye.

'I've sent your waitresses to the healer. One had her tongue ripped out.' Theo closed her eyes. Aspasia swore and spat on the pile of angelic ash. Thaïs put a finger in her mouth, rooted around for a tooth shard, which she wrenched loose and threw across the ruined room.

I considered the wreckage of them. 'You'd better work out which side you're on, Sisters. You think you want a darkness? You think you want an apocalypse? You know that word means a great revealing light, right? Well, you might find yourself burned by it. You need to think very carefully about the consequences, about what you're prepared to deal with.'

They looked contrite, a little. I pointed at them, which might have been more impressive if my finger hadn't been shaking. 'And remember this: I saved your arses. Three lives are owed to me, and at some time I'll be coming to collect.'

I shambled to the door. The buzz in my skull had gone as soon as the angel burst into flames, but there was still a dull ache. My ribs and back hurt like bastards and a nerve twitched in my leg, but I didn't think anything was broken. My fingers were burned. On the upside, my nosebleed had slowed to a trickle.

I reached the ruined doorframe, turned and stared back at the trio. 'Close up here for a while, send the word out to anyone you can to go to ground. Find a safe place and hide. Will you be okay?'

'Just go, Fassbinder. You've got work to do,' snarled Aspasia.

As I headed down the stairs I pulled out my phone and called Ziggi, but he wasn't answering so I gave up and angrily hailed a cab. The taste of ashes in my mouth was strong and bitter.

Chapter Twenty-Nine

I got home around twelve, painfully aware that yet another change of clothes was required. How many outfits was I going to ruin in the course of this investigation? I threw the cinder-covered shirt and jeans in a corner. Oddly, the ash refused to brush off, and as I showered, I wondered whether it was corrosive, but no nasty rashes were popping up to suggest revenge was being taken from beyond the grave.

I dabbed aloe vera on my burned fingers and bandaged them, then gave the dagger another cleaning. The sheath had rubbed some blisters into my ankle, but I wasn't complaining; more aloe vera and more plasters sorted that out. I was just deeply grateful for the Swiss Army Knife of the Occult.

My stomach was rumbling, I put bread in the toaster, then wandered through the house while I waited. The place had been invaded, the rooms scoured, but that wasn't what was making me feel uncomfortable. It was the emptiness and silence. They had never bothered me before, not even after my grandparents died — maybe because I'd changed so little, it had always felt as though they were kind of still there. I'd liked it that way. Empty and quiet meant sanctuary, somewhere to fill as and when I wished, and with what and whom I chose. Even when Bela and I had been a couple, we'd never lived together. Except for those rare occasions when I'd been allowed to stay at his apartment at Highgate Hill, with its ultra-modern furniture, clean surfaces and Expressionist paintings, he'd mostly slept here.

Other than that, my house had always been quiet and empty, and I'd loved it.

But now it was quiet and empty and it felt wrong.

It was quiet and empty because David wasn't here; *quiet* and *empty* had become *lonely, dormant, stagnant*.

I'd got used to having him in my life and the warmth he brought so quickly that I'd begun to take his presence for granted. *Damn him*.

There was a *clang* from kitchen as the toast high-jumped. While I was eating, I contemplated whether or not the angels would return. I wondered if one might already be sitting on the fence or perched in a tree, all invisible and watchy, but my experience at Little Venice suggested that even if I couldn't see them, I would be able to sense them if they were close. I guessed the Arch's little tour through my brain might have left a trace. Did they know about that? Maybe it wasn't something that usually happened with Normals, maybe they couldn't work their voodoo on Weyrd . . . or maybe I was just strange enough that the effect on me was different. Perhaps it was an advantage.

Then again, if they realised one of their number was MIA, I was pretty sure they'd come charging over here. If they were all psychically connected, they'd already know Sapphire was soot and I wouldn't be sitting here blithely munching toast and jam. Maybe it was time to grab Lizzie and David and head somewhere they wouldn't expect us to be, like a roach motel on the outskirts of the city, or even Serena Kallos' empty home – I had her spare keys, after all.

I threw some clothes into a bag, locked up and took the now familiar route over the fence, just in case anyone was watching out front.

The back door opened slowly, but instead of being met by David's smiling face, I saw Mel's desolate one. Her left eye was puffy and blue-black, the right red-rimmed. Lizzie was sticking to her like Velcro. The little girl stared at me, tears dripping down her cheeks, and I wondered why she was so upset about having her mother home. I grinned widely and flung my arms around Mel and Lizzie, but as I stepped into the kitchen something felt wrong. A heavy, unhappy weight settled on my chest.

They hung on to me for dear life, and when we finally broke apart I said softly, 'Did you escape? Or did they let you go?'

Mel mumbled something, her face buried in Lizzie's tousled head.

I was beginning to feel very strange. 'What's that?'

She lifted her head and repeated, 'They swapped,' speaking hesitantly, carefully, as if the words were sharp and she might cut herself.

'*Swapped?*' My vision telescoped down to the single point of Mel's despairing face. 'Swapped *who*?'

She started crying, then Lizzie began to hiccough and sob and I strode past them, listening to the sounds of the house beneath their weeping, but I detected nothing, found not a trace of a man roaming around, in one of the spare rooms, going to the loo, washing his hands, coming out to greet me, asking what I'd found, what had happened, how I'd acquired my latest collection of bumps and bruises.

I turned back to them, swallowed, and demanded, 'Where's David?'

After that first wave of numbing fear, there was rage. The fear didn't dissipate, but it was overwhelmed by the welling tide of anger. I grasped Mel's shoulders and squeezed until I could feel muscle and bone, until she cried out, 'V, you're hurting me!'

Lizzie's terrified expression told me I'd become one of the monsters she'd been warned about.

Letting go, I stumbled away, stopping only when the leather couch caught me. I fell backwards and blinked and blinked and blinked as I tried to breathe. Though I wanted to ask rational questions, to find a solution, when I opened my mouth the only sound that issued was a wail.

The next time I paid attention to anything was when the sofa cushions shifted and Lizzie settled beside me. She put a hand on my arm. In her eyes was understanding, and a guilt centuries older than she was. I wrapped an arm around her and she leaned into me.

'It's my fault,' she whispered so her mother, busying herself in the kitchen, wouldn't hear. 'I wished so hard for Mum to come home I didn't think what it might cost.'

'Oh, sweetheart, no. It's not your fault.' I swam up from my own misery. '*None* of this is your fault, okay? Tell me it's not your fault.'

'It's not my fault,' she said in a very small, uncertain voice. 'But—'

'No, buts, Lizzie. Not ever,' I said as Mel carried two mugs into the room. Chamomile steam tickled my nose as I took a sip. I didn't feel any calmer and I hated the taste, but it gave me something to focus on. My hands shook and I considered the chances of me dropping the mug were pretty good. We sat for a while, sipping tea that I wished was gin and not saying anything, but in my head there were voices, lots of them. Thankfully, the most sensible was also the loudest, the one warning me that my life was circling precariously near the drain and I didn't have time to waste on self-pity; that tears would solve nothing; that I couldn't afford to fall apart just because all of *this* was cutting too close to my own bones.

Eventually I managed a shuddering breath and said, 'Care to fill me in?'

Mel's voice was tremulous as she started, 'There was this girl – there was a knock at the door and this blonde girl was waiting. It took me a moment to realise how young she was because she was plastered in really awful heavy make-up. She was acting so nervous, looking guilty – honestly, I thought she was casing the joint, but then she asked, "Why's bloody Verity Fassbinder not home?" I didn't know what you'd want me to say, so I just told her you were at work, then she handed me an envelope and said to make sure you got it. But it was like she panicked then, because she just took to her heels and bolted.'

I'd really hoped Sally had left Brisbane, gone somewhere safe, but I had this dreadful feeling that the girl had no aptitude for finding safe places.

Mel was still speaking. 'I closed the door and was putting the letter on the hall table when someone else knocked and I thought it must be the girl again, but it wasn't. It was a blonde woman – she had this weird birthmark on her neck – and a young man with her, really skinny and sick-looking, with a bandage on his left forearm – but God, V, he *stank*.' She wiped a hand across her forehead as if to rub a headache away. 'The woman asked to come inside, sweet as pie, but I was really creeped out by the stench and anyway, I didn't know her, or the guy, and when I asked *why*, she dropped all pretence of being nice and just *forced* her way in.

'I . . . I grabbed the guy's arm and the dressing came away, and' – she shuddered, looking sick – 'he screamed and screamed, and I swear I saw him *change* . . . Honest, V, I wasn't hallucinating; it was almost like his shape blurred, as if his body was falling apart . . .

'Then the woman back-handed me and I fell over, and that cow started kicking me in the guts until I thought I was going to vomit. I must've blacked out for a moment, then I came to and she was re-bandaging the boy's arm and yelling, "*Hold it together!*" I thought perhaps she was focused on him and I tried to sit up, but she must've had eyes in the back of her head because before I knew what'd hit me, I got Tasered, then she laid into me again until I really did pass out from the pain.'

Mel was trying hard to keep herself calm, for her sake as much for Lizzie's. She sounded very matter-of-fact as she described waking up blindfolded. 'I was lying on a bed, my wrists had been tied to the metal bed-head. The woman kept interrogating me, about what you could do, about your father – and I don't think she believed me when I said I didn't know a damn thing about your dad, that I'd never met him because he'd died when you were a kid. I couldn't hear much – there was traffic, but a long way away, and sometimes people talking in another room – but it felt like there was someone else in the room with me, just watching and listening – not the stinking young man, though.'

After the first day, she'd been mostly left alone. The woman had stopped questioning her, but she started feeding her the occasional cold McCaptive Meal. Mel didn't say she'd just about given up all hope, but I was pretty sure that's how she'd been feeling when the woman suddenly untied her and bundled her into what felt like the back of a van. She was still blindfolded, and she'd been driven around for ages, and when the vehicle finally stopped she was dragged out and marched along a path, then made to stand there while someone banged on a door.

'Someone jammed a gun into my side – well, I don't know if it really was a gun, but it was cold and hard—'

Mel's voice was shaking, and I held her hand; I really needed her to finish the story, although I was pretty sure I knew what happened next. At last she whispered, 'I heard a man's voice, a nice voice, but sounding all tense – and then I heard Lizzie, and the woman said, "You've got two choices: either you swap places or you let the little girl watch her mother die", and I think I screamed then . . .'

That really was no choice.

I concentrated on Mel's tale, examining the details and what they told me. The dagger had obviously done considerable damage to Donovan Baker, which made me happy. And interestingly, his companion sounded very much like the Concrete Blonde – so less his victim than I'd thought; looked like the kid had had a girlfriend after all.

If they'd taken Mel to get information about me, she couldn't have given them anything even if she'd wanted to. Maybe they'd taken her for leverage too, to make me stop what I was doing, and when they realised they'd made a mistake, the bar had to be raised somehow. They needed a more valuable piece on the chessboard . . . but why not take David in the first place? Had he not been around when they first came calling, and they'd not wanted to go away empty-handed? Or had they come when they *knew* I wouldn't be there? They could have learned about David from Mel; she knew he existed, that I felt something for him. And Ziggi and Bela knew about him . . . but I couldn't imagine who they'd tell . . . so that suggested I was being watched.

'He said to hurry,' Mel quavered finally. 'David said. If you wouldn't mind.'

In spite of everything, I smiled – and stopped at the sudden sound of a ruckus on the front porch, a familiar voice swearing loudly and an equally familiar voice cursing at even greater volume.

'Open it,' I told Mel, who was looking scared, and she did so, then stepped aside sharply as a thin body fell inside.

Ziggi stumbled in close behind. 'Look what I found,' he said proudly.

Rose Wilkes called him more names as she struggled to her feet, but she stopped in her tracks when she saw Mel and all the disappointment in the world dripped from her mouth as she said, 'Oh, fuck, you're back,' as if her sister had been on a holiday she herself had wanted to take. I'd never before seen Mel lose her temper, but now she drew back a fist and decked Rose with a single blow. It was the one bright spot in my day.

Lizzie, still sitting next to me, peered at her mother with wide eyes. 'You said violence never solved anything, Mum.'

Mel breathed out and shook her hand. 'No, baby, it doesn't, but sometimes it's the only thing that makes you feel better.'

Chapter Thirty

'How could you think it was me? What have I *ever* done to you?'

The icy silence was ten minutes old, so even this grumpy challenge was a relief.

'I didn't *think* it was you, I just . . . asked.' And was fervently wishing with all my heart that I hadn't.

The eye in the back of his head was not forgiving. All I'd said was, *Is it possible you've told someone something about me that you shouldn't have?* But I might as well have said, *To whom hast thou been betraying me, varlet?* for the reaction I got. On the upside, when he'd answered, '*What the fuck are you talking about?*', it jerked a response out of Rose, lying on the floor with a bloodied nose. Her very unwise snorting and smirking instantly gained my attention.

I lifted her up by the shirt and shook her, really hoping she'd confess everything, but what she actually said was, 'Put me down, bitch!' which didn't help matters. So I shook her a bit more until she started crying and gave me what I wanted. In between the sobbing and the wiping away of red-tinted snot, Rose blurted out the tale of how she'd met this blonde woman in a bar who'd offered actual cash money for any tidbits Rose could provide about my movements – *anything* about me, in fact, even the boring stuff. She'd been given a throwaway mobile to text all and any information to a number that was most probably just another disposable. I liberated the phone, ignoring her vocal disapproval, and found just one number saved to it. It made me so mad; Rose didn't know why she was betraying me, and she didn't care either. She just wanted the money the woman with the dark red birthmark had been leaving every couple of days, posting the envelopes through the letterbox of the vacant house across the street where Rose had been squatting. Her clunker of a car had been hidden under a tarp out back .

Rose denied having anything to do with Mel's kidnapping, and I had to believe her, although she was positively miffed that her sister was back, because she really wasn't that good a liar.

Perhaps I shouldn't have been surprised at Mel's willingness and efficiency in trussing up Rose Wilkes like a rolled roast before locking her in a cupboard.

Before Ziggi could circle back to his '*What did you mean by that?*' huff I'd had another thought. 'Where's Sally's letter?' I asked Mel.

The small table in the hall was as bare as it had been when I'd first discovered Mel was missing, but Lizzie was on it, doing what the adults wouldn't have thought to and reaching under the couch.

'Here it is!' she cried, brandishing the envelope. She also recovered a five-dollar note, four two-dollar coins, a fur-covered lollipop and a single hot pink stiletto belonging to a Barbie she'd long ago discarded as boring.

The dirt and crease-marks notwithstanding, the envelope was obviously expensive: the creamiest of cream fabric paper with a raised ripple texture. There was no stamp, no name, no address for either recipient or sender. It had been closed tight with a big glob of red wax, nothing imprinted in it, sloppily applied as if by an uncaring and inexperienced hand. It sure seemed like Sally's work.

Cracking the seal revealed an equally expensive-looking, badly folded sheet inside with a list of thirteen names, all in an exquisite script made almost unreadable by flourishes and curlicues that most certainly weren't Sally's style. But when your handwriting is as bad as mine, you become a cryptology specialist; I could have had a great career as a pharmacist. Mercado White appeared midway down. I recognised a few more old Weyrd families, and another few *nouveau riche*. One name in particular stood out. I wasn't sure if I was surprised or not.

Then it was just a matter of convincing Ziggi to drive, even though what he really wanted to do was fight with me. He gave in with ill grace and continued the silent treatment as soon as we got in the cab.

'I'm sorry,' I sighed. 'I didn't mean you'd done it on purpose, just maybe you'd been chatting to someone who might have chatted to someone else, and in the manner of these things, it made its way to the ears of someone it shouldn't.'

'So now you think I'm some kind of *chatterbox*?'

I refrained from asking if it was his time of the month and settled for placating him the only way I knew how. 'I should have known better and I'm sorry. I'll make it up to you, just as soon as Little Venice re-opens.'

'Little Venice is closed? What did you *do*?'

Clearly I'd made things worse.

I assured him it wasn't my fault – it really wasn't, although I did give what might have been a slightly self-serving version of the angelic visit to the café. He grumbled, but without any actual words of dissent or disgust, which was a clear sign of thawing. As I was about to continue peace negotiations, my phone squeaked and McIntyre's ID flashed up. I felt irrationally happy and thankful she was returning calls at last.

But the voice wasn't Rhonda's.

'Is this Verity?' Soft, tentative tones.

'Who is this?'

The woman sniffed, as if she'd been crying a lot. 'Ellie – Ellen Baxter. We met at the morgue.'

The tattooed tech. Rhonda's girlfriend. 'Oh, hi. Where's McIntyre?' I asked. 'I need to speak to her; we've got some problems. Some new ones.'

'She can't talk; that's why I'm calling.' Her voice shook. 'Rhonda's sick.'

'Is she okay?' I said, wishing I could stop the words even as they left my mouth. I assumed my First Prize for Stupidest Question of the Year would be in the mail.

'No – she's got throat cancer. She's been admitted to the Royal Brisbane. She started coughing at home last night and couldn't stop. It was horrible; she was struggling to breathe, there was blood coming up, and—'

'Shit. Oh shit.' It felt like a hammer-blow to an already broken limb. 'I'm so sorry. Is she—?'

'She's sedated. I don't know when she can come home. *If*. If she can . . .' She started weeping in earnest, and it took me a moment to work out she'd said, 'I thought she was going to die.'

'Oh, Ellen.'

'It came on so fast . . . I mean, she's been ill, but she's been having chemo – she's been *responding* well. Then this . . . It got worse after she talked to that angel.'

The dying and the mad can see angels. That day in her office I'd told her they hung around churches. She'd gone looking for them . . . 'Ellie, what happened?' I asked urgently. 'Do you know which one – which angel?'

'He wanted . . . She asked him to heal her – she *begged*, and he just laughed. He said we were all so *small*, so *unimportant*, that we weren't special, and one less of us would make no difference.' Her tone took on an edge of righteous anger. 'She's *believed*, her whole life, despite all that anti-gay shit, and that's what he told her! But then . . .'

I waited, letting her talk at her own pace. 'He said everything had a price. That he'd help her if she'd help him.'

'What was the price?'

'The baby – the one you've been looking for. He wanted Rhonda to tell him when you found it, to tell him everything you'd said, everywhere you'd been.' She took a deep breath, then added, 'She didn't, you know, she didn't tell him anything.'

'She wouldn't,' I agreed. Rhonda McIntyre was a grumpy, tough old bat and I knew, without a shadow of doubt, that even if she had known where the baby was, she wouldn't give up the child's life. *Any* child's life.

'Ellie, did she say anything about how the angel looked? Was there a gemstone on his breastplate?'

She paused, thinking. 'Blue. She said it was blue.'

Brisbane's own special boy. He hadn't rummaged through her brain, which made me think the Arch was the only one who could do that. She must have found Sapphire when he was alone, waiting for the others. The angel had pissed her off, so she'd made sure Ellie told me everything, because she figured the worst thing she could possibly do was to set me on him. He'd made her illness worse, but she'd put her revenge in motion. I smiled, strangely proud of her faith in me.

'I don't know what I'm going to do,' Ellen whispered.

I knew how she felt. 'Stay by her side – be there when she wakes. Talk to her, hold her hand. She'll know you're around, and that's the best thing you can do for her. And let her know . . .' I swallowed, hard, then said firmly, 'Let her know I'll make them all bleed.'

She was bawling when I hung up, and I was pretty close myself. I leaned against the headrest. Apparently the Universe felt obliged to add a few more concrete blocks to the load already on my chest.

'You okay?' Ziggi asked.

'No. No, I am not.' Then I wailed, 'Oh, shit, Ziggi, when will it end?' I pulled myself together and gave him the side of the conversation he hadn't heard and we fell silent again, less uncomfortably now.

Then he circled back to David, his intentions good. 'They won't kill him, you know. They didn't kill Mel. There's no leverage in the dead.'

'That's great. You should be a guidance counsellor,' I snapped, and that was the end of our friendly chat. I closed my eyes until at last he said, 'We're here,' and I felt us pulling to a stop. When we got out of the cab, I went to the driver's side, reached in and wrapped my arms around Ziggi's waist, muttering, 'I'm sorry.'

'I know.' He stroked my hair just like my father used to before the world turned upside down.

Bela was waiting outside the rectory. There were another six Weyrd, lounging in the late afternoon sun, slouched against walls, sitting on the loveseat in the front garden and hanging from tree branches – including Hairy Jerry and Monobrow Mike, the pair who'd let Mercado White get away. They'd all let their glamours slip and were sporting the leathery wings, thick furs, scaly skins and bone plates they usually kept firmly under wraps. Eyes glowed a little too brightly, some red torches, others green and blue; ears were either overly developed or little more than niches set high on the sides of skulls. They watched us – no, they watched *me*. The sun was behind the building, giving it a kind of halo.

'I'm sorry about—' Bela stopped when he saw my face. Everything had already been said when I'd called in the goon squad. He cleared his throat. 'You want company in there?'

'Nope, I've got this. Just make sure all the exits are covered.' I didn't want any distractions, but mostly I didn't want anyone standing between me and whatever I had to do to get David back. The front door opened; Father Tony, his expression sombre, stood aside to let me pass, then touched my arm.

'This is a place of refuge,' he said, as if reminding me to eat my greens.

'Father, she bought wine made from the tears of children; they died during the harvest. Would you like me to give her a pat on the head?'

His hand fell away. 'Just . . . try not to . . . break anything. I don't want Miriam to get upset.' Behind me he closed the door to sitting room rather reluctantly.

The lumpy chairs with their over-stuffed cushions were in the same position, but only one was occupied. Eleanor Aviva wore a stylish wrap dress of blood-red, and a new handbag nestled in her lap. Around her neck was a fetching iron collar to dampen her powers and keep her from disappearing.

She smiled, stroked the choker. 'Ms Fassbinder, lovely to see you again so soon. Do you like my latest accessory?'

'Did Mercado know that you were a fellow client of the Winemaker?'

'No small talk for little Verity Fassbinder!' She laughed, and it wasn't especially unpleasant. 'My dear, did Mercado strike you as one to keep his mouth shut if he could save his own skin by giving up someone else's?'

'Good point.'

'His ancestors were weasels, you know.'

'How appropriate.' I sat across from her on a chair that felt like concrete sculpted to look soft. The discomfort helped me concentrate, dulled the throbbing anxiety slightly. 'So.'

'So, indeed.' She eyed me as if time was on her side.

'So, you know more than you've told.' I stared, trying to detect anything untoward, but for all intents and purposes she was an attractive, elegant middle-aged woman with great taste in handbags. Was she too young to be a contemporary of Magda Nadasy, or was that just another cunning glamour?

'Most people do.'

'How about I ask questions and you answer in a full and frank fashion?' Much though I wanted to hurt her, that wouldn't have done any good. What my acquaintance with Eleanor Aviva had taught me so far was that she didn't spook easily. She'd waited confidently as the whole Winemaker scandal came to a head around her and brazened it out. After Magda's death she had probably thought it was all over. 'Feel free to offer any insights to help me or make your peers consider you more favourably.'

'Oh, you sweet thing.' She laughed again. 'Ask away.'

'You were a client of Madame Nadasy's?'

'Yes, but I wasn't aware it was her. I always dealt with that urchin.' She sighed. 'I know it was naughty, but I hadn't had anything like that in such a long time. The road to hell is paved not with good intentions but with nostalgia. However, my dear, I don't think this track will get you very far.'

'And you'd suggest?'

'What would you give for information relating to Vadim Nadasy and his little pet?'

'I'm just the hired help. I can't make any deals about your fate.'

'Ah, but our darling Zvez— . . . Bela will listen to you. We both know that.'

I was aware of no such thing, but I kept my lips sealed as I thought furiously. If I could use her delusion for my own ends, I would. 'If what you tell me pays off, then I'll put in a good word.'

'Can't say fairer than that.' She sat up straight. 'You wondered, no doubt, why Nadasy didn't kill Baker himself.'

'You know I did.'

'Did you know there was a woman's body – in addition to the males – found in Baker's house after it was blown up?'

'Yes, Dusana's.'

She shook her head. 'It's the only body that counts, really.' She grinned, and her teeth were bright white and terribly sharp. Why is it always the teeth?

If Dusana hadn't died . . .

As if reading my mind, her smile widened. 'Everyone assumed it was her, but it was, I think, some friend of the pool boy, the gardener or the tennis instructor. Someone no one looked for, someone mistaken for the lady of the house. But whoever it was, it was *not* Vadim's daughter. And no one investigated too closely because dear Anders greased the right palms in the right manner.'

'She's *alive*?' I asked.

'Mr Baker was fed up, you see. He knew he'd never get away with killing her – he was as terrified of Nadasy as the rest of us – but he wanted to do *something*. His wife had gone out of her way to humiliate and torment him and he wanted to start over, but on his terms. Beginnings are *so* hard, that's why we always try to go back to them, to change them, make things move differently. To make things go our way.'

'So what did he do?'

'He paid someone a fantastical sum to cast a spell to enchant the girl, to make her into something more . . . static . . . more *manageable* . . .'

'And Nadasy?'

'Oh, he confronted Baker, threatened him – Anders is a horrible little man, but he's stubborn. He let Nadasy know that Dusana was alive, but he said if *he* died, she would too. That was his bargaining chip, you see; that's how he was able to keep Vadim at bay. He tormented him with the knowledge that without Anders, he'd never find his darling daughter, never have the chance to release her. Hope is so corrosive, isn't it?'

'And that's why he stopped asking the Council to punish Baker.'

She giggled, an odd sound coming from her. 'Then Vadim disappeared and everyone assumed he'd given up. But I think he went off to learn darker magic, to become more powerful so he could find Dusana himself and break the binding. He wanted to become someone feared not just by us but by the Normals too: those who walk so bravely in daylight.'

'Who cast the spell?' The more she said about Nadasy, the more my fear for David swelled, but I had to push it down for the moment and concentrate.

She pursed her lips. 'What you need to understand, and I trust you'll take this into consideration when you speak to dear Bela, is that Nadasy had been talking for some time about taking back the world, both night and day. He talked of staging a coup, leading a revolution against the Normals. He was stirring things up, finding those Weyrd willing to listen to his ridiculous ideas. So, when a certain person was approached by Anders Baker, looking for a means to put his new beginning into action, perhaps that person thought of a way to help distract Nadasy from his goals – to make the wheels fall off, as it were.'

'You.'

'Clever child.' Her smile never wavered. 'Nadasy was a great snob, not just about Normals, but about Weyrd too: half of us weren't good enough for him, our bloodlines insufficiently regal. Not all of us can have the blood of the Bathorys – inbred, every one, I promise you – running through our veins. Our breeding doesn't affect our power or our potential; a peasant might as easily bring down an empire as a prince.'

I could have sworn speculation gleamed in her eyes as she said *peasant*.

'And Dusana? Where is she?'

'Have you not seen Baker's mermaid? A fairly tasteless piece, I always thought, but one must work with the tools one has.' She watched her own fingers playing with the gold spider pendant dangling from her bag. It had rubies for eyes, eight of them.

Understanding started to creep up my neck like multiple tiny sticky feet.

'Lifelike, isn't it?' Her gaze met mine, flashing red. How did she look under her glamour? How many legs might be apparent if she let it slip, just for a moment; how many fangs might jut from her mouth?

'You . . .' In my imagination I superimposed the bronze mermaid's face over the portrait in Baker's sitting room; the features, now in context, matched perfectly. 'You turned her into *that*? You left her like that for more than fifteen years?'

'I never liked her. She was as uppity as her father. Besides' – she gestured eloquently with bejewelled fingers – 'Baker offered a *lot* of money. Hermès handbags don't come cheap.'

I licked my lips a few times. My mouth felt parched. Donovan Baker's mother had watched him his whole life. Did he know? I was willing to bet not. And Anders Baker had overseen his wife all those years. I felt queasy.

'And now Nadasy's back—'

'Well, I suspect he's learned much in his time abroad. He probably thinks he can free his daughter, if he can find her. And if Vadim's got his hands on Baker – whom I understand has disappeared – and he thinks he can get away with killing him now, then I don't trust Anders not to give me up if his other leverage is gone. My chances of survival are vastly increased by standing behind the likes of you.'

'Your faith is flattering.' I picked at a thread on the arm of my chair and found myself having to resist the urge to keep pulling until the weave broke. 'Where is Nadasy?'

'I wish I knew . . . imagine my bargaining power if I did.' She clasped her hands and rested them on the bag. 'I think that's enough. I'm very impressed at your self-control, given the trying circumstances, but I'm not sure how much patience you've got left.'

'You're smarter than you look.' I stood, kept my tone even and said, 'And remember: if anything happens to my lover, I'll come for you. It won't matter who you try to hide behind, I will tear you apart.'

At last her smile wavered and she blinked furiously. I rose and opened the door; Father Tony appeared as if by magic. I jerked my chin in his direction and he disappeared again, presumably to call Bela. Eleanor Aviva and I waited in silence. I thought about popping her head off, just to see what she looked like after death, to see if the glamour would fade and reveal her in what I suspected would be arachnid glory. I wanted to see if that might release some of my tension, let some of the distress drain away. But I didn't. I didn't have the energy. I felt sick at heart at the thought of David at the mercy of the mage and the golem. It was clear Nadasy had taken him in revenge for Magda, my loved one in return for his, and despair threatened to overwhelm me, until the sound of Bela's footsteps pulled me back.

My time with Eleanor Aviva was done.

'Good luck,' she called as I left the room. I didn't turn around.

Chapter Thirty-One

The low sun left little licks of silvery-gold on the ripples of the river; the wind bit through my jacket and turned my hands to ice as I held the dagger out over the water. I was crouched on a rocky outcrop, studiously ignoring Ziggi standing on the nice flat path behind the guardrail, sighing loudly and telling me every few minutes that he was cold and bored and utterly convinced there had to be a better way of doing this.

Stupid as I felt, this was the only option I had left. As the certainty I was wasting precious time became heavier, the harder it was not to turn around and yell rude things at my friend. But I did my best to ignore him and concentrate on the sole means I could think of to summon the Boatman. Things like the Dagger of Wilusa didn't exist in isolation: they were connected to the world like spiders at the centre of their webs. They linked to the elements, their owners, their custodians, to the acts they'd committed, sometimes to *anyone* who'd touched them . . . and the Boatman ticked at least two of those boxes. So I continued huddling determinedly as the blade vibrated and sang, much like an attack of tinnitus. If the only course to draw the Boatman out was by irritating the hell out of him, well, under the circumstances, I was okay with that.

Finally, the temperature dropped even further and the air started thickening and whitening until a fog was churning around me. A glance over my shoulder showed Ziggi as nothing more than a faint silhouette. In a frozen moment the boat and its oarsman were floating in front of me, staying in one place with no discernable effort, as close as he could get to the shore without running aground and losing all professional dignity. In the bow hunched a figure, facing away from me. I stood, feeling my knees crack, stretching out my arms to steady myself.

The Boatman's hood fluttered on the wind and I could see he was less than pleased. Then his shoulders lifted, a gesture I took to mean he was demanding to know what I wanted and why hadn't I done whatever it was I was supposed to do? Had I been able to reach him, I'd have wrung his scrawny neck.

'What do you want me to do?' I yelled.

'Stop them,' he yelled back, shaking a fist.

'*How?*' I glanced down at the figure at his feet, who was now looking up at me. A long cut had ruined Anders Baker's throat and rust-red blood covered the front of his expensive cream pullover and designer jeans. Stunned, I blurted, 'What happened to you?'

'They have no voice, not until they pass through. Do you imagine that any would remain silent on this last journey? That they would not howl their despair?' the Boatman asked. 'Voices have power, and these are powerless.'

Had Nadasy found him and learned the secret of Dusana's fate? I hoped not. As soon as I'd told Bela what I'd learned, he'd set out for Baker's place with full-on goon squad and informant in tow. What if I'd sent him into a confrontation with the mage? Though they'd been friends once, I didn't think Nadasy held too many lives sacred these days.

Maybe it wasn't Nadasy, I thought. After all, the list of folk Baker had pissed off was long. Bela had back-up; David was on his own.

David might already be dead and growing cold, said that shitty little voice in my head. *He's being tortured, maimed, broken, and it's all my fault.* I shuddered and returned my attention to the Boatman, who was looking decidedly impatient.

'I get it, you're not supposed to interfere, but the golem – do you know *anything* about it? Its master, Nadasy? They've taken—'

He was shaking his head, maybe a bit sadly, as if to say *I can manage only one crisis at a time.*

'Stop *them*, the angelics,' he said. 'They will break the sky and night will be forever. They will change the nature of death.'

Okay, so I could see he had a stake in that.

'How can I stop them if I can't fucking find them?' I shouted, losing my temper just a little with someone I definitely needed not to piss off. 'Or anyone else?'

He pointed upwards, jabbing at the air: upwards, and kind of *behind*. We were below St Mary's Church.

'Spaces are not what they seem.' The mist shifted again, thinning and dissolving into nothingness. Anders Baker turned his eyes in the direction of travel. The Boatman shook his head as if he couldn't believe he'd put faith in me.

'Spaces are not what they seem,' I muttered. I thought about City Hall and its hidden dimensions. I thought about how easy it might be to hide something in plain sight. I clambered up the rocks and as soon as I hit the path I started to run, almost knocking Ziggi over as I yelled, 'Spaces are not what they seem!'

I didn't need to check to see if he was following me.

The cliffs were deserted, no sign of any siren conclaves, angels, abseilers, or random sightseers to be seen in the last of the daylight. *No one.* It was almost as if the city's population as a whole had sensed something wasn't quite right, wasn't quite safe, and had gone home to hunker down with a cup of tea and chocolate biscuits until whatever threatened had blown over.

I ran up the stone steps, panting for breath, half-skipped, half-jogged towards St Mary's and pushed through the gate. I took the corner of the church a little too sharply and felt a pain in my knee, which I ignored; I had to keep going. Out past the garden, where the ground fell away, the sky was shot with pink and red, with silver limning the clouds. I circled the building, coming at last to where the ragged stones and missing masonry were hiding more than they revealed.

There had once been a room there.

Perhaps there still was.

I stepped forward, just as I had that night when I'd been hit by the thrown stone. The air congealed, feeling like glue against my skin, but I pressed on, blindly hoping that the ward, like so many others, wouldn't work on me, or at least not entirely. Only when my lungs began to burn did I start to doubt . . .

. . . and then I was through, gasping and stumbling into a well-lit chamber. It was warm, and to my relief there was no scent of decay. There was, however, a crib, rocking chair, changing table and baby bath, and toys had been scattered across the thick rug. The two solid walls were hung with sumptuous tapestries depicting ladies and unicorns getting on famously, both gorgeous, and perfect for keeping away the chill. A camp bed piled with blankets said someone else was spending time here too: someone who'd gone to the trouble of making it comfortable and safe.

The enchanted walls that hid the stone nursery from the outside world were transparent, and through them I could see the manse and the community hall, and the hospice beyond.

Then a gurgle came from the crib and I turned back and bent down, pushing aside the net with its lilac ribbons, embroidered purple butterflies and yellow bunnies. Sitting in the middle of creamy sheets was a violet-eyed baby girl with a ton of curly black hair, wearing only a nappy, a drooly grin and two sets of unbound wings. The pair closest to her skin were black, the others, smaller and silver, nestled just inside the first like the petals of a flower: so beautiful, so magical – and putting her in mortal danger. They were only wings, but they had turned her into a *thing*, wanted and pursued. With them, she would always be hunted.

Beside her lay a half-full bottle, still warm, which suggested her guardian wasn't long gone. Calliope Kallos was well cared for, apart from an untimely diaper issue. I wrinkled my nose and she laughed, a sound bright as bells. Fortunately, the changing table was equipped with all the necessities.

'This was not on my List of Firsts, baby.' I peeled open the nappy. 'Oh, sweet mother of crap!'

After cleaning her up with an inordinate number of wet wipes and spraying half a ton of talc everywhere, things were a little less dire.

'You'd think a divine infant might manage to poop something a bit more fragrant,' I told her, but the baby just kept laughing and dribbling. When I picked her up, she snuffled against my neck. She smelled sweet, floral, but not like powder. She smelled like Tobit; his odour of sanctity clung to her.

Jiggling her back and forth, I peered through the walls, but the only person I could see was Ziggi, puffing up the cracked asphalt drive, looking for me. Utter perplexity was writ large on his face.

'Ready for this, kid?' I marvelled at the intense colour of her eyes as she gurgled up at me. I grabbed a pink bunny rug to wrap her in, then paused. Where could I take her? Where was safe? Maybe the Rectory—

'Don't,' an angry growl pierced me, 'or I will gut you where you stand.'

I pivoted; the pile of blankets had fallen from the bed, revealing Ligeia's hiding place. She stood tall beside the crib, her wings spread to make herself more threatening, brandishing her umbrella in a white-knuckled grip. She pointed her left hand at me, grubby talons growing longer and sharper as I watched. The summer dress might be filthy beyond rescue, her feathers scraggy and moulting, but Ligeia was a terrifying sight in her protective rage.

Trying to stop my voice shaking and summon some of the confidence I'd felt when she stalked me in the Botanical Gardens, I said firmly, 'I think you'd have done it by now, Ligeia, if you meant to, like when my back was turned.' I wasn't at all sure of that, but I had to believe that it wasn't just because she preferred her prey to know what was coming. This was such a dangerous gambit: if I died here, no one could save David. Still, she didn't move, just stared at me intently.

'You know she's in danger,' I said.

'Calliope is safe *here*. I will protect her. I promised my granddaughter.'

Serena.

'I know you want to – I know you'd die for her, Ligeia, but she can't stay in here forever. How many years will you be able to hide her? The angels aren't going to go away; they aren't going to stop hunting for her. They'll keep killing people, sirens and humans alike. It'll mean more loss, more grief.'

'*You* can't protect her,' she sneered.

'I can protect her better than you did her mother,' I said meanly. That was unfair, especially since I'd let Serena down too, but I could see I'd hit home. I went on, a little more gently now, 'Maybe not me, but I know people who can.'

I hoped that was true: Bela, the Councillors, even the Norns – somebody could at least whisk her away.

Ligeia bared her teeth and took three deliberate steps towards me.

I raised my voice. 'There's got to be somewhere more secure than this!' She halted, and I added, 'Ligeia, this baby needs *a chance* – a chance to be what she wants. She needs the opportunity to grow and choose a life for herself. She's too small now to make her own decisions, but she can't stay here. I can get her to safety – we can get her out of Brisbane and away from the Arch. We can give her the choices you didn't have; the choices Eurycleia denied her daughter.'

Still she stayed silent and in an anger born of despair I yelled, 'You couldn't save Serena. You couldn't save Teles, or Raidne. Let *me* save Calliope.'

And finally the old siren's shoulders slumped and her wings drooped as her hands dropped to her sides. On her ravaged face was all the pain of defeat and loss, a look I'd been imagining on my own face at the thought of letting David down. I shook the thought away and held the baby tighter, as if she were an anchor.

'Ligeia, I'm taking her now. You can come with us, and I promise you can stay by her side, but you need to let me do this, for Callie's sake.' I waited for her to answer, to either agree or dissent, but she did neither, just appeared crushed. 'You'll find me if you need anything?'

She still didn't speak and I risked turning my back. The nape of my neck and the spot between my shoulder blades twitched as I stepped into the invisible barrier, but the return trip wasn't as bad; it took less of an effort and the burning in my lungs settled far more quickly. It didn't bother the child at all, and as we came out into the dusk she gave a delicate little baby fart that stank up the fresh air. What the hell had Ligeia been feeding her?

Ziggi, who'd planted himself at the base of one of the tall pine trees, saw us and smiled, dusting himself off as he climbed to his feet. I headed towards him, then watched as his mouth slowly turned down. I didn't have to ask why.

On the wind came the beating of enormous wings, sounding terrifyingly like a cohort of Black Hawks. A humming in my head set alight every promise I'd made to Ligeia, every chance I had of surviving, of finding David, and turned all my hopes to ash. *Something angelic this way came.*

Chapter Thirty-Two

You can't outrun an angel; I knew that without having to be told. Ziggi's cab was still down beside the river, and there weren't enough trees to duck through in the vain hope that the hordes might fly into them and come a cropper. I ran towards Ziggi as six angels dropped into the garden in front of us. One of them was larger than the others: the Archangel, deigning to show himself at last. I kept thinking about Serena and Teles and Raidne, with their skin branded, their wings torn off. Cut off from the hidden room by a flanking angel, Ziggi and I backed into the front entrance of St Mary's, a tiny covered portico, putting the pair of padlocked doors at our backs.

The entourage landed about twenty feet away. The Arch took a few steps towards us, the sound of thunder ringing every time his feet touched the ground. He dragged something in his wake: Tobit. His arms had been tied behind him and a bronze choke-chain encircled his neck. The other end was being brandished nonchalantly by the Arch. 'Worse for wear' didn't even begin to cover his condition. His gaze was desolate as it slid over us, then he fell face-down into the grass, apparently out cold.

About ten feet away, the Arch paused for effect. I had to admit he was truly a thing of beauty, even more than his disciples. Long silver hair flowed over broad shoulders; green eyes flared like the Aurora

Australis. He wore bracers and greaves that shone like jet, and his sable boots had pale pearl lacings. His chiton was black, and in the centre of the burning heart in his breastplate was a mosaic of twelve precious stones. My chest tightened: *this* was what had been in my brain outside St Stephen's.

The baby raised her head and burped, dribbled down the front of my jacket, then looked at the troop. Her little fists clenched. I thought it pretty unlikely she'd sensed they were there for her, but she wasn't oblivious to the tension crackling around us. She didn't cry, though, and I was proud of her.

I cleared my throat. 'You've been following me?'

The Arch smiled smugly and shook his handsome head. He threw the end of Tobit's chain to no one in particular, assuming someone would catch it, and the ruby-hearted ginger did. 'We did not follow you, for you would have sensed us. We followed *it*.'

He pointed to Ziggi, who appeared surprised – I wasn't sure if it was being tracked, or being called an 'it'. Perhaps it was a little of both. We must have looked blank, for the Arch said impatiently, 'Where you go, it invariably follows.'

'My friend is not an *it*! Although admittedly he does follow me a lot.'

Ziggi said helplessly, 'Sorry, V.'

I said, 'You couldn't have known.'

'Thus we come to this meeting,' began the Arch, and his smile slid from me to the baby and back again. Calliope shrank against me – she *definitely* knew something was up – and I held her more tightly. 'It appears that you have what I want.'

I took in my adversary and weighed up my chances of facing off against him or the golem. On balance I kind of preferred the golem; the golem got straight into it. But the Arch was wasting my time,

time during which I didn't know what was happening to David. For all I knew, the Arch was running down my clock. I needed to speed this up. 'Looks like it.'

He smiled again, and this time there was a real power behind it, and as that power got stronger I began to feel . . . strange . . . a kind of awe, in the oldest sense: devotion and fear and amazement, all rolled into utter belief. In short, I started to feel something I really shouldn't: I was angel-struck. The small part of my mind that was still my own marvelled at the degree of dominance this creature must have had to break through my Weyrd DNA, to affect me as easily as Tobit had David. Maybe that was my problem: the Normal part of me was my Achilles' heel.

I fought the influence, but it was like trying to escape from a sealed plastic wrapper.

'Now,' said the Archangel in a soothing and reasonable tone, 'now, you have something I want, something I *need*. But I do not wish to take it – I do not wish to leave you *bereft*. I know how these things work, these *deals*. We have been negotiating with your kind for aeons. Therefore, Verity Fassbinder, I propose a transaction: I will give you back your dead in exchange for the child.'

Beside him a mist formed, shifting about as if contained in a cylinder, until it resolved into a symphony of friendly brown hues: tan trousers pulled too high at the waist, a taupe T-shirt and a nubbly chocolate cardigan with a hole in the left elbow, one my grandmother had kept mending but which kept getting torn on the same nail on the same old deckchair. Grandy smiled from beneath his thick thatch of silver hair, his eyes grey and kind, the stubble on his chin and cheeks just as it always was, resistant even to the closest of shaves. I smelled Old Spice, just a hint.

Another white wisp crept up and morphed into a lavender

housedress with pink and white flowers, the apron she'd hand-embroidered as part of her trousseau, the fuchsia slippers I'd given her on her last birthday, so bright they could blind you at twenty paces. She smiled too, blue eyes sparkling, and I felt my heart expand. My grandparents represented safety, love. They'd been the only stable adults in my childhood, the only people I'd known, even as a grown-up, who were exactly what they seemed to be. They had no hidden agenda, no secret shape, and they loved me no matter what, even if I scared them a little. I felt my grip on Calliope loosen, my shoulder and arm muscles softening in the act of surrender.

But the Arch didn't know when to stop: a third cloud was forming, dense and thick, with none of the ethereal quality of the others. And it was tall, not as tall as the Arch, but big and broad, and strong, yet not quite right. Standing there in an ill-fitting suit with bloodied patches at the shoulders where the iron spikes had pierced his flesh, with a loose smile that showed sharp teeth and a hungry gaze that darted back and forth, as if looking for something to consume, was Grigor.

'Well? Do we have an accord?' said the Arch in his soothing voice, unable to hide the triumphant timbre.

If only he'd been more selective about the images he'd put forth. If only he'd not overplayed his hand by showing me things he knew nothing about. If only he'd stopped before the sight of my father had shocked me back to my senses. And although he didn't know it, he'd given me something to cling to: there was no sign of David amongst my dead.

Ziggi's hand was on my arm, as if he'd sensed how much I'd been tempted, but I tightened my grip on the baby and said firmly to the Archangel, 'No. No accord.'

That brought him up short, but I hadn't finished with him. 'You and your cheap tricks! You're supposed to be *looking after* the mortals – you're supposed to be *keeping watch* over us, not crying because you can't go home, not plotting to murder innocent *children*. So, no, I will not give you this child.'

'I demand the double-winged!' All charm, all conciliation, all attempts at persuasion were gone now. The pillars of wishful dust dissolved as quickly as they'd come and the Arch started taking his earth-shaking steps towards where we sheltered in the porch. The church behind us *shifted*, just a little. I pressed my back against the unyielding doors while Ziggi, in an act of sheerest optimism, took the Taser off his belt and sank into a fighting stance. Now *that* was brave. I touched Calliope's head, felt the silken hair, and turned her face away. She began a whimpering cry and I made *shhhh-shhhh* sounds, even as I expected her to be plucked from me at any moment and torn apart, but the Arch came no closer.

'He can't *take* her,' yelled a newly roused Tobit. 'You have to hand her over.'

The Arch turned to glare at him and the emerald-heart angel kicked Tobit in the head. A tooth flew, landing in the grass some way off.

'Give me the double-winged!' bellowed the Arch, his voice echoing all around us, even though it shouldn't have.

'She's ours!' Another voice, and a hissing to the left of it drew everyone's attention. That hissing noise grew and grew as Eurycleia and the conclave swarmed into the small garden. I had to give them credit: they knew what this flight had done to their sisters, and there were only thirty of them against the Arch and his five minions. The odds of a vastly reduced siren population seemed high. The women shivered, and as magics were undone, transformed, wings started unfurling, coming into the light for the first time in what I suspected was a *very* long time. The sirens fanned out, rolling their shoulders, fighters warming up their muscles. Talons grew at the tips of manicured fingers; teeth lengthened in pretty mouths; *retroussé* noses became sharper, beakish. The hissing ceased as they came to a standstill, laying claim to their ground, waiting, watching, mindful of the havoc the seraphs could wreak.

'Give me the double-winged and I shall break the sky. We shall go *home* and be free of this place.' The Arch made gigantic fists, just in case his point needed underlining. 'Give it to me, or I will destroy everyone you care about.'

He couldn't take Calliope from me, but he could do *that*. He could find David, he could find Lizzie and Mel, Bela and Ziggi, he'd hunt down the Norns and Rhonda. He and his would turn the sirens into so many shredded feathers . . .

No, he *couldn't* take Calliope from me. I had to make a sacrifice of her, give up the protection of her – but if I surrendered, she was dead. And if I surrendered, there would be only a brief reprieve for everyone else: if I surrendered, the sky would be broken and there would be night eternal. Life under that kind of reign had nothing to recommend it.

Yet as long as this child remained alive, as long as she remained as she *was*, she would always be a danger, a threat to those around her, because she'd always be a weapon. The Archangel would pursue her to the ends of the earth, I was certain of that. Calliope would never be free. She would have no chance to grow, to become something different. She'd have no opportunity to make her own decisions, to *change* . . .

The Arch advanced on us again and his movement galvanised the sirens. They rushed forward as one, like a rising tide, breaking into smaller groups until each angel was surrounded by his own pack of howling, biting, slicing bird-women, as enraged as they could possibly be, flying and clambering up monumental bodies, swinging on the angels' wings, trying to tear them off in a dreadful echo of what had been done to their sisters. Eurycleia and a phalanx faced off against the Arch, blocking his path. Behind him, I could just about make out an eerie flashing presence, so fast and fierce I couldn't be entirely sure of what I'd seen: something that whirled by in a haze of summer colours and blazing black and silver, an atavistic dance that left angels shrieking in its wake.

Eurycleia leapt, talons aimed at the Arch's beautiful face, her wings creating a tornado that buffeted Ziggi and me. He let her think she had a chance, let her get within a hair's breadth, then struck her out of the air as if she was an insect. When she came to rest on the lawn, bleeding from her mouth and nose, feathers floating about, struggling to rise, the Arch bent and closed one of his hands around her swanlike neck and lifted her high.

'Do something,' I said to Ziggi. I couldn't leave the baby, and though I wasn't fond of Eurycleia, I didn't want her slaughtered in front of her granddaughter – I didn't want her to suffer the same death Serena had. Ziggi gave me a look of reproach, but loped into the fray anyway, fumbling with the Taser. I watched as the prongs flew and hit their target, pierced the fabric of the angel's chiton, and embedded themselves in his thigh. The Arch roared and swatted Ziggi, who went down like a ton of bricks and didn't move again. I bit off my cry and thought furiously.

Ziggi's charge had achieved his aim of distracting the Arch. Eurycleia, dangling from his fist, managed to get one leg swinging and kicked him right under the chin. His head snapped back and he dropped her, but her blow had been no more than a green ant's bite to him and within moments he was poised to stomp her.

Then there came that whirlwind of ragged colour I'd glimpsed before, and the battle changed.

The Archangel froze, his face a ludicrous rictus of disbelief. His eyes met mine and I saw worlds dying in them. He toppled as slowly as a felled ghost gum tree, a hand outstretched towards me – towards Calliope.

Ligeia, suddenly, terribly, stood over the fallen angel. A sword protruded from his back, its ebony hilt studded with gold, engraved swirls and curlicues weaving up and down the blade. She withdrew the weapon, kicked the Arch over as if he weighed nothing, then plunged her hand into his chest. The beating of the heart slowed and stopped in the seconds between being pulled from between his ribs into the air and being put into the old siren's mouth. The Archangel began that same transformation his Brisbane brother had gone through, becoming a fast-burning silvery ash that was swiftly lifted on the slightest of breezes.

An intense quiet settled over the battlefield, broken only by the last shrieks of angels being torn apart by siren hands, by the wet sound of chests being prised open and bloody hearts being shared amongst the victors. To my great relief, Ziggi began to stir and swear, and Eurycleia also sat up slowly, her gaze fastened on her mother as if she had never really seen her before. As if Ligeia was terrible and wonderful and worthy of awe.

She truly was.

The Arch and his tribe were gone, but there were more angels in the world. The baby was still a danger. This was my last chance, while the sirens were preoccupied.

I knelt and put the little girl down, gently unwrapping the pink bunny rug and laying her on her tummy. I slid the Boatman's knife out of its sheath. The blade heated up almost immediately.

Chapter Thirty-Three

Tenderly I took both sets of the baby's wings in one hand, holding on tight as they twitched against my palm. Ignoring the cries from Ligeia and Eurycleia, I raised the knife, praying I had enough time before they came for me.

'I'm sorry, sweetheart, this will hurt,' I whispered, and brought the Boatman's blade down sharply. It sliced through the tendons where they attached to her back. Blood spurted, but only briefly, and only a little. Calliope gave a great howl, though the knife cauterised the cut almost immediately, so how much was pain and how much outrage, I couldn't tell.

Change transforms, makes things both less and more — different — and we all adapt in our own way. Be patient: you'll find your own way. The vision of my father the Archangel had offered me had reminded me of Grigor's words, of their value, and had given me an idea of how to make the child *anew*.

Calliope had been transformed: less than she had been, but free of that which put her life in danger. She was no longer double-winged, no longer a key, and so no longer suitable for *anyone's* arcane purposes.

In my hands, both pairs of wings, black and silver, turned to a luminous powder, which I tossed into the air like glitter.

I breathed out and resheathed the knife before re-wrapping the bawling baby against the cold and settling her on my hip. I rubbed a hand over her skin and found nothing more than a raised pink scar that looked months old.

Ziggi wobbled to his feet. One of his eyes was swollen almost shut and blood trickled from a split in his lower lip.

'You okay?' I asked and his look of disdain made me laugh in spite of everything. I pulled him into a hug with my free hand.

'We still got things to do, you know,' he said gruffly. 'Boyfriends to rescue, monsters to slay.'

'You're right,' I said, and felt horribly guilty that I'd had even a moment of relief when David was still missing. 'What was I thinking?'

'The child.' Eurycleia's imperious tone was gravelly, but no less demanding. She and Ligeia stood in front of me, and seeing them side by side, I could at last see their resemblance to each other. Tobit waited behind them, his chains gone, with the rest of the conclave, bloodied but unbowed and positively glowing with their victory. Eurycleia held out her arms for the baby she'd never bothered to see and said again, 'The child.'

Though Calliope had been giving me some reproachful glances, her crying had diminished to a grizzle and she showed no sign of throwing herself at her grandmother, or anyone else. As I surveyed the three, I wondered which of them was praying for the chance to do as Eleanor Aviva had suggested: to go back to the beginning, back to the place where it had all begun and do something differently, to change something, to make things go their own way.

Eurycleia was motivated by her regrets, but I didn't think it would change her behaviour. She would try to shape Calliope into the mould Serena had resisted. Ligeia, happily licking blood from her lips, would be no better; she'd bring the child up in the old ways, tell her about everything she was heir to, every morsel of flesh, every trickle of ichor. And Tobit . . . Tobit was completely uninterested, maybe because he thought he had no right to his daughter, or because he didn't want the responsibility. I wasn't sure, and I didn't really care.

'No,' I said, 'none of you lot. Not now, at any rate.'

I didn't need to see Eurycleia's expression to know she wasn't going to take that lying down, but as she lunged, Ligeia held her back, one clawed hand clamped on her shoulder. Mother and daughter stared at each other for long moments until the older woman said, 'She's right. Wait. We will wait.'

Eurycleia shrank, somehow. As Ligeia wiped her sword on the skirt of her dress, adding a smear of dark silver to the sedimentary layers already there, I saw the weapon up close for the first time and realised how strikingly similar it was to the Boatman's dagger, both in craftsmanship and design. She must have seen that dawning on my face because she said, 'Such things often come in pairs.'

'I'll contact you when I've made my decision,' I said.

The sword became a tattered umbrella once more and Ligeia gave a brief smile before wrapping a wiry arm around her daughter and leading Eurycleia away. The other sirens followed in their wake and soon the garden was empty except for us, some stray feathers wafting in the air and piles of ash that grew smaller with each puff of the winter wind.

I blinked. My eyeballs felt dry, as if I'd been staring for the longest time. I probably had. Looking at Tobit I realised he was roughly the same size as the Archangel. So who had he been *before*? I also realised the angel-related buzzing in my head was gone. He noticed my stare and shrank down a bit, as if embarrassed.

I looked askance at him. 'Why don't I hear a noise around you?'

'I'm not like them. I never was.' He rubbed his wrists where the now-disintegrated chains had worn them red.

'When we first spoke about your daughter and you told me about the Arch, did you know there was a prophecy? That it wasn't just a random crusade?' I demanded.

'Your opinion of me is that low?'

I looked around the garden. 'The sirens certainly cleaned up.'

'The angels were starving – too many of them in this small area and not enough faith.' He tentatively reached out a large finger to Calliope, who grabbed for it like a bird going for a worm. 'Lucky for the old lady. She wouldn't have had a chance against the Arch at his full strength.'

'Lucky for us all,' I said, but I wasn't sure about his assessment. I reckoned Ligeia could have taken out a whole legion of Archangels, given the right motivation.

Tobit shook off Calliope's tenuous grasp and started to move away, but I put up a hand to stop him. 'Hey! You're not going anywhere – Brisbane needs an angel. Probably. I might have been a bit careless with our last one.' He looked sceptical, but I hadn't finished with him. 'You owe me a big fucking favour! I know exactly what you're going to do.'

He said nothing while I told him what it was.

I slouched into the seat, Calliope clinging like a small clam. It was quiet in the gypsy cab, and warm, and I closed my eyes, savouring the knowledge that at least *one* thing was okay. One thing – not the biggest thing, no, but one thing, and for a few beats, that was fine. That was a win.

'Next?' Ziggi had never been a big fan of resting on laurels. Without opening my eyes I sighed, and the baby echoed me. The bubble broken, my fear for David rushed back in and pushed all the air out of my lungs. Though the Arch had shown me my dead and David hadn't been amongst them, that was a while ago, and it felt like ages had passed since then. Time was a knife's edge, seldom kind, and I was keenly aware that I might be chasing a ghost by now.

'I dunno. Back to the drawing board,' I muttered. Then I sat up straighter, an idea taking hold. We hadn't heard from Bela yet and he wasn't answering his phone, but I thought of Eleanor Aviva's words again: Beginnings are *so* hard, that's why we always try to go back to them, to change them, make things move differently. To make things go our way.

'Back to the beginning, Ziggi.'

He turned the key in the ignition as I started explaining. 'Ascot — the Winemaker's house. It's still there, right? You can't *erase* it, it's still glamoured. Hiding in plain sight . . .'

Chapter Thirty-Four

The house looked the same: huge, deserted, pale against the dark sky. On closer inspection, however, the paint job appeared a little grubby, not quite crisp, as if without the old witch in residence to make sure every surface was wiped and every wall washed, things had started the process of slow decay. I was willing to bet cobwebs were beginning to creep across the windows, that the curtains were becoming home to colonies of upwardly mobile insects.

And the place wasn't entirely deserted: I could see, just peeking out, the back of a Transit van: gunmetal grey, nondescript, serviceable, the sort with no windows anywhere but the cab . . . the sort that would be perfect for transporting stuff you didn't want seen, like a golem, or a kidnapped boyfriend.

'No one's been watching this place since you toasted the old lady,' Ziggi reported, adding, 'Didn't seem to be any need.' He'd turned off the headlights before we'd entered the property and now we were once again parked under the looming camphor laurels, waiting quietly, watching. Calliope had apparently forgiven me; she'd gone to sleep soon after we'd hit the road, switching between silent slumber and stunningly loud snoring. I had the awful feeling another nappy change was due, and of course I'd not had the forethought to retrieve the bag of baby stuff from the church.

'I'm going in,' I said, although part of me – a very large part of me – wanted to run away, terrified of what I might find. That part of me was certain I didn't want to know, that I couldn't handle *that* loss. I wasn't sure the other part of me disagreed much.

'Okay.' Ziggi moved to open his door.

'No, you're not coming.'

'I'm not?'

'Nope, you're going to be left holding the baby.' I reached forward and handed him the slightly damp, dozing lump. 'And you're going to keep trying to contact Bela.'

'Gotta say, this doesn't seem like a great plan.' He held Calliope as if trying to work out which way was up. As I got out, she farted and burped at the same time, just to be helpful.

'I'm making it up as I go along.' I stretched my fingers towards the sky, loosening up. 'I can't wait any longer, Ziggi. I can't leave David on his own.'

'He might not even be there.'

'I know. But I need to check this place first. If I have to, I'll start working out Plan B.' I patted his shoulder. 'Just keep trying Bela.'

'If you don't come out?'

'Then you can have my stamp collection.'

'You don't have a stamp collection.' He opened the glove box and removed another Taser with all the aplomb of a magician pulling a rabbit out of a hat.

'How many of these do you actually own?'

He grinned.

I almost refused it, then I remembered what I was facing and stuffed it into a side pocket. It was an X2, a bit more compact than the older models, but it still felt like a brick. I reached in through the window and touched the baby's smooth face. She opened her eyes and giggled.

'Good luck,' Ziggi said quietly, and as I started towards the house he added, 'Don't get yourself killed.'

It took less time to cover the distance than before, but I was different: I was stronger, fitter, and this time I had a very good idea what I was dealing with. Emotionally, though, I was in an even deeper hole. Before, it had been Lizzie's fate in my hands. I'd thought nothing could make me ache like that ever again. The height and depth and width of how wrong I'd been was breathtaking, but I was doing my best to stay calm, to stop the tiny section of my brain that had all the worst possible scenarios running on a hi-def loop.

Of course I wanted to charge in there, all metaphorical guns blazing, but just because I was hurting did not mean I was going to unplug my cortex and do every stupid thing people did when suffering such uncertainty, facing such enormous loss. If I panicked, I risked losing the most valuable thing in my life, so I pushed the pain and anxiety down and let hard determination be my map. I told myself to be brave, no matter what I found.

Up the steps, onto the verandah and to the double door. Someone had hammered a lovely piece of pine over the panel I'd broken previously. Those little ceramic pots, now filled with withered plants, were still sitting on the white iron table, so I used one to smash in the other panel of glass. People never learned.

Inside, it was dark and cold. Before, I'd been able to smell only furniture polish; now there was the odour of dust and the faint, familiar stench of something nasty that had passed by a while ago. The narrow Persian runner squelched underfoot, so I hit the torch app on my mobile and crouched. There were dark patches of wet there, not only in the expensive weave, but also on the polished wood floors. As I moved on, I glanced into the lounge and dining rooms. It looked as if several items of furniture were missing; I was sure there were empty spaces where armchairs and dining chairs had once been.

At the foot of the stairs I checked the light-coloured carpet for stains, but this one was clean — there was no way the leaking golem could have made it up there without leaving a trace, so instead I headed towards the kitchen, moving as quickly and quietly as possible. I'd almost made it when I heard that sound, that distinctive *bang-click*, and without thinking I hit the deck. I lost my grip on my mobile and it landed with a thud. The screen was cracked, but there was still a bit of a sickly glow that I could see by.

Though I'd managed to avoid the shot, I had landed face-down in a puddle of yuck and my left hand went sliding through another to thud into the skirting board so hard it felt like my fingers had exploded. Ziggi's X2 in my pocket crunched against my hip and the pain made me catch my breath. I rolled over and saw the two long metallic threads of Taser wire above me, the probes embedded in the wall. My gaze followed them back down the corridor to the front door where a lithe, muscular silhouette was throwing aside the spent weapon and cursing, but I was still trying to scramble out of the way when she came at me. In the weak light from my mobile I saw the glint of sleek blonde hair and hard blue eyes.

Anders Baker's AWOL security guard grinned and pulled a knife.

I didn't have time to get up so I kicked her legs from under her and she grunted as she fell. I really hoped she'd landed on her own weapon, but my luck wasn't that good; she reared up like a cobra and swiped the blade across my chest. It split the leather of my jacket, but didn't get through the T-shirt to the skin underneath. I did the only thing I could think of and kicked her in the groin. It didn't have quite the same effect as it would on a guy, but it did slow her down a little.

Then she regrouped, and tackled me.

Rolling over, I tried to grab her but my hand was still senseless and I missed her wrist, catching the sharp edge of the blade instead. I let go quick-smart, but not fast enough: it had already done enough damage to slice through the numbness and my palm was slicked with blood. I didn't have time to contemplate the wound because she drew back and drove the knife into my left shoulder. I managed to get my uninjured hand around her throat, and as she twisted the blade deeper and deeper, I banged her head against the wall with all my not-inconsiderable strength.

Three blows, and her skull caved in, along with part of the wood panelling. Three blows, and the knife was deep into my flesh. Three blows, and everyone else in the house knew I was here – so how long before the evil cavalry turned up?

I struggled to sit, and stared at the bleeding mess crumpled beside me. Gingerly, I felt around her squishy hairline looking for hints of horns, at her shoulder blades for stumps of wings, at the lower back for any sign of a tiny tail, to see if she'd somehow hidden what she was, but no glamour faded away as she died; she was just a *very* fit Normal, which I should have realised, because any Weyrd would've used their power against me, not just a stupid Taser, not just a stupid knife.

I didn't even know her name. She'd obviously taken up a new job after she'd left Baker's employ – or maybe she'd already been working for someone else for a while, drawing two pay cheques. Whatever information she'd given me had just been part of a lure, a game.

I wiped my face clean before tearing off a strip from the bottom of her T-shirt and stuffing it into the hole she'd made in me. I wound another piece around my left hand, hoping that would stop the bleeding long enough for me to do whatever I had to do to finish this. I leaned over and collected my phone. It was not lost on me that I'd once again been punctured.

I stood up, and nausea and lightheadedness washed over me. I had to lean against the wall until I'd pulled myself together, then I squeezed my injured hand and the pain shooting up my arm shocked me alert. David needed me. This was not the time for a nap. I moved slowly across the tiled floor into the kitchen, one step at a time, pausing to see if anyone was going to come charging in, but there was no one at all. In the pantry the secret entrance was once again unlocked, and I could see the door at the bottom of the stairs was standing ajar, letting a feeble sliver of light spill through.

Chapter Thirty-Five

The rows of wine racks at the unlit end of the basement were still there, though their contents had gone. They gave me some cover as I limped along, trying to ignore my aching hip where the Taser had bruised it. As I got closer to the illuminated area, I noticed the benches around the walls and the steel tables had been cleared away, but the furnace remained in its corner, cold as a witch's heart. Two narrow beds, an armchair, a few dining chairs and a low parquetry table with a slim laptop lying open on it – was that where the video of the golem had been uploaded? By whom? – had been added to the furnishings.

Both beds were occupied, as was the armchair.

David, identifiable by his favourite 'badger on a bike' T-shirt, was blindfolded and sitting cross-legged in the middle of one mattress. His bound hands had been roped to the metal frame, one to the top, the other to the bottom. Relief washed through me, making me feel faint – although that could have been the blood loss – and the pressure in my chest released just a little: he was alive, and from there at least, he looked unharmed. On the other bed was a worn-looking young man with middling brown hair, sitting hunched over and miserable. His clothing was filthy and an even filthier bandage had been wrapped around his left forearm. His expression pretty much summed up 'unhappy with my life choices'. I didn't know how much longer Donovan Baker would be able to assume human form.

335

Huddled beside the furnace was Sally Crown. Her bloodied legs and head were at an angle that looked unnatural to me, and she was completely still, though she might just have been deep in exhausted slumber. I was too far away to tell if she was breathing.

In the armchair sat Ursa, booted feet hanging over one armrest, jiggling happily as if waiting for the postman to deliver a long-expected parcel. Apparently there *was* a tunnel out of the Archives after all.

'Sigrid?' she called. 'Are you done?'

Ah. Sigrid. It felt better, knowing the name of someone I'd killed, though I couldn't quite say why.

When there was no answer she frowned – and looked up to see me standing at the edge of the wine racks. Her widening eyes told me I wasn't precisely who she'd been anticipating. I had no choice now, so I stepped from the shadows – there was no cover, no way I could sneak over to free David and check on Sally without her spotting me.

'Sigrid won't be joining us this evening.' I saw David jerk at the sound of my voice. His head turned blindly in my general direction.

The Archivist had obviously been expecting her minion to return in triumph, possibly with my head on a platter. She rose, surprisingly sprightly, but knocked over the silver-tipped walking stick that had been leaning against the side of her chair and it rolled enthusiastically across the floor and hit the toe of my shoe. I stood on it. I knew what it was now.

Ursa eyed the thing with annoyance and not a little fear; that combined with the shock of seeing me was apparently so unpleasant that she began to lose her form entirely.

Though I'd encountered a lot of negative reactions, this was new and extreme: it wasn't just a shifting or a simple shape-changing so much as a *peeling*; the Archivist's outer layer came off at her hairline, reminding me of a snake shedding its skin as it started folding back and away. The body grew a little taller and filled out until 'Ursa' was no more than a discarded husk to be stepped out of and kicked aside. In her place stood a vaguely familiar, kindly-looking grandfather in crumpled old-man trousers and a long-sleeved polo shirt.

The Ursa suit emitted the scent I recalled from my second visit to the Archives; what I'd thought had been stress-related was actually slow but inexorable decay. I wondered how long it had been since the real Archivist had been killed and her form stolen? How many records had Vadim Nadasy destroyed while he'd walked around in her shell, how many secrets had he pilfered?

And why had none of the other Weyrd noticed? Ursa didn't leave the Archives, I knew that from Ziggy. She wasn't a social creature, had no assistants, and mostly communicated by memo . . . so her lifestyle meant it was an easy thing for Vadim Nadasy to take over. All he'd have to do was avoid contact . . .

Ah, but me. He couldn't resist seeing his opponent, could he?

'What have you done with Sigrid?' he asked in clipped tones. I didn't answer, mostly because I didn't want to say *I bashed her head in.*

'I know you,' I said softly, trying to dredge up a memory. It was something to do with Lizzie . . . the football match . . . the old man who'd been watching the game on the day of the brawl. 'At the sports ground—'

'Dig deeper than that,' he said, a distinct sneer in his voice. And I could feel there was something else, something profoundly buried, something that still refused to come to the surface. I shook my head and he repeated, 'What have you done with Sigrid?'

'Sigrid is . . . indisposed,' I said and saw understanding flooding his face, followed quickly by rage.

'David, are you okay?' I called before the Q&A went any further.

'All things considered . . . I'm really pleased to see you. And I mean *see* in the broadest sense of the word.' Though his reply was pure smartarse I detected a relief matching my own.

'Likewise.'

'Is the girl okay? I heard them bring her in; they've been hurting her. She . . . she's been quiet for a while.'

'Why did you take her?' I asked the old man. 'Why couldn't you just leave her be?'

'Little Sally Crown,' cooed Vadim Nadasy. 'Sigrid caught her for me. Silly little Sally should have known better than to betray my poor Magda – she should have known better than to help *you*.'

'I was given to understand that you and Magda had had a falling-out.'

'Water under the bridge,' he said dismissively. 'We . . . *reconnected*. We talked about the good old days, about how all our rights and privileges had been given away by those mealy-mouthed Councillors—'

'And that's when she started her business again?' I guessed. 'But not meat this time.'

'Hasn't been a decent butcher since your idiot father got himself caught.'

'And you brought your grandson on board?'

He made an impatient noise and I noticed how the boy cringed. Donovan Baker hadn't moved when I'd come into the light; he'd just cowered on the edge of the bed. He wore jeans and a T-shirt, but everywhere something adhered to him, some skerrick of paper or chewed gum or twigs or dirt. And now I could see that his feet and hands weren't quite right: it wasn't just that they were covered in garbage, but that they were partially *made* of rubbish and filth. Halfway up his neck was a greying carapace of cigarette packets, the discoloured Winnie Blue logo still visible on some of them. Around his right wrist was the remains of a silver bag from a wine box. I could smell him too, his odour a mix of rot and old booze, sweat and piss and contamination, overpowering his grandfather's discarded shell.

'The boy offered himself,' Nadasy sneered. There was no pride in his voice, only disdain for the fact that Donovan had allowed himself to be so used. I felt for the boy, that his very human desire for affection had led him to this. 'My *grandson*. Nothing of the Weyrd about him but that little pulse, the miniscule thread of blood his mother left him, the faintest hint of what he could have been. Not like you.' His face stiffened, and it was by that expression of well-bred distaste that I finally knew him.

'You came to my grandparents' home after Grigor's arrest,' I said.

He grinned, and it was an ugly thing. 'I offered that grandmother of yours more money than she could have spent in a lifetime. I promised her you'd have the best of everything. She wasn't interested.'

'No,' I said, proudly. 'She would have seen right through you.'

I hadn't understood then why Not-Ursa had been questioning me about my childhood. He'd wanted to see if I remembered him. Keeping the mage in my sights, I bent to pick up the walking stick, then gave it a twirl. In my hands it was little more than a club, but if Nadasy got hold of it, this thing that stored his power and magnified it, we'd all be in trouble.

'Stop that!' he yelled, and it took me a moment to realise he was talking to his grandson. Donovan had been picking at his dressings. It looked like the injuries I'd inflicted on him in the tunnel had got worse. Nadasy returned his regard to me, his face creased with contempt. 'Thus I am served with such materials. Even *you* were better – even a shifting peasant's child had some puissance.'

'You're really not the cuddly type of granddad are you?' I sighed.

Despite everything the golem had done, I pitied him. 'Donovan, how are you doing?'

'I . . . I don't feel so good. I just wanted to be special. I've been so ordinary all my life. I thought . . . I thought if I were different . . .' His voice trailed off.

'You thought someone might care about you,' I finished, then addressed the old man. 'You told him he could change.'

'He didn't take much convincing.'

The boy started to sob, and his grandfather's expression hardened. 'Donovan?' I said, and he lifted his head. 'Did you kill your father?'

Vadim Nadasy exploded, '*You killed him?* We *need* him to find Dusana!'

'It wasn't me!' screamed the boy, retreating against the wall. 'It wasn't me! It was Aunty Sigrid!'

'*Aunty Sigrid?* But your father was an only child,' I said, confused.

Nadasy looked past me, discomforted, as Donovan blurted, 'She was *his* daughter – Granddad's. She was Mum's half-sister – but she was useless, like me. Part Normal.'

'Oh my, Mr Nadasy! What a nice view you must have in that glass house.' The room threatened to spin again and I leaned on the walking stick-cum-wand and tightened my injured fist to make myself focus. Still Nadasy remained silent. 'Poor old Sigrid. Not favoured, but useful: a whipped dog hoping for approval – hoping to be loved. Did you make her work for Baker in case he let anything slip about your golden child? Did you think she'd tell you?' I laughed. 'You should have thought about it from Sigrid's point of view: if Baker was gone, so were your chances of getting Dusana back, and if Dusana was gone for good, then maybe there might at last be some love for Sigrid.'

'That's preposterous,' he snapped, but I could see his colour leeching away.

'Hope is corrosive.' How right the Councillor been. I was willing to bet that once Nadasy had returned to Brisbane and set his plans in motion, Sigrid, who'd spent so many years toiling on his behalf, had realised Dusana was finally within Daddy's grasp. That must have tipped her hand: she'd killed Anders Baker, determined that the knowledge of her half-sister's whereabouts should disappear forever. But I knew where she was . . . not that I had any intention of sharing that. 'Donovan? How about you untie David for me? Then we can all walk out of here. We'll get you some help.'

'The boy won't obey you!' shouted Nadasy.

Donovan didn't move, but his glassy stare started swinging between us.

'Your weakness, Mr Nadasy, is that you can't see anyone else's angle. Everyone else is just a pawn to you. You're as bad as the angels.'

'Ah, my feathered friends—'

'You know about them?' Now I really was surprised. I'd never dreamed the two cases might be connected.

'Stupid girl! Who do you think told them about the prophecy?' He laughed, delighted to be able to demonstrate his superiority. 'Not directly, of course; they don't like my kind any better than I like yours. But whispers and rumours travel fast, and in time they always find the right ears. You killed my 'serker, so I had to find something else to eradicate the Council, just in case Donovan proved to be less than efficient.'

'Why get rid of them?' I asked. 'Because they wouldn't help you against Baker all those years ago?'

'Ancient history . . . but in some small spiteful way, yes.' He threw his shoulders back. 'Once upon a time I was very reasonable about the Normals—'

'*Reasonable* enough to get one up the duff,' I interrupted, but he ignored me.

'Back then I had faith in the Council. I believed we could live in harmony beside the primates. But then they grew too big for their boots and we could no longer move about freely, or live as we wished. We were forced to cover what we truly were with glamours, to make ourselves *ordinary*. I might have still remained tolerant, had one not dared marry *my* daughter, and when he took her away, I saw I'd been wrong to be so benevolent. We'd lost everything, discarded our great inheritance, out of misguided *compassion*.'

'Did you feel that way when you fathered Sigrid?'

He continued to ignore me. 'And Anders Baker, so smug when he told me what he'd done, so self-satisfied when he taunted me . . . oh, I wanted to take him apart slowly, but I couldn't risk losing my Dusana forever.'

'You left, though . . .' I prompted, hoping he'd get lost in his tale. Every extra minute was a minute closer to Bela finding us . . . if only Ziggi could get hold of him. I looked at Donovan, hoping he'd lean across and untie at least one of David's bonds, but the boy was too sunk in his own misery to move. Over by the furnace I thought I saw Sally's foot twitch – but it was so brief, so fast. It could have been my imagination because I so badly wanted her to be alive.

Nadasy obliged, saying, 'I travelled. I made myself humble, apprenticed myself to whoever would teach me their secrets, their deepest, darkest magics. I sought all possible means to take someone else's sorcery apart so I would know how to tear the veils they'd wrapped around my daughter.' He shook his head. 'So many years . . .'

I took a couple of steps towards David, but Nadasy raised a finger and waggled *uh-uh* at me.

'But you came home. You must have found what you needed . . .'

'In part,' he admitted. 'I knew how to break the spell that had changed her form, but not where she was, or how she was concealed. And Sigrid failed to discover that.' He drew himself up. 'Still, we had other plans, Magda and I: we summoned the 'serker to remove the Council so that we could fill the breach . . . and then you came along and ruined *everything*. A good battle plan must be fluid and we wanted to deal with you in a special way, so when this idiot grandson presented himself . . .'

'Why not just kill me outright?'

He looked genuinely surprised. 'Where's the suffering in that? Oh my dear, you underestimate how *very* annoying you've been. You're constantly in the way, digging where you're not wanted, always at the beck and call of Zvezdomir Tepes, turning over stones and letting the light shine where it shouldn't.'

And I recalled the Winemaker's words: 'You've made some trouble for us!' At the time I thought she'd meant for her and Sally, but now I realised Magda would never have elevated Sally to her level. Sally was no partner, merely an implement.

'After you murdered my poor wife, I knew I couldn't do it on my own, but I am nothing if not a *strategist*. I have always made it my aim to read every great grimoire there was to be found, every record of prophecy and doom I ever came across. And I recalled that of the double-winged, of the river-city when, months and months ago, I caught whispers of the angel and the siren keeping company and realised how that could be used to my advantage. I'd put the tale out so it might be heard by the other angels, the *angry* ones . . . I let it tempt them here with a promise of breaking the sky. All of that was set in train long ago! Let the angels run home and we'll see how well the apes will do against the natural selection of the night.' He glared at me. 'You were still getting in the way, but at least the boy's activities kept you out of my hair. And soon the angels will do their work, you'll be dead and my Magda will be avenged and then—'

'Yes, so . . . about the angels . . .'

His face went slack and then taut again, as if someone else was playing his muscles. I was going to enjoy this bit.

'The double-winged is no longer the double-winged, so there'll be no angel-induced apocalypse, no eternal night, no perpetual-darkness theme park – and I'm afraid that means no Lordship of the Weyrd for you.' To underscore my point, I raised the walking stick-wand and snapped it over my knee, which was worth every ounce of the not-inconsiderable pain. The two pieces made a very satisfactory clatter as they fell onto the polished concrete floor. From the hollow centre a mix of something wet and dry and red leaked.

Nadasy roared at his grandson, 'Kill him first, so she can *watch*!'

Chapter Thirty-Six

But Donovan wasn't paying attention. He was staring down at his hands of flesh and detritus, his dripping tears making *plink-plink* sounds on the paper and plastic. Nadasy charged towards him, utterly enraged, and I took the opportunity to bolt over to David.

I tore the blindfold from his eyes, accidentally pulling out a hank of hair that had been tied into the knot, but he manfully swallowed a major swear as I kissed him quickly, then produced the dagger and began to hack at the tethers on his left wrist.

'Careful,' he said quietly. 'Not that I want to tell you how to do your job.'

I rolled my eyes, got through the first rope and started on the second before throwing a glance at Nadasy and Donovan.

The old man had pulled the boy to his feet and was shaking him violently, shrieking at him, words that sounded a little like German, a little like Russian. Whilst mostly incomprehensible to me, I suspected it was a list of his grandson's shortcomings. At first Donovan's expression was pure terror . . . until there was a sudden flash and a change so fast that I'd have missed it if I'd blinked: an instant when he lit up with hatred, when all his disappointments and betrayals and losses showed and welled and spilled.

Vadim Nadasy had achieved what Anders Baker had failed to do – he'd made everything that was Donovan Baker disappear for good.

The whirlwind rose and I caught a glimpse of Nadasy's face in the seconds before he was lifted and whipped around in the cyclone of his grandson's making. His aspect was more disbelief than fear, as if he couldn't comprehend that the world was not bending to his will. And then he was gone.

Unfortunately, that meant the golem was looking for its next meal.

The rope finally parted with a reluctant pop, demonstrating that the Dagger of Wilusa was better suited to cutting flesh than anything else. David scrambled off the mattress as I kept my eye on the golem, which was swaying back and forth uncertainly in front of us.

'Check on Sally,' I said to David, and held the knife in plain sight as I addressed what had been Donovan Baker. 'You remember this, don't you?'

Unsurprisingly there was no answer, other than an increased *whirring* and *burring*. Behind me, David swallowed a sob as he said, 'She's gone.'

He grunted as he picked her up, though she couldn't have weighed too much, skinny as she was. When – *if* – we had a chance later on, I'd tell him how much I loved him for not leaving the poor broken girl alone.

'Stay behind me,' I said.

'But it's keeping us from the door.'

'Trust me: I almost know what I'm doing.' I didn't risk looking at him, just started backing away, trusting him to do as I'd asked. I made sure to stay between David and the golem as the creature herded us into the corner, always moving erratically, first coming closer, then dropping back. Not-Ursa had said the golem would eventually burn out after its human core was gone, but s/he might have been lying – and even if it was true, how long would it take? Maybe we had minutes, but we sure didn't have hours or days to spare.

'Be ready to run,' I said in a low voice.

'So ready.'

In my pocket, I felt the weight of Ziggi's Taser. With my free hand I wrestled it out. The casing was cracked and the golem didn't really have much substance for the probes to hook into, but there was plenty of paper matter, and the whole thing stank of old booze. All I could do was pray and pull the trigger.

The bang was loud in the confined space. It took an age for the wires to shoot forth, for the darts to find their target, for the golem and its collection of highly flammable refuse to ignite . . .

But then time sped up and the creature became a whirling dervish of flame.

Fire is a wonderful thing. It carries sacrifices up. It purifies and cleanses. It gets rid of rubbish.

I yelled, 'Run!' and didn't have to repeat myself. We bolted towards the door, through the shadowed avenue of the wine racks, pursued by an inferno of smoke and blaze. For a panicked moment I couldn't see the exit in the darkness, then it was there, almost as if summoned by fear. We passed through it like horses out of the starting gate, David first and me right behind him, and as I slammed the door shut I heard the commotion of falling wine racks, and something thrashing about amongst them.

Then at last the racket fell silent. I put my ear to the metal door and listened. I thought I detected the crackle of flames as they took hold of the splintered wreckage. I waited a few minutes, just to be sure, just until I could feel the growing heat from the other side, then I looked at David, waiting patiently at the top of the stairs with his pitiful burden.

It could all burn. I had what I needed.

Chapter Thirty-Seven

The emo-Weyrd waitress brought our order. Her tongue had been healed, and all she had to show for her adventure was a slight lisp. Mind you, it hadn't improved her attitude; she was no more friendly or personable than she'd been before. But Aspasia had given me a curt nod on our arrival, and Theo had waved us in with a smile. I assumed Thaïs had reverted to form and was embedded in her Delphic cave upstairs.

Rhonda had paid for our food with what could best be described as intense ill grace – disappointingly, not only had my saving of the Norns' collective arses not translated into free meals forever, but prices had been increased to cover the cost of repairs . . . Still, I was happy to note our servings were considerably larger than usual. We sat out under the canopy, next to one of the braziers, and I was a little surprised to find I was pleased to see new little snakes dangling above us like skinny *piñatas*.

'Thirty-five bucks for this?' grumbled Rhonda.

'Hey, I used up an angel favour for you. This is the very least you can do.'

She grumbled again, but didn't contradict me. She looked good – her eyes were bright and her skin was creamy, less lined. She'd even put on a bit of make-up and found a hairdresser who didn't have a vendetta against her – but I was wise enough not to mention that.

I looked at the crucifix she still wore and she said testily, 'I can hardly *not* believe now. I saw an angel. I spoke to an angel, admittedly a pretty shitty one. A better angel came into my room and healed me. It would be a bit stupid to suddenly stop believing after I've had actual proof.'

'Annoying, isn't it?'

'So much.'

We didn't talk for a while. I was beginning to think the caramel marshmallow log might have become a bit of an addiction. Rhonda was working her way through a new creation: a three-layer thing of lemon mascarpone, mead jelly and marshmallow mousse the Sisters had called 'Angel's Blessing'. It was a bit rich, I thought, in all senses.

'Did your boyfriend dump you, what with you being a danger to everyone's health?'

'I suppose a change in your general attitude was just too much of a miracle to hope for?' I didn't ask about Ellen, who'd dropped McIntyre off, given me a huge grin and a wave, then gone to find a parking space. That had been twenty minutes ago; I imagined she and Ziggi were currently engaged in a death-match over the only space available.

'Well, did he? He did, didn't he?' To her credit, she sounded angry about it.

'No, he didn't dump me. And I didn't dump him. He's currently packing his possessions into boxes so he can rent out his apartment and move in with me.'

She blinked. 'That was fast. What are you, pregnant?'

I rubbed my stomach, which was definitely getting rounder, but said nothing.

She changed tack. 'How's the Kallos baby?'

I grinned. At least one thing had worked out. 'She's settling in nicely with Christos. He's a good choice, he's already on the birth certificate as the dad, and Callie adores him.'

'What about the angel and the old birds?'

'They are allowed to visit, on the strict condition that no one tries to eat Christos, or entrance him or be rude to him.'

'That's very specific.'

'There are a very specific range of behaviours with that group.' I paused. 'It's good that Tobit's hanging around, I think, both for our city and the baby.'

'And Mercado White?'

'No sign as yet – give it time. The Weyrd have long memories, and a long reach.'

'And dear old Tepes?'

'Bela is currently in a far-away, very small European country. He's checked Dusana Nadasy into some fancy-schmancy sanatorium for Weyrd suffering . . . stuff.' I suspected it was going to take a long while for the Widow Baker to work out her issues. 'He'll be back soon – he's on the Council himself now, and they've got to elect another two new members to replace Eleanor Aviva and Adriana. As well as find a new Archivist.'

'And does the latest resident of the nuthouse know that you're responsible for the deaths of her parents and her son?'

'Not as such, no.' I said. 'It sounds so bad when you say it like that – and before you ask, Mel and Lizzie are fine and off having a well-deserved holiday in Sydney.'

She gave a snort. 'Talk about frying pan into fire.'

'And Rose Wilkes has disappeared once more.' I looked out at the dark clouds scudding low across the sky. They made me think of mist, of fog, and of the Boatman, who knew so much and told so little. I'd been avoiding the river for weeks; I was pretty sure he was going to ask for his nifty knife back and I really wasn't so keen on handing it over. Never knew when I might need it again.

The sound of voices at the counter inside pulled me back: Ellie was giving Theo her order. I stood up and stretched. My hand and shoulder were stiff, and the cuts from Sigrid's blade were slowly getting better – even Louise the healer had her limits – but I felt good. I felt settled.

I leaned down and kissed Rhonda on the cheek, much to her surprise. 'See you later, you old bat.'

'So, you pregnant, or what?' she yelled as I walked out, pausing only to hug Ellie and wave goodbye to Theo and Aspasia. I stepped onto the street, into Brisbane's wintery breath, and I could feel its heartbeat bumping up through the pavement. Or maybe that was just the vibration from the cars and trucks.

A purple cab was double-parked, blocking traffic on Boundary Street, ignoring the other drivers honking horns and swearing up a blue fit. Ziggi windmilled a hand at me and I slipped into the back seat.

This was my city, my home. It was filled with my friends and people worth saving. It was my place, and I had a vigil to keep.

THE END

Verity Fassbinder will return in

Corpselight

Acknowledgements

- Thank you to Peter M. Ball and Tansy Rayner Roberts, who let me take their characters' names in vain, respectively Sally Crown and Nancy Napoleon.
- To Ron Serduik for all the support and time spent in his lovely store, which has no secret occult book rooms whatsoever. Really. No, *really*.
- To Alan Baxter and Kathleen Jennings for beta-reading.
- To Lisa Hannett and Peter M. Ball for alpha-reading.
- To Alexandra Pierce for being my first reader's reader.
- To Kate Eltham, for insisting this story had wings and Jonathan Strahan for nagging gently.
- To Haralambi Markov for providing a hard-to-pronounce name for Bela.
- Thank you to Alisa Krasnostein and Ben Payne, who first published 'Brisneyland by Night'.
- Thanks to Jo Fletcher and Stephen Jones for all their support, and special thanks to Steve for introducing me to Jo Fletcher!
- Thanks to my wonderful agent Ian Drury for 'the deal'.
- Last but not least, thank you to my wonderful family for their support, and to my beloved partner, David, who keeps me on the path and throws ideas at me when all seems dark.

Here Today

A Verity Fassbinder short story

One, two, three, four.

Beat, two, three, four.

A dirty beat, a lazy beat, a beat to settle itself beneath your skin and wriggle around for a while. The homeless guy beneath the spreading jacaranda was smacking out the rhythm on a homemade drum—an ice-cream bucket, family-sized. Vanilla.

I'd been watching for two hours, almost. Listening just as long. Hadn't been watching the homeless guy, though I'll admit I'd given him a glance. Decided he wasn't quite right, then turned away. There were a lot of not-quite-right things going on, however he wasn't one of the ones on my list. If he wasn't making trouble—the drumming was quite soothing—then I wasn't going to poke around.

Meanwhile, back to the watching. I'd been staring at a space above the Brisbane River as it churned by, displaying all its forty-eight shades of brown. I couldn't help but notice that the rapidly thinning banks were restless with animals that usually stayed in the water: frogs, toads, fish, some snakes. All looking as distinctly unhappy as such critters are able. They didn't want to stay in their element. Something was coming and they knew it.

But it wasn't the river I was supposed to be paying attention to and I had to remind myself of that every so often. Raise my eyes not quite skyward, just up until I could see the fracture in the hot-blue air. Not really noticeable, unless you knew what to look for. It had the vague purple blush of a healed-over scar, in fact, as if it was no longer active, no longer a threat. Like someone pretending they hadn't produced an especially foetid burp and then taken a few steps away as if to say, *It wasn't me*.

I'd have had a better view if I'd gone into the State Library, sat quietly in the odd viewing platform that is the Red Box, but sitting and waiting for two hours requires coffee. Coffee, as I'd discovered to my chagrin, was not easy to smuggle in. So, even if I located a good barista, my odds of getting hot beverages past Security weren't good.

Over the bridge, in the city streets, sand was piling up. Not so you'd notice immediately, but it was definitely there. Every morning it got washed down the gutters by the street cleaners as they hummed and bustled their way through the skew-whiff checkerboard of Brisbane, down into the sewers and then into the steadily-rising river. But eventually there would be too much, too much to sweep under the carpet, so to speak. Too much to ignore. The city was shifting, shrugging, struggling with what was happening to it, but no one was really paying attention. Like most big inconvenient events, there were always warning signs and always people to pretend there weren't. Always people to shriek in the aftermath about the things we didn't see coming. I wondered what else was on its way.

Whatever it was, apocalypse big or small, Armageddon or not, life still went on. The place still breathed and so did we—we existed, we moved, we rose and went to work, came home, ate, hugged our children, and went to sleep. Stuff still needed doing, lost items needed to be found, cases that confounded the cops still needed to be investigated by someone. And yours truly still needed to pay the bills.

The click of heels got my attention although it took me a moment to locate the source. Long legs, muscular and sun-bronzed, feet jammed into a pair of shoes that probably cost more than my entire outfit. Who am I kidding? More than my entire wardrobe. I'm not a fashionista—basically, clothes are just there to cover the horrible nakeds as far as I'm concerned—but I could certainly appreciate the footwear and the way it didn't clash with the soft folds of the equally expensive dress, a triumph in golds and greens and smoky blues. There was a handbag to match the shoes—if I owned a handbag like that I'd have to live in it to justify the cost. I looked up and took in the face: all sheer angles, blonde shoulder-length hair, make-up applied so perfectly that you almost didn't know it was there. The woman gave me a smile as she breezed past, her perfume wafting along on the wind and blood-warm air. On its heels was a stink of decay, regurgitated up from the river, I thought. I breathed shallowly for a while.

My natural low-level jealousy was tempered by the knowledge that I would never have the energy required to go into that level of personal maintenance. Or the money. I didn't begrudge her and she was a bright relief on an otherwise bankrupt kind of a day.

The rhythm of the drumming had picked up and I pitched a glance towards the homeless guy. Nope, nothing happening there, just a burst of enthusiasm for the tune. He shook his head from side to side, a dog distracted by nothing in particular, the shredded scarf he'd wrapped around his bearded face flapped gaily like ribbons on a maypole. His lips had curved into a slight smile and his eyes were closed. Yep, transported.

'Fassbinder, I'm fairly sure,' came a clipped voice, 'that you're not supposed to be here.'

'I'm a member of the public,' I said evenly. 'This is the State Library, belonging to the people of the state. I'm one of them. Until I get a repo notice, I'll continue to visit as and when I please.'

She was young, Sammi Allerson, new to her position of authority and she hadn't quite worked out how to deal with people like me. I wasn't going to make it easy on her. To be fair, she'd been *very* new at her job a few months back and had witnessed an incident in which I was involved; books were damaged, people were slightly singed and the tea cup collection on the Queensland Terrace was irreparably, errr, diminished. Back in the old days, librarians had been able to turn evildoers to ash with a single glare. Apparently no one was left to teach the new ones the knack. Allerson tried for a good few seconds to get the upper hand, but it was never going to work—an old school book ninja would have kicked my arse in the blink of an eye. Amateurs.

I looked upwards to the Terrace, imagining I could see one of the few pieces of porcelain that had survived my activities, a large vase, willow pattern blue and white. Once upon a time, it was as ubiquitous as steak knives in Australian households; now the leftovers of Nanna's crockery were as scarce as hen's teeth. I suspected if the vase hadn't remained intact, I might not have made it out of the Library alive.

An added complication: we'd dated the same guy at the same time, although we'd not known about it then. The relationship didn't stick, but the animosity did.

Sammi did something with her mouth that in a three year old would definitely be a pout, but in a twenty-something was just pathetic, and leaned against the wall I was sitting on. Fidgeting with her security pass, she looked at me sideways. Her hands, on the pass, used its sharp edge to clean the dark moons of dirt from underneath her nails.

'What are you doing here?'

'Detecting. It's what I do.'

'Person or thing?'

'Don't know.'

'Dead or alive?'

'Don't know.'

'Well, what *do* you know? I'm trying to be helpful.'

I blew out a breath. 'Sorry, that's just such a new thing, I'm not sure how to react.'

She swore and pushed herself off the wall, made to stomp away. I put out a hand, gave her forearm a light touch and she stopped. I couldn't quite bring myself to apologise—not my forté, so I just told her straight, about the scar in the sky, the changes in the city, about the rising river, the call from the cop who's a little dirty, a little useless, and the disappearing families. I told her I was looking for clues and I was coming up empty.

'Whole families?' she asked and I nodded.

'Except one—kid was away for a couple of weeks over the holidays. Came home to an empty house.' I'd spoken with the girl but she had nothing to offer, so whatever happened had been done after she'd left home.

'Nothing's been found?'

I shook my head, then lifted my chin towards the break above the water.

'But someone saw the rupture, saw it tear and saw something tumble through. Something gleaming and fast and formless that bolted out of sight very quickly.'

'Who reported it?'

'Came up in the daily dispatches, some drunk got moved along by the cops while he rambled and ranted about this light, star in the east, et cetera. No one worried about it until the disappearance came up— five families that they know of so far. Your friend and mine, Detective Constable Burleigh decided there might be a link—it was beyond his ken, but someone should do something about it. You know, I never thought I'd miss McIntyre when she went on leave.'

'You're on his speed dial?'

'I don't imagine much Burleigh does involves speed, but yeah. He's caught up in this little girl lost case and, I'm quoting, "Doesn't have time for this weird fricking shit."' I thought about getting a coffee but decided I was already sufficiently twitchy. 'And look at you, all interested in the super-unnatural.'

'You think you're the only one noticing oddities? You think freaky shit isn't happening *here*?' She cast a look up at the Library's strange bulk, then leaned over to whisper, 'The books are moving.'

'For serious?'

'And they're changing. The text—it's shifting. This morning I found chunks of *Pride and Prejudice* in Patrick White's *The Vivisector*.' She shook her head. 'I just don't know what to do about them.'

Privately I thought the change could only improve White's work, but kept that to myself. Allerson was being helpful and I should try really hard not to alienate her, at least at the moment. I pulled out my wallet and flipped through the collection of cardboard slips, then handed over a sepia-toned one. The librarian took it as if it might bite.

'Maybe they can help.'

'"The Library of Lost Books",' she read out, eyebrows shooting up so high they disappeared into her hairline.

'Sometimes they can . . . fix things. Find books, reset books that have gone out of whack, make others a bit more . . . fluid in their contents. Tell Sukie I sent you.' I stood, resisted the urge to knead my backside, which had gone to sleep during my watch. 'Good luck with it.'

'Your problem? Go to the Security Office—they'll have the tapes from around the Library. Tell them I sent you.' She winced a bit at that. 'You might pick up something there. Probably not.'

'But maybe. Thanks.'

If it hadn't been for the coffee I wouldn't have seen it.

I'd watched the tape five times, seen the flash and split of the rent in the air, seen the silvery birthing tumble and streak away along the river bank until it disappeared under the boardwalk, heading in the direction of South Bank. I reached out to hit replay yet again, caught the side of the coffee cup and almost sent it over. I managed to save the situation with only minimal brown splodges on the desk and keyboard. And looking down, trying to mop up, I caught sight of *her* in the lower right-hand corner of the monitor. A flicker of a red dress passing, not hers, and then the face.

Lucy Faith Armistead, the girl who came back to nothing.

The little girl, all alone.

I checked the date stamp on the screen—just over two weeks ago, the day before she went to camp. She was just in shot, walking along, her face turned towards the river, just before the flash. Smiling at someone just out of sight—family member? Someone else?

At any rate, I needed to talk to her again.

Lucy's aunt answered the door.

We'd met the last time I spoke to her niece and she didn't seem to mind letting me in. In fact, she did it so unquestioningly that little cold fingers touched my neck and darted down my back. I shook them off, tried for a name. Anna. Anna Armistead, Lucy's father's sister. Her eyes were underscored with dark circles. Ordinary loss hits people hard enough, but the kind of eldritch loss she'd suffered . . . well, recovery wasn't easy and took a long time. The little girl would never see her parents or three siblings again. There might not be time enough in the world for her.

'Lucy's out the back, playing,' she offered. 'The police woman's there too.'

Police woman?

'I need to talk to her again. I'm really sorry—I know you're trying to help her forget and move on.' And I was sorry—I'd been through enough myself to know that forgetting was an unlikely balm. 'I need to ask her about the day she went to the Library.'

Anna blinked, nodded. 'They went there the day before she left for camp. They always did family stuff before anyone went away. Just in case . . .'

'Has she said anything? Remembered anything?'

She shook her head. 'She just wakes up crying in the middle of the night.'

I gently pushed past her, uncertain what to say, and made my way along the carpeted hallway that opened up into a kitchen, which then spilled out onto a wide back deck. I walked to the edge of the deck, leaned against the rail and peered down into the yard, picking out the bright green and yellow swing set—too new, screaming of trying too hard to be cheerful.

In the deceptive dusk light, I could see Lucy sitting on the swing, not moving any more than the merest hint of a sway. She was staring, staring down at someone crouched in front of her, someone with long, long reddish-blonde hair, jeans and a floaty crème top. On the ground beside the figure, a large orange handbag, big enough to fit a few small, yappy dogs in. Not police-issue.

I started down the stairs, the cold fingers making themselves known again. 'Lucy?'

I know that yelling out when you're sneaking up on someone is counterproductive, but something primal forced the noise out of me, even though immediately afterwards I wanted to swallow the sound. Sometimes, we do dumb things. Sometimes we just want to give the darkness a chance to run away from us. The figure shot up, not tall, turned around and gave me a brief glimpse of a pale face scattered with golden freckles, thick-rimmed glasses, a slash of a mouth pulled into a snarl. Her features were pretty enough in a geek-girl kind of way, but with an almost-round head perched on wide shoulders, barely a hint of a neck.

Then a bend of the knees, long fingers curling around the handle of the tote and a leap towards the fence, a scramble of boots and arse and legs, until she disappeared over and into the next yard. The sound of a dog barking, then whimpering in fear, then more scrambling over another nice middle-class family-home fence, and so on until the sound of something tidying up loose ends dropped away.

I crouched in front of the little girl, taking up the space where the visitor had been and looked up into the child's face.

Eyes dark as death, the skin of her face wrinkled as any British Museum mummy, lips parted, striated like dried figs, cheekbones standing out like a relief map, nostrils gaping wide. The breaths issuing from her mouth were shallow, hot and arid. I felt my heart turn small in my chest, constricting at the idea that there was nothing I could do. I held her tiny hands and watched, watched for I don't know how long until the exhalations became moist once more, the skin smoothed, the features filled out, and she struggled to pull her fingers away from my grip. I let her go, waiting for the horror to die in her eyes, for her to calm down and remember me well, and not as a threat.

When her lips, pink and full once more, opened and she began to cry, she let me gather her up and hold her while she shook, wiping her nose on her pink Hello Kitty t-shirt.

On the deck, immobile and lost, Anna watched helplessly.

That was okay.

I had a scent. I had an idea. I needed an ally.

'Is the kid okay?' Burleigh sounded like he'd been drinking for a while. I kind of hoped that was just the effect of long hours looking for his lost girl, Charlie, and not from hugging a bottle. Charitable isn't my default setting, but I decided to give it a go.

'Yeah. Got her and her aunt stashed in a safe house and I've got people watching the place.' Strictly speaking, the Ottoman Motel wasn't a safe house, but it did have a lot of occupants who (a) owed me, and (b) had more than one eye in the back of their collective heads. And those folk weren't the sort to run in the face of a possible mini-apocalypse—in fact, an apocalypse was likely to make them feel right at home, so I felt fairly sure that Lucy and Anna would be safe from any further attempts on the kid's life.

I'd questioned her closely, but she'd had nothing more to tell me. I'd been coming at it all wrong—I thought she'd seen something, but that wasn't it at all. What had come through—and I knew what it was now—had seen her. Had seen the whole family and worked out that that was the place to start. Followed them home, waited, and watched, but in waiting it had missed Lucy. Then moved on to other families—just how many we couldn't be sure—and gone back for Lucy. Say what you will, but cuckoos are thorough; it's all or nothing. It only takes one to work its way through a city, tunnelling through the population as efficiently as a mole undermines a field.

And it shouldn't have been here. Shouldn't have been able to get through. Apart from the fact they were supposed to be extinct—a quick call to Sukie told me that. But whatever was going on in the city was weakening the walls *between*, making the barriers thin, making a breach between us and the howling void where bad things live, easier and easier.

'Okay. That's okay then.'

'No, Burleigh, it's fucking not okay.' Which was what I'd been explaining to him for fifteen minutes. 'This thing eats its way through families.'

'Yeah, yeah, yeah, like one of those succubus things.'

'No, not like that. This thing isn't after sex. It wants attention. All the attention anyone might ever focus on anything—this thing wants it all. It will sit in front of a person and suck everything out of them just for the buzz of utter, concentrated, undivided attention. That's why their mothers leave them in other nests. Get out of your fucking concrete midden and get moving!'

'But there's just one. It's going to have to wait, Fassbinder. I've got every bastard breathing down my neck about this lost kid. Even that arse of a Premier was on the phone, trying to tell me my fucking job. Chances are, I'm here today, gone tomorrow. This thing, this weird shit, is just going to have to wait in line.'

I was silent, long enough to reign in my temper and long enough for him to think twice about pissing me off too much.

'Look,' he said, paused, started again. 'Look: you take care of this. Do whatever you have to and I will cover your arse. Just make it go away, okay? Just do it.'

I hung up without thanking him for the *carte blanche*. Burleigh wasn't a bad guy, and he wasn't the worst copper I'd dealt with. He was just lazy and unprepared for the kinds of bizarre he was having to handle. Like most people he just preferred to ignore the things that didn't fit into the everyday. I, apparently, had no such option. I was the go-to-girl for weird shit.

Yay, me.

I headed back towards the Library precinct. As I got closer I could hear the rhythm of the ice-cream bucket drum, still going strong. It gave me hope and I picked up my pace.

'I can't believe you talked me into this.'

I'm not a patient woman, and hearing this for the tenth time was wearing away at my nerves. Still, I gritted my teeth and said, 'And I appreciate it. And you won't regret it. You're helping me and you're helping Burleigh, and you're helping the city. It's all good.'

'How is this all good? How the fuck is this all good?' she hissed. 'If anything happens to that thing, my boss will skin me alive.'

I knew her boss, and yeah, there was a good chance Mona would do precisely that and use the skin to cover a book. Beside Sammi was the blue and white vase, recently liberated from the Queensland Terrace by her own fair hand; next to it, a Collins diary, A5 size. On the concrete expanse between us (crouched down behind a combination of drought-resistant shrubs and some brickwork barriers) and where the land drops away to the boardwalk and the black ribbon of the river, was a small figure, standing solitary in the pool of light from one of the street lamps.

A tiny piece of dangling bait, tethered by the circle of yellow, and wearing a pink Hello Kitty t-shirt.

Christ, I hoped it worked.

Normally at that time there'd be people wandering around, stealing the wi-fi in the Library atrium, stealing kisses in the shadows that embrace the building, but not then, and not for a lot of nights in a row. People might have been pretending everything was okay, but that didn't mean they wanted to venture outside into the darkness. I was listening so hard to the silence that my ears ached.

Then, *click, click, click.*

My tiny scapegoat's head tilted, just a little, but she kept her face down, shadowed. I think I saw her shake, but couldn't be sure; maybe just my imagination.

From the opposite direction, *click, click, click*.

And the smell: expensive perfume with an undercurrent of rot, a liming of decay. I recognised it from the elegant woman that morning and from the backyard of Anna Armistead's house. Two women, one scent. It was how they recognised each other, mother to daughter. Two of them; it was how they could cover so much ground, so quickly, so many families.

Terrible, horrible efficiency all converging on one fragile lure.

The clicking sound was doubled; quadrupled. Not just the tap-tap-tap of heels, but voices, clicks and whirs of greeting and greed, anticipation. I elbowed Sammi, breaking her out of her staring trance, and she passed me the vase, whispering 'Be careful'.

I mouthed *fuck off* but it was too late. Even her softest whisper had alerted the cuckoos, their heads swivelling, searching. It didn't slow them down, though, they kept moving towards the bait, faster and faster, long fingers reaching, eyes growing larger, gleaming yellow, lips sliding back, ready to begin the process of draining every last drop of attention out of their victim. A few more steps, a few more steps, that was all I needed.

That's when the scapegoat's nerve broke and she released a high-pitched scream that stopped the cuckoos in their tracks. Biting down on a curse, I stood and aimed the mouth of the vase at the pair of them, hoping they were both within range. I could hear the fetish rolling around inside the jar, anxious for company. First the mother, then the daughter, both were pulled and elongated as if caught in a wind tunnel. Clothes torn and shredded, handbags and shoes flew towards me like weapons, but the vase swallowed them whole, its maw expanding to receive whatever came its way. The two cuckoos didn't go quietly but they did go.

Allerson slapped the Collins diary over the mouth of the jar and I struggled to hold the whole construct steady as it kicked and bucked, the thing inside it warring with the captive meat, doing its work as the Maker had assured me it would. He'd stake his life on it, he'd said. Mostly I hung onto it because I couldn't bear the thought of having to listen to the librarian whine if it got broken.

Eventually, the storm subsided. The shaking stopped and all I could feel was something slushy and heavy swirling about inside. I sat heavily on the cement; the heat of the day was still radiating up through it. Allerson was doing something that appeared to be a snoopy dance. The scapegoat came towards me, stubby finger pointed at me like a weapon, profanity pouring from lips that usually wore a lurid shade of purple lipstick. Sukie had agreed to forego the make-up this time and shrug on Lucy's clothes. The scent, I had bet, would bring the cuckoos out. Sukie might only have been three foot five tall, but her temper was six foot seven. I owed her big time.

'That was too fucking close, Fassbinder! What were you playing at?'

I thought she might just kick me while I was down, but she restrained herself, which I appreciated. Behind her the darkness split and the homeless guy loped up, grinning from ear to ear. He pointed at the vase.

'Mine?'

'Your *ju-ju* worked, so as promised, whatever's left is yours,' I agreed and as Sammi began to protest, I dropped the makeshift lid and gently upended the vase. A pungent mix of fleshy sludge hit the concrete, smacking like wet frogs on tiles. The smell was unique to say the least. A crop of spiders with more legs than I could count, crawled out of the meaty mess. My new friend sat down next to the shifting stinking mass and began to eat. His hands, now that I looked at them closely, had only three spade-like digits, each tipped with a shiny sharp nail.

I stood and handed the vase back to Allerson, who held it as far away from herself as she could, spluttering, 'That's disgusting.'

I wasn't sure if she meant the meal or the state of the vase.

'All I promised was that it would be in one piece.' I pulled out my phone and dialled Burleigh.

It rang out. I gave up. I guessed it could wait.

He'd probably still be here tomorrow.